FAIR GAME

FAIR

GAME

SARIE MACKAY

LANTERN LODGE
PUBLISHING

2010

While some public servants and other notable figures in this book are drawn from the pages of Central Montana's past, the characters created here for the reader's entertainment are entirely fictional, and any resemblance they may bear to real individuals is purely coincidental.

Library of Congress Control Number: 2010906196

ISBN: 978-0-9789259-2-5

Cover Design and Illustration: Jenny Zimmerman
Book Design and Production: Judy Gilats
Printed in the United States

Effective magic is transcendent nature.
GEORGE ELIOT, *Middlemarch*

Chapter One

Aboard the *Campania*

JUNE 1895

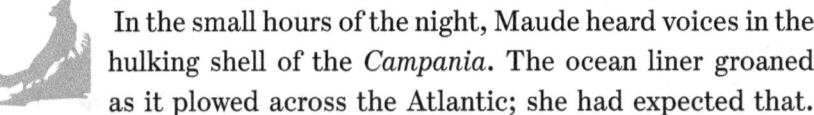 In the small hours of the night, Maude heard voices in the hulking shell of the *Campania*. The ocean liner groaned as it plowed across the Atlantic; she had expected that. But there were all manner of voices. Distant lowing like the cattle in the hills of Altyre Wood; mutterings that could have been old Dame Wrigley as she pounded her herb-pastes on the banks of the Findhorn; or short, tense notes like the yipping of the manor hounds as they tore after a stag.

But tonight, the voice that haunted her dreams was the raspy burr of the swaggering Laird McNaughton, whose deep-set eyes followed her whether she went foredeck or aft. It didn't matter if she sat on one of the chaises allotted to second-class passengers, or if she went to her favorite spot near one of the mammoth red smokestacks and curled up in a pile of ropes with her book. He'd materialize nearby, lingering until she sensed him. Her blue eyes would lift, drawn up to verify his presence, then dart away, repelled.

At thirteen, she felt herself on the edge of a dark mystery, like the night shepherd on the rocky heath above her home back in Morayshire who was paid not to sleep. She knew one thing: it would be worse for her if she did not treat Laird McNaughton the same as she treated everyone else on this long, pitching voyage.

She woke in a sweat, flinging out her arms involuntarily, reaching for something that might be bolted down, rooted to *terra firma*.

It was still dark, but a lamp had been lit far down the corridor, casting just enough light for her to see the familiar, grainy knots in the oak veneer next to her bed. They looked like a wolf's face. There were the curious mad eyes and long snout that had become so familiar in the four weeks they had been at sea. Loosening the neck ribbons of her damp muslin gown to admit some air, she rolled onto her elbow and looked across the room into her grandmother's narrow berth.

Dark gray eyes glittered back at her from the small, wizened face. "It's awake y'are, at last. I dinnae like pullin' folks from their dreams, but I near rattled ye from that one."

Maude stared. "Gran. Seeing into my dreams—it's not possible."

Gran Ailse smiled. "Any fool could see it warn't a pleasant place ye'd gone to."

Maude flopped back down on her narrow bunk, whispering, "Tell me something pleasant. Tell me what Aunt Morag says in her letters from Montana."

"Ye ne'er tire hearing of it, child." The old woman kept her voice low. "Speakin' on yer aunt, I've been thinking lately ye micht weel wind up looking more like Morag than like yer own mother. That mass o'curls the color of molasses. And when I look in yer eyes I see Morag's, blue as the noonday sky. She says the sky in Montana is bluer than 'tis in Scotland. And she talks aboot the green, wavin' grass clean up tae the horses' bellies, so deep they cannae find the sheep . . ."

Maude let her grandmother's words stroke her like the morning draft of air sifting down the corridor, across the coarse blanket of her tiny bunk. Gran always knitted up the human world and the natural world so tight and neat.

Could Montana be all Morag said it was? How could anything be as wonderful as Scotland, where spring poured into summer like a green river? Just last month she had hiked the damp path above Torrieston with her younger brother Rory while their father shared a pipe and a farewell laugh at the mill in the gorge, where the burn shimmered black as the granite beneath. She and Rory had run along the sodden trail, excited by the humus tang of spring, cold and rich in their nostrils.

When they flushed a ptarmigan that set them both hollering, Maude slowed, stroking each of the stately beeches with her fingertips. Then she stopped altogether, talking to them, tracing their gooseflesh bark, patched here and there with velvet moss the color of emeralds. Rory dashed back, catching her arm, and dragged her through the coppery duff of leaves up the hillside to a clearing where they gained a view of the valley. Breathing hard, they looked down on a pool of white mist, thick as milk, broken by pointed firs and the stone steeple of Pluscarden Abbey.

No, she thought with a tight and aching chest, *Montana can't be as lovely as Scotland, but I'm going to be brave about all of this. I'm the oldest of all the Graham children and I've got to show it. I'll be just as brave as Gran.*

By now the sea air had cooled her gown, so she pulled the wool blanket up around her chin. Another six days, she tallied on her fingers, another week crashing through the waves and avoiding the arrogant laird. Gran's storying faded into the background as she wandered farther off in thought. What an unfortunate coincidence that not only were he and his sons on board the *Campania*, they were also bound for Fergus County to set themselves up in sheep ranching. But then, it seemed that half of Scotland was on its way to Montana.

Tall and regal, the widower McNaughton made a lot of women turn their heads. He had a bold baritone voice Maude could hear whenever she walked past the mahogany-paneled first-class smoking room. He held people in his thrall when he spoke. But why must he be on the *Campania*? The mighty McNaughtons were rich enough in Scotland; they didn't need to come to America.

Her father's friends must have thought so too. That evening, as dinner came to a close and the second-class men clumped up in the hallway to leave the dining room, Hugh Gilmore, puffing on his pipe, unfolded a handbill and stuffed it into John Graham's palm. "The laird and his boys could strike it plenty rich up in Alaska if they'd a mind to. This page here tells aboot the Valdez Trail, the surest route to the gold fields."

John Graham tipped his chin down and a lock of wavy hair slipped across his forehead. It was a pose Maude knew well, one that generally preceded a good-natured rejoinder. "I didnae know you were lookin' out for the McNaughtons so kindly, Hugh."

Hugh's jaw slid out a notch. "Dinnae be cagey with me, Graham. What does someone like him see in the grasslands of Montana?"

"What do you and I see there?"

"You know damn well it's nae the same. Manor-born and manor-bred. You cannae look at him the way you look at the rest of us."

"Whether you and I like it or not, a lot of wealthy Englishmen and Scots are setting themselves up as wool growers and cattlemen in America." John lifted one broad shoulder. "Why should a well-heeled fellow like McNaughton with a braw bunch o' lads be any different?"

The men drifted out onto the deck, some grumbling, some laughing. Maude's mother, Catriona, retreated with the younger children toward the sleeping rooms. Maude stole out into the open, hoping to hear more of the conversation, but the men were some distance away, clotted in a tight circle. Resigned, she leaned against a rail, watching the *Campania*'s upper lights glimmer to life, like torches on the ramparts of a castle.

The footsteps behind her did not concern her until they were close. A muscular body grazed hers. McNaughton was past her before she realized what had happened. He turned, flicking a finger against his tweed cap. "Evenin' to you—Miss Graham, is't?"

She felt the hair curling at the base of her neck, but inhaled sharply and let the salt breeze blow the fear out of her face. "Good evening, Laird McNaughton," she said, then pivoted on her heel and walked away.

She couldn't possibly tell her mother or father, whose bunks lay on the opposite side of the ship with her younger brothers, Rory and Mac, and the little girls. She didn't want to "mak' a tether aboot it," as Gran might say. She liked bunking with Gran and being the oldest, being trusted. No, in dealing with this arrogant old fool, she'd put him neatly in his place. She'd thrust out her chin and go about her business, as the good and brave Grahams had always done.

Maude loved to watch her father with his friends when they held court among a cluster of barrels near the smokestacks in the afternoon. They'd congregate late in the day, summoned when the sun swelled into a huge crimson disk over the sheet-metal blue of the sea. She always saw her father's shoulders in the center of the enclave, and smiled at the way his great tousled brown and gray head moved this way and that as he gestured his way through a tale.

At this hour of the day, the patriarchs of the Gilmores, the Fitzpatricks, and the Shaws all gathered there, fathers of middling means who had much in common: long histories in the hills of Moray, knowledge of the "verra mad ways of sheep," and deep loyalties to families and friends.

Sometimes a seasoned shepherd named Kibbey would play his fiddle, and when the drink flowed freely enough, people would begin to dance. John Graham in his plaid vest and she in her long dark skirt and crisp white petticoat would take to an open expanse of polished wood and teach a faerie reel or haymakers' jig to their wayfaring companions.

This cool afternoon, all was quiet. The rosy sun grew dim, but Maude continued reading in her nest among the ropes, now and then peering up at the men over the pages of her book, watching her father's quick grin and catching bits of ribald humor as they blew past her on the sea air. She had come to the part in *The Mill on the Floss* where Maggie Tulliver's father had fallen from his horse, and poor Maggie was rushing home from Miss Furniss's boarding school, not knowing whether she would find her father dead or alive.

The soft blue of evening melted over the ship, and the electric lights blinked on as they did each evening at seven, but she was deep in her book. One by one, the others left the deck for drinks in the saloon, dinner, or time with family.

She didn't hear the rustle of the silk-lined jacket or the faint grind of waxed boots, although there was a breath of something that came over her at that moment—something that made the hair rise along her forearms. She'd always had a keen ability to pick things out of the air, and just now she lifted her chin and flared her nostrils, pushing the dark curls away from her face. It was whiskey, more whiskey than her father ever drank in a sitting, mixed with stale tobacco, heavily scenting someone's clothes and hair.

Strong fingers curled over her face like an iron mask and a sinewy arm pinned her slender ones to her sides. Her book tumbled away, breaking the binding. As Laird Thomas McNaughton flung her to the floor, her skull struck the planking so hard that an explosion seemed to go off inside her head. Sparks flew into her field of vision and blackness converged from the edges, like nightfall coming too soon.

Even as she fought for consciousness, she was sharply aware of the moment when his fingers left her mouth. A scream gargled up in her throat, but his hand was quickly there again, stuffing something dry and grassy between her teeth, over her tongue, and halfway down her throat. Gagging and wild-eyed, she knew she must not struggle any further against the choking mass or she would lose any ability to fight.

She stared hard at the sweating forehead and averted eyes of a man who wanted only one thing. His knees were on her forearms, but her legs thrashed wildly behind his back and she bucked beneath him like a barnyard animal.

"That's a good vixen," he grunted, "just keep that up and we'll have a grand time." His hands worked furiously at his trousers, then yanked her skirts up to her waist. "Ye know what I want. Showin' me those fine lace petticoats. Those legs . . . those damn fine ankles!"

He drew a steel knife from his vest and flayed her underclothes up the leg and midline. Moving his knees between her thighs, he smacked them aside. Then, with powerful hands locked on her upper arms, he laid into her.

Maude's blue eyes glazed as pain seared her core. She was dying, she knew it. She'd never see her mother or Gran Ailse again. Dead, on the way to America. Her head thrashed from side to side and vomit rose in her throat, mixing with the coarse fibers of the stuff in her mouth. As the swelling mass began to fill her windpipe, her neck arched in a spasm.

Driven by survival's final impulse, she coughed and gagged, but the assault on her body was so violent that all reason left her. She could do nothing but lie there like a rag doll, her body slumping along the cold deck.

He cried out. In the dim, distant place where she was, she knew he had drained himself inside her. Grunting, he pulled away, tugging hard on her breasts as he rose.

"My Maude! Ye're mine now, ken it. Forever. If ye tell a single soul, I'll take ye again. Mickle hard it'll be for me to leave the likes of ye alone, so dinnae make it any harder. Hear that? I'm *yer laird*, now and always."

She lay still, staring up at the impossible sight of a tall, red-haired man whose creased white shirttails flapped in the night wind. She kept her face passive, her breath a faint wheeze in her nose. Somehow, with each ragged inhalation came knowledge, knowledge that sounded like Gran's voice telling her to be quiet and show no fear. It grew into a whispering chorus, Gran's voice and many others, all wise women, touching her with tenderness and truth.

McNaughton caught the look on her face and stared, momentarily transfixed. Then, with a bark of laughter, he glanced at his watch and yanked up his trousers. Even when he had straightened his garments and disappeared, she lay stiff as clay. *Was he . . . could he be gone?*

The cold air settled on her wet thighs. She let her eyes drift to the side. Nothing, only the steely blue of evening stretching out across the sea. Her shaking arms were free, she realized, free to reach up to her face and dig the stuff out of her mouth, making way for the vomit and her terrified, gasping sobs. *It did not take him long to spend himself, praise God and the ancient ones.*

Leaning on one elbow, she stared at the puddle of emesis and batted at the strings of it hanging from her mouth. In the middle of the slime lay the stuff he had used to silence her—a frayed wad of hemp rope.

She spun around on one hip, looking for him, but he was gone. With inept, spastic movements, she poked her torn pantaloons into her waistband and brought her skirts down around her boot tops. Struggling to stand, she found that her legs would not hold her. Her knees buckled and she fell to the side, clutching at a brass cleat on the wall. Staring out at the rail of the ship and the black water beyond, she thought, *I hadn't ought to get near that. As unsteady as I am, I'll slip between those rails and be lost forever. But truly, why should I not crawl to that edge and slide over, straightaway, into the dark sea?*

Chapter Two
Judith Basin, Montana
MAY 1908

 "This one maun be dried," said Ailse. "It's toxic if eaten fraish, mind ye." She handed a clump of the herb known as boneset to Maude, who laid it in her basket alongside the other fragrant greens.

"You're going too fast, Gran. My pencil broke and I need to write these things down." Maude took a penknife from her pocket and sat down on a boulder, whittling the pencil tip back into shape.

Boneset, dried, for fever, she scrawled. Her fingers were still cold, even though the sun had been up for an hour. The hem of her long cheviot skirt and the soles of her boots were damp with summer dew. She knew better than to argue with Ailse, however, when it came to the gathering of simples—plants of unique healing virtue. Dawn, or "streek o' day," as Gran put it, was plainly best.

"I'll remind ye of whate'er ye forget," croaked Ailse. "Just get them in the ground at that new place of yourn afore dark, so they dinnae wilt. Ye call it a caibin, but it's a fancy hoose as far as I can see."

Ailse leaned forward all the time now, using her walking stick everywhere she went. Only a few dark hairs showed in the silvery white locks she wore in braids pinned around her head.

Maude loved that her grandmother was both mysterious as a fay and strong as a standing stone. Over the past dozen years in America, the old woman had expended no effort in grinding off the burr of her Scots tongue the way Maude's mother and father had. The old country ways coursed vigorously through Ailse, like a stream—or burn, as the old woman would say—foaming along a Highland channel. Maude's own speech, like that of her younger brothers and sisters, had become plain American English, although in moments of passion she'd tumble back to the voice of her childhood, gliding slowly over a vowel or nettling roughly against a consonant.

When she took her grandmother to town, people peeked from beneath their hat brims or cast over-the-shoulder looks at the little crone in her high-button boots and black worsted. Maude observed all this with amusement, knowing that Ailse had more knowledge in her gnarled little finger than half of them might accumulate in a lifetime.

Many were the nights that Maude, hearing a rider pounding up Stony Creek Lane, had risen from her bed to see a panicked rancher standing hat in hand at Ailse's door, bidding her come help with a difficult birth or ease a child's burning fever. She knew that people sometimes referred to Ailse as a "rabbit-catcher," an old-country term for midwife, and she suspected that the word "witch" even went around, but Ailse was never bothered by any of it.

"Mornin', Mizz Ailsie," the town ladies would say, thinking her name was some Scots derivative of Elsie. The men would nod and touch their hats. In spite of the gossip, respect for Ailse MacDougall ran deep in Fergus County.

Smiling, Maude watched her grandmother amble slowly up the garden path. She patted the surface of the broad boulder. "Sit with me a spell, Gran. You're breathing hard."

"Tut, dinnae squawk about my breathin'. At least I still hae wind movin' in and out." But she sat down just the same, resting her knobby hands on the head of her stick.

The two women were quiet for a moment, listening to birdsong and watching the summer landscape awaken. Then Ailse's head lifted. "Lookit there, far on top o' Birch Bluff."

Maude raised her hand to shield her eyes from the rising sun. There, on the ridgeline, were two dog-like figures. "Coyotes?"

"Nae, mickle stout for coyotes. That's the great gray wolf, the one they call the Adrad. And that be his mate. I can tell, e'en wi' the sun behind her like this. She's big and pure bleck. Ah, they're gone. Quick as they came."

Maude continued staring at the empty ridge, the wolves still present in her mind's eye: the strong, forward ears, the horizontal plume of tail. The great gray wolf was the stuff of legend in Fergus County, eluding rifle, steel trap, and poison.

She thought of her father, who listened with a placid expression to all the opinions going around about wolves. When he returned last May from the Stockgrowers Convention, he shared stories at dinner. "Even though livestock depredation has begun to subside," he said, "the ranchers blame the government for not setting aside enough tax dollars for bounties. By some queer mathematics, this only fuels their hatred for the few remaining wolves." John Graham rode the middle ground, whether it was at the Mint Bar in downtown Lewistown or on the lawn after services at St. James Episcopal.

"I can't help wishing the big gray will never be killed." The words tumbled out of Maude, sounding blasphemous and righteous at the same time. She plucked at the fabric of her skirt. "I'd never say that in town."

"Dinnae be sorry. The wolves belonged here once, like the buffalo and the Indian." Ailse rocked from side to side, the silver tendrils of hair shifting in the morning air. "There's nae doot some o' the bounty-killin' has made sense over the years, but now it's a dark fever all my simples cannae cure." She turned her gaze on Maude. "Enough o' that. Ye getting along weel over yonder?"

Maude sighed and brought her attention back to the garden. "I love it, Gran. More than I can say. Kettle Creek just outside my door, the wind sighing in the fir trees at night. Father was so generous, giving me that land."

"What's a hundred acres! He's come a far piece, that boy has, since he stood at the end of our lane in Morayshire, twenty-some year gane, turnin' his hat into a mush o' felt, hopin' tae get a glimpse o' my Catriona." She surveyed the horizon from right to left. "Just how much land has he got?"

"It's over thirty-five hundred acres now," said Maude.

"Hoot, is that all?" Gran flung a hand in the air.

Maude toyed with a red clover bud. "You know, it occurred to me last night as I lay in bed that he may have done it to give me dower lands." The round head popped off the stem and flew into the grass. "I mean, I realize he did it out of care for me, but I'm sure the dowry idea crossed his mind. At my advanced age, they're worried about impending spinsterhood. What's the old saying? 'My son be my son till he get a wife, but my daughter's my daughter all the days of her life.'"

The crepe-like skin around Ailse's eyes hooded as she trained her gaze on Maude. "I cannae argue wi' the idea o' dower lands. He minds the traditions, John does. Right and proper. But why couldnae he hae given ye some aither piece than the one next tae that damn fool McNaughton's ranch?"

Maude took a slow breath, then let it out in a thin stream, listening to the murmurous haunt of the bees. The silence deepened as the years slipped away and the voyage on the *Campania* came back.

"I can smell the ocean just now," said Gran, "like it was yestere'en."

Maude turned to her sharply. These moments of connection between them were commonplace, but they never stopped feeling uncanny. Gran kept her eyes straight ahead, as though conjuring the image of the assault, right now, in the garden.

"I was reading *The Mill on the Floss* when it happened," Maude said softly.

"Aye, I can see that little green book plain as day in my mind." Ailse's hands tightened on her stick.

"It was a long time later that I finally finished the book. In the end, the main character, Maggie Tulliver, drowns. She had dishonored her family, and the author must have thought it was the only thing to do with her." Maude gave a bitter laugh.

Ailse's hand came off her stick and clasped Maude's forearm like the talons of a raven. "Ye listen tae me, Maude Graham. There's nae one drop of dishonor in yer portion of this, ye hear me? A hare, white as snaw, that's what ye were, caught in the foulest trap twa human hands can set. If your father had e'er found out what happened, he would ha' kilt McNaughton. If there be guilt in any of this, aside from what belongs tae that red bastard, it lies wi' your mither and me. We ne'er kenned how tae find justice for ye."

"Hush, Gran. It's long past." Maude lifted both hands and parted the air in an unconscious way, as if sweeping away the film of unwelcome memories.

Gran let out a little sniff. "Ah, would ye look at that! The girl isnae quite as modern as she thinks."

"What do you mean?"

"I'll tell ye another time. But Maude . . ." Her face was grave as she lay her hand, gently this time, on Maude's arm. "He doesnae trouble ye?"

Maude compressed her lips and watched a blue bottle fly crawl along the tip of her boot.

"What is't? Ye cannae lie tae your Gran. Ye could spin a yarn ten mile long tae your mither and father, but nivver tae me."

"He drives by in that buggy of his. You'd think with him being married to that widow from Stanford these eight years would make things different, like he wouldn't think of me. And you know my place is on the side road. He doesn't need to pass there, but he does just the same." She stopped, feeling a chill run over her arms despite the warming sun. "The worst thing is, Gran, *I think about him*. As disgusting as he is, I feel bound to him. Cursed." She swallowed hard. "It's vile."

Maude felt her stomach churn. She was unwilling to tell her grandmother that she sometimes knew, in the darkest part of her soul, that since McNaughton had once possessed her, she didn't want him to ignore her completely. After all, she was ruined; no one else would ever want her. She couldn't begin to understand him, but the workings of her own mind were even more bitter and terrifying.

Ailse sat in silence for a long moment. "As far as him not thinkin' on ye because he's wed, I wish I could say that stops his kind frae lookin' 'round. The simple truth is, he willnae stop. I'll make ye a bundle of special things. For protection."

Maude's eyes were on the Snowy Mountains to the west. Another laugh escaped her.

Gran frowned. "It makes nae difference tae me if ye believe in my little whims just now or not. But will ye take the protection bundle? For yer auld Gran?"

The black eyes were bright. As Maude felt them boring into her, her throat thickened. Slipping her arms around Ailse's bird-like frame, she said, "Of course I'll take it. And for what it's worth, I believe in you more than you know."

The old woman nodded. "Good. I can feel it in ye, Maude. The MacDougall gift. Special wits. It's there, nae doot aboot it. Once ye feel it risin' in ye, there's nae turnin' back." She stubbed her stick into the ground and rose. "Just a wee bit o' burdock I'll be needin' first, and a slip o' cedar, and a scrap o' muslin tae bind it all. But we didnae finish gatherin' our simples. Ye ha'nt got enough in that basket. I'll be back."

She left Maude alone and, leaning on her cane, lurched away into the depths of her garden, muttering sing-song as she went, "Feverfew, arnica, coltsfoot, gentian, wolfbane . . ."

Wolfbane, thought Maude. *Aconitum. Purple flowers, fern-like leaves. Does it really help keep the wolves away? And will Gran's bundle of protection herbs keep McNaughton away? Something tells me we'll need our garden charms, our special wits, and far more.* She sucked in her cheeks, stood up, and brushed herself off.

This was the first time she had been back to Stony Creek in over a month. Gran's long lane, right now a patchwork of sun-streaked pine needles and violet morning shadows, had been carefully laid out so that Maude's mother, Catriona MacDougall Graham, would always be able to see Gran's cottage from the veranda of the big house. The low lambing sheds, known as jugs, lay a few hundred yards to the east, and the whole place was surrounded by aspen groves and neatly fenced sheep pastures.

No one would argue that the Graham ranch wasn't beautiful. Christened Stony Creek after the brook that drained out of the foothills of the Snowies into the swift and clear Big Spring Creek, it had become one of the leading sheep ranches in the county. Yet as lovely and revered as her family's ranch had become, Maude breathed a silent sigh of relief that she no longer lived here. The affectionate concern of her parents, even her younger brothers, had grown into a smothering miasma.

But here she was, back again, and it was no surprise that she had come first to Gran Ailse's cottage, tucked up in the meadow— the place where there would be no inquiries or reproofs, only quiet acceptance and the healing scents of the garden rising from every step.

Finished at last with the herbal gatherings, and with the muslin bundle of protective herbs tucked in her pocket, she kissed Ailse good-bye. As she neared the big house, she stowed her basket among the rocks in the creek, where the cold water would flow through the withes and keep everything fresh.

Catriona's new loom had arrived last month, and Maude had yet to see any of the brilliant woolens spilling daily off the new contraption, coaxed by her mother's skilled fingers.

"You made this one already?" Maude ran her hands over a length of teal and mallard green plaid. "It's so fine." She watched as the loom harness took ruby-colored filler strands of fine wool and darted them through sky blue warp threads. As her mother rowed the beater bar with dancing hands, the resulting cloth was neither ruby nor blue, but a new creation of rosy violet.

"How is it over at your new place, really?" Her mother kept her eyes on her work, but Maude saw in them a taut, restrained inquiry she knew very well.

"You should come. You'll think it's crude because it's a log house, but it's what I wanted. Having two stories makes it quite elegant, and the front porch is divine."

"Your brothers finished your porch furniture, did they?" She paused, then added, "Maude, I just don't want things to be any harder for you than they already are. Now that you've set yourself on the very outskirts of society, it will be harder to meet . . . people. There was that pretty little place in town—"

"Let's not have this conversation," Maude said, studying her mother. *She's so transparent, and she doesn't even know it. Her vigilance is so obvious, so unremitting. How she yearns to take control, to somehow overcome my black flaw.*

Oblivious, Catriona stepped away from the loom to wind a skein of loose yarn, her hand making rhythmic circles in the air. "We just want you to be happy."

Maude stared at the trailing yarn. "I saw him."

Catriona's teeth caught her lower lip. "Where? Not close?"

"Don't worry. He drove by in his buggy and stopped where the main road intersects Kettle Creek." She turned toward the window. "But sometimes, Mother, when I lie in bed, I smell him, even though he's miles away. It's almost as though I know precisely where he is all the time. I hate it. To blazes with him. I just wish I knew what it says about *me*."

Catriona laced and unlaced her fingers, flustered by this un-orthodoxy. Maude watched as her mother's face bloomed into a violent shade of pink. "I . . . I swear to Almighty God I wish that man was dead. I've imagined every manner of accident that could befall him. If it didn't mean prison for me and a lifetime away from the children, I would have killed him myself long ago."

Maude thought, yes, it would be easier to kill him than to find answers to my questions. "Father would kill him."

"Maude." Catriona's fingers clutched at Maude's sleeve. "Yes. Yes, he would. He would kill him and he'd pay the worst possible consequences. It's enough that—"

Maude finished the sentence. "It's enough that you and Gran and I know." She pulled away. "We'll never stop concluding there is nothing to be done. Don't you see, I want my rage to grow. I want to hate him more. But instead, I go on living in a private world *with* him."

Maude bent her gaze away, away from the hands that rested

inert and white on the bright band of selvage at the edge of the loom. "If you were me, wouldn't you want to know why he is so often there, just at the edge of your mind—the most repulsive man you've ever known?" She toyed with a ruby-toned strand, knowing her mother would not answer. With a wan smile, she shrugged and turned toward the kitchen. "I'll put the kettle on, then I'll go out and find those ragamuffins you call your daughters."

Out in the afternoon sun, she strode across the compacted dust and gravel, letting the sage-scented wind blow some of the ache out of her. A bluebird darted from one fencepost to another along the lane leading to the road, and the breeze moved white scuds of cloud over the Snowies.

She surveyed the long sweep of lawn and the precisely ordered flower garden that followed the curve of the drive and bent to chase the walkway. This was Catriona's world, so different from Ailse's wild copse of scents and textures. Maude had long ago figured out that her mother would control anything that might yield itself to her ministrations, whether it was a climbing rose or a match between two willing souls of marriageable age.

Marry me off, would you, mother? It would ease your mind, surely. Tidy this mess up. The white clapboard house in town, the final melding with man and community. She picked up a stone and threw it at the chicken house, where it struck with a satisfying *thwack*.

She heard her sisters before she saw them. Three girls came shrieking out from behind the enormous barn, chasing the guinea hens. Mary, the oldest at seventeen, spotted her first. Slowing her step, Mary tossed her long curls and ran her hands down her bodice. In the past year, Mary's figure had blossomed handsomely and she was highly conscious of it. Maude knew that she spent her evenings with the needle and thread, tailoring her dresses to make the most of her narrowing waist and swelling bosom.

As Mary's eyes swept over Maude, taking in the split skirt and work shirt, her upper lip ruched into a curl of distaste. "Just because you're twenty-five and have your own place doesn't mean you should ignore us," she said, her eyes flashing. Mary was clearly of the Graham side, with the same liquid brown eyes and red gold hair as Rory and Fiona. Maude, Mac, and Isobel had the unlikely pairing of pale skin with dark, unruly hair that always made folks look twice.

"I heard that the Fredrichs brought you their sick sheepdog to tend. You care more about those wounded animals than you do about us," Mary went on, pulling Fiona in on one side and Isobel on the other.

Maude thought back on what it had been like to be seventeen. She did not recall ever being as vitriolic as Mary.

Fiona and Isobel stood like ladies-in-waiting on either side of their imperious sister. Emboldened by Mary's example, Fiona spoke up. "Those are the same clothes you were wearing last time you came, Sissy."

Maude took a slow breath. "You're an observant person, Fiona. You're like the deer who watches everything from the edge of the forest. Did you know, I have a doe living behind my cabin right now? I believe she's just given birth to two fawns."

A cry of delight escaped Isobel, the youngest. "Can we come and see them? Can we pet them?"

"You can come any time. I'm only a couple of miles away, for heaven's sake, and you older girls know how to manage the buggy. We can't touch the deer, but we can watch them from my secret place."

Mary placed a hand on the shoulder of each girl. "What if we wanted to spend the night?"

"I wish you would. You know I have a guest room, or we could sleep in the hayloft, if it's warm enough." She glanced at the house. "I think the scones are coming out of the oven. Would you like to join Mother and me?"

The young ones ran ahead as Maude and Mary fell into step together. Shaking out her skirts, Mary threw Maude a look. "Nate Prestwick drove Marcella Griswold home from church yesterday."

Maude was silent, listening to the crunch of their boots on the gravel. She knew Mary had not forgiven her for refusing Nate's invitation to the Christmas Ball. "Marcella's lovely," she said. "I can see why he would." She answered spontaneously, but as the words left her mouth, she felt a sinking in her chest, realizing Mary was sure to react.

"Do you *want* to be single, Maude? What is it? People ask me. I don't know what to tell them. I don't want to say, 'my sister is just peculiar.' If I went through high school and rejected every single boy, which, God forbid, I don't intend to do, people would certainly ask about me. Would you mind telling me what is wrong with Nate? His father's not rich, but he's prosperous. You couldn't find a better-looking beau. I've kept my thoughts to myself before, but I'm asking now. What on earth is it with you?"

Maude's heart pounded in her ears. She held the white-painted gate open for Mary, wanting to finish this conversation before they even got close to the house. "I can't explain it, Mary. I know you want a better answer. Maybe someday—"

"Someday *what?*" Mary snapped. "Maybe someday a wealthy prince will come riding into Lewistown and sweep you off your feet?" Mary's brow hardened over her fiery eyes. "It's because of your looks. Everyone has always held you up as such a remarkable beauty, but the talk is going the other way now, Maude. You don't know it, but people are saying you'll end up a spinster. All these years, I've wanted to be like you, but it's coming clear to me now. You're nothing but vain. What an act you are to follow! I can't stand to have my name spoken in the same breath with yours." She grabbed the gate and flung it closed, stalking up the flagstone path.

Maude glowered after her sister. *Vain, am I?* Fingering the dull brown hopsack cloth of her skirt, she shook her head and frowned. *I can't even comprehend the notion of vanity.*

Her eyes rested on the screen door as it slapped shut. *We have never been close*, she reminded herself, staring at the early blooms among her mother's roses. *The eight years between us are just too many. For God's sake, little sister, I never meant to leave you any kind of legacy.* She lifted her eyes and looked out over the meadow.

And you know, Mary, I don't believe I have. Maybe someday you'll see that . . . then again, you may not.

She took several deep breaths, wondering how families evolve the way they do, and why some siblings so effortlessly season and perfect their love for one another, while others find that love so easily curdled by envy and mistrust.

Chapter Three

On her weekly trip to Lewistown, Maude let the horse pick his way along. June in Montana was not to be rushed. The wheels of the buggy made a soft, grinding noise on the damp road, and Bobcat's shoes pinged now and then against the stones. Up ahead, a red fox slipped into the margin of the meadow, while a light breeze sang like a zither through a grove of aspens. Bluebirds, darts of color shot down from the sky that seemed to go on forever, flitted overhead. A familiar feeling came over her, an almost believable sensation that she could stop the buggy at this moment and evanesce into some kind of spirit, floating over the landscape to feel the soft, damp grass beneath her naked skin. Nature seemed to permeate her every sense; she could not tell where it left off and she began.

She shivered with joy, then searched her memory, wondering when exactly she had fallen in love with this place, with the Snowy Mountains, the sparkling sweetness of Big Spring Creek, and the wide, lush Judith Basin opening to the south. She knew she'd worried fiercely about it as a young woman: how would it compare to Scotland's rugged magic? But she was in love with Montana, and no one would ever pry her loose. She smiled as a bank of silver gray Russian olive trees cast their aromatic scent on the breeze. To the north, the dark Judith Mountains rumpled skyward, layered with cobwebby clouds.

It was a quiet Tuesday morning in Lewistown, the only sounds being distant shouts and ringing hammers as the Bohemian laborers continued their work on the Stone Church and the new St. Joseph's Hospital on the hill. On Main Street, she passed a rude frame of slender pine poles about six feet tall and twelve feet long. She recognized it as the rack that had been built last spring by some wolfers who wanted to display pelts taken on their winter hunt.

The great gray wolf has a name, she reflected. *They call him the Adrad. Gran Ailse said the name is old Scots for "feared one." The big black female ought to have a name too, even if no one else knows it. When the Adrad is sighted, she is always nearby. I'll name her Leal. I remember that much from Scotland. It means loyal.*

A cool wind rushed in the willows along the creek, pushing its way into her nostrils, strong and fragrant. As she smelled the bitter undertones of salicylic acid oozing from the willow bark, she thought of the Indians and how they used it so effectively for pain. She and Gran had learned much from the Blackfeet. But something buffeted the scent away from her, whipping a new gust of air into her core, dispersing her thoughts and making her grab the side rail. It wasn't a real wind, but it felt real—cool and green and whirling. It moaned in her ears and sent chills across her forearms as something else, something musty and old, overpowered her. What appeared in her mind was the image of a wolf. Dark, with eyes the color of an ancient bronze Scotland stone—cairngorm, her father called it.

Her rib cage expanded from an excess of air, then went flat as the sensation poured out of her, leaving her breathless. The buggy rumbled as it passed over the boards of Spring Creek Bridge, tugging her back to the present. She felt spent, as if nothing would be better than pulling Bobcat up sharply and taking a nap in the shade of the willows.

I'd like to know where the hell I go at these times, she fumed. *These are no day-dreamy reveries. They almost always herald something—news of some kind, or an incident.* She swallowed and reminded herself that these moments of prescience weren't always negative. Sometimes she found things that had been lost for weeks; other times she happened upon a wounded animal hiding in the brush. She'd had an especially strong feeling the day before her father's oil well proved out down on Salt Creek. *There's good to be had from some of my little fits*, she insisted, snapping the reins against Bobcat's rump.

Jumping down from the buggy at the post office, she saw a long spring wagon loaded with sundry construction supplies—everything from barbwire to nail boxes to fresh lumber. It occurred to her that Postmaster Pfaus might have finally hired someone to fix the spring on the screen door, which had hung disgracefully open ever since a nasty storm last spring. Stepping over the threshold, she drew back, hearing low voices in the tiny lobby.

". . . terrible shock for all of you," Pfaus was saying, hands thrust into his pockets, eyes downcast.

"She was too young, that's certain," said the stranger, who twisted around at the sound of Maude's approach.

She leaned against the door jamb, not wanting to believe what she saw. A young man stood before her, but right next to him was a dark form, glimmering and translucent, materializing into the shape of a large dog. No, not a dog—*a wolf*. Its head came clear to the man's waist, and it shifted tentatively from foot to foot, first tilting its square head up to look at the man, then training its eyes straight at her, as if trying to determine if she was friend or foe. The eyes that fixed themselves on her were cairngorm gold.

Maude stared first at the wolf, then at the face of the stranger. Everything faded away except the eyes. The man's eyes were exactly the same color as the wolf's—a pale hazel with fiery flecks of gold. Tipping her head forward, she plastered her damp hand against the bridge of her nose. She didn't want to look again, but her own eyes fought her, peering through the spokes of her fingers. The tall stranger stared at her as if she were the peculiar one.

Like a vapor, the wolf vanished and only the stranger remained, but an animal sense hung in the air all around him. Maude swallowed hard, realizing the wolf had not been real—at least not to anyone but her. As for the man, she had never wanted so much to look away from someone, yet felt so completely unable. Somewhere in the thick air that suffused the lobby, Albert Pfaus gave a little cough, wafting in from a distance. It was enough to help her ratchet her eyes to the post boxes on the wall, away from this person who seemed oddly familiar, like a painting she'd seen long ago, perhaps in another lifetime.

All of this happened in less than five seconds. Stuffing a copious bundle of mail beneath his arm, the man clapped a dark hat on his disheveled, sun-streaked hair and made for the door, sidestepping around Maude. As he did, she felt his gaze linger on her, heavy as a touch.

"You give my condolences to all your folks out there at the Rocking M," Pfaus called after him. "My God, what a terrible shame." He turned to a stack of brown packages on the floor. "You'll be wanting your parcel, Miss Graham."

Maude, still blinking from what had just transpired, watched her own hand as it hovered in midair over the package that Pfaus heaved onto the counter. She knew it was the blue calico curtains she had ordered six long weeks ago. She brought her chin up and looked at him. "What has happened?"

"You ain't heard?"

Giving her head a tiny shake, she eyed him closely.

"It's Mrs. McNaughton."

"Rowena . . . McNaughton?"

"I suppose you wouldn't have heard, since the *Argus* ain't out yet and you folks live out of town."

"She isn't ill?"

"Past ill. Gone. Apoplexy. That's what Doc Attix's nurse told my wife. Blood clot to the brain. I guess she dropped like a stone in the dining room out there at the Rocking M. That makes the laird two times a widower now. He might be rich as Croesus, but Christamighty. He just lost his boy last year, the one in the service. Malaria, you remember. No strangers to tragedy, those folks."

Gravity had drawn her hand down onto the parcel, where it now lay with a great heaviness. Rowena McNaughton dead.

Albert Pfaus droned on. ". . . hard on that new fellow who was here. Just arrived from Ohio—some relation of theirs—Elliott, his name is. For all their airs, the Rocking M is a cayuse outfit—you didn't hear that from me, mind you—but for that greenhorn to ride into this mess, I don't envy him. Nope, don't envy him one bit."

Whispering a few words of acknowledgement, she heaved the bulky package beneath her arm and swung open the door. Now it seemed that the morning sun shone too brightly on the landscape. *A beating heart has been stilled, yet still the birds sing and the wind plays in the willows. Rowena dead. McNaughton widowed again. What does it mean? What would it mean?* Her tongue felt dry against the roof of her mouth.

As she groped her way to her next errand, her mind would not register the news; instead, she was pitched back to being fifteen and standing in the kitchen at Stony Creek, making biscuits. She could even remember what she was wearing that October afternoon when someone casually mentioned that Thomas McNaughton was going to marry Rowena Doyle, a widow from the nearby town of Stanford.

When enough time passed so that no one would connect her actions to the announcement, she had thrown on her buckskin jacket and gone to the barn. There, among the stewed-up scents of hay, grain, molasses, and lanolin, watching the play of the afternoon sunbeams on the stalls and shearing slings, she tried to make sense of her mind.

The laird, who had flung her to the planking and taken her just two years ago on the wind-tossed *Campania* and declared her his, was about to marry. The relief was immense, and yet she felt a rising surge of self-loathing.

She resented the marriage in a way that disgusted her with herself, causing a bitter riot in her own viscera. He was probably the only man she would ever have relations with in her entire life, and now he was—she cringed—done with her. Why did she feel anything? Did these stirrings mean that she cared about him, this gutter slime, this vermin of a man?

She had been with him in the most vulgar, debauched, and violent way a woman could be with a man, and now she felt like *this*—disturbed, strangely anxious. It made no sense; it was revolting. Why would she have any feeling other than deliverance? Why not, at the very least, a miniscule sense of heartsease, or even personal restoration?

Instead, she seethed, *I seem to feel as connected to the foul bastard as I ever did. Even more.* She grabbed a pair of sheep shears and began sawing them back and forth. *No girl—or woman, for that's what I am now—in her right mind would ever feel this way.*

She pondered an oath to herself, at that moment, standing in the chill silence of the barn with flour and baking powder on her black muslin dress. Staring at the shears, dark bronze on the handle grips but shiny and silver bright on the blades, she sat down on a bench and rolled up her left sleeve. With the pointed tips, she slowly made three inch-long, shallow slices on the clear white skin of her forearm.

The outer world fell away as she drew the careful, slanting cuts. There was pain, but the feeling of release was sweet and pure. Her spine relaxed and she leaned into the pony wall behind her, watching the blood come. Her own sacred blood, tiny crimson rivulets, moving from one parallel incision down to the other, traveling through time. Only when a cool tear tickled her cheek did she realize she was crying. But these were not tears of pain. She had arrived, at last, at a foothold of self-knowledge.

Aloud, with only the cooing pigeons in the rafters to hear, she said, "With my own blood, on this day, I, Maude Graham, vow that I shall never marry."

Later, even within a few weeks, she felt a wash of relief that he had wed the widow Doyle. Anything, she told herself vehemently, anything to keep his attention away from her.

When the laird and his new bride drove past her in town one day, she saw that the widow from Stanford had long, curly dark hair. As she stood in their dusty wake, wondering what it meant that the laird's new wife bore a distant resemblance to her, two women standing at the entrance of Lehman's Dry Goods joked to one another, "There went the last fine figure of an eligible man in the Judith Basin. Now even he's snapped up."

Just as Mary said that day at the garden gate, Maude had finished Fergus County High School and watched her classmates—including her friend Harriet—being courted by young men from Lewistown and other small towns throughout Judith Basin. Many, like Harriet, were engaged within a month of graduation.

The following summer had been sweetened, however, with unexpected good fortune. The sting of isolation faded when news arrived that the Wyoming land parcel her father had bought on his sheep-buying trip years ago was suddenly part of an oil boom. John had mustered enough money between himself and his brother Donald in Billings to put together a small rig and a crew, and they'd brought in a small but steady well on Salt Creek, near the dusty town of Casper.

Maude remembered two things about that event. First, the money from the well enabled her parents to start construction on the big new house at Stony Creek in the fall of 1903. Second, John had brought the whole family together around the kitchen table one late August evening and told them the oil well was to be family business, and that it was not to be discussed with friends and neighbors, under any circumstances.

"If I hear about it anywhere," he said, "I'll know it was one of my own house that spoke it abroad, and there'll be hell to pay."

So the family prospered, through hard work on Stony Creek and through slow but steady oil production. The volume and quality of the ranch's livestock increased, with burgeoning bands of sheep as well as with pleasure and draft horses. A year after the big white house was built, a large two-room log bunkhouse followed, complete with its own kitchen. The old bunkhouse was demoted to a shed. They were able to hire household help, a neighborhood girl named Dora, and the Graham children had new clothes every spring and fall.

Aloof and alone, Maude began to accept the loathsome curiosity

about Thomas McNaughton that often stole upon her. She came
to understand that, at the very least, she ought not go to war with
herself over it. Sometimes, after she finished school and the daily
work of studying her mail-order medical journals and caring for
sick and injured livestock, she lay in bed at night and wondered
if the hoofbeats she heard on the road were those of his tall black
horse. At such times she often remembered the fifteen-year-old
girl who went out into the barn choked by contradictory emotions
that could not be explained in this world and perhaps not even in
the next.

*And now this has happened. Rowena is gone. Born, grown, married,
widowed, married again, and died. And here am I.*

That evening, she was up late working with yards of blue calico—
pressing, hanging, and straightening. Every now and then, as she
smoothed her hands over the hot fabric, she'd shake her head,
wondering how far and how firmly she could extend the bound-
aries of her new life.

Later still, beneath her blankets in the welcome darkness, as
the wind fell across the valley and as unnamed riders passed on
Big Spring Road, she knew—more than she ever had before—she
was not fit for any man.

"Maude, you've got to go, plain and simple. We go too far back
with the McNaughtons. You can't slap them like this. You're their
neighbor now."

"Laird McNaughton's got plenty of folks to help him with his
grief, Father."

When she heard the bite of his boots on the wood chips behind
her and felt his hand fall heavy on her shoulder, she knew she
had lost the battle. He turned her around firmly and put his
rough fingers beneath her chin. "Christ in heaven, you're more
stubborn than I ever was. We ha'nt lost all our old ways, my girl,

and as long as I'm about, we'll keep the Graham manners alive. Can I cherish some husk o' hope that when I'm dead and gone, you might carry on the tradition of aiding our neighbors in their hour of need?"

Maude's eyes filled as she stared back at him, at the brown eyes, the mass of rust and gray hair he kept stuffed under his high-crowned hat. She prayed he could not see beyond the armload of kindling to her heaving chest. She didn't want him to see, but at the same time she hated the ignorance that swam like a cloud of gnats between them. She hated the fact that she was as much to blame for that ignorance as anyone—she and her mother and Gran. Would her father die without ever knowing what had happened? And now, the thought of voluntarily presenting herself to Thomas McNaughton . . . it was a sacred misery, this thing. She tried to keep her face passive, but her lower lip trembled and her vision blurred.

Her father misread her tears. "My sweet Maudie, put that damned wood down. It's a long while yet you'll be puttin' up with your ornery old Da." He took the kindling from her and set it on the crude table under the barn eaves, then embraced her, vainly attempting to smooth the dark corkscrew locks that haloed her head.

He thinks I'm worried about him dying someday. It was hard not to laugh. Then the comforting bulk of his broad shoulders against her brow, the worn smoothness of the leather collar on his canvas jacket, and the faint scent of tobacco on his knotted bandanna overcame her. *Father. The man who has made a home for us all, and given us so much. I cannot afford to make more of this than I already have. My life,* she told herself, *is not always going to be about some godforsaken tragedy that happened twelve years ago.*

And there was something else, too. She couldn't help wondering what the soft-spoken Rowena's life with Thomas McNaughton had been like. She didn't want to hear it, but a tiny voice in her head was prompting her to go and make her private consecrations, to say what needed to be said, from her innermost self to a woman she did not know, yet with whom she felt a vaguely alarming kinship.

He held her away. "My girl, look at your tears. Are the piney woods of Kettle Creek making you lonely?"

She smiled. "Maybe I miss Stony Creek a wee bit. But I love my house. And I have my animals, don't I?"

"Ha! Sick pups and wild critters. You need some real animals that'll put bread on your table. When are you going to start yourself a flock of sheep?"

"Saints, Father, let me get my house finished. You can give me some ewes and lambs in a couple of months. Get along. I'll be at Stony Creek in the morning."

Chapter Four

She had forgotten about the receiving line, assuming she'd get through the funeral by standing unacknowledged in a sea of black crepe and countryman's drab, then slip away to her buggy after the interment. She even had a black veil from Gran to capture her wild hair and give her a grasp at anonymity.

But as the mourners filed out of the cemetery with its boundary of wrought iron, there was only one exit, that being the tall gate, with the all-male McNaughton clan standing like sentries on either side. As they left, the slow-moving line faced the laird, guests either shaking his hand or embracing him as they paid their respects. Maude shuffled behind her mother, averting her eyes until the moment came. A few steps from the gate, she swallowed her fear and made herself look at the family. Next to the patriarch stood the four surviving sons: Lewis, Blair, Grant, and Charlie.

Of all the sons, Maude liked Blair least. He was dark and lantern-jawed, resembling his father only in body and gait. Today he stood tall, right next to the laird, staring straight ahead, dry-eyed. Catriona had once mentioned something about Blair blaming the youngest son, Price, for "killing" his mother in childbirth, and feeling no remorse when the boy died last year.

The other three sons varied in stature, but all were freckled and ruddy, with the same auburn hair as their regal-looking father.

Maude felt that the one named Grant was the only McNaughton with a decent countenance.

And there was a fifth young man among them, the one from the post office. *What had the postmaster called him . . . Elliott? No wolf at his side today.* She had tried not to think about him or his spirit companion, but had finally given in to curiosity and confessed her vision to Gran Ailse. "Some folk have airthly companions, like a dog or a cat," Ailse had said. "But I've heard of spirit-familiars as weel. This fellow you saw, he micht ken he has a familiar, but he micht not."

Yes, animal companions were generally called familiars, and they were real, not materialized through prescience. The incident at the post office had been one of the strongest experiences of special wits she'd ever had. *The wolf hadn't seemed menacing*, she mused, tugging idly at a stray curl. *But what do I care about a man who consorts both with wolves and with the McNaughtons?*

The line had stopped moving entirely. Her eyes drifted back to Elliott. About six feet tall, with tanned cheekbones and wavy hair of sun-dashed brown, he bore no resemblance to the rest of them. Yet he was clearly considered part of the McNaughton group, because a length of the red and green clan plaid lay draped across his sturdy shoulders, just as it did on each of the McNaughton men.

His eyes found Maude's and stayed. For a moment she was so lost in trying to understand how he fit into this family portrait that she stared straight back, wide-eyed, almost vacant. In these few seconds, her mind registered that he was attractive. Far more attractive than his counterparts. The McNaughton plaid looked out of place on him, so much so that she had the urge to walk forward and fling it off. The peculiar sense of recognition she'd felt at the post office returned. It was not so much about his person or his appearance, but rather a concord within herself.

And there it was again, the feeling that welled up in her chest, similar to breathing but more potent, driven into her nostrils by an unearthly wind. Her heart swelled with strength, and carpets rose along a breezy, dim hall of memory.

Mary's shove was like an electric shock, blasting her back to the present. "What's the matter?" she hissed. "Move."

Maude's eyes flicked away from Elliott and his hazel gold stare. Stumbling forward with the flow of the line, nodding to the rest of the men, she thrust her hand out and waited for the impact of Thomas McNaughton's skin on hers. Once her hand lay in his tight clasp, his eyes bored into hers. "Maude." His voice was low and cool.

"My condolences, Laird." She darted her eyes across his face, glad for her veil. If there was no smile on his lips, why did she see the light of humor burning in his eyes, now, when it should be extinguished by grief?

She hated that their hands were touching. Even three seconds was too long. In withdrawing, she needed to use force. Just as he sensed her begin to twist her arm to free herself, he released her. Nausea swirled beneath her ribs. A film of saliva pooled in her mouth as she felt the air rush between their palms.

No one saw this ugly vignette between them. It was as if she lived in two spheres: a daylit one observed by the world's benevolent, oblivious populace and a dark one inhabited by only herself and Thomas McNaughton.

The forward movement of the line of mourners propelled her through the gate. Tugging her black jacket tightly around her, she hurried to her buggy, watching her feet on the verdant June grass, making certain they did not run. She knew full well that McNaughton watched her, but she did not know that an entirely new pair of eyes was upon her as well.

Early that spring, the Snowy Mountain Pack had settled into a rocky coulee deep in the forest. Leal's litter of five was born in May, as rain pattered the lush cover of spirea and as thunder pealed over the Snowy Mountains. While Adrad and the others lay curled near the front of the deep hollow, beneath the roots of a great spruce tree,

Leal quickly consumed the placentae and umbilical cords. Turning her attention to the pups, she licked each of them clean and nudged the squirming, blind forms into position near her belly.

For the next ten days, she continued licking and nosing them all, encouraging them to suckle. They nursed ten or twelve times a day, making tiny squeaks as they tumbled over one another in furious little struggles to survive.

From the very first hour, Leal could tell which were stronger and which needed extra attention. One was especially robust, plowing about from the start, but one was weaker than all the others. Something was wrong with its breathing, making it slow to crawl forward and suck. Using the side of her snout, Leal pushed it close to her slack abdomen, helping it gain nourishment. As she did with all the others, she massaged its tiny belly with her tongue, stimulating its natural impulse to urinate. But it would not thrive.

By the ninth day it was wasting. She watched it lying very still, away from the others, barely breathing. Early the twelfth morning, when the moon was still high in the night sky, she took it outside and laid it near Adrad, who would know what to do. She knew he would bury it—not like humans do, as in a funerary proceeding, but because that is what wolves do with their dying young.

After she placed the tiny pup near its father, she nuzzled her mate and let him draw his great gray head affectionately over the top of hers. Glancing again at the tiny, quiet form, she moved from paw to paw for a moment, then returned to her litter, staying with them until it was time for the pack to leave on its morning hunt.

When she emerged from the den in the silvery predawn light, the little pup was gone. She picked up a trace of its scent, and she knew she could find its burial site if she wanted to. But she would not. She was hungry. The whelping and the nursing had weakened her, and she knew she must move with the pack. It was time to hunt.

Over the past two years, several new wolves had joined them. A recent newcomer had died almost as soon as he had arrived, covered with a skin disease that made him an outcast from the moment the pack laid eyes on him.

If accepted, new wolves were integrated into the pack depending on their stature, their character traits, and their ability to contribute. The most significant arrival over the past year had been Three Toes, a pale yellowish white wolf whose left front foot had been permanently disfigured when he yanked it out of a trap.

Adrad wasted no time putting newcomers in their place. His size was hugely intimidating, but Leal knew that his decisiveness and self-assuredness were his greatest advantages. His initial battle with Three Toes last fall had been a noteworthy conflict, but the fight ended with Three Toes on his back in a posture of submission, and peace ensued between the two mature males.

In January another male had come. He was wiry and dark, resembling Leal. She knew instantly that he was attracted to her. Adrad, with his wild mane fully ruffed out and his teeth bared, advanced on the cocky newcomer, towering over him with savage confidence. The Loner chose not to fight. His ears flattened back as he dropped to the dust in a crouch, acknowledging Adrad as the dominant male.

This morning, they hunted in the early darkness, heading north and moving single file along a familiar trail, the great pines rising like the buttresses of a cathedral on either side. Scenting cattle, sheep, and deer, they kept on the deer scent. In a few weeks the elk would be calving, but right now their prey was mule deer. The trail came out into the open, bending north and following a barbwire fence.

Below them, to the right, was a flat pasture where a small herd of Hereford cows and calves stood. Adrad was in the front of the line, with Leal directly behind him. The Loner was midway back, with several of the younger wolves to the rear. As the pack trotted along the ridge, the Loner's head turned sharply to the right. Ears up, he froze, his agate-hued eyes focused on a wandering Hereford calf. A dark blur, he was down off the ridge with three younger wolves following him before Adrad and Leal knew what had happened.

Incensed by this insubordination, Adrad wheeled and gave chase. He had not been interested in cattle this morning, but this situation could not be brooked. By the time he and Leal and the rest of the pack caught up with the Loner and the others, the calf was gutted and dying, with the entire herd bellowing loudly.

Leal knew Adrad wanted to fight the Loner on the spot, but there was no time. Instead, the alpha male lifted the limp, bloody calf in his huge jaws and tore up the hill. Shouts from the ranch house blended with the cacophony of the distressed cattle; the crack of a gunshot rent the air. But by now, the wolf pack was in the trees, bolting for the dark embrace of the forest.

Later that afternoon, a thundershower dampened the grassy basin of their private coulee. The harebells, lupine, and wild geranium leaned over, sparkling in the afternoon sun. Out of nowhere, two of Leal's grown pups from last year showed up. They had been missing for over two weeks, off on a rogue hunt of their own.

They bounded into the coulee, rolling onto their backs as soon as they saw Adrad stalking toward them. As they cowered and slouched, Leal could see their protruding ribs and the hollow spaces below their eyes. Once their father was satisfied with their identity and scent, the entire pack burst into a chatter of yips and howls. Leal watched for a moment as the weary pair was set upon in a celebration of wrestling, tumbling, and licking.

Having eaten ravenously of the calf, she retreated to her litter and sprawled deep in the den, exhausted. When Adrad came in to sniff the pups and lick her face, she barely lifted her head. He left her and took his place on a sandy mound outside, a few yards from the entrance. Surveying the young ones, he heard the grunts and snarls of their ceaseless playacting. Their romping did not disturb him; on the contrary, it strengthened the Snowy Mountain Pack community. Blinking in the sun, he eyed the Loner, who lay some distance away, then shifted his gaze to the horizon beyond.

The sky hung heavy and low as Rob Elliott rode through the dense pines along the East Fork of Big Spring Creek. The blue roan's neck glistened with damp. Yesterday, an old man at Lewistown Feeds told him that June in Montana was generally like this. "Thunderstorms and gully-washers," he had opined, sluicing a stream of tobacco between his teeth. Rob tucked that lore away, along with what he'd been learning around the table at the McNaughton place since he'd arrived in May.

"This weather doesn't bother me," he said to the roan. "Reminds me of the Ohio Valley."

Coming out in the open, he craned around in the saddle to make sure the packhorse was following all right. The roll of sheep wire and the posthole digger were still tightly knotted on the sawbucks. A smile flickered across his face as he thought of the McNaughton boys surreptitiously inspecting his knots before he rode out.

"Thought I hadn't seen them, much less known what they were thinking," he muttered. "They all looked at my pack horse. I can just imagine the thoughts going through their heads. 'Some Ohio Yankee what don't know a half hitch from a hobble strap.'" The smile faded as he shook his head. *Two losses in two years*, he reflected. *A wounded lot they are, God help them in their grief. And the old man thinks to make me one of his own. Hell, they don't even know me. I bear them some filial loyalty, but they only warrant that because of our distant connection on my mother's side. I'm here in Montana because I belong here.*

The mental sketches he'd formed of the western frontier were a familiar and comfortable landscape that had been both refuge and fantasy for as far back as he could remember. The Ohio Valley, with its lush farms and snug hamlets, bred in him a love of animal husbandry and of the land, but each night in the second-story bedroom of his mother's white frame house, he'd fallen asleep counting the years until he was of proper age to go west. When his mother became gravely ill, she'd shown him the precious family things she wanted him to keep: pewter and china from the ancient Elliott farm near Edinburgh, an enormous painted trunk, pieces of her crochet and quilting, a few books.

In the spring, he took the train west. Determined not to spend any more of his homesteader fund than necessary, he carried his personal belongings in a leather pack and rolled out a few coarse blankets on the ground overnight between trains. In the baggage car, the trunk full of keepsakes would catch up with him in Montana.

At a stopover in Minot on a crisp night in May, he bedded down behind Jarvi's Wash House. He woke with a start in the moonless dark to the cries of a distant wolf pack. There was something about those ghostly wails that hit him in the gut and convinced him he'd done the right thing. The wolves were greeting him, confirming everything he'd ever sensed and believed about this long-awaited journey. Any ambivalence he fostered about leaving the safe nurturance of the shoulder-to-shoulder settlements of the Ohio Valley crackled away into the vast expanse of that cold prairie night. At dawn, waking to the strange whicker of frozen laundry slapping on the lines, he couldn't keep the eager smile off his face. The Montana border was a scant hundred miles away.

Now, as he topped a small rise, a warm and fragrant breeze swept over him. As far as his eyes could see, the waving meadow grass was threaded with blue spikes of lupine and the brilliant gold of a flower the locals called balsam root. The sky above had brewed itself into an ominous slate color, and behind him, the western horizon was a curious sight. The Big Belt Mountains were faintly visible in the western distance, but curtains of rain stood like smoky veils before them.

Below him, Castle Creek ran clear and cold past a grassy flat and a clutch of enormous boulders. An old fir tree leaned into one of them, creating a natural lean-to. *The perfect campsite. Something to tuck away for future reference, in case things get too close for comfort at the Rocking M.*

Rob swept his hand across the back of his neck and surveyed the object of this afternoon's labor: several low spots in the fence between McNaughton's land and John Graham's. Fencing was hard work, but he was good at it. Better than anyone else he had ever teamed up with. He had fenced his own 160-acre homestead up on Ruby Creek in less than two weeks. Signing on with the McNaughtons for a month or two was a means to an end; it would help him build the nest egg he needed to put some finishing touches on his place before the snow began to fly.

Two hours later, after ratcheting the top wire taut with the stretcher, he straightened up, pushed his hat back, and glanced to his right to check the rain in the distance. *Moving north, it looks like. Might miss us altogether.*

As he turned to gather up the roll of wire, something caught his eye. Through a grove of jack pine and box elder, a figure stirred in the brush. *Well, there's a good-sized flock on that hill. It's Graham's land. He probably sent someone out here to round up the sheep.*

Tilting his head for a better look through the trees, he waited for the figure to reappear. Among the fluttering leaves of box elder, it showed itself again. The person was dressed in black, on foot, and hatless. Was it a woman? If so, she was carrying something big and bulky.

Rob easily swung his leg over the fence onto the Graham's land and entered a grove of pines. As he drew closer, he saw that the black-clad figure was an elderly woman. She was carrying a bundle of sticks, making her way up a small rise toward a stretch of the same fence he had just been repairing. He could hear her mutter to the sheep in a thick Scots burr as she plodded up the flowered hill. Being well concealed, he had no fear of being seen.

A few yards from the fence, she dropped her burden and arranged the sticks and twigs in a long pile, parallel with the fence, connecting them with several other piles she had evidently placed there earlier.

Dusting off her hands, she moistened a finger between her lips and held it up to test the wind. Then, as she picked up a long black walking stick and knotted her shawl around her, she cocked her head as if she heard something. Rob was perfectly still; he knew there had been no sound except the mewing lambs and the rustling of the long grass in the wind. But the old woman turned slowly and looked straight into the pines.

Rob's eyes widened as he held his breath. *She can't see me. I'm completely obscured and the horses are over the rise, down in the next*

*gully. Besides, I'm not doing anything wrong . . . although I am on
private property.*

He watched the old woman's face. There was no trace of fear.
She seemed only to be watching, collecting what was present to
be seen—or unseen. Where did he remember her from? At the
cemetery, two weeks ago—that was it—when they buried Rowena.
She was a Graham, of course. The grandmother of the young
woman he hadn't been able to forget. He tried to think about that
day, but he felt caught in the web of the old woman's stare, unable
to piece anything together.

For another thirty seconds, the dark eyes attempted to fix him.
Then, with a little lift and drop of her tiny shoulders, she turned
and walked through the flock, poking her stick out in front of her
and leaving a green path as she went.

Chapter Five

The evening air sparkled with the sounds of laughter and family. Maude brought up the rear of the procession, carrying a picnic basket that was so heavy she had to stop every twenty yards to catch her breath.

Her mother, in a dark red dress, carried an autoharp in a worn case, and her father, his tall figure unbowed by fifty-five years, walked at her side. Rory had gone over by the creek, looking for rising trout. Maude, noticing that Mac sauntered along at a safe distance, suspected that they had fought. Fifteen months apart, so close for brothers, they had slept together as toddlers, shared a pony in grade school, and won a blue ribbon together on their first lamb. But now she couldn't keep track of when they were friends and when they were sparring.

Mary promenaded down the center of the lane in a striped dress, but couldn't resist when she saw Fiona and Isobel plunge into the tall grass and begin making daisy chains. She ran after them, snapping off the stems of oxeye daisies and clover blossoms, carefully splitting them with her teeth and plaiting them together.

Isobel had a fistful of flowers too, but spying Maude far behind the rest, she skipped back toward her, laughing as she came, then stopped a few yards from the road when a butterfly lilted close to her head. "Maudie, look, it's magic!" She threw Maude a shy look. "Well, Gran Ailse says it's faerie magic."

Maude smiled. "That's a fritillary."

"A what?"

"Fri-till-ary. That's what kind of butterfly, or faerie, has befriended you."

Isobel wove through the long grass, keeping pace with Maude, singing an old nursery song that Ailse had taught them all.

When midsummer comes, nae lone body stands
Fair maidens and lassies, let's clasp all air hands
Then do bavens and bromes, a grand bonfire make
And leap o'er it all, till the last coal I'll take."

At the meeting place, a dozen boulders formed a wide circle. Maude wasted no time in unburdening herself of the picnic basket and finding a seat on a cool piece of granite. The air was already oppressive, and she knew that within an hour, the blaze would be fierce.

"We've put dinner off long enough," said Catriona, spreading out a cloth. The family fell upon the feast of chicken, roasted potatoes, bean salad, lemonade, scones, and apple pie from last year's canning.

With a rustle of black muslin, Ailse leaned back against a stone, teacup in hand. She raised the other arm and held it up to shield her eyes from the setting sun. "Only anaither three-quarters of an hour till dark. Micht as weel light the fire, John. Trina, how aboot 'The Rose of Allendale?'"

Maude watched her father bend down to hold a match to the pile of kindling. Midsummer fires and picnics were a way of life for the Grahams and for many of the Scots immigrants in the Judith Basin: story-telling, bonfires, and late-night flirtations for the young folk. Catriona called this occasion St. John's Mass, since the Scots had long ago Christianized the ancient holiday of the solstice. Ailse, however, continued to call it *Litha*, after the old ways.

Maude was eager for the story-telling, but her grandmother's eyes were on the boys, who were devouring a second piece of pie. "Where ye be off to this night, Master Rory and young Mac?"

Catriona's head swiveled around to look at her two sons, although her soft strumming never skipped a beat.

Mac cast her a defensive look. "What?"

"I'm just waiting for you to answer your grandmother. I haven't heard a word about the neighborhood goings-on. I like to know."

Rory shoved his coppery hair back and smiled. Maude knew he was the heart's desire of Fergus County's blooming female population. Within a few weeks after Rory's birth, everyone began remarking on the striking difference between him and Maude. "He's clear sprung from the Graham side, with that red gold hair and brown eyes," a neighbor had said.

Rory's rolled-up shirtsleeves revealed strong, tanned arms as he leaned across the blanket to pluck a strand of timothy. "Fentons are having a bonfire. Big, though." He threw a deprecating glance at the small fire in the center of their family circle. "They've invited the whole county."

"All of Fergus County, now?" Catriona set aside the autoharp and began wiping the sterling flatware. "And if your brother, Mac, wants to join you in meeting the entire populace, he'll have to do it all before midnight. Do I make myself clear?"

Mac, still avoiding direct conversation with his brother, nodded. "Fine."

Rory stood up. "It'll take us a while to get there."

"Don't take Caesar. He's looking lame," said their father, rising from his seat by the fire, which, despite Rory's disparagement, was stoked to a fine blaze now.

As the young men's figures receded down the lane, the lengthening shadows contrasted with golden stripes of sunlight. A cloud of midges rose and fell like a silver wave over the meadow. Maude felt a stab of something. She knew for certain she didn't want to go to the Fentons' and stand around like a skeleton at a feast. At twenty-five, she was a spectacle and she knew it.

"The animal healer from the forest," people called her. If one overlooked the vitriol in Mary's assessments, she reflected, her sister's description of her was not too far afield. *It's true,* she admitted. *I'm on my way to becoming as much a local curiosity as Gran Ailse.*

"He's taking his fiddle, is he?" Catriona was asking.

John nodded. "That group from Judith Gap is playing, and they wanted him."

"My son a busker!"

John puffed on his pipe and grinned. "And you with that autoharp lying at your side."

"I never once played in public and you know it." Gathering up the loose napkins, Catriona shook her head. "One boy packing off with musicians and the other dreaming of railroads."

"Well now, a young man can't sit at ease till he sees a bit of the world."

"Trina, ye maun let the young one stay later," Ailse put in. "This night, the heart barely wakens by twelve o' the clock. Why, I remember twa young folk what met in a cabbage patch along the Findhorn River late one midsummer's night." She winked at Maude.

"Go on with you," Catriona sputtered, folding the napkins and creasing them with a vengeance.

John Graham found a boulder of his own, grunting as he leaned back and stretched out his legs. "I remember that night. It was cool. Not like tonight." His eyes were on the green black of the Judith Mountains, but Maude knew he was looking across the ocean to the hills of Morayshire.

"Aye, and how could ye not? Ye won the greatest applause that night, leapin' o'er that blazin' fire like ye did," said Ailse.

In the old country, young men jumped back and forth over the midsummer fires in a playful act of heroism. Whoever leaped over the highest flames was the summer's victor over evil.

"Near burnt my privates off. It's lucky you were ever born, Maude. And the rest of you bairns." He grinned and nodded to the younger girls, now making flowered headdresses for their dolls. Mary hovered between the adults and the younger girls, devoting an ear to each conversation.

"What's this about the cabbage patch?" Maude prompted Ailse.

Catriona fired a warning look at her mother. Ailse ignored her and let out a cackle. "Hah! Neither of ye thought I saw ye that night, near the old wattle shed. And ye were fools tae think I wouldnae go there with my burning wand. I maun always circle the gardens! Someone's got tae protect the growing things and animals. I'll be circling everything this night, just as I have these twelve years in America. Moray or Montana, makes nae difference."

It wasn't until she felt her mother's stare that Maude realized she was nodding her own head. She shrugged and looked away, knowing full well that when the fire in front of them burned low and her parents had gone to bed, she and Gran Ailse would lift a couple of smoking sticks from the ashes. Together, they'd circle the prim gardens hemming the main house and the crooked herb and flower paths around Ailse's cottage. The clouds of smoke would ensure a healthy growing season and harvest to come. Already she longed for the night air on her skin and the smooth-worn touch of her grandmother's hand.

"'Twas a good thing ye were wearin' your pale green muslin that night, Trina, cause ye blended right in with all those ruffled cabbages."

Maude's hand flew to her mouth as she burst out laughing.

Her mother's face went poppy red. "Ailse Mary MacDougall, have you lost all sense of decency in your dotage? Hush now!"

John was laughing too, but he turned the conversation quickly to the health of the 463 new lambs.

It was only Ailse humming, but Maude heard music beyond the thin vibration of the old woman's throat. The meadowlarks in the willow break sounded like flutes, and the tapping of the spotted flicker was as rhythmic as an ancient drummer.

John and Catriona had wandered back to the big house nearly an hour ago and had surely chased the girls to bed by now. John would retire early, and Catriona would sit in the large mohair chair in the great room and read, or make a pretense of it, until she saw the boys coming up the lane.

Maude sat on a plank between two boulders, swinging her legs. An enamel pot, its lid rattling noisily, was perched on a stone near the edge of the fire, which burned much lower now. Ailse pulled two heavy mugs from the grass, then lifted a handful of her skirt in order to grasp the bubbling pot. The aroma of the brew filled Maude's head with memories. It was mostly good English black tea from Lehman's in town, but there were other things present: orange peel, ginger, rose hips.

She took the proffered mug and held it close. The evening air was cooling fast. "They say you're a witch, you know."

Ailse arched her brows and gave a haughty little smile.

"I'm the only one who has the nerve to tell you."

Ailse stirred the fire, sending a stream of orange sparks skyward. "There's ne'er been a secret between us. But I ken what the town people say."

"So you *are* a witch." Maude compressed her lips, trying not to laugh.

"I prefer 'wise woman,' an it please ye."

Maude sipped her tea. The sun was on the horizon, a melting lozenge of madder red, and the sky was luminous with magic. "How does it work, the lineage?"

Ailse shook her head, the blue in her eyes barely visible by the dying fire. "Hard tae say. Betimes it seems tae skip generations. I've seen glimpses of sommat in Trina, but I've allus thought she was a wee bit frightened. She lets her gift come oot in aither ways, with her weaving and her flowers. But she's verra good at matchmaking, and that's nae accident."

"So it's different in us all."

"Aye. Different in us all. I see it strong in ye. Ye dinnae ken the fullness of it yet, mayhaps. It didnae come full on me until after

I married yer gran-da. The sensing of things afore they happen, I mean. That queer breeziness aboot the windpipe. Betimes I'd feel it gentle, aither times I'd feel the wind knocked oot o' me ribs."

Maude stared, unaware that she'd moved her hand up to her sternum.

"Ye ken it inside, the breathin', aye? When sommat's aboot tae happen?"

"It makes me angry, Gran. I don't think of it as a gift. And I was shocked to actually see . . . a vision, or whatever it was I saw at the post office. It scared me. I mean, if a person's going to be blessed with second sight, or special wits, as you call them, then Keeper of the Universe ought to help her use those wits."

Ailse wove her head back and forth, her lips in a firm line. "Ye've got tae wear it and bear it, like it or nae. I've seen it growin' in ye, all these years. Wee things, like ye did in the garden when we were gatherin' simples that day. Liftin' yer hands, partin' the invisible air. That cannae be taught. It's a way of movin' the cobwebs of the spirit world away tae make a path for light and goodness. Yer shadow side and yer light side. And nae, there be nae handbook. Each of us maun write our ain."

As she turned and looked at Maude, her wrinkled face broke into a wistful smile. "Betimes we wish it werenae so, this kennin'. And I used tae wish I could wield it like a spade or a spoon. It gets easier wi' time. I've gotten used tae it, the way a body learns tae ride an unruly horse." She let out a yip of a laugh. "Maybe the horse gets used tae the rider as weel. All I can say is, it takes mickle care." She paused, her dark eyes boring into Maude's over the glimmering fire. "There be one rule in't all, and that is tae harm nae one. Not e'er. But I am nae the least bit worrit about my Maudie."

Maude's gaze dropped to the shifting coals. *Lucky or cursed, here I am with this thing, this inheritance. And according to Gran, it can't be manipulated. Bits of knowledge, mere scraps, will drift in on the ether, posted by spirit sentries from the other side.*

Lifting her eyes, she looked down the long lane and saw the big house, a few squares of yellow light swimming in a sea of evening shadows. She thought of her brothers. "What about men? Does it pass through them?"

Ailse knitted her brow. "Och, I heard of some men wi' their ain gifts, in the auld country. There was a fellow over Aberdeen way what could read folks' eyes—he could tell what ye were thinkin'. But he died afore I was born."

"I don't find it in Mary, but I do sometimes wonder about Mac and Isobel."

"Your sister Mary will find love this summer."

"What?" Maude gasped.

Ailse shook her head. "See, there's an example of how it has gotten a wee bit clair for me. Mind, I said a wee bit. Aye, there's sommat stirring wi' Mary. Could be naught, but I see her with a young man." She passed her fingers across her brow. "I see his smooth hands. Watch her, Maudie."

In the silence that fell between them, the song of the meadowlarks floated through the deepening twilight. Then, Maude picked up a faint clip-clop. "Listen," she whispered. "It's a horse and buggy on the main road."

"Aye! I wondered if she'd come. It's been twa-three year."

"It's not—"

"Ye ken full well who 'tis, child. Run and fill the kettle, then we'll walk oot tae the gate tae meet your Auntie Morag."

Chapter Six

When they greeted each other at Ailse's gate, Maude buried her face in Morag's hair. The lavender scent of it took her back to that tiny kitchen in Great Falls and to those months of flailing strangeness as she tried to come to terms with the rape. Catriona, getting settled in the Judith Basin during those grim, painful days, had deposited her traumatized daughter with Morag, who was already well-established in Great Falls.

After setting the master shepherd Kibbey in charge of the construction of their house at Stony Creek, John Graham had taken the boys and had gone on an extended sheep-buying trip to Wyoming and Colorado. Weeks stretched into months as he explored wool-growing opportunities, teaching the boys about different breeds and their relative hardiness and quality, and ultimately speculating in land as well as livestock.

Catriona and Ailse helped supervise the construction crew and laid out the gardens. Morag, whose apothecary shop in Great Falls was doing a smart business, was glad to have Maude. Morag was an elixir herself, and Catriona knew it. It didn't take long for Maude to learn that Morag was stronger in some ways than her own mother. She was a towering oak, in whose branches a wounded bird could shelter from the storm.

Looking back, Maude saw how much sense it made that she'd

been taken to Great Falls to stay with her aunt, but her feelings of abandonment could not have been more vast and deep had she been left at the edge of the Arctic Circle.

Walking through the dusky midsummer gardens with Morag and Ailse, she let the cooling air brush these fractal memories from her head. Now that it was past eleven o'clock, the mystery of midsummer was deep and rich. Birdsong had ended, but every now and then, when she heard the peculiar, vibrating *whoosh* of a nighthawk, she shivered with joy.

The scent of sage filled the air, and with it she caught the heady, exotic aroma of the Russian olive trees. The tips of the burning willow wands held aloft by the three women glowed a soft orange in the night, while the moonlight shone on the silver braids crowning Ailse's head.

"Do you think Trina's still awake?" asked Morag, a note of mischief in her voice.

"We should leave her alone," said Maude.

"Why? She should be out here with us."

"Fie on't, Morag. Ye ken she willnae." Ailse shook her head.

"I'm going to go and get her. She can at least go 'round and smoke her own blessed garden, can't she?"

"She doesnae like the auld ways. She'll back into her warren like a hare."

But Morag was already on her way up the veranda steps and tiptoeing to the square-paned windows of the great room. Maude heard the light tapping of her aunt's fingernail on the glass, then a high-pitched shriek from inside.

The light snapped on and the broad door swung open. "What in God's name are you doing here?"

Morag laughed the deep, unflappable laugh that Maude remembered from years ago. "Don't be a ninny," Morag said, tilting her head at her sister. "What other night would I come?"

Catriona peered out into the darkness past her sister and saw Maude and Ailse. She leaned her head to one side and gave a breathy, "Mmm."

"Don't be so dour, lassie. Come out with us, even if it's just for a few minutes."

Catriona tugged at the ends of her shawl. "It's cold, you . . . sorceresses. Besides, bad things can happen on these solstice nights."

"You're a sorceress too. You just don't want to admit it. Put on a coat and some galoshes, then. Come out."

Catriona let out a sigh. "Just for a minute. Only because you've come all this way, though."

The porch light went off, then Catriona emerged, joining the black-clad trio. With Morag and Catriona chattering, Maude stayed a few paces behind, lost in the velvet night.

Ailse insisted on walking around the barn and corrals. "Oh, all right," said Catriona, "but what time is it?"

"It's too dark to read my watch," answered Morag. "Are you worried about the boys? We'll hear them coming well enough."

"Speak of the devil," said Maude. "I think I hear the horses now."

"Girl, you could hear a pin drop over in Meagher County," said Morag.

"Sure enough," said Catriona, "I hear something too. Gran, if you want to finish your smoke circling, you go ahead. I'm going back to the house."

"I'll stay with Gran," said Maude.

Ailse gathered Morag's wand up with her own and set out for the sheep pens, poking the ground in front of her with her long walking stick. "The night is young, Maudie. We've got mickle tae do. We're gang tae the north pasture after this."

"We are?"

"Aye. You're father's got a thousand sheep oot there—we cannae ignore them."

Maude puckered her lips and nodded.

"I've a plan."

Maude turned back slightly, sensing that the boys had arrived at the house. Ailse marched forward on skinny legs, intent on her errand.

"Gran! Wait—please."

"What is't?"

"Something's wrong. We've got to go with Mother and Morag."

Blinking like moles, they entered the brightly lit house. Everyone was in the kitchen, where Catriona bent over her eldest son, dabbing at his face with a cloth soaked in ice water. She paused and pulled back to assess the swelling, then set her jaw and began mounding fresh ice chips into a compress.

Mary, Fiona, and Isobel perched like silent sparrows in the breakfast nook. Mary had a new sateen robe which she had sashed with a perfect bow, while the younger two drew their knees up to their chins and clutched their nightgowns tightly around their ankles. Fiona's copper hair, much like Mary's in color and texture, was tied up in rag curls, but Isobel's hung in dark, loose ringlets around her shoulders. Mac stood apart from them, lounging against the cupboards, cheeks flushed, hair tousled from the ride.

"Maude, you know where the salves are in the hall closet. Run and get the jar of arnica and the gauze poultices." Catriona leaned this way and that, studying Rory's face.

"Mother," Rory said, "the Fenton women iced me until my skin was about to fall off. You don't need to keep doing it." Then, more softly, he added, "I'll be good as new in a couple of days."

"Fine. That's fine." Catriona set the knotted bag of ice down on the table with a hard crunch.

John Graham leaned against the porcelain sink that covered half of one wall. "I'd be willing to wager this was about a girl."

Rory stared at the cupboards.

"Well, that's pretty much a confirmation, isn't it?" chirped Catriona.

"Mother, some people actually *choose* their partners." Maude regretted the words as soon as they left her lips. She set the arnica salve and the gauze pads down on the table and snatched her hand away as if her mother might sprout wasp wings and sting her. When she glanced at Rory, she saw the trace of a smile.

"I told you bad things can happen on this night." Catriona was determined to get her licks in. She threw a look at Mac, shaking her head. "I don't suppose there was any way you could have—"

Rory took a deep breath. "Mother, Mac didn't even know this was happening. He was with the band. Did pretty well, too." Picking up the ice bag, he gingerly rested his face against it and began his account. Maude watched Catriona's neck stiffen at the mention of Antonia Fredrich's name. Her mother would far sooner have selected some fresh rosebud from the Young Women's Esther Circle at St. James Episcopal, certainly not a rustic hellebore sprung from the Carpathian crags, with a *babushka* for a mother.

Maude watched the two youngest girls in the breakfast nook, taking in their innocent excitement. Shoulders hunched, their mouths forming little "o" shapes, they stole quick looks at one another. They'll never forget this night, she thought, remembering what those dreamy, impressionable years had been like, so long ago.

"Let me get this straight," John summarized. "It was you and Blair McNaughton, over the Fredrich girl?"

"Yes."

"Her father," ruminated John, "his name's Jozsef. He's one of the chief stonemasons on the construction of the Stone Church, right in downtown Lewistown. I've met him. His people came here just like we did, to make a new start. America is a blend of many great peoples." He looked across the room at the baking pans on the wall as he made these remarks, but Maude knew they were directed at Catriona. He turned his focus back to Rory. "Was anyone else involved in this?"

"Against me, you mean?"

"Well, yes, that's exactly what I mean."

"No. But that new Elliott fellow over at the McNaughton place— he's some relation of theirs—he stepped in when I was down. I could have gotten up if I had just had a second more—"

"He stepped in to help you? Against Blair?"

Silent for a moment, Rory shifted the ice bag against his eye. "That's right."

"You're wiping the salve off," said Catriona, unscrewing the cap on the jar.

John Graham raked his hand across his salt-and-pepper stubble. "Interesting. I'm not sure how that will sit with the folks over at the Rocking M, but I guess that's not our business. Anyone else?"

"Anyone else what?"

"Anyone else help you, is what I am asking." John's brows went up.

"No. But Grant McNaughton was ready to throw a bucket of cold water on all three of us when we were wrangling in the dust." He paused. "Blair cursed Elliott and told him not to come back to the Rocking M tonight."

Maude backed up toward the hall until her heels met a tall cabinet. Leaning into it, her hands dropped to her sides and traced the carved molding. She was transported back to the cemetery, where it seemed she could still watch all the McNaughtons, including Rob Elliott.

Ailse grabbed her arm and motioned to Morag. "They dinnae need us," she whispered. "Come along."

Back out in the night, with the limitless sky overhead, Maude found that things made more sense, or at least the claustrophobic glut of emotions sloshing around in the kitchen slipped away, making room for her own. But despite the space offered by the wild, open air, and all the blessings of the longest day of the year, she had the jitters.

Rob Elliott had helped her brother. It was a piece of valor; she'd allow that. But she wished he hadn't been the one. Someone else would have stepped in eventually. Why did it have to be him? He should stay away. Gallantry was something the Grahams could do just fine without. The very image of him in her mind's eye made it hard for her to breathe. What if Laird McNaughton took his son Blair's part in some twisted way and decided to wreak revenge on her or her family? It was not out of the question. He drove past her house all the time, watching, waiting, out where Kettle Creek Lane joined Big Spring Road.

As she helped Morag harness the runabout in the dim light of the barn, her fingers shook. She didn't mind one bit that they were going out to the north pasture. She wanted to stay up all night, to let the wind blow this nonsense out of her.

Thomas McNaughton had done far more than use her and drain himself into her those dozen years ago. He had created a relationship with her *in absentia*. He appeared in her life, in her mind, just often enough to maintain a chokehold on her.

It struck her just now, as she tightened the harness buckles, that she was very much harnessed to him, the filthy bastard. She lay in bed at night thinking about him, about the very pores on his face and the red hairs that grew from behind his ears and blended into the graying whiskers of his closely trimmed beard. *Why, I even think about the way he must eat, masticating the peas and potatoes of his shepherd's pie, the pink drops of wine that must stain his linen napkins, and what he must wear to bed at night.*

Tears filled her eyes. *For God's sake, look what I've wrought. I have practically married myself to him. Married in shame. And I don't see how it can be undone. The more I think about it, the more confused I become. It's as if every effort I make to comprehend it is another warm exhale on a pane of cold glass through which I'm trying to see.* She swiped the wet streaks from her face and swallowed hard.

"Are we ready, Maude?" Morag, ready to douse the lantern, eyed her suspiciously.

"We're ready." She bit her lip hard and swung around the horses, stepping up into the buggy. "We'll need to go slowly. Let the horses pick their way. It's a good moon. They'll be all right."

The iron casings around the buggy wheels rang now and then when they struck a stone, but for the most part they wound their way silently through rich pastureland, grassy and soft. Maude breathed deep, letting the night settle on her.

After a mile or so, they entered her favorite part, a long stretch of aspens near the confluence of Stony Creek and Castle Creek. Above them fluttered a dark canopy of a million heart-shaped leaves, dancing against the stars and an occasional glimpse of the gibbous moon. Maude felt with the toe of her boot for the iron pot where Ailse had stowed several glowing coals from the bonfire. She figured these would be used to relight the willow wands when they reached the flock in the north pasture.

The aspen woods gave way to a grove of pine and Douglas fir. As they entered a dark tunnel of mammoth trees, a great horned owl glided low and silent just over the horse's back.

"A better omen could nae be found," said Ailse.

When the owl hooted from a neighboring tree, the three women laughed. "Who cooks for you?" said Morag, mocking his four-part call, then replied, "We be single women three, so we do our own!"

"It's not far now," said Maude. "About a quarter mile."

The horse splashed through the creek and up a small rise. Maude could see the sheep on the hill, a carpet of grayish white mounds beneath the misshapen moon. She clutched her wool cape around her shoulders, regretting that she had worn only a thin merino cardigan over her black dress. After tying the horse, she followed Ailse and Morag dutifully up the hillside.

"Here we are," said Ailse. "It's all ready. Now Maude, when ye work a protection spell like this one, ye maun always set it on a wee brae." She pointed to the sloping landscape. "If there's eldritch gangs-on—that's spirit-mischief and hauntings, mind ye—it's verra like tae start in a place such as this. We maun set the mettle of the sun-year aright."

Maude peered past Gran's bony finger into the darkness and made out the long, grassy curve of a gentle sidehill. Ailse picked up the little iron pot and dumped the coals onto the ground into a pile of tinder that she had obviously prepared earlier. A fire sprang instantly to life, not confining itself to one small area, but instead running quickly along the fenceline in a bright blaze.

Maude felt an itch of perspiration under her arms. "Ailse . . . how big a fire are we building?"

"Dinnae worry, Maudie. 'Tis only June. The grass is green and dampish. I've built a line o' tinder and sticks aboot five yards long. It's enow tae smoke the whole flock. This is how we did it on the

Findhorn when I was a wee girl." Her eyes sparkled with satisfaction as the bundles of twigs snapped and popped, catching the blaze. "And the wind be pairfect, coming right oot o' the northwest."

Maude stole a glance at Morag. Her aunt made a slight moue of her lips as if to mean, *this is a bit more than I bargained for*, but she said nothing.

The flames grew higher and brighter as they watched, with hundreds of sparks shooting up to the black heavens. All the prearranged sticks and branches were now crackling loudly. This fire was much larger than anything Maude had ever seen at their midsummer or even their Halloween festivities. Her alarm was by no means abating, but she noted the length of the fire. It was exactly what Ailse had said, about five yards long and a yard or two wide, and showed no signs of running out of control. Such a fire could never be tolerated in July or August, because the pasturelands lose all their moisture as the summer wanes, but in mid-June, she admitted, this sort of thing could be managed if closely watched.

Out of nowhere, Maude heard a man's voice.

"Get out of the way! Look out!"

She barely had time to turn around to see the source of the voice when a dark silhouette appeared and a great drenching of cold water hit her full in the chest, followed by a second, even heavier dousing. Morag was struck too, but dodged quickly away. Only Ailse was far enough away to avoid the fracas.

"What in God's name?" Maude staggered back, the front of her body soaking wet. Her cloak had been dashed back by the force of the water and her black merino sweater was molded to her breasts. Holding her dripping arms and hands out to her sides in shock, she looked down at herself, gasping.

Rob Elliott stared at the wild-looking woman in front of him. The scene itself was eerie, but this female was spellbinding. Her hair, a mass of mahogany spirals, was blowing straight up, swept into a vortex made by the northwest wind and the upward draft of the flames. In one glance he caught it all—her slender waist, her

shapely bosom plastered with thin, wet wool, her pale face . . .
and those eyes. Even the dim firelight was enough to rekindle the
memory of the first time he had seen those lupine blue eyes. It's
her, he thought. The woman at the cemetery.

She was dangerously close to the flames, and as she struggled
for her footing, she tripped on her cloak. Its edge trailed through
the embers and caught fire. Unaware, she stood there, scowling
at the man standing ten feet away with two empty buckets in
his hands. Then all she felt was a searing pain along her left
forearm.

Morag screamed, "You're on fire!"

His body struck hers, flinging her to the grass. The scent of him
filled her nostrils. He was wet too, wet to the skin, and smelled of
creek water and leather. They tumbled down the slope, thrashing
through sage and lupine and balsam. The skin of his cheek, where a
day's worth of whiskers had grown, rasped once, twice, against her
jaw. With every revolution she felt the weight of him against her,
heavy and warm, bone-on-bone, clothing and flesh—a maelstrom
of male and female, bound tight together.

A knot of surcharged feeling rose from deep within her—dark,
unknown forces thrusting up, filling her with panic. Rising, roiling,
they plowed through her core—too many things—childlike curiosity spoiled by fear, a faint pulse of wonder long ago bled out by
rage.

Her hair covered her eyes like a dark net; she couldn't see, but
she could feel and smell and hear. The pain in her forearm floated
away, replaced by the heat of his neck against her lips. She felt the
pressure of tight, corded muscles where his neck became shoulder.
A trace of salt came through to her tongue, then the confusing
smells of castile soap and sage.

He huffed softly as they whipped through the fragrant grass. His
rib cage grazed hers and he batted at her arms and her thighs—not
hard, but with the flat of his hand, firmly, covering her every inch.
His mouth was near her ear as he whispered, "Please be all right
. . . don't want you to be hurt."

When they finally stopped, there wasn't a trace of a smolder left on the cloak, though it was in tatters. Rob scrambled away and knelt beside her. "I am terribly sorry, miss. I wanted to help you. I didn't know what you were doing." He paused. "I still don't know what the hell you were doing, actually."

Maude was on her haunches, backing away. She turned her face to the dark western sky, presenting him with her cheek, where bits of grass still clung. Panting, she leaned on tented fingers, ready to run. Unable to look at him straight on, she kept a sidelong, feral eye fixed on him.

He stood up, frowning. The awareness that he was trespassing was sudden and oppressive. This woman was beautiful, yes, but in the present moment, she was strange, even peculiar. "I'll go now. Are . . . are you all right? I have a wagon. I can take you to get medical attention."

Maude shook herself and let out a puff of air, as if just now remembering where she was. She sank back into a sitting position and drew her knees up to her chest, wrapping her arms around them. Her left forearm throbbed. As her breathing slowed, she stole a look at him. In the flickering light, his nose appeared swollen and his hair was wet. "You are Rob Elliott."

"Yes."

Morag and Ailse crept up behind him. Ailse carried a discarded fencepost six inches thick.

"Gran, don't," said Maude.

Rob spun around, recoiling from the little old woman brandishing a chunk of pine twice her size. "Hold on," he said, thrusting both palms outward. "I'm a friend. You are all Graham women, I take it?"

"More or less," spat Ailse. "What's your business here?"

"I thought it was a prairie fire, for God's sake."

Morag nodded. "Understandable. This is one of your larger conflagrations, Ailse."

"Bah!"

"This is a—family custom?" Rob's eyes drifted across the

smoldering meadow to the flock of sheep. A look of comprehension softened his face.

Ailse pruned up her mouth in silence.

"I respect the old ways," Rob said, with a polite inclination of his head. "But I had made a campsite just cross the fenceline, down by the creek. I smelled smoke and—well, what the hell was I supposed to think?"

Ailse's eyebrows knitted together. "Are ye the new ane over on the McNaughton place?"

There was a beat of silence before Rob answered, "I am." His gaze returned to Maude. He extended his hand, but she averted her eyes and remained seated, arms locked around her knees.

"Well. Fine. I'll leave you to your business, then." He turned on his heel and stalked away, grabbing the buckets with a clatter and disappearing into the darkness.

Chapter Seven

Morag clinked bottles together at Ailse's cottage, searching for the burn salve. "Here 'tis." She picked up a dark amber jar, then stopped at the window sill to lift up a heavy pot of aloe vera. "Sit still. And both of you midnight mavens, not a word of this incident to Catriona."

"Of course not." Maude winced as Morag applied the first strokes of the aloe and then the pungent ointment, then relaxed as the anesthetic took effect.

Morag looked up at Ailse. "Catriona thinks you've half shot your bolt already, Ailse. This would convince her."

Ailse sighed, then leaned her walking stick in the corner and said, "Betimes I got tae bed. I think I were ne'er sae weary." She shuffled off down the hall.

"She should be tired, with all this ruckus," whispered Morag. "You'll stay here, won't you?" She grabbed a three-legged stool and sat down to wind a strip of gauze around Maude's forearm.

"The sun will be coming up in three hours," Maude yawned. "I'll collapse right here on the sofa. I can't stand the smoky smell of myself, but I am too tired to care."

Morag reached for the scissors to trim the gauze. Then, as she bent low to focus, she remarked, "That fellow Elliott is handsome."

Maude sucked her cheeks in. "You could probably find your way back to his campsite."

"You know damn well what I mean."

"Snip your gauze now, Auntie, I'm tired."

It was late afternoon by the time she turned her buggy onto the winding dirt lane known as Kettle Creek Lane. The entire trip from Stony Creek Ranch to her own place was a scant two or three miles, just long enough to sort the jumble of her thoughts.

She had slept in that morning, stretched out under a soft wool blanket on Gran's couch. Finally, at nine o'clock, she woke to the sounds and smells of Gran's baking.

In honor of Morag's visit, they got out the best china from Edinburgh and the three of them chattered like magpies over shirred eggs, tea, and scones. They talked about Rory and the Fredrich girl and how frustrated Catriona must be at not having a more active hand in this match. Then the conversation turned to their respective gardens, to what was prospering and what wasn't.

Now, as a light rain began to patter the black canvas roof of the buggy, she sighed, already missing their company. Bobcat knew Kettle Creek Lane well and stepped out nicely, but Maude began to wish she was home right now. A dim, feverish feeling crept over her. She resented the fact that people talked about Gran, that they said unkind things about her, that she was an old hag or a witch. *If the townspeople knew that we had been out in the dead of night lighting bonfires to smoke our flocks and gardens, what would they have said to that? What would they have done?* A dark anger churned in her.

Why didn't people say wicked things about Inii Aohki, the Blackfeet medicine woman who lived on the outskirts of Fort Benton and who often came to peddle her wares in Lewistown? Maude scowled. People accepted Inii and her consort, the mysterious Blackfeet elder, Medicine Badger. They not only accepted them; they granted them a decent measure of respect as members of the ancient Pikuni Tribe of the Blackfeet. It was fine if Indians were exotic or peculiar, but if whites behaved unconventionally, the court of gossip was convened. It had been better in Scotland, where country folk were often seen of a morning, collecting medicinal herbs and mosses for their stillrooms. Bonfires on hillsides or feasting on quarter-days were as typical as going to church.

Maude was glad that Inii could make a living selling elixirs and unguents she prepared from her gatherings along the river, or even from animal organs and hides. Ailse had discovered that Inii's name meant "sees water," and that Inii always liked to camp near the water. Years ago, Inii had taught Ailse a prayer, which Ailse had repeated over breakfast that very morning: "Mother Earth, have pity on us and give us food to eat; Father Sun, bless all our children, and may our paths be straight."

On the seat next to her sat a large notebook. Ailse and Morag each had numerous fat tomes like this one, full of garden lore and instructions on how to blend various herbs into healing pastes, ointments, and tisanes. Earlier that day, Maude and Morag both pored over Ailse's books. Maude had started copying recipes, such as a barberry elixir to treat intestinal flux, then one for yarrow to stanch bleeding. Ailse finally said, "Take it home with ye, child."

Next to the notebook was a heavy piece of flour sacking wrapped around a portion of Gran's aloe plant, potted and ready to grow on her own windowsill. The sight of it made her forearm throb, tripping her mind to Rob Elliott.

He had meant well. She'd made this observation at least five times since waking. He had helped Rory, and he had intended to help her as well, although she had ended up with a nasty burn. He had offered to take her to get medical help. That was a kindness. He had done the right and proper thing, she allowed, by flinging her to the ground to keep her from roasting alive.

But after all, it was entirely his fault that she caught fire in the first place.

She adjusted her grip on the reins, wiping away the damp film collecting on her palms. Why was she thinking about him? If he were some grizzled old tramp who'd pitched camp on Castle Creek, she'd have already forgotten him.

She didn't consciously call up the memory of tumbling through the grass with Rob Elliott, but there it was, edging into her mind, over and over. As the morning wind kept whiffing the rain-steeped scent of sage into her nostrils, it was impossible not to go back to the night-time embrace of the grass and flowers, then to the arms of a complete stranger who smelled of wet skin and soap and saddle leather. The scent of him was stronger than a memory. Even stronger was the sound of his voice. She could hear that whisper now, in the wind rushing over the meadow grass . . . *please be all right . . . please be all right.*

She frowned, beset by memories. Yes, it was all true. He had held her and whispered in her ear as they tumbled in an embrace of fire and water. Rolled through the summer sage, their ribs bumping and their lips against one another's throats on solstice night. *My God.*

She raised a hand to her hot face, to the tender place where his unshaven cheek had grazed her own. Something swelled inside her, at the base of her sternum. It almost made her sick to her stomach.

She shook her head, not once but twice. There was no vigor in it, only an air of dizzy dismissal. The feeling of malaise continued; she shivered violently. Fingers knotted weakly at her midsection, she thought of the muslin bag of dried peppermint in her kitchen cupboard. *Tea. This damp weather, the strangeness of last night. I need a bath, clean clothes, and a lot of hot tea.*

Passing the gate, she steered the buggy into the long straight stretch through the meadow toward her new log house nestled in a grove of cottonwoods and towering pines.

The rain had let up a bit, but a few heavy drops still spattered loudly on the bright cedar shingles. She watched as the wind moved the tips of the fir trees back and forth above the house. It made her think of her own breath. A heaviness came over her, that familiar feeling of knowing more than what was readily apparent to the eye, but not enough. *Not again.* She breathed slowly, as she had learned to do, trying to modulate the influx of air.

Then, another chill. She wondered if one of the animals had taken a turn for the worse out behind the barn. As she looked in that direction, the feeling lightened. No, she decided, it wasn't the fawns, or the wounded rabbit she'd found, although she knew she must check on them. It was something with the house. Something wasn't right. She slowed and tied up at the long fence between the house and the barn.

Leaving the horse in the harness, she walked toward the front porch, so new that it still smelled of pine pitch. As she approached, the front door opened. Leaning against the frame and holding the screen wide with the toe of his high riding boot was Laird Thomas McNaughton.

"'Twas unlocked. With all the rain and wind, I didnae think you'd mind."

"Of course I mind. Get out of here." She flung a look around, searching for a piece of kindling, a stick, anything with which to defend herself.

"Maude. Maude Graham." He came forward, letting the screen door slap softly, and took up a new position against one of the post timbers, crossing one leg behind the other. He shoved his hands into the pockets of his leather jacket, tilted his head, and appraised her. "I had nae idea you'd grow up to be such a beauty. Everyone talks about you. 'That wild-looking Graham girl,' they say. 'Someone ought to tame her.' But me, I just have a private little smile of my own while they go on."

Maude shivered. Her hands were balls of ice. She hated that the dampness made her dark bodice cling too tightly to her chest, but she held her arms still at her sides. "Get off my porch. Get off my land. Now."

"Oh, stop now. We both know you cannae make me leave. I'll be gone in a few minutes, but I'm not ready just yet." He shifted, gesturing to the porch furniture her brothers had built, then sat down in the large chair near the door. "It's raining, Maude. Come up here and sit down in one of these fine chairs so we can talk like civilized neighbors."

"I'll stay where I am." Maude forced her breath in and out while the intermittent raindrops pelted her.

"You look fine. Fine indeed."

"Say whatever you have to say."

"I've come to make a proposal."

Another shiver crawled over her skin. *He can't be serious.*

Nothing escaped McNaughton. "That's right. I'm asking you to marry me."

"You're insane."

He threw back his head and barked out a laugh that made the horse snort in its harness. "Insane? For wanting to marry the bonniest lass in Fergus County?" He stood up and scuffed across the porch, coming down the steps in determined, slow strides.

His hunting boots gleamed and his camel-colored moleskin trousers bore only a slight smudge from the ride. He came close to her, close enough so that she could smell the pomade on his hair and mustache. He reached out, lifting a long coil of her hair.

"Maude, I may be wrong, but I dinnae think so. You cannae think about marrying because when you lie in that fine lace bed of yours—and believe you me, I did see your bed—it's me you're thinking on. Night after night, year after year. Look me in the eye, lass, and tell me it isnae so." He dropped the tendril of hair and then, so quickly she could not stop him, traced his finger along the line of her jaw. "Just like one of the prized McNaughton sheep, your fair ear might as weel be notched. A bonny wee lug mark, that's what you've got, fore'er and a day."

She wanted to slap him, but something bound her hands to her sides. He was her tormentor, but he was her soothsayer too. As loathsome as they were, his words hung in the air like a prophecy. Just as she did when she poked through the putrid gore in a wounded animal's viscera, she knew she had to overcome her revulsion and summon the keenest possible attention. Fear would not serve. Not now, not ever.

She didn't know much, but what little she had lately begun to understand was that she and Tom McNaughton were engaged in some kind of unconscious dance, something they rehearsed together or apart. She'd started to wonder—although the idea seemed as ephemeral as a wisp of milkweed—if she might, by inspecting everything about the two of them closely enough, begin the long unraveling of every last knot binding her to him, knots that had grown no looser with the passage of time.

His face was close to hers. The pomade smell mixed with bay rum and a faint lanolin scent. She saw the neatly trimmed beard, the scar above his right eyebrow. She could not believe that she had been closer to him even than this—that he'd known her, taken her, *owned her still.* The taste of bile rose bitter and hot in the back of her throat.

As he reached for her upper arms, she mounted her strength, breathing in all the spirit-energy from all living things that bloomed and grew on the earth. She shoved both fists up between his advancing arms, almost clipping him on the chin. Fanning her forearms outward as hard as she could, she broke the near embrace and ducked away.

"You cannae outrun what's between us, Maude," she heard him call out as she scrambled for the porch. "That's what scares you most."

In the house, with the door barred and bolted behind her, her chest heaving, she stepped to a window and pulled the blue calico an imperceptible half inch away. As she peered through the paned glass, she saw him rod-straight, on his coal black horse, trotting down Kettle Creek Lane.

She felt safe when she had the shotgun with her. It was a damned nuisance, but that's the way it was. Now that the shearing had started at Stony Creek, with an extra crew brought in from Checkerboard, she was on the road between her place and her parents' all the time. This morning she was at home, but the rifle lay propped against the rails of a wide half-circle of fence in the meadow south of her cabin, where she and her brothers had begun a log barricade that would keep the deer away from her own hay once it was mown and stacked. After surveying the rest of the stones they'd lined out to mark the perimeter, she walked around to nudge a couple of them into the soft turf, then rested her hands on her hips.

She and Mary had found a temporary peace lately, lapsing into the polite tolerance that formed the ballast of their relationship. Haying time meant everyone fell into harness and worked together; any squabbling would have shown itself like a festering wound. "A man can't bear his kin on his back" was one of John Graham's old sayings, and the second half of this generally went something like, "and this goes double true at shearing time"—or haying time, or some such.

Maude's wide front pasture, edged with a thick band of aspens, was hidden from the road. She liked the seclusion, but at the same time, in summer when the trees fluttered with rustling foliage, she relied on her hearing to pick up the sound of a buggy or horse and rider. So, this morning when she heard the clop of hooves and the scrape of wheels on the gravel, she took up the rifle. Balling her skirt into her free hand, she leaned into a run and traversed a hundred yards to the aspen brake. Through the trees she saw the advancing buggy of Harriet Quinn, her longtime friend.

Bursting through the leaves, she waved a greeting. Harriet called out, but her frown and anxious expression made Maude's hand stop. As the buggy slowed, Maude saw Harriet's dog, a herding collie named Sport, on a blood-soaked blanket at Harriet's feet.

"My God, Hatty, what on earth?"

Harriet's reddened eyes brimmed with tears. "The old fool got into it with a wolf. Thank heaven I was right there with the rifle or he'd be dead. I think it's his shoulder, mainly. And the back of his head."

"Get up to the house. We'll work on the porch. I'll be there in one minute." Maude dashed after the buggy. In the kitchen, she found her black satchel and dug out everything she'd require: scissors, razor, chloroform, disinfectant, steel needles, and silk thread. She laid out several stacks of boiled white cloth on the wide porch table, then jumped down to help Harriet carry Sport on a stretcher fashioned from a blanket.

"Where's Monty, for heaven's sake?" Maude was already snipping away the blood-clotted fur. "Here, hold this bit of cloth against his neck. Right there. More pressure." When Harriet didn't answer, she glanced up. "Where is he?"

"In jail."

"God Almighty." She said nothing for several minutes, focusing on trimming the fur away from the larger wound. "There are no torn arteries. We can be thankful for that. Old Sport would be dead by now if that were the case." She cleansed away dirt and grass from the gash and began to lay the flaps of skin back into place.

"I suppose he got into a fight. Monty, I mean."

"If you happen to pass by the Silver Dollar, you'll see their plate glass window is shattered." Harriet let out a hiss of exasperation. "Though I'm sure it's boarded up by now, since it happened night before last."

Maude heaved a sigh. "I'm so sorry, Hatty."

"I'm lucky Strap Wilkins came out to help chop firewood this weekend. Otherwise, I don't know how I would have gotten Sport into the buggy."

"Strap's a good kid."

"He didn't say a word about Monty being in trouble, although I'm sure the whole damn town is talking about it."

"He'll be out soon, though, I should think. I mean, he didn't seriously hurt anyone, did he?"

"No. The people in the saloon said the scuffle actually started on the street. It was the Slovenian guys and the Irish guys, like it tends to be."

Maude had begun stitching and was bent low over the collie, whose breathing came slow and labored. "Hatty," she said, not looking up, "you've done everything you can to save Sport, but blood loss is something we can't always resolve. When we're done, we'll try to get some water into him. The rest is going to be up to him and Mother Nature."

Hatty sank into one of the porch chairs and nodded, tucking stray brown strands back into her braid. "I should have aimed to kill that wolf but I didn't. I don't know what's the matter with me. I just can't kill anything. I shot right over him. I hope I scared the holy hell out of him. It was barely light out. Strap came out of the bunkhouse in his long johns." She gave a little laugh. "Monty needs to get out quick, though. Someone's got to mind our place. I've got a job this week and the extra money will be such a help."

Maude kept at her work, moving quickly to the neck wound. She knew that Harriet had occasionally been called in to assist the staff at the Rocking M with holiday events, so she suspected that with the Fourth of July coming up, this might be another such engagement.

"You never knew Mrs. McNaughton very well, did you?"

"No. Our paths didn't cross much." Maude kept her head down. "She was older, you know."

"Not that much older, really. She was very kind. And Maude, she was so lonely. No, not just lonely." Harriet shifted in her chair. "I got to know her a bit these last couple of years. It won't be the same there without her." She stopped for a moment, and in that pause Maude read more to come.

"He's—the laird—rather odd. I don't think people realize it, Maude. Of course he's prominent and full of himself, but he's a peculiar man."

Maude turned to a basin of sudsy water to scrub her hands. "I guess I just don't know."

"Maude, this is to go no further, but you know I work there now and then, cleaning and serving at parties, don't you?"

Maude's eyes finally came up to meet Harriet's. She nodded.

"I found things . . . when I cleaned."

Maude stiffened. Had Harriet found anything that could possibly incriminate her, things that might in some way reveal her connection to McNaughton? She kept her voice offhand. "What kind of things?"

"Oh, Maude, they were beyond strange." She fisted her hands and held them up close to her chin, shaking her head. "Deviant things, like . . . manacles, and curious devices. In the bedroom, mind you. Oh, the manacles were finely wrought, made of sterling silver, but that made them even more horrid to me. I wanted to forget them the moment I saw them. And the other things . . . I shudder to even contemplate their purpose."

Maude's lips curled in revulsion. After a long silence, all she could say was, "That poor woman."

"After eight or ten years of that, who wouldn't have a stroke? And Maude, that's the thing. The last few times I saw her, she seemed to be wasting. So pale, with those sunken eyes. I can't help wondering if she may have done something to herself just to . . . get out of it all. It makes my skin crawl." She sat back in her chair and wrapped her arms around her ribs despite the warm day.

"He's a fiend, is what he is," she continued, shaking her head. "Be glad you're tucked away back here and don't have to deal with him. He purports to be such a grand gentleman when he's the complete opposite. I'm surprised he even wants me back on the property, because I once heard him speak harshly to Rowena for taking tea with me on one of my visits. I'm no common drudge— I'm a respectable neighbor from the Basin, even if they do pay me. She had every reason to sit down and chat with me."

Maude sat motionless, staring at the distant mountains. Then she stirred, remembering the dog. Grabbing the bulb syringe and dipping it into a pitcher full of clear water, she motioned to Harriet. "Hold his head up, Hatty."

While she dribbled a small amount of water down Sport's throat, she massaged his neck lightly. Both women gave a gasp of joy when he swallowed and gave a little whine of recognition at Harriet's voice. It took some effort to carry him inside and place him on the carpet next to the stove, but within a few minutes, the task was complete. Maude covered him first with a sterile cloth and then an old down tick.

Back on the porch, she collapsed into a chair and sipped a glass of water. "So," she asked, an impish smile on her face, "will Monty be sleeping in the house or in the bunkhouse when he comes back?"

Harriet grimaced. "I keep thinking he'll stop doing this."

Maude let out a giggle. "Remember when the Slovenian boys and the Irish boys used to fight every Friday night in that gully behind the school? They'd roll around so much that all the sagebrush would be beaten down flat on Saturday morning."

Harriet laughed and slapped her knees. "Then, remember how your brothers would go out there and look for the money that had fallen out of their pockets while they were fighting?"

"I forgot about that!" Maude laughed so hard she had to dab her eyes with her sleeve. "My mother was so humiliated when she found out. That made it even funnier."

"What about that summer we went to the open house the Wunderlins had for their fancy new mansion? It was the same summer you all built your big ranch house at Stony Creek. Your mother had every single one of you girls dressed up perfectly. I can still see Mary in her pink frock. J. T. Senior, the gold mine owner himself— can you imagine—greeted us at the door with a silver tray full of punch cups and Mary says, 'Are you the butler?' My God, the look on your mother's face!"

Maude rolled her eyes and shook her head. "Mary has always lived in a novel. She can be so . . . entertaining."

It was well past noon when Maude waved good-bye to Harriet, telling her to say a prayer or two for Sport, and that she would send word in a couple of days.

Chapter Eight

Rob left his saddle horse at the Dark Horse Livery. He'd heard that the Dark Horse had the best farrier in Lewistown, and the big blue roan had needed shoeing for a week. Continuing on, he turned his spring wagon and team toward Wiedeman's, hoping that one of the freighters had finally brought some cement so he could start chinking his cabin.

God knows there are enough freighters passing through, he observed. Even though the Central Montana Railroad had arrived in Lewistown in 1903, freight wagons drawn by oxen or mules were commonplace. Driving down Broadway, he gave a wide berth to a long train of oxen, admiring the deft strokes of the bullwhacker as he sawed his blacksnake whip through the afternoon air. "I've seen those fellows line up marbles and use that blacksnake to cut one away from the other like they were butterin' toast," Grant McNaughton had said.

He smiled as he thought of Grant. No question he was the most likeable of that brood. He'd been a good hand on some of the fencing and carpentry jobs Rob took on at the Rocking M, and the two of them quickly found an easy working rhythm. Grant worked hard but knew when to wash off the dust and sweat of the day's labors and have a laugh.

With Price gone, Charlie was the youngest now. Grant and Lewis had the relative advantage of being in the middle. It was easy to imagine pale, bookish Lewis being the butt of jokes and beatings administered by the overbearing Blair during their growing-up years. Lewis had probably survived purely on shrewdness and evasion. Grant, on the other hand, was big enough to handle himself.

Within a few hours of arriving at the Rocking M, Rob saw that hunting held a morbid fascination for Thomas McNaughton. The rambling, elegant ranch house was ornamented with stuffed pheasants, grouse, and even owls. There were plenty of bobcats, black bear, elk, and mule deer as well. Thomas McNaughton kept a card file in his ponderous maple-burl desk of taxidermists from all over the Rocky Mountain front.

When the laird first ushered him into the smoke-and-leather-scented den, Rob was awed by the sight of an entire wall lined with leaded-glass gun cabinets. Rifles and pistols from famous gunsmiths throughout Europe and the States were precisely arranged on a background of dark green velvet.

The laird had raised his arm up to the high walls and fanned his hand in a wide arc. "Sport, Rob! And I thought bonny Scotland offered a bounty o' game. Montana's a sportsman's paradise. There be but few worthy creatures I haven't taken, such as the northern gray wolf. But what the devil, when a man's gotten ever' laist one of his prey, he might as weel be dead."

The place was like a men's club. Two maids, both of them rail thin, slipped in and out of the bedrooms in the late mornings and early evenings, making up beds and collecting trays, empty glasses, or wine goblets. A third, enormous woman, known simply as Thelma, ruled the vast kitchen. After Rowena's death, these domestics comprised the only female presence in the McNaughton world.

Monday morning, when Rob announced his plans to head back to Ruby Creek to work his own outfit for a couple of weeks, the only noise at the breakfast table was the clink of sterling against china emblazoned with the "M" crest. He'd known full well it would be that way, and had plenty of time to prepare for it, sitting in front of the campfire up on Castle Creek over the weekend, trying to sort out what had happened between him and Blair and then late that night with the dark-haired Graham girl. Woman. *Damn, I still don't even know her name.*

McNaughton said nothing about Blair's black eye or the bruising across the bridge of Rob's nose. No doubt, Rob reasoned, the laird's network of informants had enlightened him.

"Of course you've got to go back up there, Rob," Thomas said finally, lifting his coffee cup as if to toast Rob's health. "A man's got to make his place. We know that as weel as anyone, dinnae we, boys?"

Blair sat at the far corner of the heavy oak table, nearly opposite his father. Rob felt tension welling from that region like smoke from a wet fire, but believed that if he left Blair alone, things would settle.

"About how many square feet you got, Rob?" asked Lewis as he removed his wire-rimmed glasses and buffed them with a corner of his napkin.

"It's pretty humble. Only about eight hundred. The barn's bigger than the house. For my equine family, you know." He let out a quick laugh. "It's a real pretty setting, though. Nice view of the Judith Mountains, and there's a small waterfall a hundred yards from the house."

Thomas watched him with deep-set, raptor eyes. There was a mild smile on his lips, but the military mien never fully relaxed. Rob waited for a comment, but none came. Instead, young Charlie spoke up. "A waterfall usually means good fishing downstream. You tried it yet?"

"You're welcome any time. All of you."

"You'd be well to stick with fishing, young Charles, than to dally at Victoria's."

The entire table fell silent. Charlie, whose face went dark red, looked down at his plate.

"Since Rob is so new, we'd best enlighten him aboot Victoria's. Charles, why don't you tell him about this fine ornament to our city? From what I understand, you could be quite specific. Which one is't you favor? Emily or Prue? Ah, it's Violet, isn't it? Fair Violet. Brisk as bottled ale." His eyes flicked up from his coffee. "So I hear."

Charlie's hands gripped the table as he bolted up, his chair falling back. He looked like he wanted to crawl across the china and lunge at his father's throat. Flinging his napkin down, he stalked out. Seconds later, the front door closed with a heavy thud.

"He's too young for the brothel," McNaughton said blandly, reaching for a strip of bacon.

Rob swallowed the eggs that had been sitting in his mouth. Grant filled up the silence with some small talk about the new rams they'd bought, and breakfast took a desultory route toward its conclusion. One by one they made their excuses and pushed away from the table. Making certain he was not left alone with either Blair or Thomas, Rob picked up his hat and nodded his thanks. "In a few weeks, then."

Outside, he pulled up the picket line where the blue roan grazed and led her to the rear of the wagon. From the corner of his eye, he saw Thomas's tall figure moving toward him across the driveway.

McNaughton's hand came down on his shoulder and squeezed. "Dinnae hesitate to ask if there's something we can give you, Rob. Keg of nails? Roll of wire?"

"No, sir, I'm fine."

The mourning doves cooed in the tall spruces lining the driveway; a dog barked down the lane. Rob busied himself with digging out a rope to tie the roan to the back of the wagon.

"We'll clearly need you when you've finished up on Ruby Creek. I've a mind to build a hunting blind and some hay sheds on the northwest end of the property. You and Grant are the best carpenters on the place. And you know I'll make it worth your while, son."

Son. Rob looked up and gave a short smile. "Thanks. I appreciate the work."

"It's nae just the work," blurted out McNaughton, stroking his mustache fretfully. "You're family, Rob. We like to have you around as much as we can."

Their eyes met, and for a brief moment Rob saw a grieving father instead of a harsh and dissipated profligate. He held out his hand and took McNaughton's in his own. "I appreciate that, sir, and I know my own mother would too, God rest her bonny soul. I'll see you in a few weeks."

Now, as he pulled up to Wiedeman's hardware and lumber outfit in Lewistown, rubbing his swollen nose, he was glad for two things: the roll of bills in his pocket and the fact that he didn't need to see Blair or his puffed-up father for a while. Right now he cared about only one thing: cement. The way his life went for the next month was entirely dependent on whether or not he could find the stuff.

"Lucky for you," said George Wiedeman, "the freighter that came in yestiddy from Fort Benton brought seven wagonloads. You could chink ten cabins if you had a mind to."

Rob peeled a bill off his bankroll and loaded six of the dense bags into his wagon. From there he went to Lehman's mercantile operation and picked up four oil lamps, several bags of feed, a crate of canned goods, bacon, coffee, and a clock. He even found a copy of Henry Thoreau's works. A little edification on summer evenings wouldn't hurt him any. Somewhere deep in his big trunk, he had a tattered old volume of Robert Burns's poetry, one that had been his mother's, but it would be months before he uncovered that.

Three hours later, he was on his way out of Lewistown, leading the newly shod blue roan behind a heavy-laden wagon, headed for Ruby Creek.

What the hell was that? Rob fumbled in the dark, groping for the matches he knew lay on the bedside table. *No,* he thought suddenly, *I'll not light the lantern. I want to listen.*

Something told him he'd be more likely to hear it again if he was quiet, if there was no lantern light. He sat on the edge of the bed for a few minutes. Nothing. He stood up, letting his eyes grow accustomed to the darkness. It didn't take long; he'd always been able to see well in the dark. Moving toward the door to the main room of the cabin, he passed through it and saw the gray rectangles of the windows on either side of the door. One window was slightly open, letting in the cool air of the summer night.

He sat down on the log bench beneath the window, watching and listening. There was the burbling gush of the stream and the faint sough of the wind as it rustled the leathery leaves of the cottonwoods. Above, the sky was thick-sown with stars.

It was an animal, he knew that. He also knew that he had heard it the night before, but he had been so dead tired from mixing cement and carrying it around in his homemade hod that he could hardly move, much less sit up in the dark and pay attention to some wild animal. His shoulder hurt like hell, but he was almost half done with the chinking and his sense of accomplishment was a better tonic than the finest wine. He'd fallen into a deep sleep each night.

He eased his aching shoulders back and tipped his head against the window frame, letting the night breeze ruffle his hair.

There . . . he heard it. No mistaking what it was. He knew that sound, although he may have only heard it once before, that night in North Dakota. Wolf. A long, throaty moan that seemed to come from the ridge a half mile away, but at the same time seemed to come from inside himself. He swallowed thickly and his breath came faster.

Yes, wolf. Now that the feeling was upon him and the image of the animal sprang into his mind, he realized he had forgotten his dreams from the night before. Two wolves—a gray and a black, running across the prairie. The pale gray male was bushy and massively strong; she was more slender, black, and just as fast. There was no sense of destination, nor were they fleeing anything—just running for the sheer joy of it, feeling the soft tufts of buffalo grass beneath their feet and letting the sagebrush strike their legs as they sped along.

The howl came again. What struck him most was how much it sounded like a voice. It wasn't quite like a human voice, no; nor was this a creature from the pages of a fable. It seemed to him at that moment that there was a sense of language, of *communication* in that wild cry.

He rose, hands fisted, wanting to understand that wild communion between the wolves, disturbed that it was so far beyond his province to comprehend. Grasping the sill, he leaned out and breathed the night air. As it entered his windpipe, he remembered something.

Eliza Elliott, his mother, used to tell him long-cherished family tales of his forebears, going back before the days of Robert the Bruce and all the nostalgic figures of Scottish legend. The story that came to Rob just now was musty and old, full of Scots-Gaelic words that had made little sense to him and his sisters as they sat around the hearth years ago.

Eliza had told him that her own grandmother, who'd lived in the forests of the Monadhliath foothills, had once saved a she-wolf's cubs from drowning in a flood. Eliza told the tale like a bedtime story, and he had never thought of it again until now.

Her mellifluous brogue came back across the years. "I ne'er knew a wolf, but 'tis curious . . . betimes I feel I hae, e'en though they say the last ane in Scotland was kilt many years afore I was bairn. I cannae help thinking the wolf had a place amaingst us, as all God's craitures do."

When the wolf howled again, he felt something inside him quiver like the string of a bow. Flexing and curling his hands, he began to pace, muttering to himself. "I know the wolf, as I know all animals, from books, and from what people have told me. I know I risk losing some of my livestock to the wolves this winter. Yet it seems we measure the wolf badly. The Indians believe in totems and spirit guides. They see themselves as nations, and the animals as still other nations."

He shook his head and sat down with a little laugh. "What talk is this?" he muttered. "Who in the hell sits up at night trying to make sense of wolves?"

He sucked in a breath and let it out. Wolf or no wolf, he was exhausted, and had to get some sleep. There was work to be done tomorrow. *I'll go back to dreaming of the wolves, or maybe I'll dream of that Miss Graham, who's more than a bit wild herself.* He let his head tip back against the sill. After a moment, he realized he was smiling.

With a grunt, he got up and rubbed his shoulder, wishing he had bought a bottle of White's Liniment, then pulled the window shut and went back to bed.

Chapter Nine

He was on the ladder, dipping his hands in a bucket of cloudy water, when he heard hoofbeats on the turf. Even though it wasn't likely to be trouble, he immediately pictured his gun on the plank table in the kitchen. No one ever showed up here at the end of Ruby Creek Trail.

In a few quick steps he was down the ladder and in the back door of the cabin, making for the front window where he could peer out unobserved. As he scraped bits of drying mortar from his sunburned wrists and forearms, he saw a paint horse coming up the rise from the creek. There was only one horse like that in Fergus County. He strolled out the front door.

"Good thing you told me where this outfit was, or I'd have turned back about an hour ago. All the way up Boyd Creek, then all the way up Ruby." Grant flashed a wide grin as he swung his leg over the pommel and surveyed the grassy flat in front of the cabin. His eyes took in the tall barn, the tidy corral, and the lines of damp chinking that striped the front and sides of the cabin.

"Get on down and have some water. I've got coffee too. Caught a mess of trout last night. You hungry?"

After a lunch of biscuits and trout fried with bacon, they finished off with a can of peaches and downed cups of iced coffee loaded with sugar. Adjourning to the back of the cabin, Rob showed Grant the remaining work.

"Well, what are we waiting for?" Grant unbuttoned his cuffs and rolled up the sleeves of his chambray shirt.

"You serious?"

"Don't tell me you've grown to love that hod so much that you won't let someone else carry it for an afternoon. You can go along after me with the rag and clean off the slop spots. Where's the trowel?"

All Rob could do was nod. *Thank God I had the foresight to buy two ladders*, he thought, scrambling to get Grant set up.

Within minutes, they had fallen into the kind of comfortable silence and the muttering small talk typical of their hours on the Rocking M. "I think Charlie's got himself a girl," Grant said, basting a slab of mortar into a deep pocket between two logs.

"I gathered that."

"Dad's right. She's one of Victoria's clutch. I guess you could tell he isn't too keen about that."

"I deduced that when Charlie got bucked off at breakfast. Her name is Violet, as I recall."

"She's pretty, I'll give her that. Tiny thing, no bigger than a minute. Anyone can see why Charlie's interested."

"Is she—I mean, do you think she'd be good for him?"

"I've seen them together and I think she really loves him. The way she looks at him, like he's the center of her world. What the laird doesn't know is that she quit the dance hall a month ago and went to work for old Mrs. LaSalle at the millinery place." He paused, dabbing at some mortar. "But with everyone knowing how you started out, it's damn hard to shake that."

"And Thomas will have more to say about it before it's over."

"You know it. I wonder sometimes—well, never mind."

Rob knew what Grant was thinking. Thomas McNaughton was a man of appetites. No one possessed of his free-ranging vigor could reside in the oak-paneled splendor of the Rocking M's gun room and be satisfied with cigars and scotch. He was probably a regular customer at Victoria's.

Rob smoothed an uneven strip. "You got a girl?"

"Hell, no. Eventually, I suppose. Blair is sure looking. With the grace of an ox, as you saw that night of the fight. He'd like to think that Antonia Fredrich fancies him, but he's pipe dreaming there. I've often wondered why the laird hasn't tried to pair him up with someone of good standing. Like that Graham girl, the older one. She's a stunner. A little strange, but beautiful. And you couldn't ask for a more respectable family."

Rob felt saliva run into the corners of his mouth. Blair and the Graham girl. The idea was insane. He scarcely knew her, but he knew something of her spirit. There was a fragility there that made pairing her with Blair seem absurd, even inhumane.

"That Graham gal. What's her name?" He kept his voice indifferent.

"Maude."

"Maude." Rob let the name roll through his mind. *Maude Graham.*

"A rum customer to some degree, as pretty as she is."

Rob waited a moment, but not too long. "Meaning?"

"I've never seen her with anyone but that midwifing granny of hers. Lives alone up on Kettle Creek. Takes care of sick and wounded animals."

"You don't think she prefers . . ."

"The fair sex?" Grant gave a huffing laugh and shrugged his shoulders. "Never heard anyone say so. No, she's just a loner. I was thinking," he went on, "the shearing's done at most of the area ranches and the wool wagons are coming into town this weekend to load their fleeces onto the train. A lot of folks will be staying overnight at the hotels or setting up tents at the park. There'll be some Fourth of July festivities. We oughta go."

"Sounds good to me." Rob cast a glance at his companion. "Is there someone you're looking for among these rustics?"

Grant's lower jaw moved out slightly and he raised his eyebrows. "Never know."

After a few more loads of mortar, Grant stripped off his shirt. "You know, Mr. Elliott, I hope the pay is good. This is hod work."

Rob let out a guffaw. "My Hereford bull imparted a strong-smelling witticism this morning that was better than that."

"I'm giving you fair warning, the humor will steadily deteriorate from here on out."

Maude watched as old Kibbey, the white-haired shepherd who'd joined their family on the *Campania*, slid newly shorn fleeces down into the holes of the shearing platform. Slowly, each six-foot-long burlap sack filled up and was tied off, then carried to the enormous storage area on the north end of the barn, where it would wait to be loaded onto the wool wagons.

As soon as the two weeks of shearing were over, her father would import a haying crew, and another kind of sunup-to-sundown work would begin. For the women, it meant nonstop cooking.

Maude's arms were laden with two baskets of scones and a linen-swathed coffeepot. She set everything down on the battered workbench and turned to watch. Mac hauled a large ewe into place and set to work. Maude recognized the ewe as one who'd lost her lamb in the spring. That face was unmistakable— dark brown with a spattering of dusty white, as if someone had tossed a sifter of flour all over her snout. Flourface, Maude called her, although her father discouraged forming attachments to the livestock.

She remembered the lamb, born with withered hind legs. They all knew the little creature would never survive. Maude had wanted to walk away that cold and rainy day, but knew she had to help graft an orphaned lamb onto Flourface, or they'd have two dead newborns instead of one. Her father quickly laid out the lifeless lamb and skinned it, pulling the tiny liver from the sac of entrails and rubbing it over the still-damp pelt. Then, with a length of sisal twine, Maude bound the dark, sticky little fleece carefully around the back and shoulders of a cast-off twin. Then, watching carefully for ten minutes, they waited to see what Flourface would do. As soon as the ewe allowed the little one to suck, they heaved a collective sigh of relief, buttoned up their coats, and went on with their business, checking for other lambs who may have been kicked away by foolish ewes, or who couldn't fasten onto the teat, or had any number of other problems.

Rory and Mac were shearing fewer sheep now than they did earlier in the week, simply because they were tired. At first they had shorn almost ten per hour, just to show everyone they could, but they'd soon settled into a pattern of six or seven.

John Graham still sheared, but the work was "murderin' hard on the back," as he put it. Years ago, he had constructed a sling that allowed him to drape himself over a heavy leather strap, shearing while his weight and that of the sheep were suspended from a beam overhead. In recent years, though, the sling only helped for a few hours. He would straighten up and lay aside the shears with a deep groan and a shake of his shaggy head.

At break time, Kibbey took a bite of his tobacco bar and worked it around to the right spot in his mouth. "These are nice heavy fleeces, Mr. Graham. Most are seven pound or mair."

John nodded. "If we can get upwards of sixteen or seventeen cents a pound, we'll be in good shape."

"I heared that some folks is starting to shear at lambing time."

"I heard that too. The logic is that if you are running sheep out on the range without a sheepherder, a shorn sheep is more likely to come back in close toward the buildings to give birth, being cold and all. Less loss to the flock. And it's a heck of a lot easier to see if a lamb is really nursing if the wool is trimmed away. Remember that year we had so many lambs who were sucking on wool instead of the teat?"

"Aye, we lairnt that just in time."

John took off his hat and ran a hand through his hair. "We've got to get another wagon and another camptender up into the hills this month."

"Sheepherders is scarce as hen's teeth anymair," said Kibbey. "But we'll find us someone."

"If we start shearing in the spring, we'll have to store all our wool somewhere until the rail agents are ready for us," Rory said, sawing his shears open and closed, frowning.

"Been thinking about that, son. Good minds think alike." John slapped Rory on the shoulder. "I'll be talking to the other sheep growers when we get to town this weekend. And the agent too. There's no rush."

Kib fished a tin can out from behind his three-legged stool and spat discreetly into it, nodding apologetically at Maude. "I heared that Sneads over Stanford way lost a calf to the wolves 'tother day," he said, casting a look at John. "That's two for them."

John's shears sang as he stroked them against his whetstone. "I'm sorry to hear that. No one can afford to lose a beef." He let out a snort. "But Park Snead's the type to make it known from here to Miles City how the wolves are decimating his herd. Christ, he's got three thousand."

"Ah, his buzz shakes no barley wi' most folks."

"No, but there's many like him, spreading hysteria about the wolves. I'll be the first to respect what the old-timers tell me about the predation they suffered twenty years back. When I first got to the Basin, Hap McCormick told me he'd lost thirty to forty head of cattle each winter to wolves in the eighties. They damn near put him under, he said. Hated them with a passion, and I can't blame him. Hap and Millie had seven kids to feed back in those days. I saw him in town just the other day. He said nowadays people can afford to be sympathetic to the wolf. But he wagged his finger under my nose and told me not to get too soft.

"Frank Porter's got a different take on it," John continued. "Frank's too old to do much except make it to church of a Sunday anymore, but he ranched the Basin many years. Knew Granville Stuart, too. Says it was a series of rough winters, not the wolves, that put cattle ranching in a bad way more than the wolves ever did, and I'm inclined to agree. And don't forget that a lot of investors pulled their money out of the state right around the time folks started using barbwire. Once the ranchers started keeping track of their fenced-in cattle, the wolves had to go, and they've been blamed for a lot ever since."

Maude handed around cinnamon scones and cups of coffee. "Father, is it true what I've heard, that the state veterinarian is inoculating captured wolves with sarcoptic mange and releasing them, the idea being that they'll take the disease back to their packs?"

Her father nodded. "That pitiful idea came out of the Stockgrowers Convention, I'm sorry to say."

"They die from exposure when their hair falls out," Maude said, shaking her head.

The only sound was the occasional bleating of the anxious sheep in the corral outside. "With respect, sir," said Kib, "we can wag our tongues o'er this till the sun goes doon. We ought to get on with the shearin'."

Rory picked up the thread of his earlier concerns. "We can talk to Mr. McManus at the wool warehouse this weekend if you like, Father. I've been talking to him on another business matter anyway."

John straightened up and looked at his son. "Have you?" He seemed about to goad Rory for more, but he made a quick survey of the full room and bent back to the task of sharpening, with only a grunt of assent.

Maude retreated to a bench. She wouldn't be going to Lewistown with the family for the weekend events. She hadn't gone the last two years, so they were used to it. The only thing she missed was late evening in the park, when the fiddlers and banjo men would make their way to the bandstand and begin to play.

The sentimental Irish and Scottish ballads were one thing, but the jigs and reels always overcame her. Every care faded in the blue summer night, beneath the electric lights strung like gemstones from tree to tree in the warm darkness.

She didn't care if she had a partner or not. She would grab her sisters, or Rory or Mac, and haul them out to the rough platform to dance. Every step and turn she'd been taught as a little girl back in Morayshire—and all the cowboy twists and hops she'd learned in Montana—they all filled her body and set her spinning. As a schoolgirl, she'd had a favorite dancing dress, dark purple with a white slip. Plain muslin, though, that slip was, undecorated—with no frills of eyelet or crochet. Since that gray evening on the *Campania*, she'd foresworn lace petticoats, haunted by guilt that she had—just as McNaughton said—stupidly brought tragedy on herself.

But she smiled now, remembering how those summer crowds would clap and shout to see "the dancing Graham girl." She missed that. *Would Fiona and Isobel have that giddy, girlish experience when they went to Lewistown? They deserved it, for heaven's sake. Would Mary give it to them? Could she?*

No, Mary was caught up in something . . . a fanciful self-consciousness unlike anything Maude had ever experienced. It was written all over her fresh face and fastidious grooming. And maybe Mary was already in love, like Ailse had warned. Whatever it was, Maude felt certain it would prevent her from showing the two younger girls a carefree time this Saturday night. Who was this "smooth-handed" young man Ailse had caught a glimpse of? *Saints*, Maude thought, *if my mother employs her matchmaking talents, we may just have to sit back and watch.*

Fiona and Isobel sulked among the scraps of fleece when they overheard the news that Maude would not be coming to Lewistown. Isobel cast a stormy eye at her and would not approach.

From her bench, Maude asked, "What if the two of you and your big sister Mary come to stay at Kettle Creek with me next weekend, after the haying? We'll be worn out and ready for a holiday. Even Mary. Summer will be over before we know it. We must make the most of it."

Fiona nodded a quick yes, pumping Isobel's arm up and down. Isobel, who chewed her lip, tilted her head away to hide the smile stealing across her face.

"Then it's settled. I'll count on you to persuade Mary. Even if you can't talk her into it, I think Mother will let you drive the spring wagon over. And I'll make sure there are some wonderful things waiting for you." She hugged them both, pressing her face into their hair.

By the sixth day of haying, there were four enormous haystacks, each the size of a small barn, towering in the wide meadow along Big Spring Road. For a week previous, the crew John Graham hired from the southern part of the Basin had taken charge of the mowing and the dump raking, forming the hay into neat windrows. Maude drew deep breaths of the sugary scent, so rich it felt like green liquor going into her lungs, as she rode the two miles to Stony Creek to help her mother and Dora with the cooking and serving.

When it came time to stack, John wasted no time in trying out his new beaver slide, built by Stony Creek's two top workers, Lou Beck and Click Hawkins. They'd learned about the big contraption from a western Montana rancher. The beaver slide was built of long, slender poles, forming a wooden framework that reminded Maude of a partially constructed house.

Rory and Mac were in charge of the buck rake, scooping the mounds of fresh-cut hay onto a shallow wooden basket that lay on the ground in front of the beaver slide. When the basket was full, it was dragged by draft horses onto another platform, then raised high over a fulcrum that flung the hay neatly into place on the stack.

When Maude was younger, she relished the job of spreading the hay around the top of each loaf-like stack, making sure the mound would rise evenly. On Friday, the last day of this year's haying, all the Graham girls took rakes and made their way onto the final stack.

They were down to the last long windrows; it would be a small mound, probably only ten feet tall. Maude rubbed her neck, longing for a bath to rinse away the grass particles sticking to her skin and hair. As she and the younger girls waited for the ponderous Belgian draft horses to draw the next load, a light scattering of raindrops fell. Mary held her hands up over her head to keep her curls from being spoiled.

Maude suppressed a laugh. As annoying as Mary was, these bits of frippery were just plain amusing. Fiona and Isobel, both in old blue muslin dresses, mashed away at a clump of hay on the far end.

She herself was wearing something entirely out of character, only because it was so hot. She had traded in her cord skirt and boxy work shirt for an old dress of her mother's, a pale green calico, sashed at the waist. The raindrops felt heavenly as they splotched onto the worn-out cotton. She arched her back, raising her tanned arms and lifting her hair for the breeze to reach her damp neck.

"Sissy, who is that?" Fiona asked, her hand up to her eyes as she peered down the road.

Maude dropped her hands and spun around. A lone rider stood in the center of Big Spring Road, some thirty yards away, watching. Despite the heat, a cold prickle ran along her arms.

Astride a speckled blue roan, he sat motionless, one hand resting on his thigh, the other one palm up, reins threaded through his fingers. He was hatless, and his chestnut hair glinted in the sun. Maude detected the trace of a crooked smile, and although she could not see his eyes, she knew very well they were hazel with flecks of gold.

How did she look to him? In this threadbare dress that must be twenty years old, probably thin enough to see daylight through? Her cheeks flamed. She dropped her head to her task and let her curls spill forward, hiding her face.

"Who is who?" asked Mary, coming down to Maude's end of the stack.

"It's just a rider, gawking at us." Maude moved to the far edge of the shifting pile and poked at a lump of hay. She cast a look back over her shoulder.

"Sissy, he's looking right at you." Fiona giggled and ran back to hold Isobel's hand. "That man's watching Maude!"

"Stop your foolishness and straighten out that clump on the right."

Mary's voice was low, prim. "Maude, do you known this man?"

"Mary, please, let's just keep working. This behavior is encouraging h—the stranger. Father's coming across the pasture." To Maude's relief, John cantered toward them on Kelley, his favorite mare. When she cast a sideways look toward the road, she saw Rob Elliott nudge his horse into a trot. Soon there was only the fading blue of his chambray shirt and the dark flag of the horse's tail.

Chapter Ten

Catriona peered out from behind the tent awning and its flapping canvas panels, which she was supposed to be holding taut while John tapped the pins into the turf. The unfamiliar young man was wearing a suit, but he had removed his jacket in the afternoon heat and had slung it over his shoulder. His dark hair was closely cropped and his attention was completely focused on Mary's upturned, smiling face as she walked at his side. He was a fine-looking man, with a crisp white collar that set off his tanned, clean-shaven face.

"Trina, mind the pin."

She snatched the canvas and snugged it up while John tapped the last stake into the ground. They had secured a good spot in the center of the park, close to the public pump but away from the Fourth of July bustle and noise. "John, look yonder," she said under her breath. "No, don't look now. You waited too long. They're coming. Help me lift this crate of lemonade out of the wagon."

"Who's coming?"

But Mary and the young man were already there, and she was smiling, her hands clasped tightly in front of her. "Mother and Dad, I want you to meet Paul. Paul Hathaway. Paul is an attorney, from Chicago. He's here on contract for the Milwaukee Railroad. They're negotiating some land changes with the Montana Railroad, isn't that right, Paul?"

"Exactly. I'm very pleased to meet you." Paul Hathaway swung his hand into John's, gripping it firmly, then turned and made a slight bow to Catriona, taking her fingers lightly. "I had the pleasure of meeting Mary last month when she was shopping in town with her friend Miss Fenton. Mr. and Mrs. Fenton were with them as well, as I am sure you will recall."

John and Catriona glanced at each other, then nodded in unison.

"Paul wanted to come to the midsummer party at the Fentons', but he had to deliver his first report in Chicago that week." Mary's cheeks glowed a furious pink.

"I was very sorry to miss it."

"We are both . . . very happy to meet you, Paul," said Catriona. "Please come and have some lemonade. John was just about to help me lift it out of the wagon."

"Then I arrived just in time," said Paul. "Allow me."

Catriona found the cups and spread out a hand-loomed cloth. Mary bent over the linen, whisking away every wrinkle. "Oh Mother, I'm glad you brought this one," she whispered. "It's my favorite."

There was a momentary blur of missteps while seating was unclear, but Catriona sailed into the breach. "Paul, you and Mary sit on this side. Please, tell Mr. Graham—John—and me about your work. Oh, here is Mary's grandmother, Ailse, and the younger girls. John, you'd better get the campstools."

Mary's tiny sigh of frustration was not lost on Catriona, who beamed at her daughter. "Isn't it nice, Mary, that Paul can meet the entire family?"

"Yes. Yes, it's nice."

Fiona and Isobel ran forward clutching bags of fresh pastries, while Ailse, clad in sober black cotton, carried a string bag clanking with various tins. She tilted her head back and narrowed her hawk eyes as she approached, watching Mary and Paul.

"We saw the Indian witch," piped Fiona.

Isobel danced a quick pirouette around one of the campstools.

"Gran Ailse bought some smelly stuff. Worse than last year, by far."

Mary sucked in a breath and glared at her sisters. Isobel's tongue darted out.

Catriona bustled around, seeing that everyone was introduced, seated, and provided with lemonade. "Mary's sister is referring to the Blackfeet medicine woman known as Inii Aohki," she purred. "She is a respected healer here. Now, Paul, back to your work."

"Yes. Well, no doubt you've heard that the Milwaukee has wanted for many years to become a transcontinental line."

John chuckled. "Everyone in Fergus County's been jawing about that for months. We've got ninety-four miles of railroad that the Milwaukee wants as bad as lightning wants thunder."

"Yes. Well, I'm here with a couple of other attorneys to look the project over. You can probably guess I'm the junior member of the team." He flashed a dazzling smile around the table, lingering on Mary. "The others are in Helena in a series of meetings with Richard Harlow, the founder of your Montana Railroad. But you already know about him."

The conversation turned to the construction of Lewistown's brand-new, brick wool warehouse, next door to the rail depot, and the volume of this year's fleece shipment—and from there to the coming night's festivities. Catriona rose and began counting dinner plates, tossing a dinner invitation to Paul over her shoulder in a declaratory tone that no one had ever refused. Then, lining out plates on the wagon's hinged sideboard and lifting the cover from the biscuit dough, she raised a hand to shield her eyes. "Is that them? Whatever have they been doing? And what has Mac got now?"

As Fiona and Isobel ran to greet Rory and Mac, the rest of the group strained to see. It was evident that Mac was carrying some kind of small animal.

John grunted. "He's been to the Blackfeet encampment, I'll wager."

"Send him back." Catriona made a warding-off motion with her flour-covered hands.

"Just wait, Trina."

It was a puppy, a mottled-gray little thing with a black face. The two girls cooed, begging to hold it. "Good grief," said Catriona, "it looks like it crawled down a stovepipe. Is it dirty or is that its real color?"

"Oh, Ma," said Mac, "that's the color of it."

"We've got four dogs at Stony Creek! What are you thinking?"

Paul and Mary hung off to the side, watching the scene with a sort of dreamy detachment. Fiona had succeeded in prying the puppy out of Mac's arms and Isobel was kissing its nose.

"Isobel, that puppy could have all manner of ticks and lice." The voice was Mary's, in a solicitous tone no one had ever heard before. Heads swiveled and stared.

"Mary's right." Catriona knitted up the empty space. "Anyway, Mac, we don't need another dog at Stony Creek."

"This dog's not going to Stony Creek Ranch."

The only sound was the soft popping of their campfire, the shouts of children at neighboring campsites, and a fiddler tuning up somewhere.

"Well, son," said John, "what did you have in mind for the braw little fellow?"

"I'm giving him to Maude." Mac's jaw jutted out. "I don't like it that she's alone up on Kettle Creek. I have dreams about her sometimes. This pup's father is big. I saw him. And the Blackfeet brave who owns him says he's smart and faithful. I want Maude to have a dog like that."

It was a long speech for Mac. John Graham studied his youngest son, soon to be nineteen. It struck him all over again, as the lowering sunlight played over the boy's mass of coffee-colored hair, how much he reminded him of Maude. "That's fine, Mac."

Ailse, perching on a campstool, clutched the head of her stick. Mac did not miss the slight curve of her lips and the crinkled skin at the corners of her eyes.

"Another ditch," said Grant, scooting his glass back across the counter at the Elkhorn Saloon. The bartender unstopped a bottle of well whiskey, filled the glass, then added a splash of water.

Rob swished down the last of his own drink and said, "Likewise."

The two of them idly watched a trio of musicians setting up in the corner. Little by little, the place was filling up. "Looks like a lively Fourth in Lewistown, Montana," Rob said, listening to the intermittent plink of the banjo.

The doorway was darkened by two brawny men, both well over six feet tall. Grant shot a glance at Rob from beneath the brim of his hat.

"Strapping lads," Rob mumbled into his glass.

"Couple o' dang draft horses."

One of them strode in and grabbed the two bar stools next to Rob and Grant while the other hobbled up behind him on crutches, keeping a bandaged foot well clear of the floor. Rob stole a quick look at the injured foot, which resembled a boiled ham. Maintaining a passive expression, he allowed his gaze to drift up the stout leg and burly midsection. When he got to the man's head, it was too late to pretend he wasn't staring.

The man screwed his face into a dark scowl. "Infection, not that it's any of your business."

"I hope you heal up just fine. Can I buy you and your friend a drink?"

The beetled brows relaxed a fraction. "Two Lewistown Lagers, then. Rattler Riggs. This here's my brother Judd." Both men had ruddy faces, chins obscured by wiry black beards, and teeth that reminded Rob of his grandfather's meerschaum pipe.

"I'm Rob Elliott and this is Grant McNaughton."

"McNaughton, eh? Guess we ended up at the thoroughbred trough."

Grant laughed. "We're leaving pretty quick and you can have the place to yourselves."

"That's good, 'cause we ain't too good at book-lickin'.'"

"Settle, Rattler, where's your manners?" Judd Riggs adjusted himself on his bar stool. Raising his glass, he went on, "Please excuse my brother. The foot doesn't help any. Got bit by a rattlesnake."

"That happens," said Grant.

"Three times in your life?"

Grant leaned into his drink. "Maybe not."

"You can see how he picked up the nickname." As he relaxed, Judd's voice grew louder. "Anyway, wolfing's our business, pitiful as it's been this last while. We're laying off for the summer. Got our fair-weather duds out of storage just yesterday, in time for the Fourth." He sipped his beer, then dropped his nose to his shirtsleeve and sniffed. "What the heck does this shirt smell like, Rattler?" He cranked around and stared at his brother.

"Camphor." His brother scowled at him "It was in the damn footlocker over the winter. Kept the bugs out. Ain't you ever smelled mothballs before?"

Judd's face cracked into a grin. "Nope. Could never get their tiny legs apart."

Bursts of laughter popped out around the bar.

"Christ, how am I supposed to get a girl when I smell like this?"

Rattler's jaw worked back and forth. Picking up his bottle, he tipped his head back and drained it.

"Pelt bounties went up, I heard," Grant offered.

Rob shifted in his seat and took a swallow of whiskey. He knew that bounties had been raised that spring, but only because a handful of wealthy cattlemen had lobbied the legislature. Just that morning he'd overheard a rancher admit to exaggerating losses on his ranch in order to justify raising the bounties. He'd walked away shaking his head, realizing that no one would be satisfied until every last wolf was dead.

"Higher bounties don't help much if there ain't no wolves left." Rattler stared straight ahead, studying the mirrored back bar and rubbing his calf.

"This winter we're going to get that big gray for sure." Judd suppressed a belch, then let it out in a long growl. "His whole pack. Must be fifteen of 'em. Almost got 'em this spring. Came that close." He held up a thumb and forefinger a half-inch apart.

Grant lifted his eyebrows. "You mean the one they call the Adrad?"

"The very same." He took a sip and regarded Grant and Rob suspiciously. "You ain't wolfers, are you?"

"No." Rob's reply was quick and firm.

Judd's focus eased back to his beer. "We'll be after that big fella again this winter."

Grant, whose eyes were trained on a splinter in his palm, commented idly, "As famous as the Adrad is, you might have a little company. It's not just wolfers after him now, but hunters, who want him for the sport of it."

Rattler leaned over, his chin lowered and one eyebrow cocked high. "It won't be some highfluential hunter with a fancy rifle what gets him. It'll be a seasoned wolfer with wore-down heels. Mark me." He tapped the bar with a beefy forefinger.

Judd nodded his assent. "I'm going to tell you boys something you might think is a plain pile o' shit, but it's true. We know that wolf and his habits. That old bugger can tell poison. Last February, we had the perfect setup. We had a cow carcass all laid out, with the liver chopped up into ten pieces all around, and we had larded the poison right into the liver pieces. What wolf in his right mind would leave that behind? We drug that damn carcass into his area, between an old elk skeleton and a stump we'd seen him mark a hunnert times. The next mornin' we come and found his big tracks everywhere and a couple o' limbs ripped off that cow, and there in a pile with gravel scratched up all over it was the goddam liver. All ten pieces of it. Never seen anythin' like it. 'I don't want yer damn poison,' he told us."

A chill ran over Rob's arms. He turned slightly, just enough not to offend, and began watching the billiard table.

Two newcomers, clean-cut types with cowboy hats, strode in, nodding to the Riggs brothers. The taller of the two flicked his finger against the brim of his hat and grinned. "Howdy there, Rattlesnake. How's the foot?"

"Shut up."

"Just askin'."

The cowboys moved to the far end of the bar, bought themselves a couple of beers, and wasted no time in joining the action at billiards. Grant said a few more words to the wolfers, then scraped his barstool closer to Rob's, watching the thickening crowd in the smoky center of the room.

"Those two new guys are slicker than sheep snot," Grant observed. "Good thing we got our rumps tanned before they showed up."

"You mean *you* got our rumps tanned. I was doing just fine."

"Lookit there, that one fellow just sank the cue ball and his partner's got his drawers in a wad over it. Holy buckets, we've got ourselves a brawl."

The two cowboys were locked in a stumbling embrace, plowing down the center of the room. Their hats sailed off as one grabbed the other's head, shoving him into a table that sent poker chips flying. In no time, their sputtering curses and gyrating punches had them rocketing around the billiard table, close to the bar and the swollen purple foot.

"I've seen enough of this helling around lately," said Rob. "If those wolfers get involved, the whole place will come down." He grabbed his whiskey, downed it in two quick gulps, then headed for the door with Grant close behind.

Out on the street and mounted on his paint, Grant wheeled to the west, but Rob cut his blue roan in a circle and headed in the opposite direction.

"What gives?"

"Let's go down to the Indian encampment," said Rob. "I've

heard about an old medicine woman who's set up shop for the weekend."

"You ailing?"

"Just come on."

They passed the park, which Rob had reconnoitered more than once that day, looking for any sign of the Graham family. He'd finally spotted them, camped near the horseshoe pits, under a vast elm. There were the younger girls and the parents, and even the old crone of a grandmother, but he saw no sign of Maude. Now riding toward the edge of town, his mind worked the knotty problem of how to make his path intersect with hers. He wasn't about to start going to church, that much was certain, and he couldn't just ride up to Stony Creek and ask about her. *Sooner or later, I'll figure it out.*

The Blackfeet encampment was a smoky, noisome place. They tied up and walked along the central pathway. The early evening sky still afforded plenty of light for commerce. Naked toddlers ran about, their silky black hair flying as they darted among the osiers and splashed in the creek. Dogs barked, iron kettles bubbled on acrid-smelling fires, and men and women traded noisily with the whites.

Grant's step slowed as they passed a wide log rack spread with soft buffalo robes and beaded deerskin. A little farther on, a tall Blackfeet brave stood near a litter of plump, mottled gray puppies, scooping one up and thrusting it out in front of Rob and Grant.

"Nice pups," Grant said.

"Real nice," said Rob, pausing to look closely at the pup, then moving on.

At the next tent, a few furs, including coyote, beaver, and wolf, changed hands as they watched. In a lean-to set well back from the trail, some men traded firearms. Just ahead, they saw the hut of the medicine woman Inii Aohki.

"I'm going to stop here for a minute," said Rob. "Not long."

"I'll be at the buffalo robes, or somewhere nearby." Grant disappeared.

Rob pushed aside the chokecherry branches on the little path to Inii's crude hut. Crouched at the fire, she rose when he approached.

"I can help you? You come in?" She didn't wait for an answer, but shuffled through the grass ahead of him and moved aside the patterned blanket that formed the door of her shelter.

It was clear that visitors were meant to sit on the split-log bench and that the fur-covered stool was for Inii. Bones, stiff and shiny eagle feathers, several white ermine pelts, and tiny skulls—culled from birds and rodents, he discerned—hung from leather lanyards at varying heights all over the canvas and hide-covered walls. Tins and jars of strange-looking pastes and powders lined the circumference of the hut. A pallet of hay and furs formed Inii's bed.

The tiny old woman had the blackest eyes he'd ever seen, peering out from a brown, shiny face. She poured a drink for him from a battered metal pitcher. Rob willed his hand not to hesitate, but he knew she could see through him.

"Water and sarvisberry juice and honey."

"Oh."

"You have no malaise."

She uses French words left over from the Métis, Rob realized. "No ma'am. I am not ill. I—I know this may sound strange coming from a white, but I hope you will listen. If it is too strange, you can tell me to leave."

"Inii listens."

"I—I want to know about the Blackfeet religion. I mean, the whites have their churches, but I have heard that the young Blackfeet men find their own religion by fasting and praying."

Inii said nothing. She simply sat on the fur-covered stool, holding her own cup of sarvisberry water.

Hopelessness washed over him. *She'll never help me. Some fool white man poking into the Blackfeet's most sacred ground.* He set his cup down and leaned forward, his fingers touching one another lightly. "You are a wise woman. Your people have been here . . . forever."

Inii's eyes narrowed, looking into the past. "Yes. My mother, Kip a Ta Kii, she saw the white man's steamboats come up the river to Fort Benton. And her mother, and her mother before her, our *nahhks* . . . grandmothers." She circled her hand in the air, palm up, as if the ancient women were all assembled right there. "Yes, forever."

Rob suddenly remembered the tobacco in his pocket. Straightening his leg to dig it out, he stammered, "I . . . I have brought you a gift. Forgive me, I meant to give it to you as soon as I came in. I know it is important to—to honor your wisdom with a gift of good tobacco." He held out the waxed paper pouch in his flat palm.

Inii's bony fingers reached out and took the tobacco, setting it aside. She did this so unceremoniously, he wondered if it was the proper kind, or if it really had the meaning it was purported to have.

"I might be crazy . . . my people would think so. But I want to learn as the Blackfeet do. Can you help me?"

"Where you live?"

"Up on Ruby Creek, at the end of the trail."

"When you decide to find spirit-self?"

"What?"

"Was it day or night when this thinking comes to you?"

"I—I believe it was night, ma'am. But it has come slowly, over a long time. I mean, I feel it . . . here." He brought his hand to his sternum, swallowing thickly. "It troubles me—otherwise I would not bother you."

"You." She leaned over and poked his knee. "How do you call yourself?"

"Rob Elliott."

Inii rose and began moving around in the hut, humming a cadence of low notes. She opened a battered rucksack and pulled out a long deerskin roll, elaborately trimmed with beading, which she unfolded to reveal dozens of herb bundles. The shelter was filled with a cloying pandemonium of heady scents. She pulled this and that item from various pouches: first a tiny bone, then a curled-up piece of something green and vaguely iridescent. A brittle sprig of gray leaves came next, then a pinch of mustard-colored powder from a small leather sac. She bound it all up in a tiny deerskin bag and knotted it tightly with a leather thong. She left it lying on her little fur-covered bench.

"For you. But first you wait. I go get friend. Elder. He is half Blackfeet, half Métis." She patted the little pouch. "Good medicine for white man." She gave a sudden yip of a laugh. "Ha! Medicine Badger. Elder, for *iitsi iitsii.*"

Inii disappeared through the doorway and left Rob alone. He tipped his head forward, grinding the heels of his hands into his eyes. *What am I doing? This just might be the dumbest thing I ever got myself into. Who is this elder, this Medicine Badger? And what was that garbled its- word she just said?*

He stared at the pouch. He hadn't planned on dealing with a man. Somehow, that changed things for him. Could he trust a Blackfeet brave? At the very least, this Medicine Badger would probably be closed and secretive.

Night was falling and the air had grown damp. He stood up and paced, considering what diplomatic steps he would have to take if he did decide to abandon this idea. The blanket billowed open and Inii was back, with a lean, middle-aged man clad in worn trousers, deerskin leggings, and a faded red flannel shirt.

After simple introductions, Inii filled a red clay pipe with Rob's tobacco. The three of them smoked, passing the pipe back and forth. At first the conversation was light, about the weather and the whites' summer celebration, but it quickly turned serious. Rob explained himself as best he could, stating that he felt connected to the wolf, to all wolves, in a way he could not comprehend, and he hoped that the Blackfeet ways might help him understand his relationship to the wolf and to all animal nations. Once he'd gotten it out, his hosts were silent, studying him with dark eyes in the smoky gloom. *They think I'm a trespasser, a senseless white who doesn't know his place.*

Medicine Badger looked at Inii for a few moments. She muttered, "He seeks the *spomiitapiks.*" She glanced at Rob and translated,

"Sky People." Shifting her eyes back to Medicine Badger, she went on. "I listened to him before you come. I think he already travels the red road, a little." She raised her thin shoulders. "You will take him?"

Medicine Badger rolled his head back and peered down his hooked nose at Rob. "If you are on the red road, like Inii says, you are not like the other whites."

Rob looked at him levelly. "I'm as white as the rest of them, but you are right, in some ways I am very different. What is the 'red road'?"

Inii held up her small, creased hand. "White men go too fast. In *iitsi iitsii*, we journey to find the *spomiitapiks*. Our spirit teachers. Medicine Badger will be your guide. You must trust him. You listen now, Rob Elliott. These are the ways of the Blackfeet."

Outside, the low sun tinted the belly of the evening clouds a salmon orange, while the mountains soaked up sleepy, wine-colored shadows from the Judith Basin. The sky overhead was a deepening blue, with one star sitting high and steady.

Chapter Eleven

Maude swatted at a horsefly. "Blast, these flies have got beaks on them." She and the two youngest girls leaned into the raspberry bushes, pulling raspberries off the long rows of canes between Stony Creek's big house and the massive sheep barn. It was easy work, with most of the berries so ripe they nearly fell off at first touch. Through the forest of prickly stalks she could see Fiona, her face a portrait of concentration while her small hands darted quickly in and out among the bristly leaves. "Fee, they don't seem to be bothering you like they do me."

"Oh, yes they are," said Fiona, "I just whip my hand around my head every two handfuls. Keeps them shooshed away."

"You've developed a system."

Fiona's brows went up and her amber brown eyes flashed cat-like through the jungle of raspberry canes. "I guess you could say that."

"I'm going to try it."

Isobel piped up. "What are you talking about? Just smack them dead when they land on you."

"That doesn't sound like our fair Isobel," Fiona shot back. "Aren't you the one who converses with animals and carries wasps outside in Mason jars when they get trapped in the house?"

"Wasps don't attack me."

"I can't believe tomorrow is Lammas Day," Fiona sighed, her

cheeks puffing out. "We just had Midsummer a few weeks ago. Did the Irish and the Scots invent all these customs just so they could drink?"

Maude laughed, then studied Fiona's face, so like Mary's save for the nose. Mary's was small and straight, where Fiona's was upturned, dusted with freckles. Fiona was grinning at her now, knowing she had asked exactly the kind of question to get Maude going.

"You're probably on to something, Fee. All I know is that for us, Lammas means making raspberry jam and then going to the Big Spring Horse Race."

"I'm glad Mary and Mother are in charge of making the jam," said Fiona, wiping her fingers on her apron. "The kitchen's like a furnace. Besides, Mary wants to be able to tell Paul, 'I made the jam' when he comes for the corn roast tomorrow night." She mimicked Mary in a high, mincing, voice, then turned her head around and scowled at the house.

"Isobel, you down there?" Maude peered through the green leaves.

"Of course I am, Sissy Maude. Where else would I be?"

"I thought the faeries ran off with you."

"Mac's going to win the horse race," Isobel proclaimed sonorously. When she took this tone, Maude listened.

"Do you really think so?" She set her overflowing basket on the grass and straightened up, arching her back in a satisfying stretch.

Isobel came around the far end of the long banquette of raspberries, wearing a bemused look. "It came to me right then. I know about horses." She skipped toward Maude, the sun dancing on her dark curls. Maude smiled; she looked like a little sprite with that head of wild hair, glossy as burnished walnut.

"Wouldn't that be grand?" Maude moved the berry baskets into the shade. "Of course, if Rory doesn't win, we'll have his wounded pride to deal with."

As she stretched out on the grass, Maude watched a yellow

warbler flit among the branches. With the bird's lilting song, a memory came back. Last year, she had passed some rare peaceful moments here with Mary when the two of them took their books into the shade on a sweltering afternoon.

She remembered Mary setting her novel aside and lying on her back. "I don't know what sort of fellow you're waiting for," Mary had said, "but I fancy a deep and troubled man, someone like Heathcliffe was for Catherine. Someone I can love passionately, as they loved."

Maude's head came up from her own book. "I don't want to ruin *Wuthering Heights* for you, but things don't turn out well for the two of them."

"Oh, bosh. Novelists have to be sensational, don't they? That's what Miss Carrothers said in English class. Tragic endings and all that. You have such a flair for the banal. Don't decide the grapes are sour for everyone."

As the yellow warbler dipped into her vision and sailed to the ridge of the barn, her eyes came back into focus. *If Mary has found her Heathcliffe, then I am delighted for her. Or at least I'll try to be.*

The screen door clattered on the house. Maude sat up to see Mary making straight for the orchard. Sweeping her yellow skirt carefully around her, Mary sat down and began talking about the upcoming race. "Rory's bent on winning," she said, twirling a loose piece of bark in her fingers. "He wants very much to impress Antonia. He doesn't need to, except Blair McNaughton's in the race, so Rory feels he must be victorious."

A line appeared between Maude's brows. *Everyone's running amok, like the characters in a Shakespearean comedy.* It occurred to her, for the first time, that she was curious about all this amorous nonsense, and it wasn't the same empirical curiosity she'd always felt about human behavior in the past. Something had shifted inside her, thrown her off balance.

Maybe I am like the fox who's decided the grapes are all sour, she speculated briefly. But the notion that she might be jealous of the rest of them filled her with a new sense of isolation. She drew back and leaned against the tree, freshly convinced of her strangeness. Glancing down the long, sinuous lane, she saw Ailse's vine-covered house, which seemed like a harbor of sanity in a storm of lovesick siblings.

"He's obsessed," Mary was saying. "He doesn't know whether to put Glasgow through his paces today or let him rest." Shading her eyes with her hand, she straightened her spine to look across the dusty driveway.

Sure enough, at the fence of the south pasture was Rory, watching Glasgow, the big bay. Slung over the fence in the hot July sun were the blanket and saddle. Horse and rider stood fifty yards apart, silently regarding one another.

Around four o'clock the western sky bruised up with dark clouds. Maude watched from Ailse's tea table in the front room as fat drops began to pelt the small, square panes. First just a few, then a rapid-fire splattering.

"Willnae last. Just enow to cool things doon." Ailse sorted papers at a small desk on the other side of the room.

"I wish these evening showers would last a little longer. We need the greening."

"The grazin' is fine oot there at yer place. Acceptable for the small flock yer raisin', all on yer own."

A leg of lightning shot down from the sky as Maude looked over her shoulder at Ailse. "You're reading my thoughts again. I'm doing all right."

"Isnae hard. Close as y'are tae me ain hairt." A few moments passed before she added, "It'll be good to have auld Kib oot there with ye. Tick Smith's near as good as Kib, and he'll help yer da just fine here for a spell."

"Yes, I'm glad Kib's coming." Even as she spoke, the western sun pierced the moody clouds over the Snowy Mountains on the western rim of their little valley. Thunder tumbled away across the hills, and the room was filled with a slanting, silvery light. Maude felt the sun warming the raspberry-stained skin on her fingers, and the sweet scents of the afternoon came fully back.

She stared as Ailse's garden, doused by the quick rain, sparkled like a thousand gemstones. The lavender heads of the monarda, shedding their burden of moisture, curved in graceful arches over the winding garden path. Tall spires of magenta loosestrife stood over billows of blazing yellow coreopsis along the jack fence, where two mountain bluebirds sat in the stillness after the storm.

She didn't need to turn and look; she knew Ailse was beside her. "At times, Gran, I feel that nature knows exactly what we need, and she gives it to us."

A long stretch of pasture at the Heinrich Schmidt ranch formed the site of the annual Big Spring Horse Race. The length of the course was a scant one-half mile, but enough people showed up each year to form a line three deep on both sides of the grassy track.

Maude's eyes were drawn to Mary and Paul; indeed, it was hard not to watch them. Their eyes seldom left one another, and whenever Mary stepped away for a moment, Paul was quick to welcome her back to his side, folding her fingers back into his own. Mary's smile was the brightest Maude had ever seen it. She waved gaily to people who normally would have merited only a polite nod.

As was his habit, Paul draped his jacket over one shoulder. Mary paraded him up and down the length of the track, making sure everyone could see how different Paul was from the gravelly streambed of Lewistown's regular folk. Paul blushed now and then, a ruddy tinge blooming up from his white rounded collar to the dark curls on his forehead.

Maude loosened her jaw and chastened herself. *Why shouldn't Mary have some pride in him? She's young and enamored to distraction. It's only natural for her to behave that way. They are happy; they have found one another in a wide world where two people seldom have such good fortune.*

She turned away, her long cotton skirt brushing the freshly mown grass. She'd allowed Fiona and Isobel to talk her into wearing a pleated blue skirt with a white shirtwaist blouse. Feeling overdressed, she held back and scanned the crowd, then realized her attire was no more festive than anyone else's. There were even a few parasols bobbing around. Releasing a long breath, she relaxed and leaned against an isolated stretch of fence, adjusting her wide straw hat against the sun.

She could see the horses and their riders milling in loops in the broad creek bottom. There was Rory on Glasgow, giving a wide berth to Blair McNaughton, seated on a powerfully muscled bay. The race was supposed to be restricted to quarter horses only, but rumor had it that the McNaughton bay had more than simple quarter horse blood in him. Was his sire part thoroughbred? No one could prove it.

She strained to spot Mac, but there were so many horses she couldn't see him at first. Yes, there he was, on Dundee, a salt-and-pepper gray that was smaller than most of the others but known at Stony Creek to be a fast starter. Rory didn't think Dundee had the staying power to stick out a half-mile race, so he had chosen the much larger Glasgow. But Mac was convinced Dundee was a winner. And, remembered Maude, Isobel agreed with him. "Mac's going to win," she had said. Maude smiled and turned to look for the girls, but instead found herself face to face with Rob Elliott.

"Good afternoon, Miss Graham."

He held his hat in his left hand, and the sun glinted gold off his wind-ruffled hair. The whole of him . . . the smile behind his amber eyes, the impossible whiteness of his teeth, the tanned cheekbones, and the corded muscling of his forearms: it was all too much; her heart quickened despite her militant thoughts.

"Good day, Mr. Elliott."

"How is your arm?"

"I'm quite recovered, thank you."

"I've been wanting to tell you how sorry I was about . . . all of that."

"It was understandable. How were you to know we were—" she

formed the rest of the sentence in her head, but censored it before it could leave her mouth. How could she say something that
sounded so odd? How does one say, 'smoking the sheep'? She
stood there, her lips parted midsentence, her mind a cloud white
blank. Somehow, she knew he was staring directly at her lips. She
had the presence of mind to close her mouth.

"My mother didn't build midsummer fires at our place in Ohio,
but she always had a fire at Halloween. I forget the old name." His
eyes felt warm on her, and a smile lifted the corners of his mouth.

"Samhain."

"That's it. Samhain. Well, I hear you have family in the race
today."

He said the name of the old quarter day so easily, pronouncing
it just right: "so-when." "My younger brothers, Rory and Mac,
are racing." She threw a look into the group of horses. "I should
be going."

He brought his hand to her arm. "I want to see you."

Her thumping heart rose into her throat. She was about to
reply, *you can't*, but her eyes darted over his face. His eyes were
hazel, yes, but they shone with curious sun sparks. "You . . . are
seeing me."

"Don't." His eyes demanded more from her.

"We live in a small town. Our paths will cross often enough."
Her breath became ragged.

"No, they won't. Not unless we intend them to." His fingers
made their way to her hand, touching the tips of hers and sliding
feather light into her palm.

His skin on her skin, the startling warm intention of it, made
her throat tighten. She wondered if he could see her heart beating
beneath the fabric of her blouse. Fascination and terror coursed
through her. Weren't they both highways to hell? The far-off vision
of someday being a regular girl, the assertion that she might stand
still and be composed . . . it was there, so close, as close as this
man and his golden sun-spark eyes. But just as she knew it would,
the darkness came, welling up like India ink. As soon as she'd been

foolish enough to entertain them, her sunlit notions were eclipsed, dissolved by the seductive familiarity of fear. She choked out the only words she knew. "I have to go."

As she picked up her skirts and ran, the hot wind felt like freedom and failure. She couldn't think about any of this; she wouldn't. Where were Isobel and Fiona? There, on the fence. Fiona lounged against the rails, twirling her copper gold curls with her finger and eying a gaggle of boys firing slingshots into a willow break.

Isobel was a spectacle—standing on the middle rail, both arms raised in the summer air, hollering, "When are they going to start?"

Maude stopped running. *Don't attract attention.* She formed her lips into a smile, still breathing hard, determined not to look back. She would find the Graham clan and immerse herself in anonymity.

Why am I incapable of reason? He's not my beau, for heaven's sake. That can never happen. And I'm not Mary, acting like some artless milkmaid. What business does he have doing this—coming here and saying these things? She lifted her chin and headed for the fence.

Isobel's straw hat was flung back and her dark hair, although tied with a broad blue ribbon, escaped around her shoulders. Her face was slightly sunburned, and, while Catriona had a fit about it, the sienna tint and the roses in her cheeks were a becoming combination.

Good Lord, Maude thought suddenly, *how did these girls grow up so fast? Fiona is fifteen, and Isobel's blooming up right behind her. It happened when none of us were looking.*

A rumble of hooves meant the horses were heading down the track for the starting line. "Sissy Maude, hurry up!" Isobel yelled at her and Fiona motioned impatiently. In a moment Maude was beside them at their family's position, about two-thirds down the track.

One of the Schmidt boys fired a pistol and a broad banner of horseflesh came shimmering toward them, turf flying and riders' arms flailing. There were eleven horses, and as Maude's heart pumped, she was grateful the Schmidts had a pasture wide enough for this grand event. Not only that, she knew the area had been carefully inspected for prairie dog and marmot holes. She held her breath and prayed for no accidents.

The crowd screamed in one constant, roaring voice. From her perspective it was hard to see who was in front, but it looked like Blair McNaughton was leading by about a length, with Rory second. But as the thunderous contingent flew past, it was very clear that Mac was even with Rory and gaining on Blair. Dundee's legs were an invisible blur; Mac crouched on his withers like a grasshopper.

Isobel spun around on the fence and flew into John Graham's arms, nearly knocking him over. "He's going to win, Father! I told you all! Mac's going to win!"

The hurrah at the finish line meant the race was over. "Hush now," cried Catriona. "They've passed the line! That old bull Heinrich's coming out with his megaphone." The crowd was full of shushing sounds and sharp whistles as everyone settled down to hear the results.

Heinrich's deep baritone voice, thick with German, came through clearly enough: "And ze vinner of zis year's Big Spring race iss . . . Mac Graham on Dundee!"

Amidst a chorus of applause and a brief patter of disappointed remarks, the Grahams made their way toward the open area. They went slowly, allowing Ailse her plodding, determined pace. Maude eyed Isobel for any signs of arrogance about her prognostication, but saw none. As she walked hand-in-hand with Fiona, who was chattering away, she glanced around, looking for Rob Elliott, but he was nowhere in sight.

When they arrived at the meadow, the riders were still astride their horses, walking their mounts to cool them down, with here and there a sporadic, rueful critique of the race. Except for Mac, whose broad smile could be seen a hundred yards off.

"I wish that boy would cut his hair," said John. "Picked up that hair business from those fiddle players in Helena."

"Don't start now, John. He's so happy. Be proud of him."

They came upon Rory first. Maude was startled to see him grinning. "I came in second," he crowed. "At least I beat Blair!" Sliding down from his saddle, he dusted himself off, then circled around his mother and lifted his hand in a wave. They turned in unison to see.

It was Antonia Fredrich, in a pale blue dress deeply dusted with lace. Maude had never seen her in close proximity. *No wonder she has turned Rory's head.* Her blond hair fell past her slender waist, long and loose but caught up in combs at the temples. She was tall and carried herself with unusual confidence. With her parents and younger siblings, she watched Rory across a few yards of meadow grass.

Maude saw the joy in her smile, the slight rise and fall of her shoulders. There was no stopping Rory, who was already halfway across the open space that separated them.

"Stop right there, Graham." Blair McNaughton's voice sliced the warm August air. "You can just turn right around and go on back with your family. Miss Fredrich's going to take a walk with me."

A scant moment passed as everyone—Rory, the Fredrich family, the Grahams—strove to calculate what was happening. A locust buzzed in a nearby pine.

"Blair," began Rory. "You need to understand that Antonia and I have—"

"Just shut your mouth right now, Graham. I don't want to hear you use Miss Fredrich's Christian name again. Do I make myself clear?"

Rory's voice was cold. "You're half looney, Blair. You'd grouse if you were hung with a new rope."

Blair's hand reached around his back and reappeared with a Colt revolver.

John Graham stepped forward. "Young man, put that thing down. There's no need for this."

Blair twisted to the right and aimed the gun at John. "That's right, come on over here, you stinking pile of so-called decency,

John Graham. Then I can nail two carcass-picking magpies instead of one."

Catriona lunged for John, grasping his shirt sleeve. "John, stop."

Blair refocused on Rory, taking two more steps. "You've gotten in my way for the last time. This goddam race was the last straw. Thought you could show me up, didn't you?" He spat on the ground. "Then your own scrawny brother beat you on that runt. I've grown up in the shadow of the almighty Grahams and I'm damned sick of it."

He cocked the hammer. Then, to everyone's amazement, Rory strode in a straight line directly toward Blair. Maude's lips parted in shock. *Rory's calling his bluff*, she realized in horror. *Blair's out of his mind. He'll kill Rory.*

Rory came on, eyes wide, fully up to Blair, grabbing his gun arm with his left hand. With his right, he powered back and drove an uppercut into Blair's jaw.

But Blair hardly budged. Still holding the gun, he pressed it into Rory's chest.

Screams piped from the women as a crowd swirled around the perimeter. Dimly, Maude heard people shouting for the sheriff. *Where the hell was Ed Martin, anyway?* She tried to keep the thought from her mind that Rory would be dead before law enforcement ever arrived.

Rory grabbed Blair's right forearm and began wrestling for the pistol. The two of them weaved back and forth, the black shape of the gun jerking up and down between their contorted faces. At that moment, John and Mac started moving in. Jozsef Fredrich moved forward too. But what no one saw was Antonia, who flew faster than any of them.

A flash of blue cotton, a blaze of golden hair. In the middle of the two fighting men, her slender arms twined with theirs. When the gun went off, Rory staggered back, blood on his chest, and Antonia lay limp in his arms.

Maude hated hospitals. If she had to pin it down to just one thing, it would be the shininess of them. She loved a good pair of Solingen scissors, mirror finish and keen edge, as well as any surgeon, and she kept hers tucked in a blue flannel bag like a religious artifact. But every single thing in a hospital was shiny, even the painted walls. It was all part of the antiseptic principle; she knew and respected that, but she didn't like it.

She alternately sat on a stone bench outside with Ailse or went to lie under an enormous elm on the lawn. Paul had caught the train back to Chicago a couple of hours ago, but John, Catriona, Mac, and the girls were inside, as well as the entire Fredrich clan.

Evening came. An occasional horse and buggy clopped past on the street. Ailse had nodded off to sleep on the bench. A young woman and her husband came out of the hospital with their new baby, ready to go home. Happy. Maude rummaged through her memory. What was that grimly apt quotation about hospitals? "Quiet, old, and gray, where life and death like friendly peddlers meet . . . "

The next person to come out was Catriona, her eyes puffed and red. "Antonia is the better of the two," she began. Maude could see her striving to tell the story with proper respect to the two families. "She's injured, to be sure, but Rory's worse. Dr. Attix says he'll be all right over time, saints be praised. I don't know what will happen with that job offer from the railroad. He was so excited," she said, suddenly distracted, fresh tears trickling along her nose. "At any rate, the bullet passed through Antonia's bicep and went into Rory's shoulder joint. That's how it was explained to us. Dr. Attix says that the shot being fired at close range was the reason for all the damage. But they are alive. Rory cried when I told him Antonia was safe." She dabbed her eyes.

Maude and Ailse stood silently with their arms around Catriona, who stiffened suddenly and lifted her chin. "Is that . . . McNaughton boy in jail?"

"I believe so, but they may rule it an accidental shooting," Maude said quietly.

Catriona's palm flew to her forehead. "Accidental? He's dangerous." She spun around, walked away, then paced back. "Oh God, what do I know? He seems troubled beyond help. What's to be done? I am so confused."

"I micht be wrong," began Ailse, "but I recollect hearin' lang ago that when that boy's mother died, he was struck hard. Trina, d'ye mind what she looked like? Can ye recall from the auld country? Lora was her name. Aye, that's it. Lady Lora McNaughton."

Catriona stood silent for a moment. "Yes, I remember Lora," she said, nodding. "I'd supplanted her so completely with Rowena, with that dark hair. But yes, Lora died when little Price was born. Blair was about ten, wasn't he? I used to see her in Aberdeen. She was very fair. Tall and blond, quite pretty." Her fingertips came to her lips. "Like . . . *Antonia*. My God, the canker that lies in the soul of that young man. This is so sad." She burst into tears again, opening up her balled handkerchief.

Maude swallowed hard and shook her head in mute acquiescence. *Blair, the oldest McNaughton boy and the one with the deepest wound. How he must have viewed Price, God rest his soul, who passed through his mother's loins and left her dead in his wake. Why, on God's green earth, must the road my family travels continually intersect with the road of the accursed McNaughtons?* She shuddered in the cooling twilight.

Chapter Twelve
SEPTEMBER 1908

There were moments when Maude wasn't sure Ajax would ever get it, but he seemed better than he was in July. He didn't nip at her new sheep anymore, not even the lambs. Old Kibbey had helped train him. There were even times when he'd traverse back and forth in true herding motion behind the flock. And when she went fishing, he would sit on the bank sometimes, instead of splashing about, scaring the fish.

Now, as she crouched on a rock across from an eddying pool in Big Spring Creek, she shot a quick look over her shoulder to see what the little rascal was doing. She didn't want him to spoil this cast. Gran had spread a blanket on a patch of grass and had lain down to rest. Nearby, Ajax chewed on a stick.

The day Mac had brought him out to Kettle Creek, she didn't know whether to laugh or cry. By eerie coincidence, the night before, during an ear-splitting thunderstorm that rattled the panes in her new house, she had wished for a dog. The next morning, as moisture dripped from the towering pines, Mac came trotting up the sodden lane, carrying a fat, soot-faced puppy from the Blackfeet.

They set him on the porch and drank steaming coffee and watched him tumble off at least four times. He would sit down and yap at them, then gambol around like a jester until they laughed.

Mac hadn't come to Kettle Creek again until September, when a few waxy yellow leaves of the cottonwoods floated down to litter her front yard. He had just finished a long weekend with their father's crew, bringing the sheep down from the mountain meadows.

"Nice boots," she called out as he slid off his horse. He wore his dungarees tucked into the new boots, in order to show the fancy tops and their pattern of stitched-on stars.

"Thanks. They turned out just like I wanted."

Maude tried not to smile as they sipped their coffee. He seemed to have changed in the three weeks since she'd last seen him. He was becoming a character in his own right.

"You could float a horseshoe in this stuff, Maudie."

She laughed. "I've been told that." Leaning back in her chair, she asked, "How's Rory doing? I haven't seen him for a month. I've been trying to get things in shape for the rams coming in."

"He's all right, I think. What chafes him worse than the pain in his shoulder is that Mrs. Fredrich won't let Antonia off their farm for two minutes, not after what happened. Wouldn't even let her go to church. Not until last Sunday, anyway."

"She'd let Rory come out there to see Antonia, wouldn't she?"

"Oh, yeah, she's allowed a few visits, all right. They like Rory." Mac bit his lip. "Mother says they're very suspicious people, those Bohemians. They believe in curses and such. When both Rory and Antonia were in the hospital and Mother thanked Dr. Attix for his help, Mrs. Fredrich got upset about it. I found out about this later, through Rory. Antonia told him that their people believe that if you thank anyone for medicine, it renders the medicine useless."

Maude rested her chin on her hand. "Antonia's healing up all right, though, isn't she?"

"Yes. Mother went over there with Rory a couple of times. She apologized to Mrs. Fredrich, who was embarrassed about the whole thing. Antonia had to translate most of the conversation, of course."

"Belief is a powerful thing."

"Yep." Mac shifted in his chair, working up to something. "Speaking of such things . . . "

"What things?"

"I have dreams, Maude. I dream about things happening to people and . . . I worry that they might come true."

Maude looked at him straight on. "Our family is plagued, or blessed, by all manner of gifts, Mac."

"Gifts?" he snorted.

"Have any of your dreams ever come true?"

Mac slumped back and looked up at the rafters. "In a way. Last summer I dreamed of Mary getting her leg broken in a horse wreck, but then she only got thrown. Just bruised. Things like that." He was silent a moment. "The only things that have ever come true, I mean, enough to startle me, have been stupid things, like one dream I had that Fee"—he always called Fiona that—"and I would find a black-and-white cat, and sure enough two days later we found a black-and-white cat. But," he added, "I also dream of things happening out here with you. In those dreams, there's someone bothering you out here, but I can never see who it is."

Maude forced both boot heels to remain still and quiet on the floor, knees together under her twill skirt. Nodding, she said, "Well, it is somewhat isolated. I really am very happy to have the puppy. He'll be a fine watchdog. But as far as your dreams go . . ." She stood up and walked to the end of the porch. "Gran says we all have to manage our 'special wits,' as she calls them."

"What do *you* manage?"

Maude turned and looked at him, her mouth skewed off to the side. "Oh, Mac, it is so hard to explain. I . . . I feel like I know things, but not in dreams like you do. I sense things right before they happen, or I feel something that is nearby that can't quite be seen. It's almost like a sense of smell or hearing, but it seems to come to me through breathing, if that makes any sense at all. And I feel things about animals, too. Something leads me to the injured creatures, thank God and the ancient ones. At least you know when yours is coming upon you—when you lie down to rest. I never know when mine is coming, or what's going to happen."

Mac drained the last of his coffee. "What do you think of Paul?"

Maude's eyes darted to his. "He's a good match for Mary, as far as I can tell," she began, thinking as she spoke that the words sounded like twaddle. "He strikes me as the type of fellow she has always wanted." After a pause, she added, "She's certainly happy."

"Yes, he seems to be as pleasant a guy as you'd ever want to meet. Nice dresser, that's certain. And you're right, Mary's completely gone on him. Mother as well."

"I'll hear more girl talk this weekend. All three of them are coming for a stayover on Friday," said Maude, tapping her fingers on a porch timber.

"Yes, I expect you'll hear plenty."

The following weekend, she did hear plenty, and had been eagerly interested at first. Mary waxed poetic about everything from Paul's well-to-do family in Chicago to his "stylishly barbered hair and intelligent, high forehead." Enthralled by his courtroom vocabulary, she went to Maude's bookshelf and looked up words like *perpend* and *bombast*. Fiona and Isobel wandered outdoors after only a few minutes, having endured their limit of Mary's rapture.

Later that evening, as Fiona and Mary spread the canvases out in the hayloft and arranged pillows and quilts for their night in the barn, Maude and Isobel spied on the doe and the fawns in the round pasture behind the house, then went to feed the crippled cottontail Maude had found in a trap last spring. The animal had become quite tame, and was willing to let Isobel play with its ears.

"Sissy Maude?"

"Hmm?" Maude pulled some soiled straw from the rabbit's pen.

"I don't like Paul."

Maude's eyes drifted slowly to Isobel, who was stroking the rabbit absently. "That's interesting. You don't care for him?"

"No."

She felt a thickness in the back of her throat. "Did something happen?"

"No. I just don't like him. I . . . can't find him when I look at him. When I look in his eyes, I mean. It's hard to explain."

The hair on Maude's arms rose up. *Special wits indeed.* "Isobel, come here."

Isobel leaned down and kissed the rabbit's head, then approached Maude, her eyes averted. Maude folded her in her arms and held her close. "It's all right, Isobel," she whispered into the dark hair. "We must let people do what they want to do, even if we are worried about them. Can you let Mary go ahead and do what she wants to do?"

Isobel caught her breath, as if she were going to cry, but she didn't. She nodded and said, "All right, Sissy, if you think it's best."

On the river, Maude cocked her forearm, eying the malicious, hanging branches of a yellow pine, and threw the fly line. She loved the fizzing sound as it zipped over the water, then the tiny *plink* as the dry fly settled. She was surprised that it even hit the surface, because on days like this, a trout would often rise to snap at the tiny feathered hook before it made contact with the water.

Scarcely a second passed and she had a strike. *Set the hook. Firm, but not too harsh.* Two minutes later, there he was, a shining gem of a rainbow trout, silver and celadon and ruby, slithering about her feet. Beneath her deft fingers, he was free in a moment and back in the river.

She lifted her palm to her nose. The smell of fish on her hands was sensual and mossy, rich and ancient. She felt momentarily drunk with the teeming magic of the river, its multicolored bottom, the cut-crystal energy of the current, and all the pulsing secrets mortals would forever strain to understand.

She looked up at the sky, brilliant blue, and heard the rustling thickness of the cottonwood leaves. *Their sound changes at this time of year. Fall is imminent, even though it's still early September. School has started. Fiona and Isobel back with their books, and Mary too. It will be hard on her, back in that "pedestrian environment," as she calls it, for a full year, with her sophisticated new swain so far away in Chicago.*

Looking back at the river, she watched the bronze pebbles on the bottom of the far pool and the fast water braiding darkly around the rocks. Lush plants fastened tenaciously to the damp boulders waved in the cool currents of air. She steeled herself and said through her teeth, "If Ailse and I are to have trout for dinner, I'm going to have to do a couple of these poor fellows in."

Suddenly thirsty, she grabbed a blue enamel cup and dipped it into the fresh water gushing between two chunks of granite. After slaking her thirst, she picked her way gingerly back to shore among the boulders to check on Gran Ailse. She was glad she had worn her gum-soled boots. On the bank, both Ailse and Ajax had fallen asleep.

Ailse lifted herself on one elbow. "Ye dinnae ketch any?"

"Oh, they're biting. I'll have some for dinner in ten minutes."

"Ye're too soft-hearted, girlie."

"Aye, Gran. Mind the pup. I'll be back."

They dawdled on their way home, enjoying the Indian summer afternoon, picking out every color of foliage. But Maude recognized a rider on Big Spring Road. It was her father, on Kelley. Oddly, he had the horse in a lope, something he never did on this rough stretch.

She touched Bobcat's dark flanks with the whip, making the buggy bounce. Gran held on tightly and Maude shoved Ajax between her left thigh and the curve of the buggy seat. Bypassing the turn to Kettle Creek, they met her father a moment later. Kelley's sides heaved and bits of lather clotted around the saddle blanket.

"It's Mary," he said, his face gray. "She's gone away with Paul. She left a note. I guess you could call it an elopement. We don't know how else to describe it. I didn't think he—well, it doesn't matter what I thought. Trina's in a bad way. She needs you both."

Maude slapped the reins on Bobcat's rump while a weary John fell in behind. *All these weeks,* she fumed, *all summer, she was tumbling further in love with him than any of us imagined. She couldn't bring herself to speak anything more than his sacred name to me, only to make cotton-headed blandishments about his hair, his eyes, his starched collars. I sat there and smiled at her, happy to see her besotted and gay, and all the while she shared nothing of her real plans. These last weeks she's been making lists in her head, lists of what she'll take and what she'll leave behind. We've had no idea. No idea.*

Anger seethed down her arms and shot through the reins. She knew Bobcat felt it pinging through the metal fittings of his bridle. The horse skittered along in a frenetic trot.

It occurred to her, not in any fashion that she wanted to entertain sensibly, but in a calamitous, startling way, the same way a person is slapped in the face, that she was hurt. As distant as she and Mary were, as comfortable as she'd been in relegating Mary to the role of an inverse, lesser opponent, she could not believe that her sister had excluded her, omitted her from the intimate channels of her life, to such an extreme degree. She felt the sting of it deeper than she ever imagined she might. But she could not stop now to reason through this; she was too angry. Her fingers hooked into the reins and she careened the buggy around the bend toward Stony Creek.

Gran's head craned sharply and she fixed a stare on Maude. "Mind the spirit round ye. The devil nivver sent a wind oot o' hell but he sailed wi' it." She faced forward again, kneading her skirt in her hands and staring at the rocky bluffs in the distance. When she spoke again, Maude could scarcely hear her. "Seventeen I was when my Jamie and I were wed."

Maude pulled back and Bobcat slowed. She reached over to take Ailse's hand, laying her palm on the skin that stretched waxen smooth and cool over the arthritic knuckles. Ailse rarely spoke of her husband. All Maude knew was that the beloved James Warwick MacDougall had died in an epidemic and was buried on a green hill in Morayshire.

"Lang syne, as they say," Ailse muttered low, looking down at Maude's hand covering her own. "Lang syne. There's things we cannae change, and this here thing with Mary and her beau be one of them. The twa are halfways tae Chicago by now, anywise." When she flashed a wry smile at Maude and lifted her hand away, Maude saw the sparkling wetness in her eyes.

Coming up the lane, they could see Mac tossing hay into the east mangers. Rory had started his new job at the Montana Railroad's wool warehouse last week—the job the railroad managers had offered him while he convalesced from his injury—so it would be evening before he heard the news. Maude wondered how Mary had contrived to escape her older brother's notice in town, considering that the warehouse was a scant block from the rail station. And what tale had she told Fiona and Isobel that morning in order to abandon them and the spring wagon at the school gate?

Inside the house, they found Catriona. Her silver-and-chestnut hair spilled carelessly out of the bun on the back of her head and her apron was skewed sideways. First she was upstairs, then down. She washed a cabbage in the kitchen sink, then went to the landing to find a quilt in the cedar closet. She traipsed out to the mudroom looking for a gallon of citronella oil, then climbed the stairs for something else.

Maude and Ailse couldn't keep up. John tried too, but abandoned them and went into his den, closing the heavy oak door behind him. Finally, Catriona sank, panting, onto the big trunk in the hallway and dropped her head into her hands.

"I suppose you'll want to see the note." Her voice was tight.

Ailse eased herself into a Windsor chair and said nothing. Maude stared out the open window, past the billowing white curtain, to the pasture beyond. "Do you want us to see it?"

Not raising her head, Catriona fished in her skirt pocket and thrust the note in Maude's direction.

Mother and Father:

If you could know the joy I feel at this moment, embarking on a
new life with the man I love, you would feel that same joy for me.
You were young and in love once, so please try to remember what
that was like. Paul and I are going to Chicago to be married, and
will contact you as soon as humanly possible. You have our most
fervent assurances that the Graham name will be held in the highest
regard now and always and that when we all meet again, we will
have much to celebrate. You have not the slightest cause for worry
or concern. Your loving and pure daughter, Mary

"My goodness." Maude wanted to say something far worse,
but the sight of her mother's heavy head prevented it. She
grimaced as she passed the note to Ailse, who had by now dug her
spectacles out of her jacket. The note was so . . . odd. But so like
the melodramatic Mary.

"She certainly struck home with it, from a mother's point of
view." Catriona's tone teetered between incredulity and sarcasm.

Maude sat down next to her mother and slipped an arm around
her. "She's seventeen, Mother. And she's not a young seventeen,
either."

Catriona's ribs began to quake. As the tears came, Ailse scuffed
into the kitchen to put the kettle on. Somehow the next few hours
passed, and blue evening fell, and the truth of it all settled like a
chill on every Graham at Stony Creek.

Chapter Thirteen

Forty-seven. They were all there, every last ewe and lamb. Maude and Kibbey, with Kibbey's expert sheep dog, Dart, and the dubious help of the pepper-coated Ajax, got the last of the sheep into the large corral behind the barn at Kettle Creek. It was a mild evening, still plenty warm enough to let them pasture out in the open, especially since John Graham had loaned Kibbey to Maude for a few weeks. But Maude knew Kibbey would be needed back at Stony Creek soon, so tonight was a good night to run them in.

Maude closed the broad gate on them and smiled when she saw Flourface blinking at her. "Ho there, funny girl. I hope your lambing goes better next spring than it did this year."

There were no rams just yet in this flock of forty-seven, only ewes and four-month-old lambs. She planned on conducting her lambing next April or May, so that meant they'd trail rams over from Stony Creek for breeding in late November. John had visited frequently in the last few weeks, walking around the flock and talking to Maude about the critical importance of clean water, how to avoid overeating problems in the new lambs, and other notes on sheep culture. Maude was glad of it. She knew it helped keep his mind off Mary.

A letter had come from her at last, telling them all that she and Paul were indeed married and happy, well-settled in Chicago.

They'd be coming back to Montana to visit at Thanksgiving. It wasn't the kind of wedding John and Catriona had wanted for Mary; no, not for the highly respected Grahams of Stony Creek.

As Maude leaned on the gate and watched Kibbey walk up the gentle slope toward his tidy white sheep wagon, she thought of her father's careworn face. It had been one thing to have their oldest daughter show every indication of remaining single, but now, with the fresh and blooming seventeen-year-old Mary having run off with a virtual stranger, and to receive word that she was truly married and gone to them, John and Catriona Graham had aged five years in less than a month.

She gave a last look at the bleating sheep and adjourned to the house, bolted the front door and slid the cross-member into place, then checked the back pantry door.

Upstairs it was hot, incredibly so for September. On half of her bed, she had spread out an old gray blanket for Ajax. In her nightgown at last, she climbed in beside him and watched his pink tongue loll out between his sharp white teeth. *Mother was right,* she thought. *He looks as though he climbed down a stovepipe, all gray and black, with no sense to his coloring at all.* She tugged gently on his triangle ears, then let her eyes drift to the green of the fir trees outside her window.

The warm breeze blew across her pillows, carrying with it the sound of Kibbey's fiddle. It had filtered in several nights running and she had begun to like it. One night, when he had played a reel, she had gotten out of bed and danced in her bare feet and white batiste gown. But this was a mournful tune, and it made her think of Mary running away, sitting on the train, kissing Paul Hathaway.

Maude was glad she'd at least gotten to know him a little bit at the corn roast and that day at the horse race before all hell broke loose. When he was joking with Rory or Mac, or bringing Mary a glass of lemonade punch, she'd watched him for the obscurity that Isobel had sensed, but she had caught only a wisp of something here and there, nothing of substance. He'd been as cordial and affable as any courting fellow ought to be.

Like her mother and father, Maude had expected the coming months and holidays to be marked with ardent visits from the well-intentioned suitor. How different her mental pictures had now become.

She pushed the fretful images from her mind and rolled onto her back. Kibbey shifted to a sweeter tune. *I ought not get accustomed to his music*, she thought dreamily. *He'll be gone in a few weeks. But it's divine. Far better than that blasted hammering that has been going on for weeks in McNaughton's forest just west of the rock coulee. What does the man need with another hunting cabin—or whatever he's building—deep in the hills above the perfect peace of my new domain?*

A shiver passed over her at the notion of him coming closer to her. Underscoring her apprehensions, a draft of cool air slipped into the room. She hooked her arm around Ajax. From out of nowhere, she drew up a dim memory of Gran whispering in Dame Wrigley's stone hovel on the banks of the Findhorn River, many years ago.

Gran and the toothless old Dame had sent her out to play, but she had instead crouched by a chink in the chimney and watched them at their hearth work, listening to their guest, a terrified scullery maid, tell the tale of how her master spoiled every virgin who worked at Buckthorn Farm. What Maude remembered most wasn't the girl's tears, or the mystery of the herbs and incantations, but the sense of bright power that welled up in the center of that unlikely threesome as they set about protecting the trembling girl from the malevolent advances of a dark and troubled soul.

Maude bit her lip. *Could I . . . bind McNaughton somehow? Should I?* It was an arcane idea, something she'd never even considered until this moment. Her eyelids grew heavy as she struggled to part the gray veil of time. *What had Ailse and Dame Wrigley said that night as they formed a circle and muttered over the crackling fire while that pale girl sat shivering in her cloak?*

Any grasp she had on the distant past began to dissolve in the face of fatigue, and within the scant space of a minute, the tune of the fiddle had carried her away on the winds of sleep.

It was a mammoth hay barn, ten yards wide by fifteen long. It would be some time, Rob reasoned, before the mucked-up edges of the hayfield destroyed by hauling logs, lumber, and shingles became grassy again, but the area ought to look pretty good by spring. He pulled his bandanna from his back pocket and wiped his forehead. *Does Tom McNaughton really appreciate the stunning beauty of these forested foothills? Hell, for that matter, could anyone? This is God's Country, no doubt about it.* He shook his head, letting the breeze riffle his hair, and scanned the view.

He stood in the middle of a vast, rolling meadow at least forty acres in size, hemmed in by dark pines all around. Above, a few white clouds scudded in a sky of blazing blue. He spied Grant near the worksite and smiled as he saw him winging stub ends of lumber into a small firewood pile. Grant was doing that for Rob's campsite deep in the woods. He'd finally accepted the fact that Rob was happier out here in his wall tent than in one of the four-poster beds at the rambling Rocking M ranch house. Grant's strong, tanned forearms gleamed in the sun. Both he and Rob had gotten stronger and leaner that summer, working hard on fence and construction projects for the ambitious laird.

To the west, the Snowy Mountains stood cool and dark, bearing no snow at all. It was just too hot. In the creek drainages, a few aspens had begun to turn, sparking the mountainsides with flecks of gold. But overall, it had been too warm for any noticeable change in the Judith Basin foliage.

Although the hill pasture seemed an unlikely place to build a hay barn, Rob could see the logic in it. The East Fork Road was a quarter mile away, and the Rocking M's main pastures only a short distance farther. Peering into the woods, he studied his and Grant's earlier project, a hunting blind for the laird, mounted snugly amongst three stout pines. It sat about fifteen feet off the ground, accessible by a ladder of neat lodgepole pine rungs.

Laird Thomas had already been on site several times, striding around in his tan breeches and crisp white shirt, inspecting first the barn and then visiting the hunting blind. A month or so earlier, he had outfitted the overgrown treehouse with two hand-tooled leather campstools, a small cupboard for his Scotch whiskey, and two mounts for his rifle and telescope. After getting it properly turned out, he peered out one of the narrow windows and grinned at Rob and Grant, then clambered down the ladder and clapped them both on the shoulders, exclaiming, "Splendid! This patch of woods sees mair mule deer and partridge than anywhere else on the Rocking M."

The laird wasn't there today, though. He hadn't been there for over a week, Rob realized with a deep exhale. The dump rakes had finished their sweep of the mountain meadow last Friday, and the drying grass lay in thick, silky windrows. The sweet, cloying scent of freshly cut hay had mellowed into the richer, heavier aroma of coming autumn and the harvest.

Rob and Grant, with the help of the Rocking M hands, had built the hay barn up and over two loaf-shaped stacks from the June cutting. Now, a crew of shirtless, sweating hayhands pitched the late-summer grass onto wagons and carted it into the mammoth shed, heaving it over the top of the June stacks.

A wishbone of Canada geese flew overhead, honking restlessly. Rob watched them for a moment, his fingers working the leather strap that held his hammer to his belt. A summer's worth of wear had softened it to the same consistency as the leather thong that bound the sacred medicine bundle around his neck. His gaze shifted back to the earth, back to the men as they set the tall wire netting for winter. He was more than ready for them to be done, to pile into the wagons and roll down the shady road through the pines.

He'd seen Medicine Badger three days ago, and they'd agreed that tonight would be the night. They would meet on the forested slopes of the Snowies, where Moss Creek emptied into Castle Creek, and travel upstream to Rob's camp. He knew better than to ask Medicine Badger to meet him there at a certain hour of the clock. Instead, they simply agreed on "supper time." Rob knew the Indian would wait for him if he was late, but something made him want to be there first, waiting at the confluence, to greet Medicine Badger.

At last the buck rake went rattling down the hill, some of the men ambling tiredly behind, their steps as heavy as the sweat-slick draft horses, others whooping and cuffing their friends, full of waggish anticipation for the weekend.

He was at liberty to go. He'd left his horse at the Rocking M, knowing it would be at least four days before he'd be ready to retrieve him. Working his way into the young growth of aspens and firs, he spooked a covey of Hungarian partridge. His dog, Cala, momentarily berserk at having so many slow-moving targets to follow, was lost for five minutes. Rob wove his way along a deer trail he knew would lead him up a slow incline to the confluence.

He found Medicine Badger resting placidly beneath a tree with a bulging elkskin bag beneath his arm. *It figures*, he thought. *The white man's sense of time may never match up with the Indian's.* The two of them set off, heading up the gentle incline toward Rob's camp. He felt odd having Medicine Badger walk behind him on the narrow trail, but with the creek on one side and boulders the size of henhouses on the other, two men could not walk abreast.

When they got to the camp, they settled in for their meal, which Rob knew was an important part of the ritual. It was too hot for a fire, but none was needed at this point. Rob grabbed a rope anchored to the crotch of a tree and lowered a canvas bag full of dried fruit, jerky, and tinned beans. Medicine Badger brought forth his offering, which consisted of some kind of corn and venison hash and a brew similar to what they'd had at the encampment—berry water sweetened with honey.

When they were finished, Medicine Badger flicked his eyes over the scene and said, "We gotta keep going."

Rob's head drew back in surprise. "We can't stay here?"

"You will learn nothing here. They will not come." He then

pointed to Cala. "Tie the dog up. I will come and take her with me in the morning. They will not come if she is with you."

"They?" Rob fought to keep his brows from coming together in a scowl. *What is this crazy Indian talking about?*

"Pretty soon we talk."

The idea of tying Cala up grated harshly on him, but he'd had to do it once or twice before, so he decided to submit. *If things don't pan out right over the next few hours,* he reasoned, *I'll come back down here and start the evening all over.*

He left Cala with a large basin of water and a pile of dried venison scraps. From the wall tent, he took a canteen and rolled up a couple of blankets. Glancing at Medicine Badger, who nodded at the trail, he faced the darkening woods and continued upstream. Cala yipped three times and was quiet.

They continued for over an hour, deeper into the pines, as the trail grew narrower and wilder. Late-season asters nodded along the stream as it tumbled over mossy rocks on its journey down the mountain. They passed a cascading waterfall that Rob never knew existed. A pine marten, slim and mysterious in its glossy brown coat, darted across a fallen log. Gray jays creaked overhead.

On their left, a scattering of dark gray boulders in a tall grove of firs caught Rob's eye. He slowed his step, and just as he did, Medicine Badger said, "Here." The Indian unburdened himself of his elkskin bag and slipped a knife from a sheath at his belt. He stepped from stone to stone across the creek and began slicing slender osiers off at the base. Each sapling was about an inch thick, growing to a dense, fern-like crest at the top.

"We need a lotta these," he grunted, motioning to Rob. "For *stiskahn.* Vision lodge." Rob came across the creek to help, but the Indian directed him to build a fire. "Make fire here," he said, pointing away from the lodge. "Make it good and hot, with some rocks in the middle. Flat and round rocks."

Rob went about this chore, but kept his eye on Medicine Badger, who went about his task with an air of rhythmic familiarity. The

Indian stubbed a few rocks into a small fire ring, then forced several saplings into the humus in a wide oval around the stones. As he began bending them into an arc and pinioning them into a dome, Rob recognized the shape of a sweat lodge. When his fire had grown into a tidy blaze, he helped Medicine Badger collect deadfall and laid it against the framework, then pieced more willow branches and clumps of damp moss over the top.

Medicine Badger rummaged inside his elskin bag and removed some odd-looking objects. One item looked like an animal's tail. "Blackhorn," he said. Rob recognized it as the shaggy tail of a buffalo. As the Indian continued these ministrations, Rob kept himself busy feeding the fire.

When it was time, the two men used thick forked sticks to transfer hot rocks from the fire to the lodge. Medicine Badger stayed inside for some time, where Rob could hear him shoving the rocks into a tight pile. At last he emerged, saying, "Sweat good." He began stripping off his clothing, indicating to Rob that he should do the same. Naked, they crawled inside the hot, smoky lodge. Rob watched Medicine Badger go about various little motions he had clearly made dozens, perhaps hundreds of times before. The Indian sprinkled a pinch of tobacco on the rocks. He took the blackhorn tail and dipped it in a battered tin pan, then drew it across the hot stones numerous times.

Rob found the heat and steam oppressive, but something about it began to lull him into a stupor. *No*, he thought, *it's not a stupor. It's some kind of languid state, and it's not at all unpleasant.*

Just as Medicine Badger had said, his initial desire to get up and escape the heat began to pass. He sank into a relaxed mood, staring into the murky darkness. Through the doorway, he could see the fire in the coming twilight. He watched the movements of Medicine Badger's lithe, muscular arms. In the dim light, his own bronzed arms looked the same.

His gaze was drawn toward the small, intricately structured fire just outside. He stared at the twigs and watched as the bark crinkled from gray to hot orange and then to white ash. His fingers traced the dark, powdery earth at his side. The composite of centuries, he thought idly. The creek outside made a soft, rushing sound that blended with the hiss of the steam. It all began to touch him, to impinge upon his senses in an almost oppressive, hypnotic way.

"You can hear them now."

Rob turned his head and considered the Indian, whose black eyes seemed to see every thought in his head. "Them," repeated Rob. This time, it was not a question.

"*Spomiitapiks*. Sky People. They speak when you listen." Medicine Badger nodded. "When you listen, you follow the red road."

Rob could not argue with him. He felt something stealing over him, something strong and irrefutable. He took a shallow breath and felt the heat scorch the back of his throat. Medicine Badger picked up a sheaf of silver green leaves lying next to him and crumbled them over the stones, where they withered and smoked. "Sage," he said, then dragged the wet blackhorn over the hot rocks. It hissed and issued a billow of steam.

Weak from days of physical exertion, fatigued from the climb up the mountain, and now weary from the heat and the sweat running off his body, Rob inhaled the aromatic scent of the sage and let his mind go. The pungent fragrance took him to far-off, exotic lands where men had made arduous and fantastic journeys through the millennia. *In the end*, he mused, *do we not all seek the same thing?*

He found himself nodding. He was exhausted, but at the same time free of any concern. Cala crossed his mind. He could see her tied to her tree, but he knew she was all right. Medicine Badger would go to her soon.

He saw a road rising up before him, but it was not the white man's road. It was a narrow path, leading up a mountain where the setting sun cast a vermillion blaze over an amphitheater of granite, alpine grasses, and dark spires of spruce. An eagle swept silently overhead. He felt the lofty winds brush against him, ruffling his hair. As currents of air sang in his ears, he felt certain there were voices in that wind. Despite his blinking delirium, he knew the Indian was right. He strained to hear the words of the spirits.

"You gotta get out now."

His head lolling to the side, dry lips parted, Rob had sense enough to plant his hands in the dirt and crawl toward the door. This simple act was harder than he expected. His elbows threatened to buckle. Gasping with effort, he had to concentrate in order to make the muscles of his forearms work. Medicine Badger followed him. When they were out, the Indian placed a sweaty arm around his ribs and steadied him as he weaved toward the little stream. They sat on separate rocks in dished-out places in Moss Creek, rinsing themselves off, letting their heads clear. The sun was no longer visible, but the sky was well illuminated, a pale cerulean blue, dwindling to a soft ribbon of gold behind the pines. It was so warm that within minutes, their bodies were dry.

"I'm gonna make the circle." Medicine Badger stood up and pulled on his trousers, then went to the small clearing and scribed a circle in the soft earth. He built another small fire ring in the center, then sat down and waited. As soon as Rob was within the circle, he closed it with a final carving motion in the dirt.

"You prepare for the journey now," he said when Rob had dressed and laced up his boots. They sat down, feeding the small fire in front of them. "This circle is sacred. You do not leave it. No matter what. You might feel like you are leaving it, when they come for you, but you will still be inside it. When I come back in four days, I gotta find you inside this circle."

Rob listened in complete silence. He felt like the sweat had cleaned not only the outside of him but the inside as well. He kept his eyes on Medicine Badger, determined to pay close attention.

"I leave you no food or water. You will have blankets and the stuff to make fire. That's all. On the fourth morning I come back and I light the fire if it is out and I smoke you with sage. You tell me then what has happened to you, but you don't tell anyone else.

"Wild things will come to you. You will not know if they are real. Maybe they will be real, but maybe not. But anything that comes to you has the intention of coming. If an animal comes to you, it is the Creator in the form of that animal. You heard them in the sweat."

"I . . . I think so. I heard something important about fire, and what it means. And the red road. I heard the wind."

"Yeah." For the first time, Medicine Badger smiled. "You heard them. The Sky People. They are your spirit guides. They will tell you what you need to do. If you need a message from the wolf, like you think you do, you will hear it. The Sky People are all around us. We gotta be quiet so we can hear what is going on. When we stop listening, they stop talking."

A strong chill swept over Rob. Medicine Badger continued talking for some time, about the place of humans and animals on the earth, and telling stories of the raven and the beaver, who brought great medicine to the Blackfeet. Finally, when the Indian was done, Rob nodded, glancing at the medicine bundle Inii had prepared for him. Although the pouch was little more than a scrap of deerskin filled with herbs, feathers, and animal bones, Rob knew it was critically important. He picked it up and looped the thong around his neck.

Medicine Badger rose and wiped his hands against his thighs. "Make a mark every morning when you wake up and see the sun rise. On the fourth day I will come. Now I gotta go and take your dog so you will not worry."

And before Rob could say a word, he was gone, with only a low-hanging fir branch stirring in his wake.

Chapter Fourteen

Beads of sweat clustered in his eyebrows, trickling down onto his lids and stinging his eyes. Rob had no idea what time it was, but he knew morning was a long way off. He glanced at the log on which he'd been keeping track of the days. Two gashes. He'd spent two nights in the forest. At least he thought so. It could very well be three. His mind had grown infirm; he no longer trusted his judgment. The low fire hissed, casting scissored shadows on the mammoth boulders around his camp. The boulders they had chosen for protection now seemed like the backdrop to some lurid drama at which he was a helpless spectator.

What made me think this experience would be tame and simple? Thank God the Indian took Cala. The blue roan is safe too, pasturing among the Rocking M's herd with plenty of grass and water.

It occurred to him that he could die here, disoriented and alone. At least there was water nearby if he really felt he couldn't last any longer. He flung his head into his hands. *What an asinine excuse for a greenhorn I am. I'm no Blackfeet brave! I am just plain guilty, guilty of the worst kind of arrogance. All in some damned fool notion that I might understand why the wolves won't stay out of my bloody dreams. A white man dabbling in Indian ways . . . it's basely naïve, stupid. I'll be lucky not to conjure Old Scratch himself with my tinkering in pagan ways. Better off living with tortuous dreams for the rest of my life.*

He pinched the bridge of his nose, trying to focus, then looked around vapidly. *I never thought it would be like this. I am in a stupor, yet at the same time I feel that I am not missing anything, that I am seeing more than what is actually here. The night is thick with sound and scent. There is almost too much to see, to sense . . . I'll be lucky to make it till sunrise and manage my ravings. What if Medicine Badger never comes back?* He swiped at his eyes, trying to remember. *Why was this so damned important?*

He twitched convulsively at every breath of wind, every rustle of leaves on the forest floor. *What did the leaping fire-shadows mean?* Tall and lean, animated and proud, one moment they looked like white men, the next they looked like the Blackfeet at an ancient sun-dance. He knew they were shadows made by ragged spears of buckbrush, but at the same time he couldn't deny they were more than mere shadows. One figure shot its arm up in the air, beckoning to him, then jerked toward the woods, pointing into the darkness.

Rob snapped his head around, watching, probing the forest, staring past the rough bark of the first visible trunks to the next wall of dim gray pillars into the wild blackness. *Was something there?* "They will come," Medicine Badger had said.

His hearing sharpened, his eyesight keener than ever before, he listened and waited. *Nothing. Or is something there waiting, just waiting for me to stop watching?* Slowly he turned back to the fire, thrusting a couple more pieces of dry pine into its glowing orange core. He scooted himself around so that his back was against a tall boulder.

Tipping his head back, he stared up through the opening in the black fringe of pines where a thin silver bowl of new moon gleamed. An eerie stillness settled over everything. Even the trickling sound of the creek plashing over the rocks faded from his hearing. Silence, everywhere. Then he felt it.

It started in the base of his spine, a kind of rhythm, soft, like the breath of the earth. *Is this something I feel*, he wondered, *or something I am hearing?* Nothing was real anymore. His gaze traveled back down from the dark tips of the pines, through their lofty branches where the sparks of the fire died in the warm night air, down, down, back to the campsite, in the middle of a vast universe of wildness, to the tiny, dwindling fire at the center of it all.

He was transfixed by the fire, which he now could see had a respiration of its own. Every puff of ash, every soft susurration of gas escaping from the long-burning logs, moved in rhythm with the vibration he felt in his spine, and now at the base of his neck. It began radiating into his shoulder blades, pure energy and strength. The vision of the red path from the sweat lodge flared to life around him, brilliant in the setting sun, luminous with crimson warmth. He was there, on the sacred road.

What he heard next came as no surprise. It felt completely natural, just as it always did in his dreams. He knew it was coming. For centuries, he had always known. The howl was soft and long, garrulous and easy, almost like a laugh. And this time, he knew what it meant. Any trace of mystery was gone. The vibration moved through his hips and flowed into his legs, across his shoulders and down into his arms. He pitched forward, his body rocking with the pulse rising from the very dirt beneath him.

The howl came again. Rob leaped to his feet, kicking gravel and stones onto the fire. Medicine Badger's sober injunction to stay inside the circle flew away like the bat darting among the branches high above. They had come, just as the Indian said they would. Not only had they come, they had called him. He was off, running soundlessly through the woods.

Bones. Some were scattered around, nearly picked clean with just a few bits of dessicated red flesh stretched and dangling here and there. Others had been dragged into the shade several yards away, clumped and gnarled in a nest of fur and gore.

Rob's eyes were slits. At first he couldn't see anything except the sticky bones and a few gnats buzzing in the half-light. His tongue was thick, dry. He knew this feeling. *Too much to drink, that was it. Must have passed out. Drank too much with someone, probably Grant. But where am I?*

It was barely sunrise, he could tell that much. *What a damned idiot I am.* He tried to move, but his entire body was chilled and stiff. And weak, incredibly weak. The predawn cold had sunk well into his joints, but it was something else too. *Whiskey, maybe. What the hell was it? Where did I spend the night?*

A sudden yipping and growling made him strain his head a few degrees toward the bones. *Cala, thank God.* He rubbed his eyes, trying to focus his blurred vision. *Is it Cala?* If it was, she wasn't alone. There was another pup with her. No, not just one, several of them. They were lined up on the far side of the bloody lump of fur and flesh, yanking away, ripping bits of flesh off the carcass. He heard determined grunts as their little jaws clamped and jerked, then the sound of teeth cracking into bones. A dark, bushy form loomed behind the pups, then retreated at a slow trot.

Holy Christ. Rob's blood surged hard and his heart moved into his throat. *It can't be. Those aren't dogs. They're . . . can they be? Yes. Wolves.*

He froze and checked the position of his body, making sure it was exactly the same as it had been from the moment he first gained consciousness. With his cheek pillowed on a patch of buffalo grass, he took in as much of his surroundings as possible. Moving his eyes in a radius, he scanned the scene without moving his head.

A pink glow on the horizon, just above the tips of the dark firs, told him the sun would soon rise. The bones and the pups meant that he was in a wolf den, their sacred space. How he had come to be here was a riddle he was just beginning to unravel. On a mound of boulders a short distance away, several mature wolves stood, surveying the rocky glen. In a stretch of meadow below, five or six more young wolves scuffled in mock battle.

Last night. Where was I? The campsite, yes. I fasted at least two days—or was it three? The strange, dancing shadows came back to him. Now he remembered rising suddenly from his seat by the fire, called by voices from the woods.

He jerked his head and winced with pain. Every muscle and joint had been pushed to its limit and beyond. As he stiffened and let out a silent gasp, an enormous gray wolf on a rock outcropping high above him began to howl. Rob laid his head back down to get a better look.

Could this be the one they call the Adrad? His skin crawled with such intensity he could hardly lie still. He didn't know whether to get up and limp away, or claw his way as silently as possible into the underbrush.

A medium-sized black and a large pale wolf, both males, joined in. Soon their predawn chorus was taken up by others from all around the glen. Even the battling youngsters stopped their horse-play and sat back on their haunches to howl.

That's it. The midnight howl of a wolf had come to him at the campfire, and he had set off. He could barely remember, but he knew he had run. For a long time, too. *It seemed he had run with the wolves themselves, but how could that be?* He remembered blood. A battle. *Had he witnessed a kill?* He shifted his eyes down, along the length of his arm. What was left of his shirt hung in a few bloody strips.

Following what seemed an impossible and yet terribly logical line of thought, his eyes flickered from the tattered shirt to the carcass under the tree. As much as he didn't want to know it, his mind flooded with the knowledge of what kind of animal that mangled carcass had once been.

The wind shifted, carrying to him the warm scent of elk blood. Two of the wolf pups lost interest in the carcass and wandered toward him, full of curiosity. One was especially bold, a broad-chested little thing with a big square head. Rob knew what would happen next. The dark form that had shadowed the pups a few minutes before reappeared, a massive black female. She came straight toward him, almost mowing the pups down with her huge paws.

Circling Rob, Leal sniffed brazenly at his crotch and at the seat of his pants. Rob lay still, breathing slowly in and out. *Will this be the end of me, out here, somewhere in the wild back country of Fergus County? Or hell, maybe I've run with the wolves clear to Meagher County. Torn to bits by a wolf pack, bits so small no one but the hawks and coyotes will ever find what's left of me.* In spite of it all, he was surprised at how little fear he felt. *Well, if this is what becomes of me, then so be it.*

Leal's gaze was incandescent, golden. As Rob stared back at the face of coal-black fur and fathomless eyes, he thought with his gut, not with his mind. The longing he had felt that night on Ruby Creek, seated at his window and listening to wolf-song, surged through him, bringing back his desire to understand and to know. He looked hard into the wolf's eyes.

It was as if this urge had driven him all his life . . . even longer. As soon as he recognized the ancient longing in himself, something passed in the air between him and the black female. It hit him in two places at once, between the eyes and in the chest, like a gust of icy wind. *I know you*, it said. It was as if he said it to her and she said it to him, all in one instant, together.

It could not have lasted more than two or three seconds. His head tipped to the side, like a dog's. He may as well have looked in a mirror, because the wolf did exactly the same thing. But by the time he felt the first rushing astonishment of what was happening between them, he was staring at Leal's bushy tail as she whirled back to her pups, gumming them roughly about the neck with her wide, powerful jaws, shoving them toward the dusty area near the carcass.

Stunned and groggy, Rob knew he had to go. He was weak and well past feeling his own thirst, but he knew damn well he needed water, and that any moments of lucidity he still possessed would drain away with every passing hour. *I'll sink into delirium—if I'm not there already—and lose my sense of direction. I've got to act now, with what strength I still have. Medicine Badger. Cala. What day is it?*

He rolled cautiously to his side and propped himself up on one knee, looking around. From their various vantage points, the wolves twitched their ears and gave notice of him, but none made a move. Within minutes, he was in the forest, alone.

She ought not be so worried. After all, the lamb was a full four months old, not a wobbly little thing any more. How it had gotten away from the flock was anyone's guess. Her heart stuck in her mouth as she crested every little rise or came around a boulder. She could well imagine the pitiful remains in her mind: head flung back with sightless eyes, fleece rent apart, little black legs askew, a bloody midsection gashed open by a wolf, coyote, or even a black bear.

Bobcat picked his way intently along the deer trail as though he sensed the meaning of her search. "If it wasn't so blasted hot," she muttered, "I wouldn't be so worried." They were out in the wide open section of her land, in a remote corner that ran flat a long ways before wedging up into a rock coulee. Kibbey was out of sight, nearly a mile away, with the flock. The two of them had decided that if she had not returned within an hour, he would come looking for her.

As she approached the place where the deer trail curved sharply up into the coulee, her field of vision was blocked by a rocky shoulder of land forming the mouth of what must have been a river many centuries ago. The coulee was a forbidding place, a highway of rough, tumbled stones that led nowhere and dwindled into the forest. She was glad most of it was on McNaughton's land; she had no use for it. As she urged Bobcat on, a feeling rushed over her, like a breath of wind—but of course, there was no wind. She knew the feeling too well. Now it was almost certain she would find something just ahead. Working to modulate her breath, she felt hotter than ever. She reached up to adjust her wide-brimmed hat, wiping away the dampness under the crown.

The heat bounced off the boulders at the foremost edge of the rock bluff. Grasshoppers popped out of the crisp grass around Bobcat's hooves. She strained her eyes as the full range of the vast boulder field came into view. There, only fifteen yards ahead, was the lamb.

Maude immediately dismounted so that the horse would not frighten the timid creature. She had plenty of experience catching lambs and knew just how to approach this one. Within minutes she had a lead on him and was headed back toward her horse, clucking and chatting to coax him. If he gave her any trouble, she'd hobble him and pick him up, but she hoped it wouldn't come to that. The little fellow appeared no worse for wear, but clearly needed water.

Looking out across the boulder field, where waves of heat shimmered over the toss of granite, she was grateful he hadn't stumbled any farther than he had. Then, the rush of air fluttered over her forearms and chest again. In the sea of buff and gray, an out-of-place object caught her eye. It was the color, more than anything . . . the color and the texture. And the shape. Yes, the shape. It didn't fit. *What is it? Could it be a limb? Yes. It's rather like a deer.*

She saw a scattering of magpies flap and settle in the rocks, then lift again and circle in the sky. *They're waiting. Waiting for something to die. It must be a deer.*

She strained her eyes and shook her head. Even though she could see little of interest but the wheeling magpies, now joined by a couple of ravens, something wasn't right. The limb, she realized, with a sickening twist of her gut, was too bulky to be a deer's leg.

She looked down at the lamb, whose tongue showed between his teeth, then back out at the boulder field. *If I'm going to investigate, I have to do it fast.* She tied the lamb to a clump of sage and started out, planting each step carefully among the rocks, hiking up her skirts and finding stable footing as she went, watching for rattlesnakes but knowing one could strike regardless of how much care she took.

Within a few minutes she was close enough to see that the object she had spied was indeed a human leg. She lifted her skirts even higher, jumping and running. Her hat fell back, held only by the ribbon around her neck.

A man, unconscious, lay on his back on a narrow stretch of flat ground among the boulders. His face was covered in dirt and filth, his hair was matted with pine sap and duff, and his chest was marked by numerous deep, bloody scratches. Clad only in boots and a pair of tan trousers, there was also a small scrap of leather attached to a thong dangling from his neck. Pine needles and bits of dried grass were crusted to his skin in dark streaks wherever the blood and sweat had dried under the withering sun. And there was the smell of blood mingled with other strange scents she could not quite identify—wild, musky draughts that gave her a sense of being far from home, when she knew she was right in her own backyard.

The scene was peculiar, but what was strangest of all to Maude at that moment was not the fact that a near-dead half-breed lay on her property on the hottest day of 1908, but that she felt she knew him. Yet staring at him, she had no idea who he was.

Covered in filth as he was, near naked and full of stench, she couldn't imagine how anyone had come to be here, in this condition. She knew there were bums and hobos who rode the railroad and took odd jobs on Basin ranches. *This has to be one of them*, she concluded. *Whoever he is, he needs immediate attention.*

Twenty minutes later she and Kibbey reappeared, hauling her small spring wagon. The last time she had harnessed Bobcat to this wagon in a dreadful hurry was in February, as she moved a full-grown doe out of the river when it had fallen through the ice. The doe had died, despite her efforts to save it.

As she and Kibbey tied Bobcat off on a bleached snag, she thought of the irony. Here she was in the opposite situation, in the blast furnace of late summer, thinking to save a man dying of heat exhaustion. *Who in the hell is this fool?*

"He's over here," she said, leading the way. "I think we can manage him if you get the legs and I take the shoulders."

Kibbey nodded, stepping around to grasp the man's ankles. As Maude went up to the head, she squatted down with her canteen to dribble a few drops of moisture into the man's mouth. As the water fell onto his lips, she looked hard into his face. *The jawline . . . the nose.*

"Blue blazes, it's that man Elliott!" She snatched her hands away and stared. Every moment she'd ever seen him pulsed into her mind . . . the night on the creek, her flaming cheeks when he'd seen her on the haystack, and then weeks ago at the horse race. But the smoky details of that first time on the creek nearly overcame her. The two of them locked in that sudden embrace, rolling, tumbling through the June grass, his body fitting into hers, the grape-sweet lupine brushing her cheeks, his lips so close to her ear.

The sight of his burning red skin beneath the film of dirt and organic matter slapped her back to the present. She returned the canteen to his cracked lips, holding it as steady as she could. The water dribbled out, some of it making it into his mouth.

Kibbey, who had never heard Maude speak in this heated manner, retreated from Elliott's ankles. "He's a ne'er-do-weel?"

Maude shook her head. "I'll tell you later. Let's hurry and get him into the wagon. As you can see, he's no lightweight." She crouched down and hooked her arms under Rob's shoulders, while Kibbey moved up between Rob's legs and clamped onto his knees.

Grunting and taking uneven, heavy steps, they made slow progress over the rocks to the waiting wagon and heaved the limp form onto the wooden bed.

Kibbey tugged at Rob's shoulders and balanced him in the wagon box so that Bobcat would have a proper load. "Looks like your infirmary will hae another patient for a wee bit," he said, climbing on. Their pace was rapid, making the wagon rattle and the wheels crunch on the stubbly brush. After a few minutes, Kibbey spoke up loudly. "You ken this fellow Elliott?"

"Hardly. We met on Midsummer Eve."

"Och."

Maude's head jerked. "It's not like that." She bit out the words. "Not the traditional meeting, not at all. He was camping up the creek when Gran Ailse started a fire to smoke the sheep."

"So that's why the grass was all bleck oot there." He chuckled, his cheeks crinkling up around his blue eyes. "Devil kick me halfway to kirk for nae figuring that one. Ailse is the grand dame of the auld ways."

Maude smiled. "Yes, she would have brought a barrow full of Moray dirt over here if she could have."

"Aye, that's our Ailse. So this lad got in yer road that night, aye?"

"So to speak."

"He doesnae look weel now."

"No, he certainly does not." Maude turned in the wagon seat and appraised the sprawling form. *What in God's name happened to him? He looks like he's been in a fight with a wild animal. He even smells like a wild animal. And now, regardless of everything, I've got to do whatever I can for him.*

Her mind raced over the first steps of treatment. Trying to rush him to the hospital in Lewistown was a preposterous idea. He needed to be cooled down immediately, given water and rest. She could dress the closed wounds with barberry and arnica, cleanse and bind the others. The best place would be the dark corner of her barn. Shaded by fir trees and protected by a rocky bluff, it was cooler than her house. There was a cot there already, where her hired hands sometimes slept.

She drove the wagon right into the shade of the barn. "I fear there may be more to this ailment than simple heat exhaustion," she said as they lowered Rob onto the cot. "I'm going into the house to get my medicine box. Kibbey, I'll need your help. First, we've got to get those work boots off. I've loosened the laces, but while I'm in the house, will you pull them off? It's our first step in cooling him down. I also want you to look at his legs above the boot line and see if you can see any signs of snakebite. If you have to . . . take his trousers off, please do so. It's best that I'm not here for that. The undergarments can stay in place, of course. There are some blankets right there on the shelf, so that you can keep him . . . decent."

Kibbey, who was gazing at Rob's legs, taking all this in, had barely opened his mouth to respond when Maude spun on her heel and strode out of the barn. He ran a callused hand through his thatch of white hair and said, "Weel, Maister Elliott, 'pairs I'm to be your nairsy-maid." He hobbled over to the end of the cot and, with skilled hands, went to work.

Maude set her medicine box down at the well between the house and barn and pumped two buckets full of water, then hurried to the cool room in the corner. Kibbey had left to check on a bloated lamb, but before he did, he reported to Maude that he'd found no evidence of snakebite. This was good, but it only deepened the mystery of Rob Elliott's predicament.

Setting to work, she did a preliminary rinse of every inch of his face and hair in order to cool the brain, then moved on. At this stage, she ignored the cuts and scratches. Treating those would come later. As she washed him, she stopped at the navel, noting the marked line where the dark suntan of his torso stopped sharply and gave way to the white skin normally covered by his trousers. She left the merino blanket in place, then dropped to the end of the cot and worked from his feet to his thighs.

As night crept in, she was thankful for the kerosene lanterns Kibbey had hung to light her work. She dabbed a sponge into the clear drinking water and wrung it into Rob's mouth every few minutes, making sure he got just enough.

Viewing his anatomy, she studied the fitness in his torso, nodding with satisfaction at the advantage a healthy body gave to a patient's potential for recovery. The conformation of his arms struck her immediately. The deltoids were especially well developed, dipping into a tight swale before mounding into the rise of biceps. Wincing as she discovered a bloody gash on the right upper arm, she dabbed a piece of flannel into her witch hazel solution to cleanse the scratch. *Thorn, or a low-hanging branch*, she speculated. *Perfect muscling, really. Like something from one of my textbooks, or a museum.*

Carefully removing the amulet from his neck, she set it on an overturned crate. Coming back to his chest, she ran her hands across another deep, clotted scratch near his sternum. She let her hand rest there, feeling the pulse of his heart through the flesh. The look of the skin across his pectoral muscles, like bronze satin glistening with drops of water from her sponge, sent a tightness surging through her. She stared at him, remembering what he'd said to her at the horse race . . . the twinkling light in his gold green eyes, the silken touch of his fingers on her palm, and the violent feeling it had stirred in her. *Rob Elliott.* Her belly cramped and a hot flame licked at her insides, sharp as hunger.

Whipping her hand away, she blurted, "Sweet Saint Brigid." She flung a look over her shoulder, hoping Kibbey had not come back. He was nowhere in sight.

Glancing at Rob's feverish face, she whispered, "Thank God you're unconscious."

A red stain flooded into her cheeks. She grabbed a bit of flour sacking and fanned herself. Something new had boiled up within her. *What business does this man have coming onto my property and collapsing in a near-dead state? What right does he have throwing himself upon my charity like this, making my life revolve around him for what will probably be at least a week? If he lives, that is.*

Her mouth twisted into a worried curl. She didn't like the fact that she was breathing harder than normal, didn't like it one bit. Nor did it please her that her heart was fluttering like a bird in the cage of her chest.

She steadied her breath and brushed the dampness from her upper lip. *My hands already smell like him, my clothes and hair as well. It's one thing to bring home a wounded animal, but humans are perfectly able to care for themselves. How in the name of sweet Mother Earth did he get himself into this state, and why couldn't he have done it somewhere else?*

She stiffened her spine and gave her head a shake, trying to view him simply as a patient who must be cared for—no more, no less. Massaging some castile shampoo into his matted hair, she rinsed it clean with a moist towel, taking care not to dampen the bedding. Then she wiped away the last dark bits of soil from the corners of his eyes, the edges of his mouth, and the sides of his nostrils.

The damp, whiskey-colored hair curled around his high, sunburned forehead. The planes of his face were symmetrical and sculpted; his lips, although dry and cracked, were full. The upper lip bore a marked indentation in the center, which she now traced with a piece of flannel soaked in lanolin oil. Out of nowhere, Morag's voice echoed in her head, "That Elliott fellow, he's handsome."

"Pah!" she said out loud. "I'll give him the same care I'd give any patient—period." Laying her cheek against his forehead, she pulled away, frowning. He was too warm. She heard Kibbey come up behind her. "I'm convinced now, Kibbey. It's some kind of fever in addition to the heat. I don't know if he got into some bad water or what. I'm going to mix up a solution and I'll need you to help me get it into him. It'll be mostly water, but I'll add a bit of something to help bring the fever down."

Kibbey nodded and sat down on a nail keg. Turning to her medicine box, Maude pulled out a mortar and pestle and several squares of gauze, then dug through jars of powders, bark, and berries. After several minutes of grinding and pouring, a pale solution was distilling through several layers of gauze into a glass jar.

"Sommat of Ailse's tradition?" asked Kibbey, nodding at the beaker.

Maude smiled. "I'm using a little of the new and a bit of the old tonight. We'll use modern aspirin. But I'll dose him with a bit of Ailse's favorite willow bark and honey fever-reducer too."

Kibbey lifted Rob's upper body far enough for them to shove another blanket under his shoulders. They used a piece of rubber tubing to dribble a small amount of the liquid between his lips.

"We'll need to give him plain water in this fashion all through the night, I'm afraid," said Maude. "Or we'll lose him. He's just too dehydrated. Are you game?"

"I've done it for a sheep; why couldnae I do it for a man?"

Chapter Fifteen

"I dinnae like coming over wi' Fiona and Isobel in that spring wagon," said Ailse, rubbing her low back. "I'm short enow as it is, and my rig-bane gets pounded out good in that dratted thing." She poked her stick into the aspen leaves littering the ground along the path from Maude's house to the barn. "Twa days of frost, and would ye look at this?"

"You said you had a letter from Mary?" Maude tried to steer Ailse away from the mouth of the barn toward the corral, where Fiona and Isobel were belling a lamb that persisted in wandering off. It was the same lamb that had led Maude to Rob Elliott on that blazing afternoon ten days ago.

But Ailse saw Kibbey inside the barn, splitting kindling. Maude watched as her grandmother's brow wrinkled up. "Kib, ye staying down here at the barn now? Dinnae like yer auld sheep wagon when there's a wee nip in the air?"

"Why Ailse, what brings ye o'er this way?" Kib straightened up and a broad smile creased his face. "And I like my wagon fine, dinnae be worrit aboot that."

"I miss my Maudie, 'tis all. And we've a new letter from Mary. 'Pairs the twa of them have settled in Milwaukee. Aye, and Kib, John sends me wi' a message, by the bye. He needs ye tae doctor that fool buck with the bent hairn. Seems he's got that stomach ailment. I mixed up the mash but I cannae help him right weel. Ye can ride back o'er with me and the bairns in this here bone-basher if ye like." She tossed her hand toward the spring wagon.

Kib's grin widened and he lifted the wool cap on his head. "At yer sairvice, Miss Ailse."

As Maude watched Ailse move farther into the barn, she knew it was too late. Sure enough, in the dusky shadows, Rob's form became visible. A beam of sunlight, filled with flickering motes, fell upon him as he shook a forkful of hay into one of the mangers. He stopped and leaned on the hayfork, breathing hard.

Ailse ratcheted her head around to peer at Maude, then looked quickly down toward the pasture. "Aye Kib, 'tis a fine day, mair for this welcome coolness." She turned and walked slowly out of the barn.

Maude followed sedately, then, as soon as they were out of earshot, sputtered, "Gran, it's not what you think—"

"Maude, I keep me ain cart grease for me ain cart wheels, ye know that."

"Gran, listen to me. This has nothing to do with cart grease and moralizing, for heaven's sake. That man—Rob Elliott—turned up in the rock coulee with ravens circling over him a week and a half ago. I think he was on a vision quest, you know, the Blackfeet way. With no food or water for several days, he was near death when Kib and I found him. He shouldn't even be up and out of bed, but he's a stubborn fool. Anyway, in his delirium, all he talked about was his dog and the Blackfeet elder, Medicine Badger. I had to send Kib to the encampment to find the Indian. Turns out Medicine Badger had gone looking for Elliott but couldn't find him."

"He's healing up all right?"

"Yes, I . . . suppose."

"Ye dinnae seem fair sure."

"He won't talk about what happened."

Ailse nodded. "Ye cannae make him talk. I think it's against the Indian custom."

"I'm not sure I want him to anyway." Maude tossed her head,

scowling. Her dark curls danced on the breeze. "That's the last thing I need."

Gran squinted. "Twa folk what have stories tae tell but what willnae."

"What was that you said about cart grease?" Maude's blue eyes blazed. "Besides, he's a McNaughton, isn't he? That's all I need to know."

Ailse gripped her stick and stabbed the ground. "Maude Graham. I willnae be here forever and we both ken it. When I told ye a moment agae that I'd keep my ain counsel, I meant I'd keep it if't seemed I was standin' in the path of ye makin' friends with a decent lad. Ye ken naething aboot this man. If the laird crawled oot of a filthy midden heap, that's one thing, but that doesnae mean this fellow did as weel. Dinnae harden yerself beyond all savin', my blessed Maudie. Ye ken fair weel yer auld Gran wants yer happiness mair than anything on this bonny green airth." Her dark eyes glittered.

Maude's throat thickened and she bit her lip. "Gran." She flung her arms around the old woman and hugged her while her own chest quaked. "Oh Gran, I'd give anything to be normal, to be like Mary—well, a bit like Mary—or like the two younger girls will be some day. You have no idea."

Ailse's free hand combed through the river of wild hair. "Naething's harder than tae do what we fear, Maude. I cannae tell ye when to try. Only yerself can say. Now, let's gae on intae the house and read this letter frae your sister."

Maude poured the tea and sat down with the letter, which was one full page of expensive light blue vellum. The matching envelope was postmarked "Milwaukee." The letter was essential Mary, full of the kind of impertinent optimism and buoyancy that had always been her trademark.

They had been married by a justice of the peace in Chicago, with very little ceremony. This stirred doubts in Maude, since Mary loved elegant things and had always wanted a fine dress and veil, with flowers and a priest and so on. But the letter detailed Paul's good taste and how elegantly he had outfitted them both for their nuptials—her in an ivory shantung tea suit with pearls, the skirt in the newest style with no less than fifteen gores, and he in gray wool with a four-in-hand. A young couple, good friends of Paul's, had stood up with them at the justice of the peace, and the newlyweds had spent their first week in an elegant hotel downtown while Paul hunted for the ideal cottage in the suburbs. But, as it turned out, Mary continued, Paul had been given an outstanding opportunity as a partner in a new firm in Milwaukee, so they had relocated and were renting a fine apartment "on a tree-lined boulevard in a lovely neighborhood." She closed the letter with a promise to write again soon.

"How did Mother like the letter?"

"Fell upon it like a starving woman," said Ailse. "I suspect it'll be like that every time. I hope the twa o' them do come home for Thanksgiving, like Mary said they would."

"I can't imagine how Father will receive Paul. Father is so . . . subdued since all this happened. I think there is vast anger there, buried deep. Or maybe not so deep."

Ailse shook her head. "Maybe when he sees the twa of them thegither, bonny and braw and happy, he can begin tae put some o' that tae rights in his ain mind."

"What other news of Stony Creek, then? How is Mac and his music? I assume Rory is liking his work with the warehouse and the railroad. All is well with him and Antonia, I hope? Has Mother blessed them wholeheartedly? She was in favor of Mary and Paul, but she lost control of that match in a big way, so I've been wondering how well she's been managing the notion of Rory and the colorful Fredrichs. Not that she can really control any of us."

"Your dear Mac is weel. He's been playing that fiddle a great deal mair often. Played at a wedding this weekend past. Seems like he told me a fellow with a band frae Helena is comin' oot this way tae hear him at Mabon time."

Maude knew Ailse meant the first day of autumn, which in the old country many folks still called Mabon. "There has never been any doubt in my mind that he would become a musician," said Maude, smiling as she stirred sugar into her tea.

"And Rory is seeing the Fredrich lass, but I ken trouble there. That same McNaughton lad—Blair, is't?—still fancies her. Befair that's o'er, it'll be a tale langer than twa drinks, sure."

Maude let out a long breath. It did seem that Blair McNaughton was cut from the same bolt of cloth as his father.

As she waved goodbye to Ailse, Kibbey, and the girls, she wondered if Ailse would have so blithely requested Kibbey's departure if she had known Rob Elliott was on the property. The thought made her cross, because she quickly realized the irony that Ailse's discovery of Rob may very well have made the old woman *more* eager to remove all extraneous guests.

She scanned her mental list of chores. She had already put a chicken into the oven to roast, along with some potatoes. Numerous pieces of linen still flapped on the line, but first she wanted to remove the bell from the lamb. The two girls had just needed something to keep them busy, and Maude didn't want to hear a bell ringing all night when she was trying to sleep. The little fellow could be fitted with the bell again when the flock went back out to pasture.

Once the leather strap and bell were removed, she tucked them under the barn eaves on a stack of wood, scrupulously avoiding the barn door. As she turned around to head for the clothesline, she nearly bumped into Rob Elliott.

"Why don't you give me that bell and strap and I'll put them in the barn? The wind's picking up and the sky's pretty dark to the west."

"I guess that's wise." She grabbed the strap and bell and held them out to him.

He took them, watching her. "Kibbey and I have gotten a pretty good load of wood chopped. I can bring some of it over by your kitchen door."

She looked him full in the face. Even though charcoal clouds mounded in the west, the evening sun shone on his bronze hair, picking up gold lights from a summer's worth of labor. "Mr. Elliott, you don't want to set yourself back. Not right when you are about ready to go home."

"I think I can manage a few loads. I was pretty fit before all this happened, you know."

"You work for your Uncle, Thomas McNaughton?" Maude ventured the first personal question of their acquaintance and immediately regretted it. *I don't want to know anything about this man,* she railed at herself. *What would I want to know about a damned McNaughton?*

"I work sometimes for Thomas McNaughton, you're right about that, but he's not my uncle. We are distantly related, back in Scotland, by marriage." His reply was matter-of-fact.

"Oh."

"I'll be bringing some of that wood over."

"Fine. Thank you. There—there will be some dinner in a little while. You can come inside for dinner tonight, since you have no company . . . out here."

"That's kind of you."

An hour later, as she set the table, she didn't like fretting over whether he'd wonder if she was using her good china for him or not. Overcome by a fierce compulsion to make sure he didn't think she was trying to impress him, she considered digging the meanest gray enamel plates out of the bottom drawer and clattering them onto the table so he'd know he was no one special. She stopped and shook her head, realizing she must be going batty to even be thinking about such things. *Why can't I just set the table like a sane person?*

She forced herself to do what she would normally do. She got the solid white Buffalo china plates out of the cupboard, set out the everyday flatware, put the pressed-glass pitcher and glasses out, put the green beans and potatoes into their respective bowls, and set the steaming chicken on the table, giving it a few boning cuts to make it easier to serve.

When she passed the hallway mirror on her way to the door to call him to dinner, she forced herself not to look.

He came in, holding onto the door as it closed with a soft click behind him. They sat down, and after she encouraged him to serve himself, she spread the *Fergus County Argus* out on an empty space on the table to her left.

"They've got a mechanical drawing here of what Henry Ford's first automobile is supposed to look like," she said. "It's going to come off the assembly line sometime this fall. Can you imagine?"

"It'll be a while before any of those horseless carriages make it to the Judith Basin. Potatoes?"

"Thank you, yes. And here's something about Robert Peary's latest assault on the North Pole. They'll be wintering on Ellesmere Island. It quotes Peary saying that he will rely heavily on the wise counsel of his faithful Inuit Indian guides . . ." Maude's voice trailed off and a blush rose from the collar of her blue work blouse. *Indian guides. Does he think I'm dropping hints about his time in the forest? That I want him to tell me the whole story? I don't need to know. Don't care, really.* She pierced a bit of chicken with her fork.

"What do you do when Kibbey gets called away from here, like today, and you have to run this place all by yourself?" He looked at her steadily.

Maude flattened the paper on the table. "Kibbey's new here. He's usually at my folks' place, Stony Creek. I've done fine here since this place was built."

"Which was when?"

"L—last spring."

Rob nodded his head and took a mouthful of food. "Chicken's good," he said after a moment.

"I manage here just fine, thank you for your concern."

"I'm sure you do." He took his napkin and dipped it in his water glass. "Lean over here a bit."

"I beg your pardon?"

"I said, lean over." He reached over and boldly cupped her chin in his hand. It was the first time he had ever touched her like this and he liked it. She had done all the touching out there in the barn while he lay on his back, helpless and delirious. Now he was getting strong again, and it felt good, being able to do something as simple as crossing the corner of the table right now to hold her jaw in his callused hand. It was much different from that accidental night on the creek when her cloak had caught fire and he went tumbling down the hill with her—although that was a right fine memory.

Before she knew what had happened, he had used the corner of his napkin to wipe away a blot of stove ash from her cheek. He held the napkin up for her to see. "Soot," was all he said.

Her lips parted in surprise. He wondered what made them that deep color, the color of ripe raspberries. He wanted to drop the napkin and return his hand to her face, this time to run his thumb across those lips.

Her eyes were wide and staring, filled with what he might describe as curiosity. At this moment she was more like a child than any woman he had ever met, yet he knew that in a fraction of a second, the velvet darkness of indignation would fall over those eyes with all the drama of a theater curtain and their connection would be gone. *Stay with me*, he whispered with his eyes. *Don't go.* He sent the message softly, with his breath, with the warmth of his skin, hoping she would feel it with her heart more than with her mind. And she did stay, longer than the fraction of a second he had dared to expect. One second . . . two, perhaps even three.

Her hand came up, whipping her hair away from her face. Then it went outward toward the water pitcher. He couldn't help noticing the tremor in the pitcher when she picked it up to pour herself another glass. He tried not to smile.

"I'll give you a ride to McNaughton's lane tomorrow." She was flipping through the *Argus* again.

"Do you know the McNaughtons well?"

"I think if we leave around ten o'clock, that would work out best."

When she heard wagon wheels on Kettle Creek Lane at nine o'clock the next morning, she was annoyed. *Who is it now?* The sheep had been let out to graze and she was now bathed and fully dressed, wearing a dark brown wool skirt and white high-necked blouse, but she needed the time between now and ten o'clock to get the buggy ready.

Given the fact that he's leaving, she reasoned, *I could probably ask Rob to help me. No, on second thought, I can't do that, not after that conversation at dinner.* And she didn't like thinking of him as "Rob," she decided in that moment. *Let his surname be enough.*

The dishes from her light breakfast still needed washing and the bed was unmade. Ajax had chewed up a piece of stove kindling in the night and there were wood chips all over the rug in the parlor, so she still had to take care of that. When she went to the front door and flung it open, her eyes were blazing.

Like an arrogant ghost, he didn't wait to be invited in. The autumn wind blew his imported cologne scent deep into her house and an eddy of dried leaves scuttled past his polished boots as he stepped over her threshold.

"The coffee smells right gusty, as my auld faither used to say. Right gusty." He pulled his hat off and smoothed the wavy red hair shot with streaks of silver. "Thought I'd pay a call on my bonny lass this fine morning."

She could not help but back away, hating him with every step. Hating him for the fear he inspired in her still. He was inside her house, strolling into her dining room as if he owned the place.

She hated herself, too. She loathed the way she felt connected to him, as though she had become his chattel those many years ago on the rolling sea. She despised herself for feeling filthy and ruined, but there it was. No one could argue what had happened between them. McNaughton was right about one thing. He may as well have branded her. She felt the sting of it right now, as if the iron had freshly seared her hip.

Her chin jutted out. She could just redirect him to the barn, where he could collect Rob Elliott and be on his way. But something stopped her. Something in the way Rob had spoken about the laird made her wonder if there was less of a bond of kinship between them than she had thought. She was glad of it, although she didn't have time to stop and consider why.

She strode toward the kitchen, but spun around suddenly, confronting him. "You're not here for coffee. What on earth do you want?"

"Maude. You know better than to ask me that question. Yer old laird, of all people." He leaned against the door frame. "You look so fine this morning. Like a schoolgirl, with your hair up like that. That fine white blouse, all buttoned up. I fancy you have a petticoat or two beneath that lang skairt."

Maude swallowed. Behind her on one side lay a bank of drawers and a linen closet. On the other, the stairs led up to her bedroom.

"Aye, like a schoolgirl." His voice grew soft and quiet, as if he were talking to a wild animal. "What a proper lass you must ha' been all through school in Lewistown, with all those other lasses from the farms and ranches who'd never felt a man's member between their fine white legs. But you knew how it felt, didn't you? You knew all along, when they were all tittering oot behind the schoolhouse, all curious o'er their wedding nights someday, there was my Maude, who kenned it all too well."

Her heart was in her throat. She tried to swallow, to put together in her mind what she ought to be doing, but nothing made sense. Her spine loosened and her mouth filled with drool. She felt like an animal that needed to be put down. Oh, to be dead. How wonderful it would be to be released; to never feel anything again, for all eternity.

He moved closer, backing her up to the steps, continuing in his husky voice, reaching out to run his finger along her jaw. She was frozen, as frozen as she had been at thirteen on the deck of the *Campania*.

"Maude Graham." He was whispering now. "Maude Graham sat in class all day with her proper dresses and her fine dark curls. She did her lessons with her pairfect penmanship and her feigned virginity, with her sinless friends, and they all thought she kenned nothing of carnal things . . . but underneath her high-buttoned blouses like this one here, and underneath her lang skirts like this"—he reached down to firmly slide his hand from her knee to her hipbone—"underneath it all, she was lying, her body was lying, because she kenned a whole world of secrets, dark secrets that she and only one man had devised, on a wild ocean lang ago. You remember, Maude. Our secrets." His voice grew hard. "I find you fair, lassie, mickle fair. Fair game, that's what you are. You think to keep me out of your life, girl? You may as well bail the sea with a creel."

Her shirt buttons hailed to the floor as he ripped her blouse down over her shoulders, pinioning her arms to her sides. His lips were wet on her neck and his hands were deep into her chemise and corset, grasping at her exposed breasts. As he laid her onto the stairs, she flailed beneath him. She cried out, but her screams were stifled by her own gagging and sobbing. A part of her drifted up and watched in astonishment from above, raging at the futility of it, as though this would begin and end as a private scene between the two of them into which no one but God might ever intervene. *What is wrong with me? Why can't I scream? What is that taste in my mouth?*

And indeed, it was God and the saints that McNaughton invoked. Grunting gasps escaped him as he lay on top of her, his hands everywhere on her body as he murmured loudly, "Sweet Mary and Joseph! Maude, you've got to marry me. It's the only way. You're mine!"

He kissed her breasts, then shoved one hand up her skirt to pry her flexed legs apart, then retreated, now forking both muscular arms beneath her to carry her up the stairs.

Maude's head lolled back as she fought to free one hand from the binding strips of her torn blouse. Kicking wildly with both legs, she wedged herself crosswise into the stairwell, making it impossible for him to ascend. He laughed, lifting her up into the air and destroying her leverage. "The mair mischief, the better sport," he muttered, grinning at her and thumping up the stairs.

She ripped one arm free and pawed at her mouth, digging away at whatever was gagging her. But there was nothing there. Frantic, she struggled to comprehend what was happening. Surely something was in her mouth. She could feel it against her palate and teeth. She could taste it. Fibrous, like rope. *No! It's the memory of the hemp rope, on the deck of the Campania.*

I have no rope in my mouth now, she raged at herself. *I can scream.* She took a ragged, gasping inhale and poured the air out, forcing her vocal chords to work. It took everything she had to disgorge that breath and make noise, but she did it. It sounded odd, not like her own voice at all, but like a banshee, a hell-harpy.

At the harsh, braying sound, McNaughton nearly dropped her, but he was only momentarily deterred. Shoving through the bedroom door, he rolled her out of his arms, unloading her onto her bed, then unbuckled his trousers and lunged.

Ajax started barking on the back porch and wouldn't stop. She thought she heard Cala answer from the barn. Maude kept hollering, knowing that Rob Elliott would be at the door any minute. McNaughton crawled on top of her, his breath in her face. She looked up at the eyes she had stared into thirteen years ago.

But the pounding at the back door began, loud and strong. McNaughton pulled away as though drenched by ice water. His fingers were still tight on Maude's upper arms, but he was rigid, calculating. Maude held her breath as she watched his flaring nostrils, his disheveled hair. She could read his mind.

Not only was someone at the door, McNaughton realized, but whoever it was would most definitely recognize the well-known Rocking M crest on the finely enameled buggy. His fingers loosened their grip.

"Listen to me, you bastard," Maude gasped as she spun off the far side of the bed, clutching the bedsheet over herself. "Rob Elliott is here. He was wounded. I helped him. That's all you need to know. Go downstairs and tell him you've come for him. Make up some lie about all the noise. You're good at that. Just go. I hate your filthy guts."

"Rob! I understand you've had a bit o' rough luck. Here we thought you were trying to catch all the trout in Moss Creek, enjoying a bachelor's high life. What on airth?"

McNaughton stepped out onto the back porch and tried to prevent Ajax from slithering between his legs, but the dog dashed into the house. He closed the door abruptly behind him. "Come along, Rob, I'll take you to your horse and wagon down at the Rocking M. But are you well, boy?"

Rob didn't like the "boy" part much. He stepped to the side and reached for the doorknob. "I need to speak with Mau—Miss Graham. I need to thank her for her kindness."

"Nay, lad, the poor woman had a bat in the abovestairs guest room. Didn't you hear all the ruckus? I came visiting at just the right moment, but not afore she had fair contact with the creature. Said she feels so filthy after handling the varmint, she needs to take another bath. She begged you to excuse her."

As McNaughton put a bold arm around Rob's shoulders and escorted him down the steps, Rob's spine went stiff. There was something going on that he was being shut out of, and he didn't like it. Maude, the animal healer, needing to bathe after touching a bat?

Hastily reviewing the events of the last few minutes, he glanced sideways at McNaughton and took in his better-than-usual attire. The silk neckerchief at the throat, the cologne, and the protectiveness he displayed regarding Maude.

If I didn't know any better, he thought with a sudden tang of bitterness, *I'd say the two of them were having some kind of lover's quarrel in there. Lovers.* His mind raced over the details. *This might go a long ways in explaining why Maude has been so distant ever since I've known her. Tried to know her, is more like it.*

Maude and McNaughton? Hell, it could be. What a muttonhead I've been, thinking that she wouldn't have men lined up all the way

*down Kettle Creek Lane. But McNaughton, with Rowena scarcely
three months under the sod? Well, why not—stranger things have
happened. McNaughton could have had his eye on Maude for years
and now, with Rowena gone, he would surely want to seize a long-
coveted prize before anyone else. But Christ in his nightie, the man's
old. Maude Graham and Thomas McNaughton? No.*

He stalked toward Cala, who was sitting near the fence with
her brows puckered. Hefting her under one arm, he grabbed the
small bundle of his belongings in his other hand. "Yes, I'd much
appreciate a ride to pick up my horse and wagon. I owe you a little
rent, being that my wagon and saddle have been in your barn for
so long."

"Fie on the rent notion. After you built me that grand hay barn
and hunting blind? As for your saddle, I had one of the hired lads
give it a good laither with saddle soap and mink oil."

"Kind of you, but not necessary."

They climbed into the buggy, where Rob found a spot for Cala
on the floorboards.

"A laird looks after his people, family and friends alike, Rob.
Which leads back to my question about what befell you."

"I got into some foul water, that's all. Miss Graham and her
hired man found me. I was in a bad way. She's a healer. A good
one."

"Aye, she's got that from her auld Gran, the one that folks call
a witch. I've known that family a long time. We settled this valley
together, back in ninety-five."

Rob gave a brisk nod, watching a few yellow aspen leaves blow
loose from their branches as the buggy spun along a smooth strip.
"You've known the Grahams since then?"

"Even before. We were all on the same steamship coming over
from Liverpool."

Rob swallowed and kept his eyes on the stripes of wheel tracks
in the road. "What's Grant up to?"

"He's in Lewistown today. I think you'll miss him, unless you
stay the night. You're always welcome, Rob."

"Thanks. I need to strike camp, though. I've neglected my own place for too long. I'm sure you understand."

"Aye, a man's got to look out for his own interests." McNaughton struck a match on his boot sole and cupped his hands around a cigar. He pulled another from his breast pocket, offering it to Rob.

"No, thanks." Rob took a long, slow inhale of the cool autumn air, concealing his agitated respiration. He wanted to breathe out the noxious thoughts crowding his head, pictures of McNaughton connected in some bizarre romantic alliance with Maude Graham.

Staring straight ahead, he assessed the man sitting beside him. *He cuts a dashing figure, yes. Add to that, he was in high feather financially even before he came to America, so he'd be a fine catch in anyone's estimation.*

But whenever Rob took Maude's image and tried to paste it alongside McNaughton in his mind, to see her laughing and happy with the stiff and self-important Scot, the portrait collapsed. It felt wrong in every sense.

Swirling into this, like the ribbons of smoke coming off the laird's cigar, were thoughts of his dark nights in the forest. He hoped someday he'd be able to straighten out in his mind what in the hell had actually happened, because his memories of it couldn't possibly be real.

Chapter Sixteen

Leal saw hints of autumn everywhere. It was not here yet, but it was coming. As the wind blew the cottonwood leaves in the afternoon, they made a dry, scratchy sound. The grass had gone yellow, and the sunsets were changing. On the deer trails in the forest, she'd come upon bear sign, stained dark purple with chokecherries. Most noticeable of all, the earth smelled warm and dry, and all the animals' leavings had a different scent.

Her pups, although growing big and strong, still required protection and constant watching. The brawny one who had first bowled his way out of the den one misty morning in late May was as inquisitive as ever, always leading the others. He looked like his father, with a deep chest and a large, well-proportioned head. Just now he was trotting around with a scrap of elk hide, boastful, as if he'd killed the elk calf himself.

From her perch on a knoll, Leal looked on as an adult female of lower status headed the brazen pup off before he blundered into the wide meadow beyond the play area. All the adults worked together to manage the new litter. This slender white female had been with Adrad a long time, but he had not chosen her as his mate. Perpetually uncertain of herself, she went through a temporary change each year when Leal gave birth to a new litter, rising to the role of governess and helpmeet for a few active months. Head down and meaning business, she followed the pup closely as he dragged the elk hide back to his littermates.

As cocky as the little fellow was, he showed great promise. Several times in the last two weeks he had caught field mice entirely on his own, and just yesterday he had pounced on a slow-moving partridge, although he had not known how to kill it. Each time he spied a rabbit shooting through the sage, his body would stiffen and his siblings would pile up behind him, craning to see what he saw.

Three months from now, although they would not be big enough to track on their own, the pups could follow the adults on a hunt. Now, as summer leaned into autumn, their daily play simulated adult activities. While they engaged in carefree romping, forelegs splayed, rumps and tails high, there were also mock battles, with growling and clattering fangs. Little by little, life became more serious. As their elders had done before them, these pups would say good-bye to the summer hours of playing in the creek and chasing bumblebees. By the time the first snowflakes appeared in the pale October sky, they would think and run as a pack, with a collective consciousness.

The next day was warm, almost hot. Midmorning, Leal went to the perimeter to mark the roots of the weathered stump she visited several times a day. As she turned back, she saw the bold pup trotting out into the forbidden field, bent on some prey only he could see. Quickly, she surveyed the open meadow for any sign of danger. Seeing none, she set off at a lope, her eyes fixed on the foolish youngster. This was a dangerously exposed area, where any predator could appear without warning.

A dark shadow moved across the grass between her and the pup. The moment she saw it, primal impulses sent blood coursing into every muscle of her body. Her long, powerful legs dug into the turf and her black form melted across the field. She moved so fast that the wind blurred her eyes, but to her, she could not move fast enough. The golden eagle's shadow grew broad, dark as a cloud, as he descended. He was silent, enormous. She saw his hideous yellow feet, the black claws, the parted beak and strange tongue.

She sped forward at a dead run. *Not my pup.*

His talons struck before she got there, sinking hard into the soft flesh of the furry shoulders. A startled yip pierced the sky. Leal could not see them, but the other wolves were coming too. Right now, she acted alone. She was aloft, powered by hindquarters trained for this very moment. Flying ten feet into the air, she clamped the white trap of her teeth onto the bony part of the eagle's dark wing. In an explosion of feathers, the bird struggled to wrench itself free. Burdened by both the pup and Leal's ninety pounds, he flapped only a few seconds and fell to the earth, pulling his black talons from the yowling pup.

Lips drawn back, snarling, with loops of spittle whirling about her head, Leal went after the huge bird, intent on mauling it to death, but it dragged itself into flight, shedding long, dark feathers as it went. She turned to her pup, and as she did, a half-dozen members of the pack arrived, with Adrad in the lead. His huge snout traveled the length of the young wolf, then he washed its bleeding shoulders with quick swipes of his big pink tongue.

The quivering thing could not stand. Leal sank to the ground, lying next to him, sniffing, licking. She stayed with him in the meadow as, one by one, the others retreated. Adrad stalked part-way back, his hackles raised, then stood and waited. The pup, seeing the pack leave, was not about to stay behind. Lurching to his feet, he let out a squeal of pain and was silent. Leal walked slowly in front of him, twisting her head around every five or six paces. By the time they were halfway across the meadow, he was even with his mother's shoulder.

Satisfied, Adrad walked ahead of them. The wounds on the pup's shoulders had begun to clot, although the V-shaped puncture on his left side still seeped a seam of blood down his leg. His step was uneven, but his head was high. As Leal glanced down at him, she noticed that every few yards, he lifted his eyes and looked at the sky. And that is how he became Sky Watcher.

The sky was a pearl gray and the wind blew from the west as Maude drove the buggy into Lewistown. *Next year*, she vowed privately, *I'll have my own garden and I won't have to hope and pray for whatever wilted castoffs I can find in Hopkins' produce section. With September long gone, I'll be lucky to find a single squash.*

Main Street was busy. There was the rasping sound of a saw as a crew of workers cut new siding for a storefront. As she twisted around to watch, two blanketed Indians shuffled out into the street directly in front of her, making her rein Bobcat in sharply. A frisson of irritation went through her, followed by guilt. *Father's right. We may have settled the west, but we've started an eternal disaster of trying to figure out who belongs where.*

Two women in old-fashioned sunbonnets peered into the windows of LaSalle's Millinery. A huge freight wagon rumbled past, carrying a load of sandstone. The driver was Bohemian; there was no mistaking the broad forehead and high cheekbones. Maude wondered if he worked for Jozsef Fredrich. A string of pack horses clopped along, their panniers jammed and knotted tight. The four or five men in the lead shouted jokes and passed a flask. Noticing the pickaxes and the sluice pans, Maude knew they were probably headed for the gold camps up around the tiny community of Maiden.

Even the hitching rails at the grocer's were crowded. Spying a decent space at last, she guided Bobcat in. When she stepped down, she saw two large, dark-haired men grunting and shoving boxes of canned goods into a spring wagon.

"When we come back next month, it'll be wolfing time," one of them said. "We're gonna beat last year's kill, Judd, you wait and see. Gonna bag that big one. But dammit, I can't recall if Wiedeman's carries strychnine."

"Might. If'n they don't, Powers' is sure to. Bein' that they've got traps and guns, they're more likely to have the poison. Glad we left some of those bitches alive last year. Was hard to do, but it'll mean more good pelts this winter."

Maude stared, unwilling to believe what she had just heard. The men, bent on jimmying a crate into a tight spot, hadn't noticed her. Her gaze moved to the forward part of the wagon box where a wolf pelt had slipped from the broad seat. The flattened head of the wolf dangled, waxen slit eyes staring up at her. The breeze caught its thick neck ruff of tawny fur, blowing the rust and ocher shades aside to show the silvery undercoat.

She shook her head and backed away. In that moment, wolfing changed from an easy means of milking a government program to a maniacal, perverted thing. She stared at the stiff face that had sighted jackrabbits, deer, and grouse. *Inii Aohki says they once fed on bison calves. Now we've destroyed the bison. We've taken the grazing land where the rabbits and grouse once lived. Is it any wonder they have turned to livestock for food?*

She imagined this animal alive, running as only wolves do, its huge tufted paws falling softly on the snowy plains of the Judith Basin. *I learn so much from every animal I encounter, but I shall never learn from you, nor from your brothers and sisters. You will all be gone before I come close to understanding your place in this land.*

She had to think about her hand, because it involuntarily moved toward the pelt. As one of the men turned to look at her, a slow grin spread over his stubbled face. She hastened away, flinging her scarf around her as the brisk wind sent leaves scraping along the board sidewalk. Inside the dry goods store, she groped with shaking fingers for a basket.

Several minutes passed before she could focus on her business. Alone in a back aisle, she set the basket down on a case of beer and looked around herself furtively. *No one.* Quickly, she swept the air around her with her hands, whisking away a vapor of darkness, then grabbed her basket and went on. *That's what Gran teases me about*, she realized. *I don't even remember when I started doing it. I just do it to clear things away, like that sad business outside just now.*

Within ten minutes, she had finished at the grocer's and had moved on to Wiedeman's. Bobcat's harness rigging needed two new buckles, and Wiedeman's had the best tack in town. As she stared at the buckle display, she realized that fastening them to the harness rigging would be no easy chore. Kibbey would have to be conscripted.

A loud noise from the next aisle shook her from these ponderings. It was the unmistakable brittle crash of breaking glass. Rounding the corner, she saw a crouching man trying to collect several pieces of a shattered windowpane. His head was down. All that was visible was his chestnut hair and his hands, fingers forked out in quick, grasping movements, as if he could collect every shard of glass before anyone saw the glittering mess.

She smiled. How embarrassing. Then she saw the drops of blood, pinging fast on the floor next to his hand. "Sir, you've cut yourself. Let me help you."

The head came up. Rob Elliott.

"*Cailleach*," whispered Maude. As the word came out, she couldn't remember the last time she had said it, or even heard it. It was the name of the most ancient Scots goddess, mother of all deities. An exasperated gasp escaped her. "Is this all you know how to do, is injure yourself?"

A stock clerk materialized with a dustpan and broom. "Excuse me, sir, if you'll just move a bit . . ."

Rob fired a hard glare at Maude, then turned to the clerk. "I'd be happy to do that."

"Gosh, no. This is the third time that has happened since I started working here. In fact, it's the store's fault. Those seven-buh-tens oughn't be on that shelf up there. We're going to redo this section. Manager's out to coffee just now, but I know he'll want to talk to you. Lookit the blood on you, sir."

Maude dug into her bag and, finding her white handkerchief, raised it toward Rob's forehead.

"Don't." He pulled a blue bandanna from his back pocket and lifted it up, then handed it to her. "I can't see where to put it. Would you . . ."

"Come over here by the boots and sit."

Rob made an impatient sound with his tongue and teeth, took two strides to the bench, and sat.

Maude briskly went about her business, applying pressure to the cut.

Rob's eyes darted to the stock clerk again. "I can do that."

"No sirree."

In the ensuing silence, the brisk sounds of the broom and the clink of glass on the metal dustpan seemed inordinately loud.

Rob's eyes moved from side to side and finally settled on Maude's jacket, flapping in front of him, and then on her waist. Her dark cotton blouse had flat mother-of-pearl buttons, and one of them rested right on the waistband of her skirt, shifting slightly as she moved her arm to stanch the blood. Her waistband wasn't tight, but gapped slightly. His eyes moved down, watching the skirt follow the form of her hips until it fell away in a dozen pleats.

He didn't know much about Maude Graham, but he would bet money that she wasn't the type to wear a lot of stiff undergarments. Her skin, he reasoned, was just beneath that fabric. He wanted to put both hands there, around that waist, to feel her moving, to get a better sense of the size of her.

"I need some witch hazel," she grumbled. "Or some alcohol, at the very least. Where is that manager? This is really the store's fault, just like the boy said."

Rob pulled his head away from her hand and rose, taking the bandanna from her.

"Keep that on," she commanded, her chin lifting as she watched him rise.

He searched the lupine blue eyes while the memory of all the nights he had shoved her out of his mind flared inside him like summer lightning. *Is she the laird's woman? Has she lain with him? Well, the old red bastard can go straight to hell.*

In one swift motion, he brought his right arm around her shoulders. His left hand came up behind her head. Then his mouth was on hers, soft and hard at the same time, finding her, the woman who had not left his heart since that June day at the cemetery. He wanted never to leave her, not now, not ever. He pushed against her and breathed her in, all lavender and pine, crushing himself against the smooth wetness of her lips.

Maude's hands flew up to his arms, in part to keep her balance, in part for reasons she could not have identified or admitted. The harness buckles jingled to the floor.

In the first seconds that Rob's lips touched hers, their two mouths connected and fit with eerie familiarity. His arms tightened around her and he brought his torso in, connecting his body to hers. She felt him, and the core of her fluttered toward him so fiercely that she caught her breath. Their teeth bumped. The strangeness of it knocked her senseless. Her knees buckled, and her hands clutched his arms to keep herself from falling.

He lifted his face away, just an inch or two, while their breath mixed in the air between them. His eyes on hers, his lips still parted and wet, he stared at her with the light of discovery burning in his eyes. A trace of a crooked smile danced around his mouth. He wanted to take her and kiss her again, harder, until they were both delirious, but something made him wait. "Maude Graham."

She lifted her hands from his arms, then fumbled at her scarf as she sat down on the bench. Once seated, she saw the buckles on the floor and leaned to pick them up, her hand shaking. Finally, looking up at him, she compressed her lips. Working to make the words come out evenly, she said, "The blood's clotted."

"That's all you can say?"

"What do you expect me to say, for heaven's sake?"

"You've never even called me by my name."

"That's what you want me to do, call you by your name?"

"It would be a start."

"Mr. Elliott."

"Mr. Elliott?"

"Well?"

"For Christ's sake."

She stood up. "Well. Well, we've had dinner together."

"Yes, we have." Rob was chewing the inside of his cheek. He had to say it. "Who else do you dine with?"

"What's that supposed to mean?"

"Is there someone else?"

"What are you implying? That I have a lover?"

Rob drew a slow breath and stared at her. Her lips were red from the kiss. She looked half the virago, half the frightened hare. "I'll tell you straight out. When I left your house in September, Laird McNaughton escorted me off the place by giving me every indication that he was your . . . gentleman friend. He put me in my place right well, and I've had more than a month to wonder exactly what he means to you."

The heat coming from Maude's bosom rose up her neck and throat. She knew that her furious blush, along with her speechlessness, would confirm Rob Elliott's suspicions about her and McNaughton.

She kept her eyes on his and set her voice as hard as granite. "You are most sadly mistaken in believing the laird, who has delusions of grandeur, if not godhood. Now, if you'll excuse me, I have just been insulted."

She snatched at her skirts and turned. But before she could take a step, strong fingers fastened themselves around her upper arm. "Maude. Maude Graham. I like saying your name, even if you don't like saying mine. That's not going to change. Before you stomp out of here like a little girl throwing a tantrum, look me in the eye and tell me you don't think I had every right to ask you that question."

Maude saw Rob at that moment, his serious hazel eyes and the crust of darkening blood high on his forehead. But she also saw the display rack of deerskin gloves behind him, the gleaming trash can bristling with lawn rakes off to the left, and the embossed tin ceiling running on for what seemed like miles. It was all rarefied— her whole world, every molecule and atom. Her heart was in her throat; tears pooled in her eyes. Her chest had iron bands around it, and she wondered if a twenty-five-year-old woman could have a heart attack. She opened her mouth to speak, and as she did, she took Rob's hand in her trembling fingers and removed it, gently, from her arm. "I . . . I'll see you later. *Rob*."

Her fingers, now bloodless and cold, struggled to hold the reins as she drove the buggy around Lewistown, weaving a dazed path in and out of the well-heeled avenues known as the Silk Stocking District. Bobcat picked his way along. Whenever they came to an intersection, she was forced to make a decision one way or another. The wind was light, thankfully, making occasional dervishes of fallen leaves on the lonely streets and in the gutters. Finally, after three-quarters of an hour, she felt calm enough to start for home.

Rob Elliott. The saints are throwing us together. And he seems to have considerable intentions in the matter too. That kiss. The delirium of it! She wouldn't think about it. It was too much. Her fingers went to her lips and her heart raced, bringing back the steel bands.

She huffed out a quick breath, now remembering that she had wanted to stop and see Rory at the wool warehouse near the Depot. Maybe that would ground her again, just a little. What could be more temporal, more earthly, than a brother?

"Release me from this lunacy," she said to no one in particular, then slapped the reins on Bobcat's rump and set out for First Avenue South.

She found Rory hunched over a stack of pink shipping receipts, the thin October sun forming a pale rectangle on his oak desk. He didn't see her in the doorway until she let out a little cough. He gave a start, then rose with a smile. "It must be grocery day."

Maude smiled back. "You pay more attention to my life than I thought." She took in his starched white shirt and thick knitted vest. Although his robust summer tan had faded during his convalescence, he looked well. "Mrs. Fredrich make that vest?"

He nodded, smoothing it over his rib cage.

"I haven't seen you for a while. How's the shoulder?"

"Getting there. Wish it hadn't been my right side, that's all."

She nodded. "And Antonia?"

His face tightened. "All right, I suppose, if anyone can say that about a beautiful woman being torn up by a bullet."

"She is every bit as beautiful as she ever was, Rory, and you know it. Don't let this tarnish your love for one another in any way." She pointed to a chair. "May I?"

"Oh, sure."

"What news from Stony Creek?" It felt good to ask. She missed the girls, and Ailse.

"Not a whole lot. Fee and Izzy are back in the school harness pretty good now. Ailse is fine, though she pines when you don't show up. Mac's been playing the mining camps almost every weekend, which worries Mother some. But she's all right. He's getting darned good. Our new telephone's ringing off the hook with people wanting his band to come and play. Girls are calling too. I have to admit, Mac looks every inch the romantic hero with those long locks and fancy boots. Old John can't stand it. Says he's about to yank the phone out of the wall, but you know he won't."

"Mac." Maude shook her head fondly. "Well, I'm glad they haven't run those lines out to Kettle Creek. I'm not at all ready for a telephone."

"You and Ailse. She thinks the "tally-phone" is the queerest thing in the world. Anyway, Mother's finished with the applesauce and is canning something else now—I think it's pumpkin—left and right." He moved a sheaf of papers on the desk, looking for something. "All Hallows is right around the corner, isn't it? Or whatever you and Ailse call it."

"Samhain."

"You've got that distant look in your eye already," Rory said, shaking his head. He pulled a half-sheet of paper out from under the piles on his desk. "I . . . uh, would like your opinion on something."

"Really?"

"Yes." He cleared his throat and reshuffled some papers. "Well, you see, I've got this friend, Jack Spaulding, who works with the

Milwaukee Railroad. Because the Central Montana Railroad is merging with the Milwaukee, I end up having telegraph or telephone contact with Jack once a week or more. Interstate Commerce Commission stuff and all that."

"Go on." Maude felt the edge of suspicion. Rory was agitated, there was no doubt about it. His elbows rested on his knees as he sat in the chair opposite her, eyes downcast. "Rory?"

His eyes flicked up. "Well, maybe I shouldn't have done this, but I did. I asked Jack to find out if there's an attorney in Milwaukee by the name of Paul Hathaway. One of Mary's letters said he'd been given a position with a new firm there, remember?"

Maude's eyes were fastened on him. "What did Jack find?"

"That's just it, Maude, he didn't find a damn thing. There's no Paul Hathaway there. And there aren't any new law firms there. Not one in the last four years, anyway."

"But Mary's letters are postmarked from Milwaukee. I've seen them."

"I know."

"Saints. What does this mean?"

"We have no way of knowing what it means, Maude. I don't know whether to tell Mother and Father, or what I should do."

"You ought not tell them. Of that I am certain." She inhaled a long breath and let it out. "What made you decide to ask Jack this question in the first place?"

Rory scooted his chair back, stood, and walked to the dusty window. Rubbing a spot clean with the heel of his hand, he peered out at the windy sky. "I have no idea. I just had a peculiar feeling about Mary. Her letters strike me as odd. I mean, she's always been melodramatic, but the letters seem so artificial. Mother devours them like magazine stories."

Maude watched a fly buzzing dully on the ceiling, wondering what Mary might be staring at just now, in her strange life in Milwaukee. "I know." She rubbed her forehead. "She's coming home next month. How will we keep up the charade? This is so perplexing. Do you think he might have left her?" A knot of fierce anger formed inside her. *Wait,* she told herself, taking a slow, uneven breath. *Wait for information.*

"I don't know what to think. Maybe he's still with her, but perhaps he's just not an attorney, like he purported to be."

"Wasn't he working on contract for the Milwaukee when she met him?" She paused, thinking. "I mean, if we can believe him. Can you ask your friend Jack to find out about that?"

"I will. But bear in mind Jack only works *with* the Milwaukee Railroad. He's actually employed by the U.S. Government, as an agent of Interstate Commerce. He just happens to be stationed in Milwaukee. But I think he can still find out more about Paul. Or whoever Mary married."

Chapter Seventeen

 John Graham put his feet up in front of the fire at Stony Creek and took a sip of whiskey. The *Fergus County Argus* lay across his lap, momentarily discarded.

Catriona had several things left to do before she could sit down and enjoy Mary's latest letter, but she glanced at her husband as she toted a stack of linens up to the landing closet. His head was tipped back into the worn spot on his massive leather chair and he was staring at the flames, lost in thought.

Finally, when the last of the sheets and towels were tucked away and the five bushels of just-picked apples were stowed on the enclosed back porch, safe from the raccoons and skunks, she pulled off her apron and sank heavily onto the mohair chaise across from John's big leather chair. "I'll be glad when Dora gets back from visiting her mother in Butte, that's all I have to say. I can't keep up."

Sifting through a pile of papers on the end table, she lifted a formal-looking postcard. "Here's an announcement about the dedication of the new St. Joe's Hospital this Sunday. We ought to go."

"Ought to do a lot of things."

"We'll be conspicuously absent."

John grunted. "They'll never miss us. The Catholics are coming down by the squadron from Great Falls. We gave our donation to the building program and we're paid up." He scowled and swirled down the ice in his drink. "Is that another letter from our Milwaukee girl?"

"Yes." Catriona slipped on her reading glasses. "You seem to have something on your mind. How was town?"

"All right." He folded his newspaper and tossed it into a wicker basket, then leaned his head back again for another long study of the ceiling. "I ran into Tom McNaughton outside the Bright Hotel," he said finally. "He insisted on buying me a drink."

"Insisted?"

"Well, you know he and I are cordial, but we aren't *friends*."

"So did you have the drink?"

"Yes."

"And?"

"He has the notion that he'd like to marry our oldest daughter."

"Good God."

John stood up, straightened his gray wool vest, and paced to the other end of the room. "Tom McNaughton. That toplofty, pompous ass. Even if marrying him would give Maude a world of advantages, I could never turn her over to him. And Rowena in her grave only four months."

"John—" Catriona nearly choked out the words. "Maude . . . doesn't . . . fancy him."

"Of course she doesn't. He's too damned old for her. She's sweet on this Elliott boy, isn't she? She ought to be."

"What did you say . . . to McNaughton?"

"I used every slippery figure of speech I could think of without extinguishing his manhood outright. I told him I respected him for coming to me, but I also said Maude was no longer living under my roof and she had a right to choose a husband for herself." He grabbed his pipe from the end table and poked a few shreds of tobacco into the bowl, then took a stick of kindling and rammed it into the fire until it flamed up orange and hot.

Catriona modulated her breath and relaxed her hold on Mary's letter, which she had crushed in her right hand.

As he sucked on the pipe stem, John eyed Catriona over the glow. "I asked him if he had spoken to her about this. He said he'd only just begun to express an interest in her and he felt the next proper step would be to come to me."

He walked the length of the living room again, then pivoted at the far end, staring out at the darkening sky. "You know, Trina, I can't help wondering if this is just some high-hatted strategy of his to begin getting his hands on Stony Creek. With him for a neighbor, a man can never lay back and rest. I never told you this . . . remember a couple of years ago, when the homesteaders with small holdings had a chance to annex another one hundred and sixty acres apiece, all they had to do was go down to the land office and sign up?

"Well," he continued, "Tom McNaughton knew that those Scandinavians on the south end of his land couldn't read. He wanted that property the land office was holding and he bribed Willie Franks not to go out and tell Lindvall and Ekstrand about the annexing deal."

His wife stared into the fire, saying nothing.

"The man's got a dark heart," John muttered.

Catriona turned her head away, that he would not see her lip quiver. *Darker than you'll ever know.* Forcing her memories back into the gray mists of time, she smoothed Mary's letter and took a breath.

"John, we have to be calm about this. We don't want to speculate what goes on in that egomaniacal head of his. This bit of nonsense isn't going to go any further, because Maude doesn't care for him a whit. You mustn't say anything to her about this. Promise me you won't."

"Of course not. But you never answered me about her and the Elliott boy. Man. He's not a boy. He's not blood kin to McNaughton, is he?" He shot her an arrow-sharp glance.

"No. There's some distant connection by marriage, that's all."

A smile curved John's lips. "You're the resident matchmaker. Are those two going to get together?"

Catriona raised her eyebrows and shrugged, but her heartbeat quickened. "He's a handsome boy with a winning way. I know my girls, John Graham. This will all work out like a fine old Scots ballad, just you wait and see."

She arranged her skirts and sat back. But as she peeled back the envelope and began to read Mary's letter, she had to hold her forearm close to her hip to steady her shaking hand.

"If we were tae do it proper, we'd assemble on the greatest eminence in all Fairgus County," said Ailse, seated at the small maple table in her cottage.

"Well, yes. That would be fine indeed." Maude decided tact was the better part of valor in this discussion about the placement of their Samhain bonfire. Ailse was hardly able to climb Judith Peak, the county's highest point. "But Birch Bluff is a grand eminence, and it has been our Stony Creek Ranch tradition for ten years, after all."

"In Moray the lads would lie doon near the fire tae let the smoke roll o'er them. Muckle indeed, those boys wanted tae be part o' the mystical ways of Samhain. The bairns o' today dinnae understand. The smoke o' these ancient fires is like a muck midden heap. Does nae good till it be spread aboot."

Maude smiled. "I won't tell our girls that you're likening the smoke to manure. I doubt it would help your cause."

Ailse let out a cackle, then grew serious again. "E'en Catriona didnae set oot a glass o' spirits for the departed last year. I always get oot the finest crystal and pour some claret for whoever micht pass in the night. Ye maun do it yourself, now that you have that bonny caibin." She waved her hand grandly. "Look oot the window, Maudie. It's the beginnin' and the endin' of all things. The leaves have near fallen frae all the trees, and Mither Airth is fallin' asleep. Life comes bonny weel again in the spring, but we are enterin' a time o' sacred rest. I mind years gane by and my ain Gran Callie, sitting nigh her peat fire in that wee stone hoose on the Findhorn. 'At Samhain,' she tauld me, 'the veil 'tween this warld and the next is mickle thin. We maun listen sharp to hear the counsel of them that's gane befair.'"

Maude looked out the window, remembering. "The spirits are flying about, and the bonfire makes sure that only the good spirits come close."

"Aye, and just like the solstice fire, the smoke protects us and all that is ours." Gran was filling small muslin bags with a mixture of rosemary and mint leaves. The fresh scent filled the entire room. Maude suspected these fragrant bags might show up in the Christmas stockings, but she didn't ask about that.

"Why do some of the Christians dislike All Hallows so much?"

Ailse's brow creased. "'Twas fair easy for them to confuse the spirits of the beloved departed with weel-feart demons. It seemed like wicked conjuring to them whene'er we sought the wise counsel o' the daid. And worse, Gran Callie tauld me that e'en the kindest deities o' the auld faith seemed like evil spirits to the Christians. Frae there, I suppose 'twere a short leap for them in their judging."

Maude sighed. "I'm glad we observe these special old traditions, and it doesn't interfere with my gladness for Christ."

She let her eyes drift back to the scene outside the window. In the foreground, a lone Canada goose lingered in a field of corn stubble. The distant mountains were dark rumplings of green, with low wisps of clouds scarfing their summits. She heard a faint gunshot and knew someone had found a deer.

Fall had come to the Judith Basin, and All Hallows was a week away. She had spent that morning carving jack-o-lanterns with Fiona and Isobel. But, for the first time in her life, she wasn't thinking about the grand bonfire on Birch Bluff, and the varying sizes of twigs, sticks, and logs she always mentally cataloged as Number Ones, Twos, and Threes. She wasn't thinking about who would ride in which wagon, and about the heavy blankets they'd need. She was thinking about a man.

Would these sawing twinges deep in her belly ever stop? It felt like her senses were being twisted right out of her. She'd be halfway through a chore and forget what she was doing. When she analyzed the thoughts coursing through her mind, they invariably consisted of some fantasy about running into Rob Elliott. Or she'd find herself daydreaming about whatever he might be doing at the moment. Based on her experience with him, she'd drawn what seemed like a reasonable conclusion that he was accident-prone. She'd repeatedly invoke the saints to keep him from breaking an arm or falling from his horse. Something had happened to her appetite, too. For the first time in her life, food had become irrelevant.

"Aye, there's mickle to be learnt frae people all o'er the warld." Ailse was saying. She knotted another bag and said, "'Pairs I'm oot o' claith, so I'll bide a moment. I fancy a bit o' calico for the rest." She studied Maude from across the room, then got up to poke some more kindling into the kitchen stove. "Somethin' aboot ye, Maude, tells me that ye micht ha' seen Rob Elliott o' late."

"What?"

"Ye cannae fool yer auld Gran."

"Stop saying that."

"I won't force ye tae speak on't."

Maude hugged a pillow close to her chest and continued staring out the window. With a sinking heart, she thought of Mary, and suspected she'd spent several weeks last summer feeling exactly this way about Paul. *What in life was ever more than a gamble?* She felt a slight smile of irony turn the corners of her mouth as she realized that at last, she and Mary had something in common. *But do we? Heaven only knows what Mary's situation has now become.*

Something about the dark line of pointed firs on the Snowies, rimming the distant horizon of the valley, was comforting. They were constant, when precious few things ever were.

"Ye look a mite pale," Ailse said in a soft voice.

Maude turned to look at her. "I suppose I am," she replied, biting her lip.

"When I met . . . my Jamie, I clean stopped eating. I didnae think it mattered, till one day I swooned on a bridge and near fell in the Findhorn."

Maude felt something quicken inside her as an image of a young Ailse passed before her eyes, lasting no more than a second. This tiny, white-haired, arthritic woman was once a lithe and winsome girl so in love that she couldn't eat, so enraptured that she grew dizzy while crossing a bridge, fainted, and nearly fell into a river. All for the love of James Warwick MacDougall.

"Thar's nae fleeing fate, Maudie."

Ailse stood by the stove, turning the lid-lifter over in her hand, but Maude could see from across the room that her eyes were wet with tears. She rose and went to her grandmother, throwing her arms around her. "Oh Gran, you remember it all, don't you?"

"O' course I do. Like 'twas yesterday." Ailse set the lifter down and fumbled for her linen hankie, then dabbed her eyes. "I can still see that wild hair that he couldnae keep under his plaid cap. Summat like yourn, child. God rest my Jamie's soul. Love ne'er leaves a pairson, Maudie, nae matter how auld they be. I see love hanging round ye now, like a purple cloud o' heather."

"That's what this is, for certain? What about 'pearls before swine,' and all that?" Maude raked both hands through her hair and flung them in the air.

Ailse pushed the ringlets back from Maude's face. "We take our chances, every laist one o' us. And it *is* love, this thing that's got hold of ye so bauld and strong. Whither ye wanted it or nae, it has found ye at laist."

After almost an entire hour spent checking on her sheep, examining two that seemed to be coughing, then isolating one lamb who was especially stiff, Maude hung her wool jacket on the familiar peg near the back door at Kettle Creek and adjourned to the kitchen, slumping back in the chair next to the stove. Through the west window, she saw roseate glints of the sinking sun through the dark pines on McNaughton's land. The stiff wind that had set into the Basin a week ago had not abated. All around, she heard the rush of the Douglas firs and the moan of the tall cottonwoods. It was a tenebrous evening, just what one would expect at this time of year, and it suited her mood.

Tomorrow was Saturday, and Samhain, and she had promised to take Ailse to town for more calico cloth. Why Ailse wanted to do this on Samhain was beyond her, but the holiday mood seemed to have taken hold of the old woman and Maude was not going to dampen it.

She picked up the notebook in which she had been scribbling for the past two nights. Many sheets had already been torn from it and tossed in crumpled balls into the kitchen fire. What survived in the pages of the notebook, with dozens of cross-hatchings and blots, was a rambling, circuitous attempt to tell Rob Elliott why she could never marry him. It was a vague essay, of that she was keenly aware.

"He hasn't asked you to marry him, you vain thing," she whispered out loud. "A kiss in a hardware store. What does that mean?"

The horrid altercation with McNaughton last August blasted into her mind. He had told her then and there how much she knew of sin and animal coupling. He was right about that. As much as she had repressed the rape, thrown the memory of it overboard to drown in the brine, she had relived it too. Relived it many more times than even she could count.

She *did* know sin. And there was no way she was going to tell that to Rob Elliott. She was simply going to have to deflect him, to let him know that she was not available. Ever. Anything was better than the alternative. Courtship? Feigning innocence? She leaned forward, dropping her head into her hands. Tears came, startling her. She had not cried in so long. They dripped in fat splotches onto the notebook.

This, she realized, *this decision to refuse him, means I shall never marry*. Even though she'd made an adolescent blood oath, this was the first time in her adult life that she had ever faced it. *Well,* she admitted, *it's the first time the situation has ever presented itself. The first time I've ever allowed it to. I didn't ask for Rob Elliott to come into my life. I didn't ask for love. And now that it is here, I must make this decision. I am making it.*

Knowing that Rob Elliott considered McNaughton a rival made it even worse. If he were to know that the laird had taken her . . . a wave of nausea gripped her, and she reached for an empty basin on the floor. She retched once, gripping her stomach, glad she hadn't eaten since noon.

The notebook slipped and fell. She sat back, her forehead damp and cold. "Where are my special wits when I need them?" she demanded aloud. "Here it is the eve of Samhain, when the spirits of the departed are supposed to be thick about us. All of you, my ancestors, tell me what to do!"

She sat silent, listening, but in truth she didn't expect anything. The granddaughter of Ailse MacDougall knew better than to expect a wraith to coalesce and hover over the kitchen table. She knew that whatever knowledge from the spirit world she'd gain this evening, or any other time she was reduced to pleading, would more than likely come as a simple prompting of her own heart. Oh, certainly, there were the times when the hair would rise up on her arms, or she'd feel the deepening of her breath and the sudden knowing of a thing, but that never happened because she demanded it. Those real spirit-sensings were something far beyond her own personal will.

The crackle and pop of the fire in the stove, the muffled ticking of the clock in the dining room, and the moaning of the wind—nothing more. She let her eyes drift lazily around the room, indulging in a brief moment of admiration for how the place had turned out. The blue curtains, the deep golden luster of the oak bead board cabinets, the frosted silver of the galvanized countertops. *Not a bad retreat for the local spinster*, she thought, her throat thickening.

Her eyes flickered to the window, where the sun had dwindled to little more than a blush above the distant hill. She studied the alpine darkness for a moment, and, as she did, a twinkle of light caught her eye. Ratcheting forward in her chair, she tilted her head to the side. The light grew brighter for a moment, then disappeared.

There is only one thing it could be, she concluded, *and that is a lantern. Clearly, it was on McNaughton's land.* She knew he had a hunting camp up there somewhere. *It is deer and elk season,* she reminded herself, *and those hills are probably crawling with the McNaughton boys and even some high-toned guests from back east.*

She bent and picked up the notebook, smoothing its pages. She didn't want to write the letter now. She didn't want to see Rob Elliott, or cross paths with him, because it would mean finality, disaster. She only wanted to think about him, to remember that kiss, his lips hot and wet on hers, the way his arms felt around her, and how his hand had found its way into the hollow between her shoulder blades. Just the thought of his touch sent a current of something indescribable up through her core and across her breasts. She shivered and hugged herself. *If this is what Mary felt for Paul . . . well, I understand her now better than I ever have.*

Staring at the white page, she scrawled the words, "I could tell him all." As soon as she did, her fingers opened and she dropped the pen on the table. The same black clouds that filled her mind at the horse race—that pressed on her chest and made it hard to breathe—came again. She swallowed hard and closed her eyes, shaking her head and pulling away from the darkness. It was so much sweeter to simply think about him, about how she felt when she looked in his eyes.

What is he doing right now? What is his place like, up there on Ruby Creek? Has he built it entirely himself? She knew so little about him. She should have asked him questions, so many questions, when he was here last summer. She had lost her chance, wasting that time they had. It would never come again. The scant amount of information she did have would need to last her the rest of her life. *Was he raising sheep or cattle? Maybe horses? Where did he come from?* He was a Scot, she knew that much.

Just now, it seemed that she might find a way, if she worked very hard, to live without him. The thought sent a white spear of pain through her, but she picked up the notebook and clutched it to her chest and let her eyes brim. She had been alone so long. She knew how to be alone—it was something she did very well—and it was something she had vowed to make a lifetime of. She had plenty of courage about this business of solitude. She'd proven that to herself a long time ago.

After all, the thought of Rob, of him taking her in his arms and kissing her, was a warm dream, a place she could go in moments that did not require rational thought. Right now, she could feel his fingertips in her palm at the horse race on that sunny day. She felt the brisk, awakening brush of his unshaven cheek against her face on solstice night. Knowing he wanted to be with her filled her with a joy she thought she'd never experience, never in her entire life. She would always have these private indulgences; no one could ever take them away. *I can bring back such moments whenever I like,* she told herself. *In the quiet sanctuary of my home, I shall spend evenings like this one, remembering and dreaming. Perhaps it shall not be unbearable.*

She lay the notebook on the table and let her head fall back, concocting a story of Rob Elliott in her mind, content to spend the evening weaving a tale that required neither pen nor paper.

A light rain pattered the roof of the hunting blind, but McNaughton could hear them a quarter mile through the woods, drinking his best Ben Wyvis scotch and singing old hunting songs. They had gotten two bull elk that day and everyone was in a fine fettle. When he slipped out the door, a blaze was roaring in the big lodge fireplace and the cook had fed them all with beef roast and potatoes baked with Roquefort.

I know that tune well, he reflected, stroking his mustache. *Yes, it's thoroughly English, but I've sung it a dozen times on visits to*

Jim Morgan's place in West Virginia. He mimed the words as the boisterous singing cascaded down the damp, pine-covered slope:

So we'll all go a-hunting today;
all nature looks smiling and gay . . .
Let's join the glad throng that goes laughing along,
and we'll all go a-hunting today!

Yes, he remembered that tune "bloody well," as Morgan would say in his booming bass voice. He remembered Morgan's fine Georgian house back east, and his flirtatious, buxom little wife in her low-cut gowns. He shifted on his campstool and began humming along with the men. The martial beat of the hunting song formed a rhythm in his belly as he recalled thundering rides through the wooded slopes of Morgan's acreage, pursuing a dark little minx of a gray fox. They never did catch her that day.

"Come out, come out, my little vixen," he whispered.

He turned the focus ring on the telescope to sharpen his subject. The scope was aimed with precision, so he took care not to bump the tripod. His fingers were chilled, but it didn't matter. With one hand, he held the telescope steady, and with the other, he reached over and extinguished the kerosene lantern.

He could see her now, in that chair by the stove. This was the best view, he had found. Her kitchen had by far better lighting than the bedroom, where she drew the shades too often. Sometimes she would sit there by the stove in her nightgown. Not tonight, though. For a moment it seemed that her eyes flashed in his direction. But now she was leaning back in her chair, just sitting there, looking the most idle he'd ever seen her.

The telescope was German, and the crystal lens was an especially fine piece of work. He saw that her lips were parted, and he could watch the rise and fall of her breathing. He remembered laying his hands on her in September, ripping the buttons from her blouse. A blouse quite similar to the one she was wearing now. Touching her flesh that day, seeing the shadow between her round breasts—it had driven him mad. A woman of lovely attributes indeed. And then Elliott had come.

Maude had lovely attributes, yes, but there was something else. There was such a sense of *waiting* about her . . . waiting to be taken. He let go of the telescope, his thoughts scattering. *Rowena's been gone five months now*, he calculated quickly. *There be nae windows in a shroud. Folks in town may blather all they like, but a man can take a wife six months after being widowed.* His eyes moved from side to side in the darkness, forming a plan.

Then, turning back to the telescope, a smile curved his lips as he watched her lean lazily back in her chair. He envisioned her instead at the long dining table at the Rocking M, not in the shirtwaists and skirts she always wore, but in fine gowns, silky things that would be cast aside each night next to his massive walnut bed.

His hands warmed, perspiration gathering on his palms. His loins began to ache, unbearably so. After a few moments, he knew he couldn't climb down the ladder and go back to the lodge like this. *Damn it to hell.*

"That woman knows full well what she's doing to me," he muttered through clenched teeth, fumbling with his belt buckle. Maude Graham was the prize of Fergus County. He wanted her and he'd have her, but right now he hated her for making him take care of this business on his own.

Chapter Eighteen

Ailse was still hopping mad as the covered buggy rolled down the lane toward the big house at Stony Creek. Maude was angry too, and the drive back to Stony Creek had done little to settle her nerves. At the sight of the buggy window a few inches from her face, she gritted her teeth. The spider-web crack covered the entire pane of glass. She didn't look forward to explaining this to her father, who'd been kind enough to let them use his favorite closed buggy on this chilly autumn day.

They'd talked about it all the way back, trying to reason through why a group of schoolboys would have turned ugly on a Saturday morning.

First Maude had blamed herself, saying, "We shouldn't have hitched up around the corner from Main, near that empty lot."

"Fie! 'Tis nae the damned sixteen hunnerts. We can hitch our fine buggy where e'er we please." Ailse stewed a moment, shaking her head. "But I should hae kenned it when I saw the ravens in the cottonwoods on the way tae town. Always a sign o' conflict."

It had all happened so fast. They'd finished their shopping, and Maude was laden with Ailse's new bundle of cloth as well as a bulky hatbox from LaSalle's, containing a broad-brimmed hat for Catriona's birthday next week.

Neither she nor Ailse thought much about the gang of ragtag boys pitching stones into the newly dug foundation, until one of them called out, "It's the old witch woman!"

Another one, much taller, drawled, "And she's got her apprentice with her, the one that don't have a comb to her name."

"Hurry and get in," Maude had said, but Gran stood her ground, holding up her old blackthorn stick and winding up with a handsome curse. "They've got stones," Maude sputtered.

For a moment, Ailse's baleful stare had a chilling effect on the ruffians. One of the youngest even dropped his rock. But the older one took a step toward the buggy. Maude saw him thrust out his jaw and set his hips.

"Get in, would you?" Maude flung her parcels into the back compartment. "Or I'll come round and throw you in myself."

A stone fell with a skittering thud a few feet in front of the horse, who snorted and reared. This was all it took to convince Ailse, who scrambled around and shut her door with a frantic snap. Maude had barely closed her own and sent a sharp ripple along the reins when a rock hit the window with a loud crack. She hunched her shoulders but kept command of the horse, wheeling him sharply away as another rock hit the back of the buggy.

Ailse opened her door an inch and cut loose, squawking like a chicken. "By all the saints and the ancients, I wish I was witch enow to turn ye faul ratkins into corbies! May yer parents hear wind o' this and feed ye naught but hog slew for twa month hence! And a hiding fra' yer faither's belt besides!"

Maude grabbed her arm as the buggy careened around the corner. "Get your head back in here, you daftie. They'll chase us out of town!"

On the drive home, her insides churned. Part of her wished she had picked up rocks and thrown them right back. *Ailse is right,* she thought, jutting out her lip, *we aren't living in Salem under the influence of Cotton Mather. But, on the other hand, we did the right thing by getting out of there as quickly as we did. It's a dark afternoon, and All Hallows' Eve to boot. There was mischief about, and we were as likely a target as any.*

She looked down at her dress as they drove home, shaking her head at the irony that she had worn a striped blue wool skirt with a fitted jacket. It was the most stylish thing she owned, and she had chosen it because she thought she might see Rob Elliott.

She had berated herself as she put it on, but she wore it anyway. She even went to the mirror to see what the suit did to her blue eyes. She intended to say good-bye to him. But couldn't she have one handful of sweet moments before their little affair ended, before she consigned it to a swift death? And then she hadn't seen him after all. Instead she had been run out of town, both she and her proud Scots grandmother, like pariahs.

Usually John Graham waited until five to have a whiskey, but he poured himself one at three-fifteen when he saw the buggy window and heard the story. "I'll see Sheriff Martin first thing Monday," was all he said. Catriona, still in her rose-trimmed apron, sat with compressed lips at her loom, which clacked and whirred louder than ever.

Ed Martin would proceed with due diligence, Maude knew, but this would be a hard case to pursue. Whose child would ever confess? She and Ailse wrote down what they could remember about the incident and laid the papers on John's desk.

Fiona and Isobel clung to Maude, holding her hands on either side. "You look so beautiful today, Sissy," said Isobel. "How could anyone be mean to you?"

"My sweet Isobel." Maude looked down into the adoring eyes.

Fiona chirped, "Can I have that suit when you don't want it anymore? Do you think it would look as good on me as it does on you? I mean, redheads look good in blue too, don't they? Mary always looked good in blue, so I should too."

"Of course you look good in blue, Fiona, so why don't we just start looking for a suit for you of your very own?"

"Not in Lewistown."

"I have the new Bloomingdale's catalog."

"You never told me."

"Now you have to come round to see me again, don't you?"

Mac came in, holding his violin case and wearing a peculiar expression. "I—was just packing my saddlebags to head up to

Maiden for our performance tonight. There's a fellow outside in a buckboard. Says he's here to see—uh—Maude."

The clacking loom slowed and stopped. Maude's hands disengaged from Isobel's and Fiona's and flew to her breastbone. The younger girls turned and peered up at her. Ailse, who nodded in a rocker near the fire, let out a slow, breathy, "Aye." John Graham's whiskey glass found his magazine-littered chairside table.

Maude dropped her hands to her sides and smiled brightly. "I'll be right there." Under no circumstances did she want Rob Elliott—for surely that is who this caller must be—admitted to the zoological consortium now assembled in the living room.

In a moment she was on the porch; he was standing on the bottom step.

"Welcome to Stony Creek."

"I've come with some All Hallows gifts for your family, if you'll permit me."

The clouds that had covered the sky all day now formed layers of orange and dusky purple, and the angling sun came through the aspens in long golden stripes across the lawn, striking his buckboard, the horse behind him, his shoulders, and his hair. His face was partly in shadow, but she could see that he was smiling. Her eyes quickly sought the place on his forehead where he'd been cut. It was healing nicely—only a dash of red, fading away.

His even white teeth showed; his hazel eyes sparkled in the glancing light. He just stood there, grinning at her.

"You found the place," she offered.

"It wasn't hard. Everyone knows your family."

"I guess that's Father's doing." She shivered when she thought of what had just happened in town, remembering that she and Ailse were known for things other than the Graham's prosperous woolgrowing.

"It's chilly." He came up the steps, taking his coat off. "I've never seen you in anything but black or brown. Except that day at the races. You look beautiful."

"Mr. Elliott—"

"Don't." He draped the jacket around her shoulders. "Can't I say what I think?"

Her heartbeat seemed audible. Everything was moving too quickly, in a direction she couldn't control. The jacket still held the warmth of him. It melted down through her shoulders, into her chest and upper arms.

The leaf piles smoldering in the ditch sent up wafts of tart smoke that nipped at her nostrils like incense. She thanked heaven for both the smoke and the cool air on her face; they were the only things keeping her sober under the intoxicating influence of him next to her. She was unable to utter the most commonplace remark, or even to reason her way toward some small gesture of hospitality. She stood there feeling foolish, unable to do anything but smile. *Is he standing too close to me? No, I want him closer still.*

From behind, there was a peculiar scratching and then a sudden tapping and giggling. She turned sharply to see Fiona and Isobel swish the curtains quickly shut. She tossed her head as an exasperated sound escaped her lips.

Rob gave a nod of acknowledgment. "I'll get the cider and the other things. I'd like to get off on the right foot here if that's at all possible."

Her smile faded as she remembered her vow, her position in life. The die had been cast long ago, and she had accepted the outcome. Awash with guilt, she stayed rooted to the porch planks. *What was there to do except let him deliver his gifts, then talk to him later? Get rid of him, that was the goal, wasn't it?* She tapped her lips with her fingers.

The wide front door swung open and Catriona appeared. The apron was gone; her chestnut and silver hair was combed and pinned. She was in her element. Maude could hear the teakettle whistling in the kitchen. Catriona swept down the steps and in a twinkling was at the buckboard, introducing herself, pumping his arm, helping him with the jugs of cider.

John, well-trained through the years, had shuffled out to the porch himself and came up alongside Maude, swirling his whiskey.

"He's welcome to join us for the evening's festivities. We've got plenty of food. And he can stay in the bunkhouse. Kibbey knows him from last summer on your place, right?"

Maude nodded dumbly, then turned to look at her father. Something about his eyes, grown paler with the years, brought to mind the evening hue of the Atlantic Ocean. It didn't seem so bad just now, that shade. She swallowed. "I'll let him know you extended the invitation."

Much later, when everyone had retired, their clothes and hair so thickly scented with bonfire smoke Maude wondered if they'd ever wash clean, she and Rob stood alone in one of the empty corrals. Alone, that is, except for the two horses who tossed hay exuberantly from the manger onto the ground, as if holding their own Samhain feast.

She and Rob had been the ones to put away the spring wagon, while Catriona and the younger girls bore the blankets and foodstuffs back to the house. John had made it clear to Kibbey that Rob was expected to stay in the bunkhouse, so a lantern burned bright on the other side of the orchard, where Kibbey performed his evening ablutions. Maude could hear the creak of the pump handle and the gush of water.

"That's Ailse's cottage, clear over there, across the meadow." She pointed into the velvet darkness to a place where tiny windows glowed amber bright among a dark lace of branches. "I'll sleep there tonight."

"I suppose they'd look rather askance at my driving you home to Kettle Creek."

"The good Episcopalians John and Catriona Graham? Rather."

The silence settled around them, the only sounds being the grinding of the horses' teeth and their shifting from hoof to hoof. Then, as sharp and sweet as the autumn wind, there was Kibbey's violin.

"Ah, it's an old jig. *Tiocfaidh Tu*. I love this one." Her boots began working in the dirt as she swayed from side to side, her head nodding. "Do you dance, Mr. Elliott?" She could barely see his face, but there was enough light for her to discern his surprise. She didn't care if he danced or not; she was already lost in the music, moving without him.

Rob made no reply. She felt a firm hand slide around her waist and another slap into her right palm, and suddenly she was flying around the corral. The fiddle notes went high and fast, lilting into the night sky, skittering out over the meadow. She and Rob twirled and gamboled across the dirt, kicking it up in little clods here and there, but for the most part sailing across it as though it were a dance floor. Maude threw back her head and laughed aloud. *The corral is perfect*, she realized. *Its surface is firm, dampened just enough by the cold October nights. A ballroom couldn't be any better.*

Rob spun her around and released her with one hand, only to grab hold of her solidly, spot-on, with the other. She hadn't had a drop to drink, but she was dizzy with delight. She had never met a better dancer. *Saints, he even puts my father to shame.* He twirled her, then reeled her in close and held her, trotting forward and back, making her burst into laughter as he held both her hands fast. She was convinced she'd tip over backward, but didn't.

When the tune ended with a quick saw of the bow up and down, he released her and bowed. "You are a splendid thing," he said. "Wherever did you learn?"

"Where did I? Look at *you!*" Breathless, she gasped out the words, then peeled off her leather coat and slung it over the gate. "To be honest, I've danced ever since I can remember. My father taught me, bless him. If I don't have a partner, I dance alone. It will always be that way with me, if need be." She stiffened.

The violin came again, this time a waltz. "I swear that old buzzard is doing this on purpose," she muttered.

"I gave him three dollars."

"*What?*"

"Just kidding." Rob had gathered her up again, but the wide arcs and the vigor of the jig were gone; the new tempo was slow and sweet. She strained to remember the name of the waltz, but soon it didn't matter. Her shoulders seemed to follow his, pinioned by invisible sinews through a thin slice of air. And so it was all the way down her torso. Everything was aligned, connected.

Their hips touched, sending messages at exactly the right instant, making the dance fluid and warm. She felt the heat most of all. Perspiring herself, she could feel the damp of his body coming through his woolen shirt.

A thunderbolt of memory shot into her and she saw him lying on the cot in the barn at Kettle Creek. Tonight, beneath the wool shirt, next to her breasts and belly, was the same muscular chest rippling down to a lean beltline, the area that she had traced with curious fingers that hot evening. And now, just as their bodies seemed to sense the next steps in the dance, he knew where she had gone with her thoughts. His right hand slid down her back and pressed her spine to him.

It was exactly what she wanted him to do at that moment. She let out the tiniest huff of breath. With a fierce, burrowing motion, he used his jaw to push aside her hair. He found her mouth, kissing her hard and deep. She glimpsed the stars, and was gone. There was nothing but him, all wetness and warmth and sensation. She raised her hand to the back of his head, sinking her fingers into his hair, pulling him close, kissing back hard.

He pulled away roughly and said, "You feel it, don't you? For God's sake, tell me you feel it. You and me, Maude." Then his lips were on hers again, his hands were locked in her hair. She melted into him, little sobs of wonder and anguish trapped in her throat.

He stopped, folding his arms around her. "Oh God, Maude. I can never leave you."

Her face dropped onto his chest and her tears fell on his jacket.

The violin crooned low, so soft they could barely hear it. The air stilled and Maude felt something. *No*, she thought, *it's nothing; I'm so incoherent right now I can't trust any of my senses, whether it's the pure and simple gray matter between my ears or what Gran would call "special wits."*

Rob held her, stroking her hair, swaying slightly from side to side as the violin pealed out its dying strains. A chill ran over her but she willed herself not to shiver. The night air filled her core, coursing into her like a fluid, the way it always did when she was gathering messages from the ether. Forcing her breath into a steady, in-and-out rhythm, she let herself rock back and forth in Rob's arms. All she could do was wait. What was it this time? What was about to happen?

There it was. On a distant hill, a mile or more to the east, a low and throaty bay rising into a plaintive howl. And then something else happened, something she could never have expected or anticipated. Rob's body went rigid. The hand that had been stroking her hair dropped to her arm and latched on, unconscious.

As she drew her head back and looked at him, his chin lifted and his eyes grew bright and alert, fixed on the black mass of hills, searching. There was a look about him just now, a look of such agony and joy, she was spellbound. She wanted the moment to stay. *Let me study this. Let me know you.*

He had never looked more real, more wonderful to her than he did at that moment, but there was something frightening too. He seemed to have quickened, as though a red-hot poker had stirred his blood. What did the howl mean to him? She and Gran had talked of familiars, animals who meant special things to certain people. It was usually a domestic creature—a cat, or a horse. But a wolf?

He caught his breath, then compressed his lips and dragged his eyes back to her face.

Maude's knitted brows began to relax, but one of them rose, forming an arch as dark and ominous as a runic inscription. "What just happened?"

In an instant, he became unreadable. "Wolf. You heard it. It was east, toward the Snowies."

"Don't you try to hoodwink a Graham. You know they say we're witches."

Rob licked his lips. "Hoodwink? What are you saying?"

"Something's going on with you."

"Something's going on with me, you say."

She glowered at him.

He looked away. "Well, it's . . . getting close to wolfing season."

"Don't tell me you're a wolfer?"

"Don't you think they're predators?" He eased his eyes back onto her face, studying her.

"Of course they're predators. In nature's grand order, they happen to be carnivores. We kill the ones who come after our sheep. I just don't believe in exterminating every last wolf in the whole state. Nor does my father."

The howl came again, and this time it was answered from a bluff across the valley. Maude watched Rob's eyes travel across the horizon, tracking the dark points of the firs against the starlit sky, mapping where he thought the alpha male might be, where his mate was. He swiped his hand across the back of his neck and came back to her.

"Maude, there are things . . . things I can't fully explain to you, not yet. Hell, I can't even explain them to myself. I just know this country is where I'm supposed to be, and I know I'm supposed to be with you. It's late, and I know you've got to go. Poor old Kib's got to get to bed, and I know he's waiting for me. But tell me one thing. Tell me you'll try us out. Give you and me a chance."

Maude put both hands up to her temples. Whatever Rob was holding back, it was nothing compared to the secrets she'd buried in her own cairn of stones long ago. *In fact,* she reasoned crazily, *any skeletons he has in his closet would make things easier for me, wouldn't they?*

She looked away, feeling more lost than ever. Give the two of them a chance? However magical this Samhain night had been, she couldn't erase a lifetime of regret with a midnight jig in a barnyard.

"I . . . I don't know," she stammered. "You yourself are telling me there are pieces of you that you can't share with me, and I . . . in all fairness to you . . . I just don't know if there's any hope for us. I have reasons of my own. You . . . must respect that, please." Even in the shadow of the barn, where the darkness was deep and forgiving, she could feel the red paint of shame creeping up her neck.

But the light filtering through the apple orchard was enough for her to see the contour of his jaw shift. She felt his anger rising, bubbling up as he considered the possibility that she may be in love with McNaughton after all. Her stomach shifted and saliva rose in her mouth as she considered the advantage of letting him believe it. It would be like pulling the trigger when a horse was down, never to rise again. *Mercy. If I care enough for him, I ought to have mercy. It's so hard, so very hard, but sometimes a person has to do the hardest thing.*

He grabbed her arms and brought her out of the shadows. Positioning her where the pale, wavering beams of Kibbey's lantern were strongest, he took her chin in his hand and held it steady. "I want you, Maude Graham, to look me in the eye and tell me you are in love with Thomas McNaughton."

Her eyes searched his face. For a tiny second, she framed the lie in her mind. It was one thing to struggle with the nighttime intrusions from the past, when silence and solitude left her vulnerable to raking, scorching memories. But when had she ever granted McNaughton admittance to the daily sunlit garden of her thoughts? A well-crafted lie. Maybe this perverse method was exactly what she needed to achieve her noble end.

Hot tears sprang up. She closed her eyes, willing the moisture back in, but it trickled down her cheeks. Lie to him? She couldn't do it.

Rob touched her face. "He hurt you, didn't he?" The words fell from his mouth like stones.

"Ssshhh!" Maude's eyes flew open. *No words, no words.* She didn't know what to say; she just had to silence him. "No. Don't speak." She took his hand from her face. "It's late. I have to go. So do you." And she was gone.

Chapter Nineteen

Standing on the platform at the Lewistown Train Depot as the clock ticked close to the 7:40 arrival time, Catriona and John were as smartly outfitted as Maude had ever seen them. After hearing Mary go on for months in her letters about the fashions she'd seen in Chicago and Milwaukee, Catriona had yielded to the purchase of a new suit from the Bloomingdale's catalog. A recent check from the Salt Creek oil rig had helped with that.

Her mother's ensemble was a fine-textured worsted-wool affair, dark gray with the latest yoked skirt. John had consented to a new waistcoat, but he insisted on wearing his usual shearling jacket, and therefore, according to Catriona, he still looked like "an old cuss from the Basin."

Maude didn't blame him one bit. She clutched her own black merino coat around her, for the wind was out of the north and the thermometer had dipped to seventeen degrees. Isobel and Fiona were inside the depot, kneeling on a window bench, huffing their breath onto the panes and drawing musical notes and turkeys. Ailse had stayed home next to the wood stove, suffering with rheumatism.

Maude looked at Catriona's new handbag, knowing that it contained Mary's most recent letter, with all the details of her train travel.

Rory and Antonia were there too, huddled in the corner, out of the path of the wind. Maude watched them with unconcealed interest, happy that they'd announced their plans to get married at Easter. Rory's eyes met hers and held them for a moment. A few days previous, in Rory's office, they'd had a conversation about his friend Jack in Milwaukee.

"Jack says there was indeed a Paul Hathaway doing work for the Milwaukee Railroad last summer, on contract in Montana," Rory had said. "He confirmed that with some of his friends on staff in the personnel offices. But Paul wasn't from Chicago. On his employment contract, he listed Syracuse, New York, as his place of residence. This is going to take a while to figure out, Maude."

Maude sat and frowned. "Was he a real attorney?"

"We think so. Or I should say, we're hoping so."

She shook her head. "We know one thing . . . we know he's a liar. Mary was so in love with him last summer. I want her to be happy, but honestly, I don't know how I'd behave if he actually showed up here." She plastered her hand against her mouth and spoke through her fingers. "Would I want him to, even if it made her happy?"

"I feel pretty much the same way."

"We'll have to be polite to him if he does."

"That's what I keep telling myself." Rory slammed a drawer shut on his desk. "But someone's got to get the truth out of him, Maude. And I don't know as it'll be Father."

Maude had driven home that day wondering how much truth would be forged out of Mary's visit and how much her sister would rigidly withhold. Clutching her stomach with one hand and keeping a weak grip on the reins with the other, she stewed over how to proceed once Mary got here. After all, she had no idea how much Mary knew about her own husband. There was always the chance, too, that Rory and Jack's information was off, missing one crucial scrap of intelligence that would redeem Paul and knit the whole picture back into a sensible portrait of a young couple just starting out. The new law firm Paul spoke of, for example, could exist just beyond the city limits of Milwaukee, too new to be included in any of the directories.

But as they stood on the platform with the November wind blowing tiny snowflakes out of the dark north, something bore down on Maude, making her more and more convinced that Paul Hathaway wouldn't be on the train. She cast a look over her shoulder at the two girls inside the brilliantly lit depot.

"I can't find him when I look at him," Isobel had said that afternoon last August. Maude's heart swelled with feeling as she watched the girls, who laughed as they added tail feathers to a round-bellied turkey etched into the window fog. Isobel had detected something insincere in the handsome, dark-haired Paul. *Isobel, Isobel. What episodes of pain and joy will your special wits eventually bring you?*

And what of Fiona? Maude studied the older girl, who now regaled Isobel with a cross-eyed pilgrim. While not prone to the feverish sensationalism they all saw in Mary, Fiona had begun to resemble her older sister. "Two pennies struck at the same mint," their father had said. Maude knew that Fee, more than anyone, was breathless about seeing Mary.

Fiona viewed Paul as one of Mary's many acquisitions, like her French parasol or the fine new horse that had been mentioned in a letter. Oh, she liked him all right. She'd known almost from the start that he was Mary's chosen one, and that made him just grand. But over the last few months, he had become the staid furniture of Mary's new life, and she couldn't wait to get Mary away from him. She wanted to get the sense of her, to feel how she was the same and how she had changed. What was the big city like, really? And perhaps, just perhaps, some of Mary's new clothes might fit a fifteen-going-on-sixteen girl.

When the whistle split the night air, both girls jumped off the bench and burst through the double doors leading to the platform. Pulling on their mittens, they sidled up to Maude.

"She'll be comin' round the mountain when she comes, she'll

be comin' round the mountain when she comes!" Fiona and Isobel sang a few loud bars, making Catriona grin.

With Thanksgiving only two days away, the train was packed. Mary must have been sitting near the front, because after only a moment or two, she descended the steps and was caught in her mother's arms. Maude was there, hugging her sister close, followed by the two younger girls and then Rory and Antonia.

"Where's Paul?" asked John, craning his neck down the crowded platform in the direction of the baggage car. "Gone for your luggage, I suspect."

"Paul will be along on a later train," Mary announced, grasping her mother's arm. "There's just so much going on in our lives. The young attorney and his busy bride, you know. We are pulled in so many directions we've learned to divide and conquer." She flashed a wide smile.

She turned to Maude. "Don't you love my hat? Beaver felt with pheasant feathers. Perfect styling for this time of year." Mary's eyes were bright and her cheeks were flushed pink. Maude had to admit she looked exceptionally well, better than she'd expected.

"The Milwaukee is in the best financial shape it has ever been," she went on, returning her focus to John and Catriona, "and the railroad captains are looking for new investors. Paul's very busy— traveling with that aim. Their focus is on the West, so they'd like to see him move out here, actually."

"Montana?" John's voice scooped with incredulity. Catriona tilted her head, her eyes fully on Mary.

"Well . . . perhaps. Somewhere in the Rocky Mountain region." Mary picked a stray bit of wool off the sleeve of her long coffee brown coat, which looked brand-new.

Rory's eyes darted to Maude's. She gave him a warning look and returned her gaze to Mary.

"I'll go after your bags," he offered. Then, seeing Mary focus on Antonia, he said, "You remember Antonia. We're to be married next spring."

"Of course! Mother wrote to me about it. Congratulations."

She embraced Antonia, kissing her. Then, in a softer voice, she added, "If you would get my bag, Rory, that would be so kind. There's just the one."

"It seems Maude's acquired an admirer too, just recently," said Catriona.

Mary turned to look at Maude. "How lovely for you, at last."

Maude's eyes rested on her sister long enough to plumb the depth of meaning behind the remark, then shifted to Catriona. "I do not believe this tiny spark that seems to have caught everyone's notice will be kindled into a flame, so let's chat about something else."

Rory approached, lugging a simple black trunk. Maude couldn't keep her mind from racing. *Why is there only one bag? Knowing Mary as we all do—Ailse had once called her "our bonnie peacock"— she wouldn't return from Milwaukee and Chicago without parading a trove of acquisitions, even if they are the modest trifles of a new bride.*

Maude couldn't read Mary any better than she ever had. Her sister's theatrics were polished, amplified by the drama of homecoming. She took a long, deep breath of the crisp November air and turned her attention to the oncoming snow. Mesmerized by the dancing, fiery white specks against the tall light posts lining the railway platform, she reached a gloved hand up and parted the air in front of her, as if moving a curtain that was blocking her view. It wasn't until she had made the gesture that she realized she'd done it. She cast her eyes quickly around to see if anyone had noticed, but all eyes were on Mary.

"Your older sister," Catriona was saying as she snugged her arm into Mary's and proceeded into the station, "is uncomfortable with being the focus of an honorable man's romantic attentions. I say she ought to relax and enjoy it."

Maude heard her mother say these words, and her rational self knew she was surging into the bright depot with her merry family, but as Catriona spoke, she felt herself and Mary transported, swept away from everyone. She saw the two of them alone in a golden autumn field, facing one another in silence, where all was sunshine save for a shadow on Mary's face as a raven glided overhead.

The small spread on Ruby Creek was shaping up. Rob had spoken to his neighbors, the Ingersolls, about sharing their hired man, an industrious young man named Roy Akeley, for one day a week. The arrangement was working well.

Just that morning Rob had ridden back over to the Ingersolls' and talked with the old man, Per Ingersoll, about how he'd applied for his brand back in 1890. After a long visit over stout black coffee, Rob felt satisfied that his paperwork was in order. He'd post it to the State Livestock Commission in Helena the following Monday.

A month earlier, Per had agreed to sell him fifteen Hereford cow-calf pairs. The old gent had even hinted about needing a partner in a year or so, which surprised Rob. But glancing at Hildy Ingersoll, bent over the large porcelain sink, he'd seen the flicker of a smile.

We'll wait and see, Rob told himself as he rode back down the Ingersolls' lane, taking in a waterlogged roof here and a sagging perimeter fence there. With a gloved hand, he tipped his hat back and grinned up at the irony of the telephone line. *Glad they've got one,* he thought. *I suppose I'm next, seeing that they did string the line all the way to the end of the road. But one thing at a time.*

The way he saw it, he had just gotten Ruby Creek fully outfitted. He had finally unpacked the enormous trunk that had always sat at the foot of his mother's bed in their house in the Ohio Valley.

It had been a journey, that unpacking. A lot of blankets and woolens, numerous pieces of his mother's pewter and china. There were quite a few books, including the one he remembered best: *Selected Poems of Robert Burns.* Dark green and worn, the book felt dense and heavy in his hand, just how he remembered it.

Deep in the center of the trunk, wrapped in a soft blanket, was a rectangular gilt-edged mirror. Nothing gaudy, just a simple thing to hang over a washbasin. It had been his father's shaving mirror. He could still see his mother, Eliza, reaching up and tracing her fingers along its edge, lost in the days when she still had "her Brodie."

When he got back to Ruby Creek, he stoked the fire in the woodstove and grabbed a hammer to hang the mirror in the kitchen, next to the calendar he'd gotten from Wiedeman's. For the third time that day, he was reminded that Thanksgiving was only a couple of days away. A week ago, a note had come from the laird, not only inviting him to Thanksgiving dinner but also suggesting that he stay on to hunt the northern forest of the Rocking M for holiday-season game. It was signed, "Uncle Thomas."

Truth be told, Rob wouldn't mind seeing Grant McNaughton, but he'd just as soon share a beer with him at the Elkhorn or the Blue Goose. Still, the hunting proposal tantalized him. He returned to the stove, lifted the lid, and rearranged the crumbling orange logs. Begrudgingly, he allowed that the McNaughtons could, in a vague way, be described as "his people." Thus, the offer of dinner at the Rocking M had some measure of appeal, but it fell far short of the invitation for which he'd been hoping.

The Snowy Mountain Pack made a slow retreat to the coulees north of Coffee Creek. Leal and Adrad knew there were elk just south of the Missouri, and with the bitter snows coming in from the north, the pack would do well to settle in where water and food were at least a little more plentiful. What motivated them most of all, however, was the loss of the Loner three days ago. He had been caught in a steel trap baited with raw meat. Adrad and Leal had seen him die. Worse, several of their pups had seen him die. He had been dark, not quite as black as Leal, but having the young ones view the death of a dark-colored wolf had been hard. Leal had seen how they looked at him, then jerked their puzzled faces up to her. She didn't want any of the pack to go that way—not this year, not ever.

Leal's four pups of last spring were strong, led by the bold and intelligent Sky Watcher. None, however, were the size of her pups from the year before, who were by now as large as herself. Adrad remained the largest and most famous wolf in the region. The pack had numbered seventeen, but with the loss of the Loner, they were now at sixteen.

Neither parent wanted to lose a single pup to the traps, or to the terrible, convulsive death that came from the bad meat put out by the men who hunted and skinned wolves, taking their furs and leaving their flesh to freeze and dessicate on the windswept prairie.

As they migrated northwest to the coulees and cliffs south of the Missouri, they circled widely around the fenced areas of the humans and their livestock, keeping many miles away from the noisy places where their buildings and pungent scents were thickly clustered.

About halfway to Coffee Creek, along a small ravine near the Judith Mountains where red cattle grazed, Leal picked up a familiar scent. She stopped, one forefoot raised, and turned her yellow eyes to the left, looking downhill and south to a thick grove of pines and cottonwoods along a creek. She knew immediately that this was where the kindred man lived. Her tail plumed up and her dark nostrils quivered as she whiffed the smoke from his cabin fire. Something stirred in her, something old, a pulse that lay between memory and instinct. She had to pause there for a moment, just to be sure.

Adrad, on a small rise just ahead of her, turned to look back, the wind ruffling the thick gray fur on his shoulders. He shook himself and yawned nervously, but regarded her with respect because he too remembered the kindred man who had run with them on that strange night in the warm season.

The pups milled around and stopped, studying her and raising their noses to the scents of smoke, horses, and livestock. But Leal was finished. She knew what she needed to know: the kindred man lived. She turned and loped on.

Chapter Twenty

Maude lost the battle with Catriona over whether or not to invite Rob Elliott to Thanksgiving dinner.

"I don't know what kind of household Laird McNaughton is running at the Rocking M now that Rowena's gone, God rest her soul, but there's no doubt we can give that boy a better dinner over here. We sure can't leave him alone up on Ruby Creek. And Mary would like to meet him, wouldn't you, Mary?"

Mary raised her lashes, revealing eyes the same color as the well-steeped pekoe in her teacup. Setting the cup down with a clink, she replied, "Yes, of course I should like to meet him. His name is Rob?"

Maude gave a wooden nod and glanced at Ailse, who was stationed in the pressed-back oak chair next to the stove, darning a flour sack dishtowel.

"Father Wakefield spoke on this very thing last Sunday," Catriona continued. "He urged us all to bring someone new into our homes this Thanksgiving and make them welcome. He said that if the person were new to the community, then so much the better."

Maude looked up at the ceiling fixture and tilted her head in her mother's direction. "Mother, as Gran would say, let's leave the kirk in the kirkyard. I don't need Father Wakefield's advice in this matter."

"I just don't know what's holding you back, Maude Graham!" Catriona's voice stung like vinegar.

Maude shot up, her napkin wadded in her fist, and glared at her mother. Knowing, or suspecting, what she did about the state of Mary's marriage, and remembering how Catriona had fluttered around last summer over that carpet knight Paul Hathaway, she had enough volcanic asperity to tell her mother that she wasn't fit to even pretend to be a marriage broker. Quivering with intensity, Maude was held back only by Ailse's cautionary stare.

Catriona stopped her bread kneading and wiped her hands on her apron. Sniffing, she amended her tone. "Well . . . I didn't mean to be harsh, Maude. It's just, look at your sister now, and how she's got a fine marriage going for her. Can you blame your mother for wanting every one of her girls to be happy?"

Maude stole a look at Mary, who sat slope-shouldered, toying with a spoon.

"And here you've got a right handsome suitor plainly courting you, after all this time. What's a mother expected to think? You can't say he isn't a good man. We can all see it plain as day. I remember your own Granda, Jamie MacDougall, God rest his soul— you've got his wild hair, you know it right well—I can still hear him muttering over his pipe. 'Better to say *here 'tis than there it went.*' Yes, I hear him like it was yesterday."

Maude's eyes locked with Ailse's again, then her chin dropped. She let a long, silent sigh escape. "It's fine, Mother. I'll invite him." She folded her napkin and set it on the table. "I'll place the call before I leave. I believe his neighbor has a telephone."

Mary stood to clear the dishes from the table and, as she did, Maude watched the morning light fall across her sister's shoulders and bodice. In that moment, as Mary turned toward the sink with her hands full of Catriona's rose-printed china, Maude knew that her sister was pregnant.

Maude frowned, then smiled, then frowned again. Earlier that day, Isobel had ridden to her house and unfurled a note, like a town crier. "Rob Elliott will come to Thanksgiving dinner with us on two conditions—that you let him whip the cream for the pumpkin pie and that you let him escort you home when dinner's done."

"I suppose Mother has already acceded to these conditions on my behalf."

"Actually, it was Father."

"Well, they are behaving in concert then."

Isobel sat on Rooster, one of her favorites, looking down at Maude. "Is Rob Elliott a bad fellow, Sissy Maude?"

Maude's lower lip puckered up and she went quickly to Isobel, leaning against her slender, trousered leg as the warm afternoon sun beamed down on them. "Heavens, no, he's not a bad fellow. I just feel like I am in a fishbowl and everyone's watching me. Izzy, I'm far older than most girls ought to be when they're courted. I've gotten so used to being alone. I'm just a little . . . scared to try being with someone."

"I think . . . I think I would be afraid of it too." Isobel slipped her fingers deep into Maude's hair and left them there for a moment, then pulled Rooster away and trotted back down the lane.

For the rest of the day, Maude continually found herself arrested in the middle of a task, daydreaming, wondering what the holiday would be like. From there, it was impossible to suppress the thorny questions that sprang into these scenic meditations: *Where am I leading Rob Elliott? What am I doing? What have I already done?*

The platter, heavy with turkey, the large casseroles of mashed potatoes and sweet potato gratin, and a half dozen additional hot pieces of crockery, once seated on the heavy damask tablecloth, released the pleasant cedar scent the fabric harbored from its long stay in the closet. The entire Graham house, so fragrant and full of sensation, sent Maude's head reeling. For once, she was grateful for Catriona's mysterious seating program. Rob had been placed on the opposite side of the table, at an angle from her.

"But Rooster doesn't like the south pasture, Father," Isobel was saying.

John Graham eyed her. "Did you take tea with that nitwit gelding? How do you know what he thinks?"

Isobel was silent, then tossed her dark hair. "He doesn't like that pasture because of what happened to Oban year before last. And we can't talk about that because Fee will cry, and we mustn't do that, not on Thanksgiving."

"We'll save this discussion for later," intervened Catriona, who sailed on to the topic of Clementine, Winston Churchill's new bride, whose wedding dress had appeared in the November issue of *McCall's*. The delicacy of the lace, and whether or not it was Venetian or Brussels, became the discourse for several minutes.

As Maude's eyes traveled around the table, she encountered Rob's dark, auguring gaze often, and while his glances and suppressed smiles made her hands turn cold, she also had to resist the urge to fan herself with her napkin. The ground between them was no longer level; it was shifting wildly. She had lost her compass. Before, it had been so easy to declare herself disinterested. Now, she didn't want him to stay away. She knew that an unkind word or a harsh look would affect him. One thing had become clear to her: she didn't like the idea of a world without Rob Elliott. Not one bit. He had come, making it plain to her and to everyone that he wanted her, and now everything was different. Topsy-turvy, yes, but she'd begun to have moments of lunacy, when she felt like absolutely nothing mattered except the next time she could lay eyes on him, touch him.

Just now, it made her crazy to realize that she wanted him to look at her. It had never mattered before, but when she cast her eyes in his direction and saw that he was not looking at her, she was disappointed. Discovering this made her feel more foolish than she had ever felt in her life. *I will not look at him*, she told herself. But time and again her eyes flicked across the abundant landscape of the Thanksgiving table to find him.

She was glad she couldn't see Rory from where she sat. If their eyes met, she feared the air would crackle with their shared knowledge of Mary's strange little world. As the commerce of dinner progressed, Catriona's attempts to engage Mary in any form of conversation met with paltry success.

Feeling the bright focus of her mother's frequent looks, however, Mary's lips finally curved into a smile as she offered, "About the lace on Mrs. Churchill's gown . . . it's surely Brussels. Venetian lace has a more sculpted look."

Maude listened politely, glad that Mary was making some kind of foray. She glanced around the table, assessing empty plates and flickers of restlessness. *Yes, it's time to serve the pumpkin pie.* She leaned forward, preparing to push back her chair.

"I believe you're right," Catriona replied. "You know, when I showed the article to Mrs. Wakefield's sister-in-law, the one from England, she told me that Clementine Churchill's parentage is in question. She said the bride's mother, Lady Hozier, bore Clementine out of wedlock. Can you imagine?"

Maude could not stop the rotation of her head toward Mary. Mary's fingers were poised like those of a pianist, clawlike, on the edge of the table. Her eyes were fixed on the top edge of her plate as if it were the face of a clock striking twelve.

"Ailse," Mary said, reaching for her water glass, "I miss your recipe for rosemary-lemon tea. Might I borrow your wonderful book to copy some things?"

"I dinnae have it, child. Your sister has got it oot on Kettle Creek."

"You . . . you can come out and stay with me an evening, Mary," Maude put in. "Copy all you want. I am not quite finished with it, but I would love some company. Speaking of company, why don't the two youngest girls—and Rob—come to the kitchen and help me get the pie."

Like a dusty road, the Milky Way coursed through the indigo heavens above them. On either side of the buggy, the harrowed earth was dark, broken here and there by pale acres of corn stubble and untilled fields of sagebrush. Bobcat plodded along, but both Maude and Rob watched his ears spindling back and forth as he gave notice of the fact that Rob's blue roan was tied to the rear of the buggy. Cala lay curled up tight on the seat next to Rob.

"There's plenty of bite in the air, but not a hint of snow," Rob said.

"You sound disappointed." Maude shivered. The thermometer said 12 degrees above zero when they left Stony Creek.

"I wouldn't mind a dusting of snow tomorrow or the next day. I'm going hunting. West of your place."

Maude let this comment and all its implications register. Rob would be on the laird's land, more than likely in the company of one or more of the McNaughtons. She forced some warmth into her voice, trying to dispel the fractious energy she felt building in the thin column of air between them. "Yes, snow will help, in that case. You're after elk, I presume."

"An elk would be nice. I'm going with Grant." There had been talk of adding other hunters to the party, but so far he only knew that Grant—and perhaps the laird—were coming.

"Grant. He's one of the middle ones. He's always been—pleasant."

Rob nodded but kept still. He was being allowed, for the first time, an apprentice's understanding of what lay between this woman and the McNaughton clan. He looked straight ahead, but was fully focused on her through the peripheral field of his vision. Her pale profile against the dark landscape, the few dancing curls that had escaped her hood, the slight upturn of her nose. He breathed in the scent of her: lavender and soap, whiffs of ginger and clove from the morning's baking, her warm skin. He could almost feel her blood moving underneath.

It came to him that, as much as she scrupulously avoided the subject of her relations with the McNaughtons, he would just as soon avoid it tonight too. As they drew up in front of her cabin at Kettle Creek, Rob jumped down. "The place will be cold. You go in and get the stove going. I'll put the buggy away and get the horses settled."

By the time he joined her in the kitchen, the room had begun to warm up. Maude had uncorked a bottle of her best Scotch whiskey and two glasses stood on the table. Rob's cowboy hat came off the minute he closed the kitchen door behind him. As he set it on the metal countertop, Maude saw that he had something else in his other hand: a book.

"Whiskey?"

"Aye."

"Aye?"

"I'm in the mood for a little Robert Burns. Do you mind?"

"Not at all." Maude smiled and poured.

"It's still pretty chilly in here. If we close the lid on the woodbox, we could both sit on it and be near the stove."

"We could." Maude grabbed a couple of pads off the chairs and tossed them on the woodbox, sat down, and looked up at Rob. "To Scotland's bard." She raised her glass and clinked it against his.

The whiskey heated her throat as it went down, and the stove was warm on her right side. Rob sat down and began flipping through the book. "I'll start with a bit of whimsy. Here's 'To a Mouse.'"

Maude watched him, the way he held the worn old volume, reading closely but lifting his eyes from the page every now and then to make sure she was paying attention. He kicked his right leg out for emphasis every few lines, and leaned into the parts he clearly knew well.

When he finished, he leaned over and kissed her lightly, then gave her one of his crooked smiles and caught her hand in his. She smiled back, realizing that his good humor sparked a new kind of joy in her.

"Here's a sillier one, by far. 'No Churchman Am I.'"

As he read the sing-song passages of the irreverent ballad, she tried not to look so often at his thighs, lean and muscular beneath his dark trousers. His hand still held hers. She felt and saw the strength of the long, sturdy fingers, the callus on the inner curve of the left thumb, and one on the inside of the forefinger.

He set the book down to finish his whiskey. She was not far behind. Tipping the bottle, she filled them each half-full again, then leaned back against the wall.

"Now for a special one. Something I have chosen just for you." When he glanced over at her, his eyes were alight with interest, but the playfulness had been replaced with something new. "This is called 'How Green the Groves.'"

Maude listened in earnest, but as he began to read, Isobel's voice came to her. *Is Rob Elliott a bad sort of fellow?* Tiny lines formed between her eyebrows as she realized that the mere traffic of living can make it extraordinarily difficult for two people to come together. She pushed these worries out of her mind and focused on Rob's voice, which lay somewhere, she decided, between a tenor and a baritone.

The shepherd in the flowery glen, in shepherd's phrase will woo:

Here he stopped and picked up his glass. Over the brim, his eyes burned into hers. When he set it down, he did not look at the book, but finished the stanza looking directly at her. Her stomach twisted beneath her ribs.

The courtier tells a finer tale, but is his heart as true!

She inhaled sharply here, making a move as if to rise, but his hand landed heavily on her arm, holding her next to him. Returning to the page, he read the final lines:

These wild-wood flowers I've pulled, to deck that spotless breast o' thine:
The courtiers' gems may witness love, but, tis na love like mine.

Rob set the book on his lap and took the glass from her hand, setting it at the edge of the woodbox. Leaning into her, he rested his forehead lightly against hers and said, "Maude Graham, you are the most beautiful woman on the face of the earth."

He tilted his head slightly and kissed her tenderly, then deeper, letting his lips slide over hers. Maude lifted her face and pushed forward, meeting him, rising from a long darkness. Her fingers traveled up his arms, curving around his biceps through the flannel. She felt she was discovering a work of art, feeling the contours of a masterpiece for the first time. It was delicious, this feeling. She could not believe this was happening to her.

There was a thud as the book slid to the floor. Rob drew away and gave her an apologetic smile. "We cannae let the bard be falling doon."

A rush of cool air washed over Maude as he scrambled down onto the floor. "The binding didn't break, I hope."

"No. But it's . . . I'm not sure."

Maude leaned over, looking down at him. He was on one knee and had retrieved the book, but two folded pieces of paper had fluttered out and had slid underneath the kitchen table. She scooted off the woodbox and crouched down to help him.

As soon as she touched one slip of paper, she knew it was old— very old. The corner crumbled in her fingers as she clumsily tried to pick it up. Using more caution, she carefully lifted it with a fingernail, then set it on the tabletop. Rob succeeded in picking up the other piece and laid it alongside.

"This book was my mother's. I can only assume that, whatever these are, they were placed here by her own hand."

He picked up one paper, which looked like a story, written in fine, tight penmanship. Sitting down, he moved the kerosene lantern close and began reading.

Maude pulled the other one toward her, the one she'd damaged slightly. It was much older and appeared to be a fragment of a poster or a handbill. It read:

Nae Mair Blude Shall be Spilt. Murd'ring Blacke Beast Kilt on River Findhorn. 10 February 1743. Laird MacIntosh hath Awarded the Hunter McQueen with Land Tract. Tis Herebye Announced The Last Wolfe in Bonnye Scotland is Deade.

Sinking slowly into her chair, she watched Rob devour the page in front of him. Finally, he slumped back and slid both the paper and the lantern toward her. With tentative fingers, she moved it closer and began to read the neat, feminine hand.

This story was told to me in person by my father-in-law, Gifford Elliott, two years before his death in the autumn of 1866. It was told to him by his own mother, Sarah MacInnes Elliott, who was raised on the MacInnes family lands on the far reaches of the River Findhorn. Sarah's mother, Chloris, saved a litter of wolf pups from a terrible deluge one spring and from that time forward, a peculiar friendship existed between her and the wolves. Indeed, it seems to have spread to all her descendants. I know that my son Rob may someday find this record, and if he does, it is my belief that he was meant to. —E. E.

That Highland spring of 1743, it didn't matter that it was late April, the snow had come anyway, a great, heavy mass of it, cloaking the stony bluffs and the river bottoms the night before. McQueen had risen after midnight, so encouraged was he by the white flakes falling from the dark sky. Tracking would be easy, and he was fair certain of his prey this time.

What did it matter that the loathsome animal hadn't really killed any children in the Grampian hills? At the bonfire, his sister Meg whispered to him that only one child had died, and that was from a fall from a cliff. The wild things had come later and had fed on the body. But for McQueen, it would be better if folks continued believing that the Great Black Wolf had done it. The Laird MacIntosh had promised a land grant and a casket of gold to the man that brought home the head of the Great Black.

As night began to fade and the walls of the ravine became visible, the snow stopped and a thick fog poured in. "The last wolf in Scotland, are ye?" muttered McQueen under his breath as he kept his eyes down, focusing on the paw prints that stood out like ink on parchment. Each impression was enormous, wider than McQueen's own foot and just as long. But the wolf was tired; McQueen could see it in his shortening stride. Aye, you're an auld bastard, y'are. And ye ken I'm comin' for ye.

The wolf tracks veered suddenly to the right, toward a cleft in the massive charcoal gray outcropping of rock. McQueen slunk quickly behind an oak, knowing that the wolf was probably circling 'round. If it only weren't so damned foggy. Just as his hand went to his knife, a barrel of dark fur and muscle came from a granite ledge overhead.

The wolf knocked him easily to the ground, cuffing his forehead and slicing the skin so that blood ran warm and red into his eyes. McQueen's knife slashed again and again. He felt a surge of brutal lust as it struck a rib. But the wolf was slipping through his hands, turning to look at McQueen over a shoulder of coal black fur, glaring with amber eyes and making the most sinister growl McQueen had ever heard.

McQueen made a lunge for him, heaving himself on the enormous shaggy back, clinging and stabbing. Man and wolf rolled and tumbled in the snow and rocky cobbles of the shallow creek bed, blood welling everywhere in the slush. McQueen felt a great slash on his upper thigh, nearly ridding him of his privates as the wolf dealt him a powerful blow.

Crying out, "You'll not keep me from the Laird's reward!" he fastened himself on the fur ruff behind the wolf's head. In the fray, he couldn't be certain, but he thought he felt something there, something like a rope around the beast's neck, and sure enough, he held it fast, for whatever 'twas, he knew it was going to help him end the life of the Great Black.

With his left hand clinging to the rope, he drew his sharp dirk across the wolf's throat. When blood spilled over his knuckles, he knew the stroke was good. The movements of the Great Black slowed to a stagger. With McQueen still clinging to it, the wolf dragged him around the river bed for nearly a quarter of an hour, finally falling to its knees in the churned mass of snow, mud, and blood.

McQueen fell with it and lay staring at it face to face. Its golden eyes were heavy-lidded, dimming as if some vast distance were beginning to separate the two of them. A strange and peculiar familiarity came over McQueen, as if he knew the wolf the way one knows a man. And here that man lay dying in his arms. The wolf's gaze seemed to soften even further, as if to say, "I had no quarrel with you."

"Bah!" McQueen scoffed, "Ye're going to meet the de'il, y'are."
He tore his eyes away and began withdrawing his arm from beneath
the great head. He uncurled his fingers from whatever it was that
had allowed him to hold onto the animal so tightly. Sitting up, he
felt for the rope around the animal's neck, struggling to see it, but
the fur was too thick and dark. As he worked it around, the Great
Black let out a long and ragged exhale. The broad chest and vast
rib cage were still at last.

When McQueen had parted the thick black fur and had the rope
where he could get a good look at it, he found it wasn't a rope at
all. It was a long piece of tightly woven wool plaid, tied like a neat
collar, dirty and faded with time. It was hard to imagine how it
could have ever gotten there, and why. But he could plainly tell two
things. It was a tartan, and it was MacInnes green.

The room was still except for the soft crackle of the pine logs
in the stove. Rob had gotten both their glasses from the wood
box and was sipping his whiskey, a dark look on his face. Maude
reached for hers.

"I suppose you think me somewhat peculiar."

Maude's mouth felt like a bell without a clapper. *Peculiar?* The
last twelve years unfurled in front of her, a private world into which
no one had been admitted. *I am, at last, healing old and bitter
wounds, and I've found ways of providing a meaningful service in the
world. How might I be judged if the world knew my story?*

As Rob sat still, drilling his gaze into the tabletop, it occurred
to her that she rarely formed opinions about others, at least not
consciously. She couldn't form one now about Rob and didn't
know how to tell him so. Her silence, though, spoke for her.

He flung his head back. "I know what you're thinking. You're
thinking about the night we danced in the barnyard, when the wolf
howled in the hills."

"I wasn't thinking about that."

"Weren't you? Weren't you wondering what the howl meant to
me? Isn't there enough wolfish folklore out there to scare the spirit
of Christ Jesus out of anyone?"

"I thought you could hold your whiskey better than this."

Rob laughed and shoved his hands into his hair. "Anyone with any sense would kick me out."

"Why? Because you have a connection with animals? So does my sister. You heard her at dinner, about the horse that won't go to the south pasture because of another horse that kicked a metal shed there and then bled to death from a gash. Witches have animal friends. They're called familiars. You forget how many times my kin and I have been called witches. There's a broom over by the woodbox, but I've never flown it. Can't say as I'd mind, though."

Rob stared at her for more than a minute. The clock ticked loudly. Finally he said, "You and yours don't frighten me as much as I worry myself, Maude. It's hard to explain."

Don't I know it, Maude thought. Repressing a wild urge to laugh, she got up and went to the Victrola, digging around in the shelves for the right music cylinder. A moment later, the tender strains of a Mendelssohn violin concerto filled the kitchen. When she turned to look at him, she was smiling and her blue eyes were sparkling. "Sometimes," she said, leaning against the wall, "we have to wait for the words to come."

Rob had never seen her so unguarded, so provocative. He shoved back his chair and, in two strides, was standing in front of her, his hands on her arms.

"I thought music soothed the savage beast," she said.

"Don't be so sure about that." He reached up and touched her face, tracing his hands over her lips. "I've never seen you like this."

"No, I have never seen *you* like this."

"Are we getting to know one another?"

A vapor of hesitation floated over Maude, but she waved it away. "Perhaps."

"Don't pull back now, Maude Graham. I won't let you." He slipped one firm hand around her waist and with the other, grasped her right hand, swinging her into a slow, rhythmic dance around the table.

The whiskey had worked its way into her every limb, making her drift into the sweet, mournful lilt of the violin. She loved the way her feet just seemed to know where his were going. It was like that night in the corral, only different. That night had been sheer frolic, but tonight was new, potently magnetic.

The tension between them mounted. She felt molded to his body like a piece of India rubber, but she also felt taut enough to snap. Something ached inside her that she'd never felt before. The feel of his hand against the small of her back set a fire deep in her belly.

As he pressed her hipbones against his groin, the sensation exploded. She put her hands on his shoulders and pushed back, looking at him. She had perhaps two seconds to study his hazel eyes, then his lips found hers. All she could feel were the hard grazes of the stubble on his jaw against her chin and his hands clutching deep in her hair.

Her own hands amazed her, working their way over his shoulders and back, fingers knotting into his belt loops, trying as hard as she could to bring him closer. She wanted him tight against her, so close that he could never leave.

"Maude, Maude." He whispered her name over and over as his lips slipped from her mouth to the hollow of her neck. As his hands ran from her narrow waist to the swell of her breasts, she gasped out loud.

"Upstairs," she said, taking his hand. Rob grabbed the lantern, and in a clatter of boots they ascended. Next to the broad white bed, their hands worked the buttons on each other's clothes. Maude slipped out of her blouse as Rob flung his flannel shirt over the bedpost.

"Christ in his nightie, it's cold in here. Get under the covers and we'll finish this business where it's warmer."

Laughing, they climbed beneath the Hudson's Bay blanket and the down tick. When the last article of clothing was discarded on the floor, Maude lay between the crisp muslin sheets of her familiar white bed and felt a chill dance over every limb. Her past rose like a spectre. Maddeningly, her next thought was of Eve in the Garden, startled by her own nakedness. The dark place between her thighs begged to be covered, and she knew her hand had shifted modestly, protectively, toward her groin.

Her heart beat a snare-like tattoo inside her head and her self-consciousness increased to a crescendo. The accumulated cold of the bedclothes crept in and wrapped its fingers around her heart.

Rob propped his head up on one hand and studied her by lantern light. "We don't have to do this, Maude."

"I—I want to."

"I think you do. But is tonight the right time?"

She drew a sharp breath. "Downstairs I was so certain. A locomotive couldn't have stopped me." Her throat tightened as she remembered McNaughton crouched over her just months ago, right here on her own bed. She blinked fiercely, squinting away the details of the laird's face. From nowhere, tears came, spilling out of the corners of her eyes onto the pillow.

"Maude, on my life, I would never frighten you or hurt you."

"It's not you, for God's sake!" Stifling a sob, she could not disguise her anger.

Rob's eyes darkened as he pondered her. "Does this have something to do with Tom McNaughton?"

"If you care anything about me, you will not ask me . . . that," Maude choked out the words and rolled away.

Rob stared at the dark spirals of hair falling across her shoulder blades. After several moments, he reached over and turned the wick down on the lantern and watched it gutter. Moving into the center of the bed, he arranged a bit of the sheet between himself and Maude. Then he took hold of her firmly by the hips and tugged her close. It was a long while before he slept.

Chapter Twenty-One

 In the morning, with the room even colder than the night before, the pocket of air their bodies shared beneath the covers was a warm nest. It was, Maude found, more comfortable than anything she could have imagined.

As soon as she lifted her eyelids to see the pale hues of the November morning, she knew Rob was awake too. She felt him stretch his legs, then dovetail them back into position next to hers. As he did, she felt the morning hardness of him against her backside. The evidence of his arousal sent a spasm through her core.

Quickly, before she had time to engage her mind, she reached for his hand and brought it around to her chest, placing it on her breast. The moment his fingers traced the shape of her, she gasped and the ache inside her grew.

Their hands began feverishly exploring. When the covers were pushed back, cold air poured over their naked skin. As Rob yanked the down tick high up around them, Maude rolled onto her back. He took in the full length of her, running his hand down between her breasts and stopping just below her navel.

"The most beautiful woman in the world," he whispered, moving on top of her, kissing his way up the midline of her torso.

Maude hooked her fingers around his upper arms and drew his face to hers. "I want you."

He lurched forward, kissing her and easing himself into her at the same time. Startled by the sensation of him inside her, Maude rocketed back through time. *Moist sea air, the flash of torn pantaloons, that hemp rope.* Her insides convulsed and she bucked.

"I am hurting you."

She trained her mind on the present. "Just . . . go slowly. Kiss me."

He did kiss her slowly at first, his mouth covering hers wetly. He kissed her cheeks, her eyelids. The stubble on his cheeks caught her lips and chafed them, ripping her thoughts away from what was happening inside. He found her mouth again and kissed her deeply, his tongue moving in, encouraging hers. The texture of him, the way he felt against her, rose up like a velvet wave, washing away all active thought. Then there was a new universe of skin and slipperiness and scent and warmth, and she was lost in it.

Her low belly twisted with desire as she felt herself respond to him. Gasping with surprise, she had the awestruck sensation that her body had a will of its own and was teaching her to hold him there. Once her mind and body fixed themselves on this extraordinary task, she and Rob were irrevocably united. In the private consciousness that now existed between them, she knew he was trying to be gentle, but then he moved, and the more he moved, the less gentle he was able to be.

But it was all right. Now that she was here, with him this way, she realized that lovemaking was not entirely about gentleness. She was a woman with a man. In the next instant, she knew there was an element of beautiful madness to this. Her eyes opened wide. They clung fiercely to each other, sweating, driving for a closeness that went far deeper than skin. Like everyone who has ever drunk from this cup, she wanted her fill. Every aspect of him was wonderful to her at that moment, and she was wonderful too. Then, with a wild cry from both of them, it was over.

Their good-bye kiss had left her wanting to go back upstairs, but Maude's knowledge of her body told her that once was all she could afford at this time in her cycle. This morning was all they could have, for now.

It was odd to see him riding away. Riding away to the McNaughton place, especially. Cala flung backward glances at Ajax, but Rob had trained her to follow his horse. Ajax whimpered, but he too stayed where he belonged.

Maude knew Rob had wanted to talk to her about his family's history. He'd carried several loads of firewood from the barnyard to the house while she cooked breakfast of eggs and side pork. As they ate, he hinted that his experience last summer with Medicine Badger had been a clumsy attempt to figure out why he was so connected to the wolves.

She knew from personal experience that explaining one's special wits was not easy, and further, she had a deep conviction that these matters should never be fully explained. Special wits are just that—gifts from one's spirit guides—and as such they are the most sacred possessions one will ever know.

"I think your family thinks you don't care much for me," Rob said as he tightened the cinch on his blue roan while the two dogs scuffled on the barn floor. "I can't figure where they got that notion." His face was downcast, but she could see the ghost of a smile on his lips.

She felt hot. "I suppose this will be a favorite topic between us for quite some time."

"I suppose."

She fingered a latigo strap on a nearby saddle and watched the dogs, waiting for her blush to fade. "Well, my family will get the picture soon enough. Mother worries excessively about me ending up a spinster." She paused, running the latigo slowly through her fingers. "I'm not the one she needs to be worrying about."

"What does that mean?"

"Well, the plain truth is, I'm concerned about Mary. But I'll tell you about that when you get back."

Now that she had given Rob Elliott free admittance to the range of her thoughts, she was amazed at how much space he occupied.

It gave her a measure of comfort that he wouldn't be far away over the next week. While the hunting party scoured the forests and bluffs of the enormous land tracts of the Rocking M, he would still be within five or six miles of her place. At least one evening, he told her, they'd take a break from braving the cold in canvas wall tents and would stay instead at the laird's posh hunting lodge that lay in the forest west of her sheep pasture.

With her arms wrapped around herself, she watched him ride away. Her world had been turned on its ear, and she laughed out loud. She wanted to tell everyone; she wanted to tell no one. Everything that had transpired in the last twenty-four hours was as remarkable as if the moon had come down to rest on the roof of the barn. *Magic indeed,* she thought. *I'm as giddy as a girl. Hadn't thought it possible. Never, really.* She looked at Ajax, who stared up at her. "For now," she instructed him and herself, "until I feel a bit less intoxicated, all this magic and moonlight will stay in my heart."

Mary was coming this week, she remembered, to copy recipes from Ailse's big book. Morag had written from Great Falls, announcing that she'd be arriving by train to spend a whole month with Ailse, leading up to Christmas. Maude was glad. She was tempted to take Ailse and Morag into her confidence about Mary's situation, but she hesitated. It would be hard for Ailse not to tell Catriona.

Using an iron poker to break the ice on the sheep watering troughs, she wondered how she'd break the ice with Mary and get to the heart of what was happening with her. She smiled wryly as she remembered something Catriona often said about women's typical willingness to talk to each other. "Count on it, a woman will tell another woman just about anything if it involves the man she loves."

As she watched the sheep mill toward the trough, she saw Flourface, the flock's true iconoclast, standing off to the side, as if she didn't need food or drink. Reaching for the gate, she said aloud, "I'm afraid, Mother, that our Mary is the exception who proves the rule."

I've got to get into Lewistown and talk to Rory, she decided. *If there is any news about Paul Hathaway, I need to hear it before Mary's visit.*

"We still don't know if he's an attorney or not. We know he studied law in New York State and that he's most recently from Syracuse. We don't have any idea where he is now. We do know that the Milwaukee police are looking for him because he left numerous unpaid debts." Rory showed Maude the latest telegram from his friend Jack. "Paul's a first-class bounder, Maude. I'd use another word, but . . ."

"What—what about Mary's departure from Milwaukee? I hate to even ask that, but was she living under the name of Mrs. Paul Hathaway and does she bear any of Paul's legal responsibilities because of it?"

"Our sister has actually borne up very smartly under all of this. She must have seen the worst coming. If they ever were legally married, she took back her own name when she got an apartment. I don't know exactly what kind of a place it is, but it's up above a German restaurant. She has been waiting on tables at the restaurant and doing seamstress work in her off hours."

"Holy Saint Brigid. Mother will die if she ever finds out."

"I'm worried about Father. He'll kill the man."

Maude nodded slowly. "You know, Rory, I am less concerned about revenge than I am about caring for Mary and helping her shed the lie that she is living. The sooner I can help her confide in us, the sooner our entire family can heal."

Rory tilted his head to the side and raked a hand through his copper hair. "Honor is a big thing with me."

"Be that as it may," Maude said, fixing him with a hard look, "there are legal authorities out there who can chase this man down. We have a sister to take care of, and parents who are going to take this poorly when they learn the truth." She stopped, knowing that she had an even larger portion of the truth than Rory did, and that all hell was going to break loose when the full story of Mary's pregnancy came out. When it did, her brother's taste for revenge would be sharply whetted.

"Well, you do what you feel is best and I guess I'll do likewise."

Maude sighed. "May I borrow that telegram?"

"Sure. Keep it at your place for now. I don't want Mother and Dad to see it until we have a plan."

"Your mother and Mac took the girls to pick up Morag at the station this morning," said John, "but they're due back any minute. Ailse didn't go, so you might go over to see her. She's having a spell with her back."

Maude found Ailse finishing the rosemary-mint sachets she had started at Samhain. "Who's going to mind Morag's apothecary shop while she's here for the holidays?"

"She's got a wee helper to bide there. Not a young 'un, mind ye, but thin as a sapling. A widow she's been teaching. In her letter tae me, Morag said she was missin' me sairly, and she said a woman's business isn't always the most important thing she has tae do."

Maude smiled. "It will be wonderful to have her here. I miss Morag too." She pulled a chair up next to Ailse and took a breath. "You know, Mary's coming to spend the night tonight. I'm a little worried about her."

Ailse peered over her spectacles. "Aye. I dinnae ken what tae make on't, but there's an ill wind blowin'. I have a sense that she's with child."

Maude let out a heavy sigh. "I should have known you might be ahead of me. I'm convinced of it, Gran."

The jingling sound of the covered buggy's harness came from the lane. "They're here." Ailse eased herself out of her chair. "I'm glad I put the kettle on. We'll talk mair, lass. 'Tis nae secret that

Mary cannae show her soul easily, and the twa o' ye han't been great guns o' friends, but see what ye can make on't tonight."

The door opened and Catriona, Morag, Mary, Fiona, and Isobel poured in on a draft of cold air while Mac led the horses toward the barn. Mary quickly offered to make the tea, almost bumping Maude out of the way in her eagerness. Maude was glad to simply listen to Catriona and Morag catch up, and to talk to Fiona and Isobel about their favorite horses, friends, and school.

The time went quickly. The sun had begun its descent when Maude and Mary pulled her buggy out of the barn, where Bobcat waited in relative warmth. Maude threw in Mary's carpetbag, which seemed a bit heavy for a one-night stay. She dismissed this observation, and the two of them climbed in.

"I'm happy that you're coming, Mary. I have a pot roast with some potatoes in the oven for later. It will be wonderful to have you there."

"Pot roast. Sounds divine—thank you so much. I hope you didn't go to too much trouble."

"Not at all. The guest room is one of the warmest rooms in the house. I think you'll enjoy it. It is well heated by the kitchen stove."

"Have you . . . enjoyed Ailse's book? There's so much knowledge there, it's amazing. A treasure trove of simple healing."

"It is wonderful. I started out wanting to copy the entire thing, but I realized that could take years."

"I'll do as much as I can this evening." Mary sounded as pert and chipper as Maude had heard her since her return. "At least that will be a start."

Maude had no intention of introducing the topic of Paul at this point. She wanted to get Mary to her house, have dinner and perhaps a relaxing glass of blackberry cordial or a cup of tea before venturing onto such dangerous turf.

Once they had arrived at Kettle Creek, she got the horse and buggy stowed and, upon entering the house, was relieved to find that it had not cooled off significantly during the afternoon hours.

After new fires in both the downstairs and upstairs stoves were lit, the place quickly returned to cozy warmth.

Mary served herself very little food, but Maude made no comments. After dinner, Maude retrieved Ailse's big book. "Some people would call this a grimoire," she said, laying the heavy notebook on the table in front of Mary. "It is, after all, a practitioner's journal, intended for a specific field of study." She paused and stared out the window, thinking of the unpleasant stone-throwing of Halloween. "Although as many times as we've heard people call Ailse a witch, I suppose I ought not use the word grimoire, since it can indeed be associated with magic."

Mary gave a short laugh. "People make such nonsensical accusations."

"You're right about that. Anyway, go ahead and get started while I do the dishes."

"Are you sure you don't mind? I could help you."

"No, there are only a few here." As Maude started to clean up, she heard Mary setting to work. Pages flipped, then there was the scratching sound of the pen. She knew Mary was after certain recipes or perhaps a home remedy, and she also knew that she herself didn't like being interrupted while she was writing, so she kept quiet.

Maude had placed the telegram on one of the highest shelves of her kitchen cupboards, where Mary would have no reason to reach. As she put away the last dinner dishes and brought out two teacups and saucers for tea, she glanced up at it, reassuring herself that it was ready when she needed it.

After pouring the tea, she was surprised to see Mary close Ailse's voluminous book and set down her pen. Mary then folded up her own slender notebook and tied it tightly with a ribbon.

"Done so soon?"

"My eyes are tired. I'd love a cup of tea."

After a few sips, Maude took a breath and plunged in. "You know, Rory has a friend who works for the Milwaukee Railroad. His name is Jack Spaulding."

Mary's eyes had been drifting around the kitchen, but they now came to rest on Maude's face. The air between the two women seemed to cool, so Maude knew she had to speak her piece. "Rory was worried about you this fall and he asked Jack to look you and Paul up."

Mary's jawbone shifted beneath the smooth skin of her cheeks. Her tongue darted out to moisten her lips. "And?"

"I don't want to tell you anything you already know far better than I do."

"Maude, why don't you tell me what you mean? You've always tried to make me look like a fool, and you're doing it again. What have you told everyone?"

"I haven't told anyone anything. I'm trying to help you."

Mary's mouth moved into the strained shape it always took when she grew angry. "When have I ever asked for your help? When have I ever *needed* your help? My big sister, who has everything, who has been treated like a princess since the day she was born." She rose and tossed her spoon onto the table. It clattered across and fell to the floor. "There is nothing wrong with my life, you . . . witch! You've always been a hellcat. No one can understand you. Look at you—you have a good man who wants you and you're playing hard to get. Who are you waiting for, Prince Edward? This Elliott fellow is honest and good. You can see it in his eyes, in his face. You're a blasted spinster, a *deliberate* spinster, and I'll never understand you. You want to live alone out here on Kettle Creek forever. You don't believe in romance or love or anything like it. And you propose to help *me*? Don't make me laugh!"

Maude's gut churned as she strove to repress her emotions. She tried to tell herself that the words coming out of Mary's mouth said more about Mary than they did about anything else. But despite her efforts to remain calm, the hair on her forearms stood up and her heart pounded. *Mounting rage, that's what's welling up inside me, pure and simple. I mustered my courage and entered this conversation feeling love for this sister of mine. For God's sake, she's clearly in trouble and needs a sister's love. Her world is falling down around her. But I reach out to her and all she can do is launch this vicious attack.* The desire to slap some sense into Mary was rising fast, faster than she could control.

Standing on the opposite side of the table, Mary sneered and fisted her hands. Maude looked at those hands, held waist-high, just beneath breasts swelling with pregnancy. What a fool Mary was to turn away from the only friend she had. She might as well be a rabid animal, snarling in a corner. It would have been one thing if this was the only instance Maude had ever seen of this behavior, but Mary had always been like this. No matter what she had done to build Mary up, to show her that she admired her or had confidence in her, Mary had been mistrustful and had snapped at her outstretched hand, just as she was doing now.

"All right, Mary," she said, her voice as taut as a steel wire. "If you want me to be one hundred percent frank with you, I will." She turned around and reached for the telegram, then set it flatly on the table.

When she focused on the yellow paper, Mary's eyes softened as though she *had* been slapped. They rose and sought Maude's for a fragile instant, one of the few moments of complete, unguarded honesty that had ever existed between them. Then her gaze dropped by degrees to the tabletop.

> RORY GRAHAM, LEWISTOWN, MT: No sign of Hathaway since Sept. Mary using last name of Graham. Working at Hoffman's Rstrnt. Hathaway has outstanding debts thru-out Milwaukee. Last known address Syracuse NY. Some law school. No record of degree. Will keep trying. Yr friend. J.S.

Mary's face went ashen as she leaned into the wall next to the Victrola. "He could still come back," she whispered. "No one knows what might happen in the future." Her arms were at her sides now, palms out, weakly entreating.

Maude's heart broke. Still, she held her distance. She knew Mary too well. If she went to her now and took her in her arms as she longed to do, Mary could turn on her again. "You're right, Mary. No one knows what the future may bring."

"He left as soon as I—"

"As soon as?"

"He . . . left at the end of September."

"And you've been supporting yourself ever since."

"Saving up to come . . . home."

"You're home now. You're safe. We all love you."

"It . . . it is good to be home." She sank heavily into her chair. "I—I'm sorry I said those things. It's none of my business about you and Rob Elliott. You can be alone if you want."

Maude resisted the barb and the old, familiar freight that had so many times calcified her conversations with Mary. Tonight, she would keep the peace. "I am glad you think well of him. I do also." She picked up the cups and tossed the cold tea out. "I think you could use just a spot of blackberry brandy instead of this tea," she said. "It will settle your nerves, maybe help you sleep."

Mary gave an odd little laugh. "Sleep. We'll see."

As Maude eyed her sister carefully, something brushed over her, making her turn quickly to the blue calico draperies to see if a window had been left open. No, it was not a draft. She knew then what it was, and she knew what was coming next: the deepening of her breath, involuntary and yet strangely calming. It was like a shiver of the soul, the effort of her psyche to integrate everything that was happening, or that might happen.

She let the fey feeling move through her. It passed, as it always did, like a breeze whispering through an aspen grove. In a matter of a few seconds, she was pouring the brandy. Something would surely come, probably tonight, and yet she had no way of knowing what it was.

Chapter Twenty-Two

Three days into the hunt, Rob began to wonder if their little party was ever going to find the infamous elk herd that roamed the valleys scoring the McNaughtons' portion of the foothills around the Snowies.

Jake Desmarais, the laird's guide, had taken them to the elk's favorite December haunts, but by Tuesday night, Bobby Gordon, one of the guests from back east, joked that the only elk he was likely to see during this visit was the one stuck up over the fireplace at the laird's Forest Lodge.

Rob liked Gordon, but he could have done without Jim Morgan, McNaughton's friend from West Virginia. The dining tent was a convivial place, where everyone lingered as long as possible near the warmth of the square tin pack stove before shuffling off to their individual tents, but once Morgan and the laird got into their cups in the evening, the conversation invariably turned bawdy, at the expense of Morgan's wife or any other woman whose name came up.

Rob and Grant got accustomed to joining Bobby Gordon in his tent, which was larger than the other private tents, for a simple hand of poker. Each guest tent had a small stove that Desmarais fired up in the early evening, and Bobby Gordon's crackled merrily throughout the card game.

"I hunted in the Tetons last year," Gordon told them. "Got

myself a nice bull elk. I was so impressed with myself that I hiked down into the gully to admire my kill. Then the strangest thing happened. Damned if my guide didn't appear in a stand of pines about 100 yards away and start shooting at me. 'For Christ's sake, Mick,' I hollers, 'if you wanted this one, why didn't you tell me?' I grabbed my rifle, figuring I ought to shoot back."

"I would have done the same thing," said Grant.

"Well, then I hear this grunting sound behind me. Turned around and sure enough, there's the biggest damned grizzly I ever saw. Mick saved my life that day. Killed that bear with two shots."

After an hour of storying and banter, Rob adjourned to his own shelter. Pausing to look up at the sky, his lips curved into a smile as he saw that not a single star was visible. With any luck, they'd have a blanket of snow by morning and they just might find that herd.

The hunting party rose early, invigorated by the flakes coming from the dark sky and accumulating thickly on the ground. After breakfast, they rode a good mile and a half into the pines with Desmarais well in the lead, looking for elk sign. Two packers with several mules brought up the rear.

The morning sun was a fuzzy lemon yellow dot behind the falling snow when Desmarais came back at a quick trot, telling them to dismount and follow him on foot. After twenty minutes of silence, the men could hear the piercing sound of a bugling elk. Senses heightened, rifles at the ready, they fanned out according to the guide's instructions. It was their good fortune that the elk were in a narrow canyon. The men positioned themselves where each one had a fair chance of achieving a kill even after others had taken the bull of their choice.

Alert and ready, Rob sat in his perch among some rocks, downwind from the herd. Half an hour later, when the melee was over, he scrambled down into the canyon to examine the six-point bull he'd taken. The elk wasn't perfectly symmetrical, but he was darn close.

It was hard to turn his trophy kill over to the packers, but it was part of hunting party etiquette, and he knew they were skilled at their trade. The head and cape would be delivered to a taxidermist in Great Falls, and he'd see it in three months, after paying a fine price. The meat would be wrapped in white packets with his name on them, then stored at the Palace Meat Company in Lewistown, courtesy of the laird.

It was a flushed and boastful group that made its way down the mountainside toward Forest Lodge that afternoon. Silver and leather-bound flasks went around innumerable times, accompanied by many rehearsals of how the elk had poured through the mouth of the canyon, and the firing of each priceless shot.

The hour was late and, like the rest of the men, Rob was slouched in one of the well-worn leather chairs in front of the fire at Forest Lodge. The warmth of the lodge was luxury enough after three nights with nothing but canvas between him and the elements, but as he glanced around, Rob couldn't help being impressed with the well-appointed elegance of the place. Balancing his glass of claret on the plump arm of the chair, he watched the flames dance in the massive stone fireplace. Across the flagstone floor were scattered Turkish rugs of various lengths and patterns, and the dark-stained pine walls were studded with animal mounts and engraved prints of European cataracts and woodlands.

He was done with his hunt and glad of the outcome. It had been good to spend this time with Grant, and he felt he'd mended fences to some degree with the laird, although things would probably never be the same between them. He had dark suspicions about Thomas McNaughton, suspicions that seemed to only get worse with time.

The laird was as avuncular as ever, slapping him on the back after dinner and congratulating him on getting the biggest bull. Rob knew this wasn't easy for McNaughton, who almost always bagged the largest animal on any hunt in which he participated.

Now, around the fire, McNaughton took up the topic of wolfing, and waxed passionate about his plans to kill the Adrad, describing him to the out-of-state guests as "the great gray wolf that roams the Missouri Breaks and the Judith Basin, eluding capture for untold years."

"I'll get the auld gray bastard one day," McNaughton said, standing up to fill his glass again. "And it willnae be the coward's way, with strychnine. I'll take him on a level playing field."

Rob kept still, remembering the tale he'd heard at the Elkhorn Saloon about the Adrad's ability to detect poison. He felt nothing but admiration for the alpha male.

"Isn't it true," said Bobby Gordon, "that wolf predation on cattle and sheep has declined sharply since the turn of the century? I've heard that wolves are almost wiped out in Montana. Seems to me they're being killed more because they are feared than because they represent any real threat to livestock. What's the point in killing the old fellow now?"

"Been attending some kind o' classes, Bobby?" The laird winked at him and sipped his claret.

"Actually, Bobby's right." Rob spoke up, avoiding the narrow gaze of the laird. "The number of wolf pelts turned in for payment hasn't been above five thousand since 1898. At the Stockgrowers Convention last spring, the formal report was that the pelts taken last year were well below fifteen hundred. The main gripe was that the state-funded bounties have gone too low. Anymore, wolfers hate wolves simply because the job doesn't pay."

"Still," said Bobby with a shrug, "a man has the right to protect his livestock."

"No one will argue with that," returned Rob. "I've got cattle myself."

The laird gave a low chuckle. "This talk is so serious, boys. Let's not be dull. As far as the wolfies go, you can cuddle up wi' the vairmints all you want. I'm a sportsman, and there's plenty like me all o'er the world. To us, wolves are fair game, and naught will ever change that." He stood up, restless, and moved to the window on the east side of the lodge, rubbing his thigh. "I think I'll take a moonlight stroll. Entertain yourselves. What's mine is yourn." He threw on a jacket and went out into the night.

After a hand of cards, Rob's mounting curiosity drove him to the same window on the east end of the room. The sky was cloudless and a full moon glowed like a lamp above. Because the trees had been partially cleared around the lodge, a wide mantle of smooth snow lay pale and pristine among the black trunks of the pines. Smooth, that is, except for a set of footprints leading straight east into the forest. Toward Maude's place.

His palms grew moist. Moving back toward the main group, he leaned against the back of the couch for a moment, then said, "I think I'll go out for a breather—then I'll probably hit the hay. G'night."

They tossed a jest or two in his direction but thankfully stayed focused on their game. He slipped out, grabbed his mackinaw, and made his way in the same direction that McNaughton had taken. He gave McNaughton's trail a wide berth, however, in case the laird returned sooner than later from his mysterious errand.

Not quite a quarter mile from the Lodge, he glimpsed a light in the trees. "Sweet Saint Peter," he whispered to himself. "He's in his hunting blind. What in the hell?" Crouching behind a boulder, he waited. McNaughton had been gone well over half an hour, and it stood to reason he'd have to come down soon.

Ten minutes went by, then fifteen. Finally, as the wet snow soaked uncomfortably into his boots, Rob heard scraping and thumping. A long leg appeared on the lodgepole ladder. The laird appeared, hopped to the earth, then retraced his steps directly toward the Lodge. He moved through the dark woods with such familiarity that he'd clearly done it many times before.

When Rob was sure that he could approach the treehouse undetected, he circled in from the side, bringing a fresh pine bough with him to brush away any footprints. Climbing quickly up, he unfastened the latch he himself had installed that past summer, opened the narrow door, and went in.

Fumbling about, he nearly knocked over the lantern, then righted it and lit the wick. Looking around, he could see nothing that would have kept anyone entertained in the tiny little space for the thirty or forty minutes that McNaughton had just spent there. *Books? Magazines? A hunting journal, perhaps? Nothing, just the telescope, the stool, a shelf with some ammunition and a few rags.*

A possibility seeped into him, chilling him worse than the brittle December night. He glanced at the telescope, then looked away. *It's too strange*, he thought. *No, if I considered it, then why wouldn't another man, someone more desperate?*

He looked at the campstool, scooted back a foot or two from the telescope. Grabbing it, he positioned it and sat down, taking great care not to bump the tripod. Measuring his breath as carefully as he had that morning when he sighted up the elk, he leaned forward and closed his left eye, peering cautiously into the expensive instrument.

There she was. In her kitchen, by the stove. She was wearing her robe, and her hair was pinned up.

If McNaughton watched her like this, tonight, how many other times had he done it? She feels private on Kettle Creek. She has no reason to think anyone could ever see her. Probably walks about in various states of undress. He felt sick. Swallowing, he quickly sorted through all the possible consequences of the situation. *God only knows what McNaughton might be contemplating.*

Rob's jaw was so tight his head began to ache. His fingers curled into white-knuckled fists. He didn't want to terrify Maude, but should he tell her? Or at least take some overt action to keep this predator away from her? He had to get out of there and think.

He slapped the campstool upright and doused the lantern, then crammed the cold match through a crack in the window. Fastening the door latch and scrambling down the ladder, he covered his tracks and leaned into a dead run.

As his eyes adjusted to the night, his confidence grew and his stride lengthened. His feet easily found patches of ground that the snow had not touched. Like a wild animal, he left no trace of himself.

He felt more powerful than normal; that was undeniable. He didn't know if it was because the more he discovered about Thomas McNaughton, the more the man revealed himself as a reprehensible bastard, or because Rob had come to believe he'd lay down his life for Maude Graham. Maybe it had to do with the eerie family legend about wolves. Right now, he didn't have time to think about it. The woods became more and more familiar as the cold air whipped past his ears. It was this same forest, he remembered, that he had ranged so freely that fateful night with the wolves.

He overshot the Lodge on purpose so he could return from his supposed evening stroll from the opposite direction. He circled behind a cluster of enormous boulders, then leaned up against a stout white pine two hundred yards west of the Lodge.

Taking a deep breath of the alpine air, he smoothed his ruffled hair, then sauntered down the trail and found all the men, including the laird, standing on the broad back porch, smoking cigars.

"An' it please ye, what be doon in that teacup that's caught yer fancy?" Ailse regarded her youngest daughter, Morag, curiously.

Morag threw her head up and pushed back her hair. "I don't know. I don't normally look at the leaves, but something made me do it tonight. And I came up with such a strange pattern."

"Did ye swirl the tea three times widdershins?" Ailse, who had been standing near the window, came to look.

"Always. Look. Two knives and a flag. It gives me a chill." Morag pulled her shawl tighter.

Ailse clutched her stick and walked back to the window, thumping softly on the carpet as she went. The clock on the mantel struck half past ten, and a gust of wind muttered against the windowpanes. She stood there, staring straight down the lane through the double row of trees, toward the big house. "There's summat faul afoot this night, Morag. Sure as I'm Ailse MacDougall. Things are knittin' themselves thegither in my haid."

She turned around and faced Morag, both hands knotted around her stick. "The fairst thing tae worrit me was that my wee measurin' cup is gane. Ye ken, the fine glass piece ye gave me wi' the engravit calibrations. Then young Rory asked me what Mary would want from the Fredrich's rye silo, the one they say be tainted. He said Mary rode o'er yonder this Monday past. I didnae tell ye, Morag, but Maude is fair certain our Mary is wi' child. An ye ken as weel as I what a desperate lass micht want wi' moldy rye."

"Rye mold. *Ergot.* My God. It's one of the most powerful abortive agents I know." Morag's hand flew to her lips. "Not only that, when they came to the train depot, Mary had a small package from Powers' Mercantile. For all I know, she could have bought *nux vomica* as well."

"There be plenty o' that in town, with wolfing season upon us. Strychnine is cheap."

Morag inhaled raggedly. "In minute doses, strychnine sometimes works to end a pregnancy, but it's extremely dangerous and more often than not, it ends the life of the mother as well."

As the two women stared at each other, the clock ticked loudly and the wind moaned in the chimney.

"Morag, we dinnae need a ball o' crystal and scryin' tools to tell us we need to hie to Kettle Creek. Will ye help me get the buggy hitched, quiet-like?"

Within a half hour, two slender, black-clad figures were hunched in the Grahams' small buggy, bumping along the grassy back lane out of Stony Creek Ranch.

Rob lay in one of the upstairs rooms at Forest Lodge, three doors down from the master suite occupied by the laird. The place was quiet, save for the stertorous breathing of Jim Morgan in the room next to his own. The notion of sleep set Rob's jaw. He was far too busy nursing his wrath. He had managed to finish out the evening on the back porch with a brief show of good spirits. Finally alone in his own room, he had carefully noted when Desmarais moved across the lawn with a lantern, retiring to his private cabin a hundred yards away.

Now, in the dark stillness of midnight, his anger and his desire to get away devoured him. He wanted to see Maude, even if it was only for an hour. He had no reason to fear for her immediate safety, but his sudden awakening to her vulnerability and her perilous exposure to McNaughton—and *God only knows how long all this has been going on*—made him crazy.

What manner of man was McNaughton? All that Rob had witnessed tonight left no question that the man was capable of the worst kind of depraved lewdness. *Did he intend to force himself on Maude? At minimum, he was some kind of perverted hedge-creeper.* Yet Rob knew it was more. He had the measure of Tom McNaughton enough to know he was obsessed with power and conquest. If he had already hurt Maude in some way—well, the thought was untenable.

He had to see her, touch her, make sure she was all right. Tight as a spring and sorely aware that sleep would never come, he stole out of bed to examine the latches on the windows. By now the moon had passed its midpoint and was perched in the western half of the dark sky, illuminating the snow-dusted lawn around the lodge. If he could open one of the windows quietly, he could get out, go to Kettle Creek, and return undetected before sunrise.

When he turned the casement crank, there was a reedy creak. Grasping the window frame to lighten the load on the hinges, he was able to open it without a sound. Then, just when he expected complete silence, he heard music. Someone was outside, playing the damned harmonica.

Keeping his head low, he peered over the sill. There was Desmarais in his striped blanket coat, walking along the perimeter of the frozen lawn. The low tunes of a campfire song drifted up. Just as the tracker reached the upper end of the lawn, he pivoted and strolled toward the next corner, his black and tan hound prowling along behind him.

Rob sank back on his heels. Even if he could evade Desmarais by jumping from the window at the right moment, he couldn't fool the dog. Dropping his head into his hands, he cursed, vowing to leave at first light.

Chapter Twenty-Three

Maude retired earlier than usual, worn out from adversity with Mary. Sleep was slow in coming, however. She was on edge, wishing things were different. On the one hand, she had to admit that things had gone better than she'd expected, but in the long run, she'd begun to believe that she and her sister might never understand one another. She loved Mary, that much she knew, and for now, that would be the wind that filled her sails.

She took a deep breath, glad that Rob had brought a generous load of kindling into her bedroom. The little potbellied stove in the corner blazed brightly. *Was he sitting somewhere in front of a fire right now, celebrating a successful hunt?* Watching the orange glow flickering through the black cast-iron plates, she hoped he was warm and well-fed, wherever he was.

Relighting the lantern, she reached for the volume of Burns's poetry he had left on the bedside table, but her hand stopped. *Was that a noise in the kitchen? Curious. Mary went to her room a good two hours ago. I never heard a thing the entire time I took my bath in front of the stove.*

The stirring downstairs persisted. Ajax heard it too, letting out a low growl. She sat up stiffly, setting the book aside. The fey feeling she'd had earlier that evening whistled sharply through her. Shoving her feet into her slippers, she tiptoed down the stairs. At first, all seemed quiet.

Then she heard it—a mewling, gagging sound coming from the far corner. It sounded like an animal. Snatching the iron poker from the stove, she edged slowly around the table, holding the lantern high. Nighttime incursions by wildlife were not unheard of in remote areas of the Basin.

But no. There, curled and writhing in the corner, was Mary. Lurching up on one elbow, she let loose a stream of black vomit, entirely missing a large dishpan. "Get . . . away," she gurgled, glaring at her sister with bloodshot eyes.

"Mary—you're ill!"

"By . . . my own . . . hand."

Maude's mind moved like a scientist's over the scene, gathering the physical evidence, collecting the data she'd observed for weeks, remembering every detail of her sister's predicament. *Abortion. Self-induced abortion.* She fell to her knees. "What have you taken? Tell me! While you still can, Mary. Tell me what you've taken."

Mary lay back, gasping, her white gown smeared with dark emesis. Then, without warning, her arm hinged out and her fingers landed on Maude's wrist like claws, digging in with a fierceness that made Maude cry out. Mary sat bolt upright and her mouth fell open. She stared at Maude for an instant, then she folded in half, screaming.

"God have mercy on us," Maude cried, then stifled a curse. If there was any clue to be had in Mary's room, she had to find it fast. Wrenching her forearm loose, she floundered to her feet, raced down the hall, and burst through the guest room door.

Mary had not concealed anything. There in plain sight on the dresser were all the tools of poison. Maude recognized Gran Ailse's glass measuring device, and next to it lay a waxed package of strychnine from Powers' store, along with a medical journal open to a section entitled, "Therapeutic Abortion." Mary had underlined a sentence instructing the physician to administer a tincture of *nux vomica,* the Latin term for strychnine, "at a dose of 5 minims every two hours until the fetus is expelled."

She scanned the dresser for more evidence. In a brown paper wrapper were several bits of what looked like moldy, misshapen kernels of wheat. Maude stared hard, her mind raking over everything Gran had taught her. She surmised that these kernels were either wheat or rye, and that they were deformed due to a grain fungus known as ergot, traditionally used to induce abortion.

Either drug would have been dangerous enough, but Mary had taken both. Maude's mind became crystal clear. Mary had begun vomiting, yes, but Maude needed to force liquids and induce a great deal more of the same. She grabbed the medical guide and dashed to the kitchen, flopping it on the counter. She then opened her apothecary cupboard to compound the proper emetic.

Mary's screams were a nonstop, blood-curdling horror, nothing like the intermittent labor pains Maude had seen in full-term pregnant women. She became distracted, not knowing whether to turn back to the medical book to look up the effects of ergot or to proceed with the business of creating the emetic. She raised her hand to her clammy forehead and felt as if she herself was about to be sick.

A shadow in the doorway startled her, and her hand bolted automatically toward the shotgun standing in the corner. She ducked to the side, but as she did, she saw faces in the window. Ailse and Morag.

"*Cailleach!*" She flung open the door. "Get in here."

"Where is she?" Ailse spun to the left, locating Mary by her groaning.

"How—" Maude gasped.

"No matter," said Morag. "We just knew. Part simple deduction, part wise women. It's strychnine and ergot, isn't it?"

"Yes. I'm about to mix oil and milk. That's what I use for the dogs, and that's what she's going to get." She turned to the icebox and grabbed the milk jug, then reached for the large bottle of sweet oil in the cupboard. "I don't know if she's convulsing or what. I think it'll take all three of us to get this stuff down her throat."

"If she has taken both substances, I don't see how we can save the baby," said Morag, fumbling with the stopper on the oil bottle. "If we do, it will be a miracle. We may not be able to save her womb, either. I'm just praying the muscle tissue of the uterus doesn't rupture. If it does, your sister . . ."

"Hush now," said Maude. "Hold this glass steady. I've got some tubing if we have to use it." In a moment the mixture was ready. Their attempts to get Mary to sip the stuff from a small tumbler were ridiculous. Mary was so combative and delirious, most of it ended up on their clothes and on the kitchen floor.

Ailse asked, "Have ye got a wee bobbin, ye ken, for thread? We maun tie a cord round it and use't tae keep her jaws apen. The cord'll keep it frae slippin' doon her thrait."

Morag held Mary's hands while Ailse put the bobbin arrangement in Mary's mouth. Maude got the rubber tubing and the funnel ready. Whenever Mary took a breath between screams, they forced the milky stuff down. After several ounces, Mary retched, heaving into the basin.

"Again," Morag commanded, and they continued the procedure. After a grueling series of repetitions, Mary vomited twice, getting rid of even more black bile. Morag and Ailse both shook their heads when Maude, tube in hand, looked inquiringly at them.

"Pull the bobbin and let the lass be," said Ailse. "'Tis mickle hard tae watch, but she needs ever' ounce o' strength to pass this dark night and come oot t'other side." Ailse dragged herself a few feet away and motioned to Morag and Maude, who crawled toward her. In a low whisper, stealing glances at Mary, she said, "I cannae believe there is nae bleedin' yet. If she doesnae bleed, we may have caught this in time." She drew her gnarled fingers over her eyes. "Faith, I dinnae ken."

Maude sat back on her haunches, staring at her sister, who was no longer wailing, just moaning and twitching. "We can move her to the guest room now, I think."

"Let's clean her up a bit first." Morag rose and headed for the sink, returning with a ewer and a pile of dishtowels.

Clean and wrapped in Maude's muslin robe, Mary was carried

to her room and placed on the bed. With the filth gone from her red gold hair and the ivory muslin framing her face, Mary was so pale that the freckles across her cheeks and nose stood out like the delicate pattern of butterfly wings.

Morag buttoned herself into her nightgown and prepared to crawl into bed with the ashen form of her niece.

Maude's eye's searched the room and hall. "Where's Gran?"

"She's out walking 'round the house."

"Oh." Maude glanced out the window, but it was dark as pitch. Her brows peaked in momentary consternation. "Is she going deasil or widdershins?"

Morag's head turned. "Now there's a good question."

Walking three times clockwise, known as deasil, around a person or place was a practice in the Highlands, older than recorded history, supposed to bring about an auspicious outcome. Walking counterclockwise, or widdershins, was done to drive away ill will or evil spirits.

"Hard to say which might be best tonight," Morag concluded.

Hard indeed. Maude wanted to disconnect herself from what was happening with Mary, to rewind the train of events as she had rewound the thread onto a clean bobbin. She appraised the room, satisfying herself that she was really ready to leave it. The poisons were gone, the bureau was swept clean except for Mary's ribbon-bound notebook. The bed was large, with a trundle, so Ailse and Morag could be relatively comfortable there, although no one would be sleeping much.

Taking a last look at Mary from the doorway, Maude shook her head and went to the kitchen. When she heard Ailse come in the side door and go into the bedroom, she let out a sigh of relief, glad to be alone. The thoughts she had been fighting all evening broke through, filling her with bitter censure. *It seems*, she reflected, her teeth clamped tight, *that my dear sister Mary has made her bed but is unable to lie in it, so she must drag us all down with her.*

She poured a cup of coffee and hauled the medical journal in front of her. As she dropped, bone-weary, into a chair, she rested her chin on her hand, wanting to cry. *Yet*, she thought, *I am too tired to be angry. As far as women go, each one is strong and weak, and my sister is no different from the rest.*

A line formed between her brows and her jaw shifted from side to side as her thoughts darkened again. *But is Mary trying to improve herself, to work with the hand she's been dealt? As far as I can tell, the answer is no. When will she stop thinking only of herself? She is so often envious of me, yet she preens constantly, implying that I ought to be envious of her. Her outlandish notions persist despite her being belted in the face with reality . . . lofty notions of ideal love, convictions that she is entitled to success without effort. That day she stood at the garden gate and accused me of being vain . . . it was as though she was describing herself.*

I can't change her, Maude concluded, her lips in a thin line. *But I'm not going to keep exposing myself to her recklessness, either.*

She turned her attention to the journal and began reading aloud. "When ergot is administered at the full dose described in this section, it will produce contractions unlike those of normal childbed labor. The force of these abnormal contractions is significant and sustained, and will not cease until the child is expelled or until the patient is physically exhausted."

She continued, her fingers knotted in her hair. "The tissues of the womb, generally thought to be muscular and durable, are placed under great strain when subjected to the force of the ergot drug. Among the physical dangers present in the administration of this drug, lacerations and hemorrhage should be the physician's chief concern, as either may result in death."

The hand that gently shook her shoulder in the morning was Rory's. He had gone to the barn at Stony Creek very early and, seeing the missing buggy, quickly discerned that Ailse and Morag were absent. Knowing as much as he did about Mary, it was a short leap to the conclusion that there was trouble at Kettle Creek.

"In less than an hour, Mother and Dad will be here," he said. "If you can tell me what to say to them, I'll ride back and break the news so that we don't have a—a scene, I guess."

While Rory sat at the kitchen table, Maude told him everything. His auburn lashes downcast, he fidgeted with a wedge of kindling the entire time. Maude respected the bond between Rory, Mary, and Fiona. She heard him swallow at different points in her tale, and knew he was wishing Mary's pain away. At the end, he rose and walked to the window, yanking out his bandanna to blow his nose.

Morag came to the kitchen looking weary. Stoking the stove, she brewed a fresh pot of coffee. "Ailse is keeping watch," she said through a yawn. "Someone needs to stay with Mary full-time in the event she wakes up and becomes emotional. We dosed her with laudanum in the night, and we'll continue until she seems more accepting of her situation. At present, she is clearly a source of harm to herself and her child. If we don't keep her calm, we may have to consider a sanitarium, and I am sure none of us wants that, especially Mary. Someone will have to be with her constantly until we feel more confident about her frame of mind. And until we know the fate of the child."

"Rory," said Maude, "We have no choice except to tell Mother and Father the full story. I have given this a great deal of thought and I honestly feel there is nothing to be gained by keeping this from them. We need to support Mary. She has behaved foolishly, but I have to believe it is only because she is in terrible pain. She needs us now more than ever."

Rory nodded. "I agree. It'll take a while for everything to register with Mother. She has been living in a fantasy—just as much as Mary, if not more. She'll come over here as soon as she has gotten a grip on the situation. And on herself. I can't say how Father will react."

Maude bit her lip, picturing John's hands clenching and unclenching, the tousled gray hair quivering on his head as his neck muscles worked with rage. "Silently, I think."

"We can predict that much, yes." He pulled on his coat and went out into the bright morning.

"Aye, it'll be after Epiphany, sometime in January." McNaughton strutted along the back porch of Forest Lodge in the crisp morning air, hands stuffed into the pockets of his tweed jacket, pontificating on his quest for the Adrad. "I'll take my eight-millimeter Mauser and track that banshee up into Arrow Creek or where'er he cares to go. He knows I'm comin' for him. And I'll bring Desmarais with me. Best tracker there is. All you braw lads can vouch for that, aye?"

A chorus of "ayes" went up from the men, who were saddling their horses for the ride out.

"Best tracker there is," the laird repeated. "I hear the old Adrad has a bonny black bitch and a litter o' new pups. They'll slow him down. He may think he can elude the Laird o' Judith, but not for long. Aye, that pack of his will slow the old fellow down."

Rob stood, head down, next to his horse in the wide corral. Every muscle in his body was tight. *Yes, old Tom, go ahead and stand there and tell everyone that great gray wolf lies around in the evenings thinking about you. Go ahead and assign a wild animal the same arrogant traits you possess. That just makes it more obvious that you think you've got heaven's own windpipe beneath your boot. If I've come to know anything, it's that none of us can truly comprehend the wolf, no more than any of us knows the eagle or the bear.*

He gave a solid tug at his cinch, trying to slow his breathing. He'd had every intention of leaving at first light, before everyone rose, but he told himself to hold steady, to act as though nothing was wrong. He'd put his feelings aside just long enough to make his farewells to Grant, promising to have a drink with him sometime over the holidays.

Powered by tension, he practically flew up into the saddle. Then, as the blue roan danced around, he tipped his hat to the laird. "Please give my heartfelt thanks to Desmarais. And Merry Christmas to everyone at the Rocking M."

"But Rob, my lad, where will ye be over Yuletide?"

"I've got plans," he shouted over his shoulder as he galloped down the hill, the roan's hooves thundering on the forest floor.

Chapter Twenty-Four

She knew exactly where she wanted to go; after all, she could find her way blindfolded after all these years. Bobcat was humpy, as her father would call it, not at all used to the saddle. "Don't get too uppity," she murmured, leaning forward to thump his neck a couple of times with the flat of her hand. "We're all-purpose folk up here on Kettle Creek."

The Basin was a still place. Now and then there was a sough of wind that felt a bit like a warm Chinook, but other than that, only the creak of saddle leather and Bobcat's hooves on the moss and pine duff. To Maude, the austere silence felt like an homage to the changing tide of the earth. Today was Yule, when the sun's road across the heavens would be shortest of all, and night would be long indeed. The cold air nipped at her cheeks and nose, waking her from the delirium of the past two days. None of this business with Mary seemed possible or plausible, but it was real, every bit of it. Throwing her hood back, she let the air wash over her. Coming here, to the place on the east edge of her property that she and Ailse called the Thick Pines, was good medicine.

It wasn't far to the spot where she and Ailse had always gathered Christmas greens, including the best bearberry—or kinnikinnick, as the Indians called it—anyone in Lewistown had ever seen. The stuff looked like the boxwood of old Scotland, and made the Graham's wreaths and Yule logs the pride of Judith Basin.

At an opening in the woods, she pulled Bobcat to a stop and cast her eyes east, where rolling hills and pine-covered bluffs obscured the compound of houses at Stony Creek. The hills and Big Spring Road far below lay in purple morning shadows, and behind them the rising sun turned the morning clouds to layers of copper and rose.

Dismounting in the dense ramble of pines and boulders where she and Gran had always done their cutting, she quickly found the loamy sections of forest floor that favored the low-growing plant. Pruning away a few lush branches, she tied them with twine and rolled their trailing ends into a loose ball, tucking them into the saddle bags.

The morning sun pierced the cloud cover for a moment and was gone again. The wheeze of a gray jay cut the air, sounding for all the world like the tin whistles she and the other children used to get in their Christmas stockings. A tear was in her eye. She wanted to see Rob. She wanted to sit across the table and look at him, to hold his hand in her palm and examine those calluses she had seen on Thanksgiving night, to ask him how he'd gotten each one.

The gray jay's call came again, but this time it was followed by what sounded like laughter. Girls laughing. Maude raised her head and turned to listen. For a moment, her mind raced over Gran Ailse's stories of the wee folk and pixies. She couldn't keep herself from glancing around the shadowy grove, where the shifting clouds and uneven spears of sunlight cast a little world of magic.

No, the laughter was far below. Big Spring Road. She took a few quick steps toward the edge of the trees and looked down. There, a few hundred yards away, were Fiona and Isobel, on their way to school, sending up a lively racket as they bounced along in the wagon.

She wanted to shout a greeting, but she knew they couldn't possibly hear. Then, just as she was about to turn and go, a patch of color on an abutment below her caught her eye. She slid behind the shelter of a juniper and watched. It was a man, lying prostrate on a broad rock ledge above the road, watching her sisters through a crenellation in the row of uneven boulders. Next to him lay two rabbits, evidently just taken from a trap. But at the moment, he was far more interested in the Graham girls than in trapping rabbits.

Maude felt like she had swallowed something vile. It bubbled in her throat, but it wouldn't come up, nor would it go down. Her hands went ice-cold.

He wore a tan coat and dark trousers. The profile of the lantern jaw, the way his left leg was stretched out, along with the conformation of thigh, hip, and torso . . . everything about him coalesced, and as it did, she felt every ounce of reason she possessed drain out of her, reamed away, replaced by scarlet rage.

In three paces she had her hands on the rifle, deftly slipping it from its scabbard. Sinking down, mindless of the wet moss and rotting leaves, she steadied herself. Her blue eyes aligned the long barrel. There was no hesitation, no shaking or tremor. She simply aimed and fired. The report filled the entire valley.

Knifing the gun back into its sheath, she whipped Bobcat's reins off the branch, slammed into the saddle, and gave him a solid kick. The horse reared, rolled his eyes white, and bolted forward.

Blair McNaughton scrambled to his feet. A layer of dust still hung in the air from where Maude's bullet struck the rocks over his head. A taunting smile twitched around his lips as Bobcat danced down the slope of loose rock.

"Thanks for parting my hair."

"You're on my land. And what the hell are you doing watching my sisters?"

He stared at her for a moment. "Everyone watches the Graham girls." The smile widened into a grin. "I'm going to be real disappointed in you if you say you didn't know that."

"Everyone? Only idle loafers with a penchant for vice. Where's your horse?"

Blair nodded to a clump of junipers some distance away. "You know what I think? I think if you were as honest as I am, you'd admit that life's pretty lonely without a bit of wickedness to spice things up now and then." He took a few bold steps toward her. "From what I've heard, you know a thing or two about wickedness."

Maude swallowed thickly. "You're daft. Get on your horse and get off my land. Your family has more than enough acreage for trapping. Don't come here again."

He shifted his weight fully onto one leg. Maude couldn't tell if he was preparing to collect his things and go, or settling in for a confrontation. "Yes," he drawled, "living with only a mob of bleating sheep can make a person go plain skite after a while. It's only human nature to want a little company."

He looked over his shoulder at her as he leaned over to pick up the rabbits, then ambled off toward his horse. Maude stayed put until he rode past her on a deer trail some distance below, heading south toward the McNaughton fence line. Only when she saw him get down, pass through the gate, and remount, did she turn Bobcat up the hill and walk slowly through the pines toward home.

Chapter Twenty-Five

The air cooled in the afternoon and tiny grains of snow floated on the air. She had just finished tacking up the first of several bundles of juniper and fir onto the porch timbers when she heard rapid hoofbeats on the lane. Rob dismounted, strode onto the porch, and captured her in his arms.

She let out a laugh, almost dropping the hammer. "Welcome back."

He kept his arms tight around her, holding her fast.

"Is everything all right?" She pushed against his chest, looking up at his face.

"Sure. I just missed you." He stared into her eyes, offering a soft smile.

She returned the smile, assessing him for a fraction of a second. "Put your poor horse in the barn, then come in."

He told her all about the hunt, avoiding any mention of what he'd discovered about McNaughton's hunting blind. After she told him about Mary, he was doubly glad he hadn't added to her burdens. They sat in silence for a while as the whisper of snow crystals blew against the windowpanes and the pitch pine popped in the wood stove.

Ajax lay stretched out, dead tired, near the stove. Rob leaned over slightly, listening. "Ajax's stomach is growling."

"Borborygmus."

"What?"

"Stomach rumbling."

"Where do you come up with this stuff?"

"It's a medical term. I read a lot."

"If you ever say that about my innards, I'll go sleep in the barn."

She drew a finger along his palm and smiled. "I'd just follow you."

His face grew serious again. "Is the baby—"

"We don't really know. We think we may have saved it, but only time will tell."

"How's your father doing?"

"He wants to kill Paul."

Rob shook his head. "If it were my daughter, I'd feel the same way."

Maude stretched her arms out on the table and put her head down. "It has been a long week. And now it's Christmas. When I went out to cut boughs this morning, it felt wrong to go through the motions of festivity, but I think the Grahams need it. I'm taking a load of them over to the big house, in case it hasn't occurred to them to put up any greens."

Rob touched her hands again, then moved to her left wrist, pushing her sleeve up to stroke her arm. "What's this?" He traced the soft skin of her forearm, gently following the pattern of three parallel scars.

Maude's chest quickly rose and fell but she did not withdraw her arm. Dragging her long lashes open, she brought her eyes up to meet his. "I—I took a blood oath once."

"A blood oath. Another family custom?"

She breathed out a little laugh. "It isn't some kind of witchy tradition, if that's what you're asking." There was a long pause, then she looked down at the scars. "No, this was something else. It was an oath I took when I entered womanhood. I . . . vowed that I would never marry."

The sun pooled on her outstretched arm, lightening the narrow band of lace on her sleeve to bright whiteness and turning the three scars to ribbons of silver. She made no attempt to cover herself. Bringing her eyes back to his, she studied his reaction.

He simply looked at her, those green amber eyes of his betraying nothing. There was a slight movement of his jaw. Anger? No, there was not enough force there to imply genuine anger. She had the sense that he was weighing what she had just told him along with other information, a great deal of other information. It was then that she began to feel ill at ease.

"That was quite some time ago." He said it softly, but his fingers ran around her wrist.

"I am not that old." She gave another laugh, jutting out her chin.

"That's not what I mean, Maude."

She wanted to joust with him; better still, she wanted to get up and suggest that they go out and finish putting up the Yule greens. Or dig out the buffalo robes for the twenty-minute buggy ride to Stony Creek.

Rob read her face in a heartbeat. "I won't ask you anything else about it. Not today. But I will ask you to think about the relative wisdom a young girl might have about the next sixty years of her life."

A spark flew off a dark, flinty place in her. Her lips came together, tight, and she forced back the dampness that threatened at the corners of her eyes. "There's a damn lot you don't know, Rob Elliott."

He bolted out of his chair and swung around the end of the table, yanking her to her feet. Bringing his face close to hers, he spoke in a fierce whisper, his voice full of something she'd never heard before. "There's even more *you* don't know, Maude, if you don't have sense enough to trust someone who would die for you."

He knew he was being rough, but he couldn't stop. Not now. Not until he knew she was completely safe. He glanced at the west window. Even at this very moment, someone might be watching. The only way to end the evil that hung like a malevolent cloud around Maude was to step fully into her life. He would be gentle when and if he could, but she was making it damned difficult.

Maude's lips quivered and the tears she'd held back came tumbling down. Her head dropped against his shoulder as she let out a tight sob. Ajax came out of his bed by the stove and wove his slender body between their legs.

"Maude, you've just got to trust me." Rob held her against his chest. "You've been alone forever and you're the bravest woman I know. I'll never take that away from you. But I'm not leaving."

It was close to eight o'clock when Catriona heard Rory come through the front door.

"We loaded thirty-nine sacks of parcels and mail onto the eastbound tonight, and it'll be even worse tomorrow," he said, collapsing into one of the oak chairs around the kitchen table. He twisted his neck and shoulders one way, then the other. "Everyone knows if their gifts are going to make it to Philly or Boston, the fourteenth is the last day they can ship. Christmas is grand, but I never looked at it from a railroad man's point of view before."

Catriona trimmed the last of several dozen pieces of string that would be laced into Christmas confections for the tree. "Think of yourself as a frontier Santa."

Rory rolled his eyes, then reached for one of the covered crocks on the stove. "Mac and Dad are still out?"

"They're out with the herders, getting the bands tightened in. I still can't believe we have four thousand sheep." She shook her head.

"They've added up, that's for sure." Rory waited a moment, then asked the question that had been on his mind all day. "Mary saw Doc Attix today, didn't she?"

Catriona gave a stiff nod. "I don't know why Fred had to call John Atchison over to consult on the case. At this rate all of Fergus County will know."

"Mother, they're ethically bound not to discuss their cases with anyone. I know that for a fact."

"But what about those nurses? That Mildred Dean is a blathering magpie." Catriona dropped the scissors into a drawer and gave it a shove with her hip.

"Mary must be a whole lot better, or you wouldn't be thinking about Mildred Dean."

Catriona folded her hands tightly over her midsection and leaned against the cupboard. "Yes. Yes, praise God in His heaven. She does seem well physically, and she's more—what is the word the doctor used—stable. We are reducing the laudanum dose. And as for the baby, Dr. Attix said he may have detected a heartbeat. I—I'm not sure, but I think I saw a ghost of interest in Mary's face when he said it. A blessing, that."

"I'll tell you what's a blessing. It's Aunt Morag. I'm darn glad she's staying on for a while. She's worth three doctors." As he dug into his mutton and carrots, Rory glanced up at his mother.

Staring into the air, she held her fingertips over her mouth. He knew she didn't realize she was shaking her head. He also knew she swam daily in disbelief about what had befallen Mary—moreover, about her own participation in her daughter's downfall. Catriona's chest rose sharply and fell. "I'll put the kettle on," she murmured, smoothing back some stray wisps of silver hair. "You—you haven't heard any more about—"

Rory cut her off, not wanting her to have to speak Paul's name. "No. How's Father doing with it all?"

"He said something about going to Milwaukee after the holidays. He wants to meet your friend Jack. Then he started talking about hiring a Pinkerton man. I don't think you can even do that. I mean, not if you're a private citizen." She lifted her hand in a futile gesture. "He's worse in the evening, after he's had a drink."

The back door seemed to blow open for a moment, but it was Mac's slender form sidling in on a blast of north wind. "Moses on a mattress, it's cold," he said. "Five below. I just looked."

"Are you picking up this foul talk from those music people? And where's your father?"

"We got the sheep in as close as we could. He and Kib culled out the weak ones and got them into the south shed. But they're coming now. Look, you can see the lantern."

Catriona went to the window and shivered. "Faith, it *is* cold. They've got enough firewood down at the bunkhouse, haven't they?"

"More than two cords. That's a lot. Mother, what does Gran mean when she says, 'a green Yule crowds the kirkyard'?" Mac pulled off his coat and slung it over a chair, blowing into his hands.

A smile lit Catriona's face. "That's what your great-grandmother Callie used to say at Christmas when she felt it wasn't cold enough to kill all the pests and cankers that made people sick. A wee bit of Scots folklore, is all." She let out a little huff. "Ailse was probably observing that we certainly haven't got that problem here in Montana."

Pulling the cloth covers off the remaining dishes, she arranged them on the table. "There. You're all set. There's one for Kib too. I'll be upstairs with Morag and Mary."

Tom McNaughton's rail trip to and from Butte passed more quickly than even he had expected. On the way to the prosperous mining city, he sat with Charlie Bair from Martinsdale, one of the few wool growers in the state more prosperous than himself. The two of them reviewed last August's outbreak of bluetongue and what could be done to prevent it next summer, concluding precious little in the end, and went through the wolf question like all self-respecting stockmen.

McNaughton took care to inquire lightly about Charlie Bair's mining interests, which he assumed were the reason for Bair's excursion to Butte. Bair warmed to the discussion, shaking his head as he reported that the big copper barons were making close to a million dollars a day on their holdings.

On the return trip forty-eight hours later, McNaughton watched as the Montana Railroad's new rotary plow chopped, inhaled, and blew out the snowdrifts, making short work of the frozen white dunes in the windswept Judith Basin. The passengers chatted noisily about the new contraption, acknowledging that with the purchase of the homely little railroad by the Milwaukee line, more modern advantages were surely on the way.

Even the first-class car was chilly, so McNaughton kept his plush shearling coat draped over his shoulders as he read the Butte *Miner*. Every now and then his hand would slip into his pocket, seeking the familiar shape of the small item there, and a hint of satisfaction would lift the corners of his mouth.

Two days later, on Christmas Eve, dressed with care in his gabardine trousers and polished boots, he ordered his elegant black-lacquered sleigh hitched up. The black stallion wasn't fit for the sleigh, so a chestnut mare was harnessed, and extra sheepskins along with a buffalo robe were thrown across the padded seat.

The runners made a sweet, violin-like sound on the road along the river. A layer of light snow overnight had brought a sense of newness to the world, and the brisk movement of the sleigh made every passing dogwood branch glisten as though it were encrusted with diamonds.

Diamonds, he thought. *What a day!* The mare took the turn up Kettle Creek Lane easily, with scarcely any suggestion from him. *It's as if she knows*, he thought. *This blessed morning, it's as if the whole world knows.* As he watched the cold, dark water of the creek shallowing under pearly panes of ice, his heart quickened with anticipation.

Maude leaned over a galvanized tub, flicking out the mucky detritus of leaves and hay. With a red wool scarf wrapped around her head and the entire world muffled under three inches of new snow, she didn't hear a thing. McNaughton jumped out of the sleigh, his long legs striding easily across the snow-covered grass. He was two yards away from her before she had fully straightened up.

"What are you doing here?"

"Maude, it's good to see you."

"What do you want?"

"Can we not wish one another a Good Yule, or Merry Christmas, as they say here in America? We've known one another a long time."

"I wish you and your family the best. You should be with them. Please be on your way. I am quite busy." She looked past him toward the south meadow.

"Maude, I've a gift for you." His hand slipped into his pocket. "I think it's time we started over, made things fresh between us. All this harsh yammering that's gone on. Cannae we be different from now on?"

Maude's head drew back as she regarded him suspiciously. The sun glimmered behind the fir trees, and as the wind moved their branches, her eyes were alternately dark as sapphires and light as the sky. "Where are you going with this talk?"

"I saw your father in town some time back." He stopped, seeming at a loss.

"What about my father?"

"Nothing about him. It's about you and me, and the future." He opened his fisted hand, then lifted the lid on a small velvet box. The sun struck a large square diamond caught in a filigree of gold. "I want you to be my wife."

Maude's jaw fell open. "You . . . spoke to my father about this?"

"Aye."

"And he said exactly what?" Her gloved hands, covered with rotten leaves and silt, began grinding the mess into a pulp between her tight fingertips.

"He said you were a woman of your own mind. As if I didn't know that." A grin spread across his face.

"Take your diamond and go."

The muscles in his face slackened; the auburn brows went up. He cocked his head to the side. "Now, Maude. Don't be rash. You know very well what has happened between the two of us. Do you think I haven't figured why you're alone out here, living like a spinster? It's because you've retired into the shade. All these years, never a sweetheart or a gallant. You know I've watched. I've ne'er stopped watching."

"My life is absolutely none of your business."

He put his hand over his heart. "Ah, but it is. I'm not a young man any more, and I've learned a thing or two. I'm saying this kindly now, but you're no blooming fresh rosebud. And we both know why. It's because I took you these many years gone by. Perhaps I shouldn't have, but there it is. What's done is done, and I mean to make an honest woman out of you. It's not out of duty either, it's because I want you. And I think there's a part of you that wants me. Don't tell me you don't think about me, because I know you do."

He reached for her chin and brought her eyes up. "Look at me and tell me you don't think about me, that you don't feel a bond with me still."

Maude stared hard and said between her teeth, "All right, Tom McNaughton. I do think about you."

A smile spread across his face. He leaned back on his heels. "There, you see?"

"But tell me this. What does it signify if I think about you?" Her voice rose against her will. She didn't want him to see that he riled her. That would mean letting him see who she really was. Nonetheless, something bore her along. As much as she wanted to beat it back, to silence it, she felt an awakening sense that this needed to be said. Not for him, no; he didn't matter. These words needed to be spoken for her, for her alone.

"What does it mean?" She stared straight at him, firing away. "Does it mean something wonderful and lovely? Is it a sign that I ought to commit my life to you because you . . . because you raped me? Is that something for a woman to build her life on? You're mad. If I think of you too often, it's not love or anything like it. It's a curse. It's the ugliest journey of survival that could ever be forced on an innocent girl. Because of you, I must find a way to break this . . . this "bond" as you call it, this thing that you did to me in the most brutal and inhumane way imaginable. I was a child, for God's sake! The fact that you think I could ever marry you only shows how demented you are."

His palm was still open. The sun glinted off the diamond. His eyes were on her, but his face was drawn. He stood silent, his lips pale. "Very well—I suppose I had that coming after all these years. But nothing can change the fact that you were mine from the beginning, Maude. Nothing will e'er change that. I'll keep the ring, for now, but I will be back." He closed the lid and slid the box into his pocket. "You can count on that."

They heard the scrape of the catchwire on the gate south of the barn. Rob Elliott appeared, a small evergreen tree hoisted on his shoulder. With his hip, he pushed the gate wide open, came through, and lay the tree down. The gate swung closed with a soft *clink*.

"Morning, Thomas. What brings you over this way?" Rob took several brisk strides and stopped next to Maude, not quite touching her. The same height as McNaughton, he met his gaze levelly.

McNaughton's eyes went from Maude to Rob and back again. Maude watched his jaw shift beneath taut, pale skin.

"It's a fine morning. I came with a brace of grouse for Miss Graham, 'tis all. A neighborly Christmas gift." He turned, adjusting his coat around his shoulders, walked, head high, back to the sleigh, and returned with a package wrapped in butcher paper.

"They were shot and plucked just yesterday. Not exactly a partridge in a pear tree, but still fit for the spirit of the season." His smile was stiff as he handed the parcel to Maude.

"Well, Rob, the boys miss seeing you. Cook brewed up a pot o' the McNaughton ginger brandy, so we'll welcome you down for a toddy any time." He tugged on his gloves. "I'll be off."

He stepped up into the sleigh, then guided the horse down the lane, disappearing among the thick stand of ivory and black aspens.

Rob pivoted around to stand directly in front of Maude. Raising his gloved hands, he held them tentatively in the air where they hovered in frustration. He wanted to lock them onto her shoulders, but finally he shook his head and dropped them to his sides. He was convinced that there was far more to all of this than Maude was telling him. *As sorry a scoundrel as Tom McNaughton is, however dark and filthy his habits, there is some part in all of this that Maude owns.* Despite everything, despite all that he felt for this solitary beauty, and as much of his soul as he had already given to the idea of a life with her, his senses were heightened and his hackles were up.

He formed his words with care. "I know you better than I did last summer when I was flat out unconscious in the back room of your barn. Right now you're trying to keep your breath even. You're trying to make sure I don't see how much he frightened you. You're trying to make sure you don't let on that he said something you don't want me to know about. You can't hide this from me anymore."

She looked away. "I asked you—"

"I know, you asked me not to discuss the matter of Tom McNaughton. I'm sorry, Maude, but I'm no longer satisfied with that. Not when he keeps coming between us."

"He's not between us!" She flung him a stormy look.

"How can you say that? You're not yourself right now, and nothing you can say to me will convince me that you are. You're a hundred miles away. He stirs you to something I can't even describe, something like . . . bad blood. I'm here looking at you and I can't tell what it is. Whether he's a stupid fool with the wrong idea or an evil snake with cunning designs too hateful to describe, he is most definitely between us, Maude."

Her nose dripped; she swiped at it with her glove. As she stared into Rob's searching eyes, she caught a flash of that scene on the

Campania deck. The idea of telling him, of confessing everything, flooded warm into her mind, sweet and wonderful, honest and complete.

How steadfast he looks just now, with the sunlight and shadow falling across his shoulders this brilliant morning. He might hear it all and take me in his arms, forgiving everything, seeing me clean and pure as the girl I once was. But the notion exploded, dashed like brittle flotsam against her granite-hard fear. "I detest Tom McNaughton." She bit the words out. "That's all you need to know. How could someone I detest come between us?"

His eyes locked onto hers. "Love and hate are dangerously close emotions, Maude. I'd feel a hell of a lot better if you were flat-out indifferent to the man." He turned away abruptly, grabbing the cut evergreen. "Someday the truth of this is all going to come out. My mother, God rest her soul, used to say, 'oil and truth will float uppermost at last.' I just hope—" he let out a huff of air and shook his head, picking up the tub with his other hand.

She wanted to say, "You hope what?" but she knew better. He was letting the subject alone, and if she had any sense, she'd let it go. He wasn't happy, but it was better to let this pass.

Rob was matter-of-fact. "After we get this tree up in your parlor, I'll ride alongside your buggy to Big Spring Road. Then I'm going up to my place to check on the cattle. Of course you'll want to be with your family tonight, on Christmas Eve. You need to be there, and I'll feel best if you are. I'll swing by Stony Creek tomorrow to see you and your folks."

The drive was mercifully brief. Maude offered light conversation about matters on Ruby Creek, asking about his plans to drill a well and to acquire another 160 acres. Instead of leaving her at the junction of Big Spring Road and Stony Creek Lane, however, Rob rode with her almost halfway up the lane, then leaned into the buggy and kissed her lightly. "Merry Christmas, Maude. I'll see you tomorrow." He wheeled his horse around and set off at a quick trot.

Maude dropped her face into her hands, listening to the sound of the blue roan's receding hoofbeats. There was a pain in her chest like she had never felt before. *What was happening?* All she knew was that the precious silken cord between her and Rob was fraying perilously; perhaps it had already snapped. Bitter tears flooded her eyes and spilled down her cheeks. "If he thinks I've got something going on with Tom McNaughton," she sputtered, "then damn him to hell. He can just ride up to Ruby Creek and rot with his stupid cattle and his annexed acres."

Everything had descended into confusion. Rob had seemed so protective of her lately, something that alternately flattered and provoked her. And now this. How things had come to this state of ruination was beyond her. McNaughton was part of her past, true, but her very distant past. Ancient history. Something to keep entombed, not something to exhume, risking the release of deadly vapors on everything dear to her. How had this vile man created so much havoc in her present-day life, a life that had been so full of new happiness?

She lifted her wet face and resisted the urge to snap the reins. She allowed Bobcat to move at his usual buggy pace down the lane, through the wide yard and into the welcoming dimness of the Stony Creek barn.

Chapter Twenty-Six

 Rob had barely reached Big Spring Road when he saw a rider approach from the north. There was no mistaking the piebald horse. Grant slowed his gelding and pulled him up nose-to-nose with Rob's roan.

"Merry Christmas, cowboy. Where you headed?"

"Back up to Ruby Creek."

"Come on down to the Rocking M for a hot brandy before you go."

"I don't think so, Grant. I've got to get."

"What's one hour? It's still early."

Rob's eyes went from Grant's face to his pommel and back again. A line of reasoning began to form in his mind. "You know, maybe I will."

He was relieved to find he was not the only guest at the Rocking M's open house. Far from it, in fact. The place was jammed with ranch hands and wealthy merchants and ranchers from Lewistown and other small hamlets around the Basin. In the great hall, Rob recognized Andrew Fergus, son of James Fergus, for whom the county was named. A number of prominent sheep ranchers were clustered around him, talking about the building materials the Milwaukee Railroad was bringing in by the carload every week. Touching his hat in a brief gesture of respect, Rob moved past, heading for the enormous den.

As he passed the front room, he glanced out the long row of

windows and saw the brothers—Blair, Grant, Lewis, and Charlie—
on the porch, laughing with some of the Rocking M workers. A
group of musicians was stationed in the dining room with fiddles
and mandolins, so the air was lively and festive. In the den, Rob saw
Tom McNaughton chatting near the gun cases with Alex Davidson,
one of the high-ranking hands from Charlie Bair's ranch.

Rob didn't know for certain, but he had a strong sense that
McNaughton had seen him. The laird, puffing on a large cigar,
opened a wooden humidor and offered one to Davidson, who put
up his hand in protest. Rob watched, then turned to the chafing pot
where the ginger brandy simmered. He knew he'd cross paths with
McNaughton soon enough. After a cup of the spiced brandy, he
felt even more equal to the task he'd set before himself. If Maude
wouldn't—or couldn't—tell him what was going on between her
and the laird, then he'd damn well find out on his own.

When an elbow landed in his ribs, he turned to find Blair standing
next to him. Blair set his drink down and stuffed his hands in his
pockets. He averted his eyes for a moment, then brought them
back to Rob. "How's things up on Ruby Creek?"

"Skiff of snow. Cattle are fat and happy. Thanks for asking." He
assessed Blair's mood, which seemed neutral. "You folks have got
yourselves a real nice party here."

Blair chewed his lip for a moment. "This music reminds me of
someone. She—" He glanced away, swallowed hard, then resumed.
"She told me once that Yule is meant for 'forgetting old wrongs.'"
He gave a half smile, but his eyes were bright.

"I'd agree with that," Rob said.

"I was up in the high country last week and . . . I saw something."
Blair spoke slowly, looking down at his drink. He was silent for
a moment as the sounds of the party continued around them. "I
found a couple of dead elk." He glanced at Rob, and Rob saw him
swallow. "They weren't just any old couple of dead elk. They were
two of the biggest bulls I've ever seen. Huge racks. But they were
locked together. They'd been fighting and they couldn't break
apart. Died like that." He stared at Rob, then flicked his eyes

away. After a moment, he added, "Say, I've got some of the good stuff in my flask. Thirty years old if it's a day."

Rob didn't need another drink, but thrust his cup forward anyway. "Sure."

After pouring, Blair tucked the flask away. Another moment passed as he gazed off into the crowd. "How 'bout we . . . let bygones be bygones?"

He swung his cup out and Rob met it with a clink, saying, "Here's to a Good Yule and a good future." With that, Blair edged his way back into the mass of smoke and laughter.

Watching the crowd close after him, Rob sipped the scotch and leaned against a massive hunt cupboard, absorbing what had just happened. Having Blair McNaughton make such a conciliatory gesture was not something he would ever have expected. Unlikely and curious as it seemed, it felt sincere, and Rob was glad of it.

"Rob, I'm glad you made it by." Thomas appeared, having edged his way through the throng in the main hall. "We would all have been disappointed to have the Yule pass without you. Here's a gift. From me and the boys." He shoved a tissue-wrapped package into Rob's hand.

"That's not—I can't . . ."

"Don't offend your host, now. Remember the Highland ways." The laird smiled and nodded.

"Thanks. Tom, I'd like to have a moment alone with you."

"A good idea. I've been thinking the same myself."

Rob studied his face, but he was nodding to a guest across the room. Then, Thomas motioned toward the drawing room off the main hall. "What's on your mind, Rob?"

"To be perfectly blunt about it, I'd like to know about the nature of your . . . friendship with Maude Graham."

They were alone in the room, which was lit only by the afternoon light from the windows. "I think," began McNaughton, laying aside his cigar, "I ought to tell you a little bit about things, starting pretty far back, if you'll humor it. You probably knew that the Grahams lived in the same shire as the McNaughtons did, back in Moray."

Rob nodded, taking the last sip of his scotch.

"You may have heard some of these tales the locals tell around here about the Grahams' eldritch ways, being that their women come from a line o' howdies—midwives and healers. Not to discredit them, mind you. There's skill there, no doubt about that. But, of course with that, there comes a bit o' this talk and that, that the womenfolk are hard to tame and so forth. 'Fell wild,' as they said back in Moray." He retrieved his cigar and took a long pull.

"No one, and certainly not me, says Maude ever dallied on the dark side, but she was a wild one from the start. She was the first born, and even though she was a good girl with the younger bairns, she couldn't help but draw attention to herself. I mean, look at her." He swallowed and looked toward the musicians down the hall, and had to clear his throat before beginning again.

"There was talk, especially among the church folk. The older she got, well . . . she was overbold with the local boys, poor lass, and would have been the shame of the family. John Graham was wise enough to see it. Good man, that. I'd been planning to come to America for some time, and I guess it wasn't any surprise when I heard the Grahams were thinking on it as well."

Rob stood silent, the empty cup in his cool hand.

McNaughton lowered his eyes and, with the toe of his boot, pushed a dying miller moth along the floor. "If the family ever knew what happened between that girl and me on the steamship coming o'er—and many times since—it would break that proud man's heart." He tamped the toe of his boot down, crushing the moth.

Rob froze, stiff as kindling. His ears felt as if they were full of cotton wool, but the laird's words penetrated nonetheless.

"I was astonished, what with her being such a young lass. But," he said, spreading out his hands in an imploring way, "I was alone back then, grieving the loss of my Lora. I'd seen the bonny girl watching me on the deck, looking up sly as a fox from the pages of her book. Other times, she'd crowd past me and push up against me with that full bosom—e'en back then it was as ripe as autumn fruit—when no one cared to look. I tell you, Rob, it was more than any man could stand. And finally the night came when she slipped into my cabin on the *Campania* and—well, decency stops me there."

As McNaughton paced to the window, Rob placed a hand on an oak colonnade to steady himself. The scotch boiled in his empty gut, and as a cold film of sweat formed on his neck, he strained not to reach up and yank at his knotted silk scarf.

McNaughton went on, "When you came 'round the barn this morning I could not have been more shocked. I had no idea you'd grown sweet on the little vixen. I'd have done anything to prevent this. God knows I should have warned you somehow. It hasn't left my mind since I came back here. It's good that you came. Good that this is all out in the open between us."

He pulled a white linen kerchief embroidered with the "M" crest from his back pocket and dabbed his nose. "Truth be known at last, I'm ashamed. 'Tis a dirty business, and I need to own my part in it. She's sorely plagued with guilt, I know, but I intend to make an honest woman of her. I can make things right for her, and I need to, damn it." He made a fist and let it fall on the table, like a father making a point about a straying child. "I care for her, make no mistake. That's why I was there this morning."

The soft strains of the violin and the ebb and flow of men's voices floated down the hall. "Now that's an irony," said McNaughton, with a humorless grunt of a laugh. "They're playin' 'What Child is This.' There's a folk tune with the same melody . . . 'Greensleeves,' it's called. About a lovely maid who was careless with her virtue. Repeatedly careless, alas."

Drawing his forefinger and thumb across his eyelids in a weary gesture, he dropped his hand and looked at Rob with a resigned expression. Then he turned and picked up his cigar, which had gone dark in the pewter ashtray.

Striking a match, he puffed once, letting the smoke drift up. "I can only begin to imagine how much fear she'd have in telling anyone about her past. Especially a handsome suitor like yourself.

But last summer, when the two of us were abovestairs together . . . surely you suspected. I tried to protect her reputation with that skite tale about the bat. But the truth will out, eh? I guess you might best describe Maude Graham and me as handfast, according to the auld ways, when that term meant bound together by circumstance and fate, and often a bit o' passion too." He pursed his lips, looking momentarily abashed. "'Twill be legal before too long. She's asked me to be patient with her, and I've granted her that."

Rob lowered his punch glass to the hall table, where it met the polished wood with scarcely a sound. "Thanks for the information. It's very . . . enlightening. I'll be on my way."

"Dinnae forget your gift, my boy." The laird held out the small package, which had lain forgotten on the table.

Rob took it and met the older man's gaze for a moment, then turned and sought the heavy brass handle of the front door and the sharp December air.

Maude drove the buggy back to Kettle Creek late Christmas afternoon, remembering little of the day. There were vague images of Mary, in her white dimity wrapper and shawl, sitting near the fireplace, of Mac glowing over his sturdy new violin case, and of Isobel twirling in her red Chesterfield coat, dark curls flying.

There was her father's quiet companionship, after the gifts were all opened, when he stood close by her at the broad window, coffee cup in hand, watching the chalk white sky and the dancing flakes just beyond the glass.

"Looks like an old-time Montana Christmas, like those first ones we had after coming over, remember, Maudie?"

But the snow began falling thicker around noon. As the thermometer held steady at eighteen degrees, the flakes took on a consistent size and rate. Maude's eyes darted down the long lane again and again, past the flanking aspens and the tidy jack fence toward Big Spring Road, watching for the blue roan and the patch of tan mackinaw.

One o'clock came, then two. Rob knew they were serving dinner at two. At quarter to three she knew he was not coming, and she couldn't bear one more soft-spoken inquiry from Catriona. Ailse's dark eyes were on her often enough, but she at least said nothing.

At the turn from Big Spring Road onto Kettle Creek Lane, Bobcat stumbled in a deep rut and nearly went down. Maude dropped the reins and grabbed the side rail, ready to jump out, but the horse righted himself and kept going.

"Damn you, Rob Elliott, I should have gone home two hours ago, but instead I waited for you," Maude blurted. Tears watered the corners of her eyes and her nose began to drip.

"Easy, boy." Her voice sounded more querulous than she wanted it to, and the very notice of this made her lip quiver. When she added, "It's not far now," she realized she was comforting herself as much as the horse, and her gloved hand flew up to stifle a sob.

She woke in the night, out of a dead sleep. The room was cold; her fire had burned low and was nearly out. When she lit a candle, she saw that the clock said twelve thirty. Scrambling out of bed, she opened the small door on the bedroom woodstove and thrust in several pieces of kindling as Ajax stretched and settled down again, his head on his paws.

Under the covers again, she stared at the snapping flames behind the grille, trying to remember the dream she'd just had. She'd been with Morag and Ailse. They were in a grassy meadow; it may have been in Scotland. It was a meadow, yes, but there were headstones here and there. Much farther apart than they'd be in a normal cemetery. And set apart from the headstones there was a circle of standing stones, just like one near Strathearn. But Rob was one of the standing stones.

Rob was a stone? She shook her head. His mouth was open, like an *O*, and the wind whistled past him, making sounds as though he was trying to talk to her, but he couldn't, because he was made of stone. She tried to remember the rest of the stones in the circle. They were what you'd expect—big slabs of granite, weathered and gray, gently tilted by the sleep of the millennia.

If she missed anything about Scotland, it was places like this. She remembered going to a familiar group of stones on summer evenings, when the scent of heather was on the air and the warm wind rippled the grass like the gentle hand of the Creator. A sense of wisdom settled on her shoulders whenever she entered the circle.

And where is that wisdom now, when I need it? Special wits indeed, she fumed, rehearsing an old litany she'd covered many times with Ailse. *What good are special wits if they only come unbidden, and can't be counted on in times of tragedy or emergency? Dear Ailse, I need to see you.*

I'll ride back to Stony Creek in the morning, she vowed. She glanced out the window, hoping for a glimpse of a star, which would mean the snow was letting up. There, among the skeletal branches of the tall cottonwoods and the fir trees, was the thin silver saucer of a new moon.

But it was Ailse who came to her. Both she and Morag came in the long-bed buggy drawn by two ale-colored Belgians. "We didn't want to fool around with the phaeton in all this snow," said Ailse, slipping off her beaver coat.

Maude went to the sink and filled the graniteware kettle. "I was going to come see you as soon as I could. I had a powerfully strong dream."

There was a short silence, then Ailse clipped out, "We ken."

Maude's head pivoted like an owl's.

"Put the kettle on and set yersel' doon. I'm not cocksure enow tae think that everything that happened in our dreams was the same as yourn, but yer Auntie and I think the signs are fair strong here."

"Was . . . was there a stone circle?"

The two older women nodded. "Like the one at Strathearn," Ailse leaned forward and spoke in a whisper. "Tell us."

Maude swallowed as a wave lifted her innards. "I'm not sure I want to go on."

"Come, come, sit doon. Morag's dream was different frae mine," Ailse said. "I wager all three of us had a variation. In mine, ye had entered the circle and had built a fire in the fire ring, and yer man Rob wanted tae follow ye in. But ye took burdock and angelica and salt frae yer pocket and cast it 'tween all the stones, binding him so that he couldnae enter. I can still see the fear on yer face."

Maude's hand was on her stomach, clutching the fabric of her shirt. She turned to Morag. "What about you?"

"Mine was just the opposite. You wanted him in the circle. But he stood outside it, and a swarm of dark sprites came, whispering in his ear. He turned away, looking at you over his shoulder, and left."

Maude's mouth was dry. "In my dream, he *was* a stone and he could not speak to me. It was awful. All I know is that something is wrong. I don't know if I'm to blame. How could I be? I'm angry. You both know he was expected for Christmas dinner. All night I wondered if something had happened to him. His horse could have thrown him; he could have broken a leg. He's accident-prone. But I stupidly feel I should have known what it was . . . I mean, I should have known what happened to him."

"Aye, the women in our family come tae rely on our airy senses," Ailse acknowledged with a shrug. "Mayhaps too much." Her expression grew more serious. "Ye're right, though. Sommat is wrong. Wrong wi' that boy. How it came tae be this way, we cannae ken."

Maude drew herself up and took a quick breath. "You've both got that official wise-woman look about you. It's obvious you're going to tell me what I ought to do, so you might as well spit it out."

Ailse puckered her lips in mock chagrin. Morag raised her dark brows and said, "I'll get oot the teacups and we'll discuss it."

Chapter Twenty-Seven

Two hours later Maude was on Bobcat, riding northeast. Her saddlebags were filled with everything Ailse and Morag thought she could possibly need. Extra gloves and socks, a heavy gray blanket, a loaf of bread, deer jerky they'd brought from Stony Creek, even pickled beets wrapped in several layers of newspaper. "Pickled beets?" she had asked, but the packing went on until the saddlebags bulged with items for every eventuality, including hard cider and festive pastries sent over from the Fredrichs and the Christmas gifts that had lain forlornly under the tree at Stony Creek, waiting for Rob. Last was the weighty little tissue-wrapped package, flecked with bits of glitter and tied with a white satin bow, which was her special gift for him.

Ailse and Morag bade her an ambivalent farewell. Still in Maude's hearing, Ailse scolded herself and Morag loudly with reminders that no unmarried woman should be sent off to the home of a bachelor without a chaperone. Morag acknowledged this was true, but reminded her mother that this was a new century and a modern age. "After all," she remarked, referring to Ailse's courtship, "it isn't 1847 anymore." Ailse, only partly mollified, closed her mouth and was silent.

She knew nothing about how to find Rob's place, save for the fact that he was located on Ruby Creek, at the end of the trail. Bobcat stepped out eagerly, glad not to be confined within the buggy traces. Ajax trotted behind. As they descended a slight decline, the aspens congregated thickly around them, black knotty eyes winking on pale bark. Chickadees darted and whispered while the chalky sky above hinted of snow. She glanced at her watch. A few minutes after noon.

"Where, exactly, are we going, Bobcat? Up Ruby Creek, to the cabin with the Herefords," she averred, with a plucky lift of her shoulders.

Roy Akeley, the hired man, had done a good job of seeing to things on Ruby Creek during Rob's absence, but one of the cattle had kicked a crack in the watering trough on the south side of the barn. Roy was still there when Rob arrived and insisted on helping him before heading back down to the Ingersoll place.

Tall and rangy, Roy bent from the waist, bailing out the icy water low enough so that the trough could be repaired. Rob emerged from the cabin where the tar bucket had been warming overnight. The two set about the task, which was more complicated than it had first appeared.

"Just like every job," said Roy, wrapping his wool scarf around his neck. "If you think it's going to take twenty minutes, it takes forty."

Rob grunted a laugh. "You got that right."

"Old man Ingersoll could barely get into the wagon to go spend the holidays with their people at Fort Benton. He's getting pretty stoved up."

"The missus is still pretty spry, though."

"Yup." Roy struggled to hold the splintered board in place. "We should have some kind of clamp here. Speaking of women, why haven't you got a girl?"

Rob's face darkened. "I thought I did, but I was mistaken. What about you? You're a fine figure. Just out of high school, aren't you?"

"I know what you mean about thinking you did but you didn't.

There was a gal I liked a lot, but evidently she had her sights set a mite higher than the likes of me. Her name was Graham."

Rob felt an inner jolt. He sharpened his focus on the daubs of tar, smearing them briskly into place. *Was another chapter of Maude's history about to open up?*

"Yup, I can still see her face and hear what she said to me that day. 'Mr. Akeley,' she said, 'I do appreciate your kindly interest, but I must decline your attentions, as my future does not lie with a cowhand from Fergus County.'" He gave a little snort at the recollection, then went on. "Sad thing is, I heard she left school for some railroad fellow. Went off to Minneapolis or someplace, then the scoundrel up and left her. I would never have done that to her. She's the prettiest redhead I ever saw."

"I know the family," said Rob, breathing more easily. "She is a nice girl and she certainly didn't deserve what happened to her."

Roy pounded on the board, shoring it up. "A heartless bird it is that flies its own nest. If I knew where that fellow was right now— well, never mind."

Rob nodded in silent agreement, then packed in the last stroke of tar. Laying another board across the front, he dragged over a spare post and propped it against the whole arrangement. "We'll keep them in the other corral for now. I'll get some clamps at Powers', though. Thanks, Roy. Give my best to Per and Hildy when they get back."

Back inside, he set to work on the frame he'd started on the small window between the kitchen and his bedroom, designed for the purpose of admitting heat from the kitchen stove. Cala curled up on her rug to watch.

As he laid out his tools, he glanced at the corner cupboard and saw the small silver picture frame that McNaughton had given him as a Christmas gift. It was heavy sterling, with the family crest stamped at the top. Just now it was hard to imagine ever wanting to use it, but maybe someday.

Mitering, skinning, hammering, sanding, leveling, varnishing . . . he kept busy, trying not to think about Maude and her sordid history. As he gripped the miter saw tightly, perhaps too tightly, his mind burned with questions he could not suppress. *Why couldn't I have seen what was going on, what had been going on for years before I arrived? Were people laughing behind their hands at me while I carried on courting her? I'm nobody's fool, for God's sake.*

The piece of trim cleaved in two and clattered to the floor before he even realized how much pressure he'd applied. As he fitted it onto the frame, he could not stop his mind from traveling the familiar channels it always did when faced with a problem. Willing or unwilling, calm or angry, he would analyze any obstacle or conundrum set before him until some facet or fissure yielded a clue. He had always been this way. Perhaps the problem would not be solved in his favor, but at long last he would make peace with it. He would arrive at a rational explanation, finally, and only then could he move on.

But why couldn't he make McNaughton's story fit with what he knew and sensed of Maude Graham? While the idea of a liaison between Maude and McNaughton had certainly seemed suspiciously plausible this past summer, he could not, as mightily as he tried, imagine a young Maude mincing her way around an ocean liner, pressing her maidenly bosom up against a mustached aristocrat old enough to be her father. Let alone knocking on the door of the old goat's private quarters long after the Graham children would all be tucked up in bed.

McNaughton's words rattled like a chain through his head: *"Last summer, when the two of us were abovestairs together, surely you suspected . . ."* Rob grimaced and whacked the nail so hard it bent. *What were they doing up there?*

Clawing out the bent nail, his mind spun to that night in June when he and Maude tumbled through the meadow grass, she on fire and he trying to save her. Her body folded in his arms, pressed against his for the first time, rolling down the hill in the scented night.

He stood quietly, the misshapen nail between his fingers, lost in remembering. That night, he'd felt as though he had come across the continent to find her. There were other reasons he had ended up in Montana, yes, but when he laid eyes on Maude Graham, he felt something definite, something as clear and sharp as he felt when the wolves called his name. He knew he was where he needed to be. The scent of the lupine and the sage wafted back to him. He felt giddy, almost drunk.

He shook his head and gave an exasperated snort. Picking a new nail out of the box, he drove it in. *All right, what if it's true? Or more likely, what if McNaughton's salacious tale held portions of the truth, and Maude had been a wanton of sorts? She wouldn't be the first young woman to lose her virtue unwisely.*

Unable to stand this train of thought, he grabbed his coat and took the tar bucket outside, heading for the barn with Cala at his heels. The snow was falling again, this time in big flakes, soft and white. Cala began barking before they even got to the corral. Rob saw the bay horse and the rider in her long coat and stopped, his hand on the catchwire. He had nothing to say. He had formed neither a position of condemnation nor forgiveness; she had not given him enough time, *damn her*. He was frozen, inept. He could not even raise a finger to his hat in greeting. All he could do was stand silently in the falling snow, wishing he had come further in solving his problem.

"You've come a long way."

She nodded, keeping her eyes on his face. He would not look at her. "I see you are in the middle of something. I can help you." She slid off her horse without waiting for a reply, tying Bobcat's reins to the corral rails.

"Just a tar job on the watering trough. I've done enough to get it through till spring, I think." He walked to the barn with her following, tucking away the sticky bucket and washing the tools with turpentine. For the entire five minutes in the barn, not a word was spoken.

As they walked back to the cabin, Rob finally looked at her. "I'm sure you didn't stop by just to see if I needed help around the place."

Maude bristled. "No, I came to get something."

"And what might that be?"

"I came to get something for myself and my family, and that is the explanation you owe all of us for not showing up for Christmas dinner when we were all expecting you." Her throat was so constricted she could hardly get the words out, but she kept her flashing eyes fastened on his.

Rob's jaw tightened. "Yes, I suppose you do deserve an explanation. Of sorts."

"What is that supposed to mean?"

"Well, Maude, I am not sure who owes who more of an explanation."

She wanted to ask him what in the hell he was talking about, but something stopped her. She was on the verge of uncovering the truth. "You appear to be upset about something." It was the gentlest reply she could muster, and it took all the humility she had.

He turned on her with an icy stare, giving his head a little shake. "I'm working on getting over my irritation entirely."

"'Entirely?'" She sucked the cold air into her nostrils as her chest rose and fell.

"I need a drink." He threw down the turpentine-soaked rag and went inside, leaving the door open for Maude and the dogs to follow. Scowling, she strode back to Bobcat, loosened the cinch, and went to the cabin, where the door stood idly open.

Closing it behind her, she walked into the kitchen. Rob had set two glasses out. It was the most hospitable gesture he'd made so far. Into each one he poured about three fingers of Scotch whiskey, then drained his glass immediately and filled it again.

Maude took her whiskey, tossed it back, and slammed the glass on the pine tabletop. "Rob, if things are over between us, then so be it. Sometimes these things happen. I don't want to give you the impression I am happy about it, because I'm not. I'm deeply disturbed, even angry. I thought we had something remarkable, something that comes along once in a lifetime, once in a century. You're the one who made me realize that, so now you're the one who's got to tell me what happened. I've a right to know, and so does my family. If you're half the man I think you are, then you'll come straight out with it."

Rob took another hearty swallow and glared at her. He filled her glass again. "I'll tell you. But first let's toast. Let's toast to the truth. No more deception. Not one shred of it."

Maude caught her breath. *God in heaven, what has happened? What does he know, and how harshly has he judged me? All those pretty words I just spoke about a sacred love that comes once in a lifetime.* She raised her hand and shoved it into her hair, looking wildly around. Her throat tightened. *What am I doing here?* Fingers from the past plucked at her. Haunting voices rose from the recesses of her mind: *He's rejecting you. Isn't this what you wanted, what you thought best?*

She glanced at him, and for a moment it seemed she did not know him at all. He struck her as a stranger, standing there with the pale afternoon light hanging about him. *Maybe it was true. Perhaps the two of them should never have met.* Her lower lip twitched and her eyes grew shiny. However much he knew her, and however much they were still vast unknown continents to one another, she wanted to drop to her knees and ask him not to hate her.

Then she was borne even farther away, whisked off on a secret wind. She was inside the stone circle at Strathearn, and where was he? A breeze came up out of memory; she could smell the sea air and the heather. The grasses lay flat and rippling. The scented wind rushed around and through her, matching her breath, telling her that whatever might happen today, all would be well. There were things she could control, and things she couldn't. She would go forward, through this day, and she would be all right.

He was waiting, watching her. She took her glass and clinked it solidly against his. "To the truth."

He pulled out a chair for her and took his own seat. "I was on my way home from your place Christmas Eve," he began, and went on to tell her the entire story, from the moment he had run into Grant on the road all the way through the laird's tales of why the Grahams had decided to leave Scotland, what had happened on the *Campania*, of how McNaughton believed that he and Maude were "handfast," and of their imminent marriage.

Maude listened to it all in stoic silence, although there were moments when she could not keep her head from moving back and forth in sheer incredulity. The part about her going to McNaughton's room on the *Campania* made her want to burst out laughing, as did the fantasy of the upcoming marriage, but she restrained herself. Laughter might not be an appropriate response at this point.

As Rob drew close to the end of the story, Maude did indeed become angry, but not with McNaughton. She felt a roil of rage at Rob for having believed such a load of rubbish. When he finished, he set his glass down and raised his eyebrows with judicial piety.

She stood and walked to the window. "I have one principal question for you."

Rob sat up a little straighter in his chair and had the fleeting thought that maybe he ought not have any more to drink. "You have a question for me?"

"Why did you so quickly assume that all of this was true?"

"Why would Tom McNaughton make it all up? He has no motive. He's obviously in love with you. Any idiot—and that apparently describes me quite well—would know there's something between you. What in blazes was going on upstairs in your room when I was at your place last summer?"

Maude watched feathery snowflakes settle on the auburn backs of the cattle bunched around the cottonwoods near the creek. She rested her hands on the smooth new wood of the door jamb. Crisp air poured off the window glass, yet on her right was the warmth of the woodstove. Cala and Ajax tussled in the front room. Bobcat was at the corral, and ought to be unsaddled and taken to the barn, but he was all right for now. She and Rob had toasted to the truth. It was time.

"Rob, I'm going to tell you what really happened between Tom McNaughton and me. When it's all over, you're going to have to decide who you want to believe. I'll make a pledge to you right here and now that I will respect your decision. I may not like your decision, but I'll respect it."

Rob looked at her and gave a curt nod, the cool light of skepticism glimmering in his eyes.

"I was three months shy of my fourteenth birthday when we came over on the *Campania*. We did not leave Scotland for the reasons McNaughton gave you. He fabricated that stuff because it bolsters his little tale of conquest. We came over just like everyone else these last ten or twenty years, because my father wanted to homestead and set us up in ranching.

"I was frightened by McNaughton but, I admit, a little fascinated too. He was a well-known figure in our rural Morayshire aristocracy, and recently widowed. It was somewhat remarkable that he and his boys were on the same ship as we were. But I paid no more attention to him than I did anyone else, even though I noticed him watching me a great deal. He was actually the one who frequently bumped into me, not the other way around.

"I often read books in quiet corners by myself . . . " here she faltered, swallowing hard, and coughed. "Although my mother and my aunt and Gran have known about this since the beginning, I have never told this to another living soul, so please forgive me if I . . . stumble a bit." The cool air coming off the glass seemed much chillier now. Staring out the window, she hugged herself, rubbing her upper arms with her hands. Unable to look at Rob, she did not know his expression had changed. He tilted forward, both hands on the table.

"On the *Campania*, I often went off to read alone. One evening I was some distance away from the crowded areas of the ship. I was foolish. I was so absorbed in my book I never saw him coming. He—took me. . ." Gasping out a sob, she let her head tilt to the side, traveling back in time. Her voice grew small and childlike. Tears ran down, forming wet ribbons on her cheeks.

"Right there on the floorboards—ruined my dress—it was blue. The pain . . . I couldn't walk. I thought I'd fall in the ocean—I was just a girl . . ."

She dropped in a heap on the floor, crying outright, her face in her hands. "My God, I've had thirteen years to figure out how to tell this story, why can't I do it without falling apart?"

Rob's chair scraped back; he took two paces toward her.

"No!" She almost shouted it, whirling around with upraised hands, holding him off, her face wet and desperate. "Go back, go back and sit down. You mustn't. Stay away till I'm done.

"The things he said to me that night never left me. He said he owned me. *Owned* me. And I believed it. I was a *girl*. I thought whoever took your maidenhead was the one you belonged to forever. What did I know? He told me I would always be his.

"I tried for so many years afterward to erase those words from my mind, from my thinking, but even in school, when other boys wanted to court me, I was convinced I could never be with anyone but him. Really, it did begin to make sense to me in a mad sort of way. That's why I cut my arm and made the oath never to marry. I felt used and put away, like something that can never be new again. When he married the widow from Stanford I didn't know what to think. But he'd still look at me the same way, so I knew he was just waiting. Waiting for the next time.

"When I got my own place—and isn't it the greatest irony of all that my father gave me land adjoining the Rocking M—I knew things would get worse. He drove by constantly, watching me. The time you were there was terrible. He tried to rape me. I know it was because his wife died—that's another matter there—and he was so full of lust he couldn't stand it. You coming to the back porch was the only thing that saved me. I heard him lying to you. I was upstairs trying to put on some clothes after he completely ripped away my shirtwaist."

"Why hasn't your father killed him, for God's sake?" Rob paced the narrow kitchen, clenching and unclenching his fists.

"My mother and grandmother and Morag knew about the rape, but they never told my father. They knew he would kill McNaughton, and they knew he'd very likely be jailed for it, perhaps for life. We were just getting started in America, and it would have devastated our chances for prosperity. We had such a big family. What would we have done without the head of our household? We women have carried this secret around with us all these years. It would have been my word against his, and I was only thirteen at the time. Besides, it happened on board a ship in the middle of the ocean. We may have been wrong, but I followed their counsel."

"So all this horse—er, flim-flam about you being handfast to him is just . . ."

"Black-hearted treachery. He is the most conniving, deceptive person I have ever known. I pray that someday I will be truly free of him. Someday."

Maude, her face averted, plucked at the braided trim on her skirt. "So now . . . now you know I was raped."

Rob rose and went to her, lifting her up off the floor. Setting her down in one of the pine chairs, he drew his own close, taking her right hand in both of his.

"I'm so sorry, Maude."

"About the rape or about believing McNaughton?"

"Both." He shook his head, looking down at the floor.

"I hope you can see why it isn't the kind of story a woman is especially eager to tell." She laughed bitterly. "You see, Rob, we have crossed our own Rubicon now. There is no turning back."

"No, there is no turning back."

"I know all of this could very well change the way you feel about me." She stared at him, willing him to meet her gaze.

He lifted his eyes to hers. "I think that might be true of some men, in their feelings for some women. It isn't true of my feelings for you."

"We toasted to the truth, remember that." Her voice was hard.

"I am remembering it."

"I don't want to get a year into something, or two years, and have you decide you aren't so sure about being with a woman who's . . . soiled."

The corners of his mouth turned up slightly.

She lifted her head, peering down her nose at him. "What humor do you find in this?"

He shook his head apologetically. "I was just thinking about you saying we had crossed the Rubicon. When Julius Caesar said it all those centuries ago, he meant it was an act of war. I was thinking, when you caught me smiling, that in our case it's an act of love."

Her lip quivered as she looked off to the side.

"But," he said, "I can see why you'd be concerned about my reaction to this story you've bottled up for so long. Maude . . . do you think you can set those concerns aside? Permanently?"

Maude inhaled sharply, then let the air out. "God, Rob. I want to try."

"Wait here." Rob disappeared into the other room and returned a moment later. "Before all this happened," he said, "when I planned to come to Stony Creek for Christmas dinner with you and your family, I had a gift for you."

He opened his palm to reveal a handkerchief of white linen and lace, tied in a loose little bundle. "Open it."

Maude did as she was told and out tumbled a ring, an oval blue topaz surrounded by tiny diamonds and set in yellow gold. "It's beautiful," she gasped.

"It was my mother's. And I believe her mother's too. I don't think either of them wore it very often, so it's well preserved. Family legend has it that the topaz was recovered from an ancient cairn, then cut and set in Edinburgh." He took the ring back from her. "Are you ready for this?"

Her lips parted and her eyes grew round. "Oh, my."

Sinking down on one knee, with the crackling woodstove behind him and the snow falling softly in the background, Rob took Maude's left hand. "Maude Graham, will you do me the honor of becoming my wife?"

Maude willed the maelstrom of wild thoughts in her head to cease. Silencing the voices that offered random reasons why she ought to say no, why he shouldn't even ask, she heard herself saying, "Yes, Rob Elliott, I will."

They stood, holding each other. Flustered, Maude wanted to laugh out loud, but she was weary to the bone and figured she had a good case of delirium. The confession, the whiskey, and the swirling giddiness of their reunion had all made her weak in the knees. She could not believe she was here, in Rob's cabin. She hadn't even had time to take it in, to get a sense of the place. She wanted to know him, to truly come to understand this man who had completely changed her life.

Rob kissed her face, tasting the salty traces of her tears. He moved to her mouth, smashing her lips against his. Breathing hard, he pulled away long enough to whisper hard into her ear. "Nothing's going to come between us again, Maude. Ever."

He kissed her softly, then deeper. Maude felt the slow, hard stroking of her heart as she slipped her arms around his waist, aware of the new weight on the fourth finger of her left hand. She pressed her palms against his beltline at the small of his back, bearing down. His thigh slipped between her legs. She stopped thinking and gave herself over to the fierce need to align herself with him, to connect the hot sparks in her belly with his. As her hips moved against his hardening groin, she lost control, fumbling now at his neckerchief, the buttons at his throat, searching for skin to touch and to kiss.

She was off her feet, scooped up by strong arms and carried to the bedroom, where they rid one another of their clothing in the crisp afternoon air and dove beneath faded quilts and flannel. Rob, so tense with lust and longing that one more touch from Maude would undo him, kissed and caressed her lavender-scented skin until she could stand it no longer. Looking at the lupine blue eyes, he fell into her, moving with her as they cried out together.

Chapter Twenty-Eight

He was quiet in the morning. She tousled his hair at breakfast, then presented him with the Christmas gift she had wrapped in white tissue some weeks before—a gold pocket watch engraved on the inside with a Robert Burns quote she'd chosen, "O whistle, and I'll come to you."

Holding her hands to his face, he said, "It's grand, Maude. I couldn't have asked for anything better. I'll treasure it all the days of my life." He tucked it into the pocket of his vest, holding his hand over it. Then, pulling their coats from the hooks by the door, he held hers up and gave a nod. "Let's go for a walk by the creek."

The wind had come in the night, sweeping the snow awry into crazy patterns, carving it into drifts and wells around the trunks of the trees and along the fence lines. The path along the creek was whisked clear. By the time they reached the frozen waterfall, Maude was breathing hard, glad to rest on a satin-smooth stretch of fallen log as nuthatches and chickadees darted in and out of a thicket of brambles.

As Rob stood next to her, looking over his land, she could smell the morning scent of him, part castile soap and part leather, and part simply Rob. The sense of who he was, physically, beneath his clothing, even beneath his skin, was so potent that she shivered. She wanted to peel off her deerskin gloves and run a hand between the buttons of his jacket, finding a place where she could reach the hard muscle of him, and make him hers all over again. She wanted him, not only because of the wringing twinges in her core, but because her happiness was multiplying by the moment. She was beside herself, lost in a senseless joy. This, she realized, is what love feels like. A foolish smile crept over her lips and she began to laugh.

He turned abruptly and sat down, tight against her. "What?"

"I'm laughing out of sheer happiness, that's all. I'm in love with you, and I want to take you back to the cabin and make love to you forever."

He ran his arm beneath hers and grabbed her hand, saying nothing. His eyes were forward, trained on the milky sheet of ice that covered the creek, where the light wind worried the snow crystals and spun them into loose ribbons. "Maude, we need to go to Stony Creek."

Her eyes shifted. It was his tone, more than the words. Still holding his hand, she pulled away slightly, in order to look at him straight on. "What's wrong?"

"I woke this morning thinking about . . . your sister."

"My sister? Do you mean Mary?"

He nodded. "I can't—we can't even come close to doing to your parents what she and Paul did to them."

She jumped up, her hands fisted. "What are you talking about? This is nothing like that."

Rob's chin dropped and he looked up at her through thick lashes. "Maude, hear me out." His jaw was set. For a moment, there was no sound but the soft lispings of the chickadees in the brush.

Maude compressed her lips. "Well, go on, then."

"I'm not going to chance, for one second, having either of your parents thinking of me the way they think of that mongrel Paul Hathaway. Right now they know you aren't at home. They know you're here. As far as your father is concerned, your virtue is in peril. I'm taking you home, and until the day we're married, I'm going to court you. Court you in broad daylight." His eyes were fixed on hers. "We all deserve that, especially you."

Maude let out a long exhale. His words had entered her like a knife blade. Something was rising out of her, some kind of vapor from the past. She felt rattled, annoyed, as if she wished she had thought of this first. *But I couldn't have*, she realized. *I never perceived in myself any virtue to defend. This is what shame has done to me.*

Her eyes drifted to the tangled thatch of the rosebushes and the winter birds fluttering in and out. She felt her hands tight at her sides as she wondered if she ought to have somehow managed her long-ago disgrace differently. *I never felt the kind of shame that makes people hang their heads and confess to someone*, she reflected. *I let the laird rule my world, and I've lived in that private hell all this time. I allowed him to write the pages of a dark script for me that I've not only lived but also sealed and hidden, so that no one could know, let alone try to help me.*

Rob had shaken those pages loose, exposing them to daylight and truth, and she had finally begun to forgive herself for being young and beautiful and, most difficult of all to admit, vulnerable.

She turned her gaze back to Rob. "You're going to . . . court me."

He nodded.

"But—"

"How about Candlemas?" His eyes twinkled.

"What?"

"Weren't you about to ask me when we could get married?"

She eyed him imperiously. "I'm supposed to be the prescient one in this relationship."

"I'm not without my magic."

"I suppose. Yes, I was about to discuss a date. Candlemas is the second of February. That's almost six weeks away." As the full meaning of this settled on her, her eyes widened. "*Rob.*"

He drew her in and whispered, "We can make it." He ran both hands into her hair and looked straight into her eyes. "You think you don't want this, but you do. You want it more than anything in the world. Someone took something precious from you a long time ago, and we need to stop right now and start mending that. We begin right now, today."

Maude's brows knitted up, her lower lip quivered, and tears spilled down her cheeks. "God in heaven, Rob, I love you."

Maude sat in the kitchen with Catriona and Mary while Rob and her father talked in the front room. Catriona circled around the broad kitchen table, too skittish to sit down. "Scones," she murmured. "I meant to make some anyway." She pulled her best apron over her head, not realizing it was inside out, and set to work.

"Isobel and Fiona are skating?" Maude toyed with a dried-out bit of kinnikinnick lying on the tabletop.

"They can't get enough of it," said Catriona. "That section of the creek your father diverted for a skating pond is smooth as a mirror. It's nice and thick, too; we looked it over to be sure. Still, Ailse and Morag went along to keep an eye on them."

"What made you decide on Candlemas?" Mary asked. She was perched near the stove, her head bent over some crochet work.

"It was Rob's idea." Maude shrugged. "He's traditional. It's the first holiday coming up and it seemed like a good time."

"What is Candlemas, anyway? I don't remember having church services for it."

"We asked Father Wakefield. According to him, it's based on an old Jewish law that women who have borne children are believed to be impure six weeks after the birth." She glanced at Mary, who raised her eyebrows.

"Be that as it may," Maude went on, "we all know that Jewish and Roman Catholic traditions are blended throughout the Bible. Candlemas marks six weeks after the birth of Christ, so it's the celebration of the Purification of the Blessed Virgin. According to tradition, church leaders are supposed to bless new candles for this service. Now, if you ask Ailse, you get another aspect of the story."

"Which is?"

"The ancients called it Imbolc. To them, it was the earliest beginnings of spring."

"Spring commencing on February 2? That's quite a stretch." Mary set her crochet work down. "Mother, would you like me to get some currants for you?"

"Thank you, Mary. Maude, isn't it wonderful how much better your sister is? Morag's pronounced her quite fit, so she's going back to Great Falls next Tuesday."

Maude watched Mary reach for the currant tin on the shelf and saw the rounded swell of her belly. Tension between her and her sister had eased slightly. "You look wonderful, Mary."

"As wonderful as one can look in these sack dresses." She slid the tin to her mother, then heaved herself back into her chair. "Perfect garb for the unwed mother to don for a spring wedding. Two spring weddings, now that we have both Maude's and Rory's."

Catriona dusted off her floured hands. "Now, Mary, I saw a lovely quotation in *Harper's* the other day. By William Thackeray, I think. Something like, 'Good humor is one of the best articles of clothing one can wear in society.'"

Mary sucked her cheeks in. "I'll try to bear that in mind, Mother. I'm sure Paul considers that when he puts on his fine things, wherever he is."

Catriona's spine stiffened.

Mary resumed her crochet work. "Wherever he is and whoever he's with."

"Someone else will feel the terrible pain of his faithlessness," Maude said. "We don't know who she is, but I feel compassion for her."

Mary's head jerked up, her amber eyes bright. "That's easy for you to say. You have someone who won't leave you. Paul never even gave me a chance."

"Mary, none of *us* will leave you, ever," said Maude. "We are your family. You don't have a husband but you have all of us. We are all so happy about your baby—so very excited."

Catriona wiped her hands on her apron and went to Mary. "Maude's right, Mary. You're so much better off without Paul. Surely you're coming to understand that, aren't you?"

Mary dipped her head. "Sometimes. Other times it's . . . awful. I think of terrible things. I picture him with someone, and see the two of them being killed in an accident. Then other times I feel as though I would take him back in a heartbeat."

"It takes a long time to come to terms with . . . betrayal," said Catriona.

Maude was glad that her mother used that word. Every chance they had, they needed to describe Paul as the villain he was.

Mary's lips parted, then closed again. "I . . . had the strangest experience."

Maude kept still. She had already said more than she should. Catriona too, was quiet for once, listening.

"It was Christmas Eve, after church." Mary stopped, digging a handkerchief out of her pocket and dabbing the corners of her eyes. "You all had gone on down the sidewalk toward the street but I lagged behind. Do you remember that, Mother?"

Catriona nodded and sat down at the broad, scarred table.

"I stopped at the crèche on the lawn. I just wanted to stand there for a moment and look at the figures of the nativity. It was snowing, and everything looked so pretty. There was only a small beam of light from one of the church windows and it happened to fall precisely on the Virgin Mother's face as she looked down on the manger."

Mary's voice broke and tears begin cascading down her cheeks. "As I stood there—right then, Mother, for the first time—the baby moved."

Catriona brought a dishtowel up to her own face, and Maude realized she too had tears in her eyes. Things had changed a great deal since October.

Mary went on, "You all called out to me to hurry up, so I had to come away, but I could hardly bear to leave. I was so full of wonder. I mean, that it happened right then, while I was looking at the Holy Mother. And the way I felt was so new to me." Mary's voice grew even more querulous. "It didn't . . . change everything, but I felt something like—hope. Hope that it may not be entirely horrible being a . . . mother." She coughed out the final word and stopped for a moment, mopping her wet cheeks.

"As we drove away, I remembered that the Virgin Mary is my namesake. Now, sometimes, when I think back on that evening, I still feel a tiny gleam of hope. Maybe there's a chance I—we—will be all right." She wiped away her tears and took a deep breath.

Maude smiled and kept silent while Catriona reached across the table and folded Mary's hands into her own. The sound of approaching footsteps put an end to their conversation. Rob came in with John Graham on his heels.

"Catriona, I'd like to introduce your future son-in-law, Rob Elliott." John slapped Rob on the back so hard that all six feet of Rob teetered for a moment. Catriona threw her arms around him, laughing.

Giving him an earnest squeeze, she said, "I don't know you well, Rob, but I know you enough to believe that you and my daughter are worthy of one another, and with that, I welcome you into my family."

Rob's face was dark on the drive to Kettle Creek. He sat with his elbows on his knees, his hands gripping the reins as though they were twin pistols.

Maude guessed what he was thinking. *If McNaughton comes back, what then?* Rob had asked her father's permission to court and marry her. He was taking the high road, and the notion of staying in her house, sleeping in her bedroom, was unconscionable to him. But she knew he wasn't about to go back to Ruby Creek. Before they left his cabin yesterday, he'd stopped by Ingersolls' and asked Roy Akeley to watch over things and feed the cattle.

The fact that he was taking McNaughton so seriously gave

Maude greater pause than ever. As the buggy rattled along Big Spring Road, she marked the rhythm of each fence post looming up and falling away, noticing how unsteady her breath had become.

Laird McNaughton wasn't just a cad; he posed a peculiar danger to her. Her eyes lost focus, seeing only a blur of white snow and sagebrush, as she tried to tell herself she was imagining it—that he was nothing but a deluded, middle-aged fool destined to be the same remote curse he'd always been. But something cold and dark lodged in her chest, and she knew things had changed. She felt, sharp and clear, a renewed sense of what she'd seen in him all those years ago—a ruthless man for whom conquest was everything.

It was as if he'd been waiting for her to reach womanhood, and now it was time to pluck the rose, to possess it completely. He'd have what he wanted, and nothing would stop him. She pulled her coat more tightly around her.

"I'll stay in the barn," Rob said finally. His voice was soft but there was an edge to it, as though he'd settled a dispute with himself. "There's no other way." He glanced at Maude, who gave a nod.

"Lucky for you there's a stove out there now. I bought it last week so I'd be ready for any problems with the new lambs this spring."

"I guess I'm your first problem of the season."

Chapter Twenty-Nine

They got into the habit, over the next few days, of playing cards on a barrelhead in Rob's little room, which was cozy enough. The stove, along with the bead board paneling Kib had installed last fall, kept the place more warm and comfortable than Maude expected.

They could have played inside the house. She'd offered, but Rob would have none of it. He agreed to have dinner in the kitchen and always helped wash dishes afterward, but as soon as the dishtowel was hung on the rod behind the door, he was on his way to the barn.

This evening, after an early dinner, plenty of pale blue afternoon light still filtered through the window into Rob's room. As the two of them played gin rummy in companionable silence, they listened to the peculiar mating calls of the great horned owls roosting in the tall spruces behind the barn.

"They almost sound like they're barking at each other," Maude said with a laugh.

Rob agreed, watching the way the two dogs cocked their heads at the owls' odd language. He lifted a card from the center pile with a flick of his thumb. "One of these afternoons, he's going to show up."

Maude tossed her head up from the game and looked at him. "We both know it."

He fanned his cards out on the barrelhead and grinned at her. "Gin."

"There's the three of clubs I was looking for. You had it all along."

He leaned back against the wall, his hands behind his head. "The last couple nights out here, Maude, I've lain awake off and on. I've worked out some ideas. Like you say, we both know he's coming. It's only a question of when. Today when I was up in the meadow looking for that fool buck ram, I kept stewing about the fact that we hadn't formed a plan yet. This is what I'm thinking we should do when that time comes."

For the next ten minutes, she listened as he sketched out his strategy. As he drew outlines of the house, barn, and corrals on the barrel with the tip of his finger, she nodded and every now and then made suggestions of her own.

The following Sunday afternoon, the sound of buggy wheels crunching on the gravel made Maude straighten up from the bundle of twigs she had just tied. She was behind the house, where the young apple trees grew near the curve of the creek. She knew Rob couldn't be far. After all, he was just looking for downed timber on the rim rocks rising up a quarter mile north. They had agreed he would be back within an hour, and that was half elapsed already.

Maude came around the side of the house, dusting her gloved hands. Sitting not five yards from the front porch was an elegant black landau, drawn by a matched pair of bays. She vaguely remembered hearing that McNaughton owned a landau, so her eyes darted across the lawn to the front porch. There, silhouetted by the electric porch lights, was a tall figure in a long coat.

McNaughton appeared to be carrying some kind of case. Knocking vigorously on the door, he stopped midstroke and turned when he heard her footsteps.

"Ah, the mistress is tending to the tasks of the manor."

"Good evening, Laird."

"Evening to you, Maude." He smiled. "I must say that's the most pleasant greeting I've ever received from you."

Maude took a cautious breath, measuring exactly how she wanted this to go.

McNaughton gestured to his carriage. "I brought my landau out for a spin. I don't believe you've ever seen it. It was custom-made in St. Louis. Come and have a look."

Maude folded her arms around her rib cage and shrank away.

"Oh, come now, I simply want to show it to you. It's a fine conveyance. Nothing like it anywhere in the state."

As Maude walked warily toward the carriage with the bronze "M" enameled on its side, her eyes darted into the pine shadows on the west side of the house. *Rob, Rob, you're part of this plan, please be watching me.* She stopped a good six feet away as McNaughton unlatched the door and flung it wide.

In spite of herself, she couldn't stop a gasp from escaping her lips. The inside was lavishly upholstered in cranberry-colored velvet, and over the top of the plush seats were two ample throws, one of sheared beaver and the other of sumptuous red fox. Bracketed to the inside walls were sconces holding small kerosene lanterns, and along the right-hand side was a brass bucket, probably for champagne.

"I've never seen the like," Maude said, backing away. "I'm sure you're quite proud of it."

McNaughton dropped his eyelids slightly. "Oh, I am. You can just imagine what a pleasant ride it is." He closed the door gently, then let his hands fall to his sides. Careful not to get too close to her, he eased himself a few steps away from the carriage.

Maude glanced at the gray eyes, watching for the ruthlessness behind the unctuous manners, but at the same time, she felt a strange tug of compassion. Just now, he was clearly using great care not to frighten her. She didn't feel as afraid as she usually did around him. She felt good—even exhilarated. Would it be so wrong, she wondered, to show him some neutrality, since he was soon going to be consigned to her past, forever? After all, he couldn't hurt her anymore. That part of her life was over. For the first time ever, she felt strong and stable in his presence. She could afford to be a little generous, at last. He was such a miserable person; she felt herself rising to something new. Could it be mercy?

"You know, Maude, after I was here the other day, I realized I must have alarmed you with that sudden proposal. It was rather rude of me. I brought a wee bit of my best Scotch whisky this evening and I wondered if we might just have a toast to consider—just to consider—beginning again, you and I."

He turned to the porch and unbuckled the carrying case, bringing out two glasses engraved with the Rocking M brand. Uncorking the bottle of whiskey, he began to pour.

"I don't care for any, thank you, so just pour for yourself."

McNaughton ignored her, filling both glasses. "None of the best from the Rocking M? What would your dear father say? He joined me for a drink not too long ago. He'd savor this as if it were liquid gold. Let's toast to your father, at least."

She waved her hand. "Laird McNaughton, I've got to speak to you about something."

"Can't you call me Tom, after all this time?"

"Whatever you like. Nonetheless, I've got to tell you something."

"Pray go ahead, my dear." Nodding deferentially, he took her hand and placed a glass of whiskey in it.

Glancing down at the drink, she gave her head a little shake and proceeded, undeterred. "Since your wife's recent passing, you've pressed me time and again for some kind of continuance of our—relationship—and I find the use of that word despicable, since what took place between us those many years ago was utter violence, not the commencement of a relationship. For some reason unknown to me, you have been unwilling to accept my position." She paused to draw a breath.

McNaughton took a long pull on his drink. "Talking about matters of the heart is never easy." He raised his glass. "A little liquid courage might make this easier for you."

Maude licked her dry lips, then took a sip. It was good whiskey. "To call this a matter of the heart is absurd. You have assaulted me not once but twice. I don't know why I even have to have this discussion with you, but it appears I must. Please know that this will be the last time.

"When you were here at Christmas," she continued, "you saw that your relative—I know he is not a blood relation to you, but you evidently have a distant connection by marriage—you saw that Rob Elliott was here."

McNaughton lifted one eyebrow. "I do recall."

Maude took another sip, and at the same time, had a fleeting sense that she was already feeling the whiskey in her knees.

"The fact of the matter is, Laird McNaughton—I will never call you by any other name—there's no point in delaying this any longer. Rob Elliott and I are to be married at Candlemas." She removed the glove from her left hand and let the blue topaz glitter in the late afternoon light. The sight of the ring filled her with even more strength and courage. She wanted to smile, but kept her expression sober.

McNaughton let out a guffaw. "I knew it. The fox has indeed been watching the henhouse. My own kinsman. Well, we'll see about this. Whatever makes you happy, Maude. To your good health, you bonny sweet lass."

He raised his glass again and looked away for a moment, a bemused look on his face as he absently studied the south pasture. "But wait," he said after a time, "I never showed you how the entire top of the landau can be removed for summer driving. It appears to be made entirely of wood, but it's actually part canvas and padded silk . . ."

Befuddled, Maude took another sip. He was taking the news much too well. As McNaughton described the carriage's elaborate roof canopy and the way it could be detached by means of numerous latches and sliding pins, she shook her head to clear her thinking. She didn't care about the damned British brass foundry and the flexible roof supports.

But McNaughton went on, gesturing and pointing. She noticed how he smiled at her every now and then in a banal sort of way. It wasn't like him. Nothing was making sense. *Where was Rob? Why was McNaughton being so compliant and jovial?* She backed up gingerly and sat down on the edge of the porch.

Rob should be here by now. They had this all planned, start to finish, exactly how it would happen if McNaughton came. But here the man was, sitting down next to her, lifting his coattails, ever the pretentious gentleman. He was seated a good three feet away, respectful, even companionable. But something had shifted. The casual smile had given way to a watchful, vigilant expression, more like the real McNaughton. *Predatory.* She felt a dull chill run up her spine.

She peered through the thickening twilight at him, and as she did, the hair rose on her arms. A familiar gust of inner wind coursed through her. *No,* she thought. *No.* A deep knowledge filled her in that old way, but this time it was cloudy, so very cloudy.

The fuzz thickened in her brain. "My drink."

"Your drink," he said, raising his glass again. "I mixed it just for you, my bonny. Got the glass ready, in a very special way, before I even arrived." His eyes scanned hers and a smile crept over his lips. "So your little world of certainty has gone a bit vertiginous, has it?" Swallowing thickly, he set his own glass down on the porch floor. He leaned into her, slipped his hands beneath her arms and stood, raising her up with him. Her head fell back.

Maude emitted something like a whimper, but the sound was stifled as his mouth crushed down on hers. When she flailed at him, her efforts tired her so much that her arms seemed to melt and the edges of her world grew smoky and dim. She could barely sense what was happening, but she felt his wet lips on hers and his tongue thrusting into her mouth, hard and probing. His left hand was on her buttocks and his right hand went inside her coat, pulling her blouse from her waistband. His fingers slipped in, frenetic and eager at finding bare skin, then quickly fanned up to cup her breast.

"No," he said, panting, "not here. Our carriage."

He lifted her ragdoll body and moved quickly to the landau, climbing easily inside and placing her on the furs. Jostled by the rude yanking of her skirt, Maude felt the shock of his cold fingers on her thighs.

"Sweet Jesus, woman, I have waited so long. Longer than that upstart Elliott, longer than anyone. But we've got to leave." He dragged his hands away from her and backed out. "By the time that whelp knows what has happened, he'll never find you."

"I already have, you bloodsucking bastard." The butt of Rob's rifle rammed into the back of McNaughton's skull with a loud crack. McNaughton pitched forward, then reeled around, his eyes burning with rage.

Flinging himself at Rob, he grabbed the gunstock and slammed the rifle across Rob's chest, shoving it up against his throat. Rob's coat and scarf kept the gun from hitting his windpipe, but the barrel plowed up and scraped hard against his jawbone. Using McNaughton's own force against him, Rob flipped the gun out of the laird's grip and into the air.

Startled, McNaughton drew back. "You won't stop me, you little piece of shite!" He charged Rob, driving a fist into his face.

Rob went down hard, blood draining from his nose. Airborne, McNaughton crashed down on top of him. But Rob rolled to the side, scrambling to his feet and landing a hail of blows into McNaughton's gut as the older man struggled to stand.

McNaughton doubled over, gasping for air. Rob came back in, putting the entire weight of his body into a driving uppercut. McNaughton tottered backward, bumping into the white-eyed, rearing horses, then sprawled onto the ground.

Stumbling to the open door of the landau, Rob grabbed Maude, who had groggily slipped one ankle out the door. Scooping her up, he half-carried, half-dragged her from the carriage to the porch and yanked open the front door. Lowering her to the kitchen floor, he turned around to watch McNaughton, who had rolled himself onto his hands and knees near the carriage.

Rob strode back to him and landed a solid kick in his ribs, toppling him back onto the frosty gravel. From there he went to the barn, cut two lengths of rope, and stalked back. Binding McNaughton's hands snugly behind him, he ordered him to his feet.

"Get inside the carriage."

McNaughton lurched up on one knee, glowering through the mud and blood crusting on his cheeks. "You don't even have the decency to let me drive myself home?"

"Decency?" Rob towered over his foe, the wind tossing his hair wildly around his face. Sparks of vengeance glittered in his eyes. In spite of himself, McNaughton caught his breath, for he thought he saw a yellow glint of something inhuman in Rob's drilling stare.

"What right do you have to use the word *decency*?" Rob spat. "I'm doing you a kindness you don't remotely deserve. Get up and get in your damned carriage, before I bloody some other part of your ugly face."

McNaughton's jaw worked back and forth as he stood up and climbed in. After he was seated, Rob whipped another piece of rope around his ankles and tied it into a snug knot. Stepping back and holding the black-lacquered door, he looked coolly at McNaughton, who turned his head away and stared off into the dusk.

"You come back here, Thomas McNaughton, and I'll kill you. Make no mistake. This is the end of the trail for us."

He closed and latched the door and went back to the barn. A moment later he emerged, leading his blue roan with only a bridle. In his free hand, he held a fly whip. Leaping agilely onto the horse, he took hold of the harness rigging and led the matched bays down the winding lane.

When he got to the East Fork Road, he pointed the team south toward the Rocking M, then swung the fly whip high and whacked both their rumps, yelling, "*Yah*! Run like the bloody devil. You've got him inside!"

The skittish horses bolted away, and the landau clattered down the dark road.

Chapter Thirty

Morag stood on the depot platform, her fat carpetbag in hand, with several Graham women clustered around her. Isobel, in her red Christmas coat and high-button boots, leaned against her aunt's free arm. Her head, crowned in clove brown curls, came just past Morag's shoulder.

"Lookit the twa of ye now," purred Ailse. "Spit and image of yer great-gran Callie."

Morag smiled down at Isobel. "Half of the Grahams got Granda Jamie's dark curls and half have the auburn stuff from John's side. Mary and Fiona got bright copper, like two lucky pennies." She reached over and ran a hand under Mary's chin.

Morag's face grew serious. "Mary, you take care of Miss Fiona, now. A bad sprain is nothing to fool with, especially one that has bruised up like hers. It was good of Maude to stay behind to look after her today."

Mary nodded. "We'll make sure she does just as you instructed. We've got Ailse to help too."

"I can still skate without Fiona, can't I?" Isobel spun away from Morag and fixed her blue eyes on Ailse.

Catriona frowned. "Isn't it enough that one of you is injured? The doctor said Fee's anklebone may even be cracked. Let's hold off on the skating a bit now."

Isobel scowled. "Mother, you heard the stationmaster say it's the best year the Basin's ever had for skating. Everyone's talking about how they've never seen so much ice on the creek."

"Now, Trina, she's got a point," said Ailse. "If the lass fancies a time or twa skatin', I'll watch her. Fiona didnae fall on the ice, mind ye. She was climbin' the bank o' that burn in her sturdy boots. These things happen."

Morag raised her eyebrows and elbowed her sister. "Be thankful, Trina. There are any number of things they could be doing that would worry you more than skating."

Turning back to Mary, Morag said quietly, "Fiona is at a somewhat . . . delicate age. You know she admires you fiercely, don't you?"

Mary's gaze was fixed on the black and gold lettering on the passenger car, which branded it as part of the greater Milwaukee rail system. Groping her way back from a distant summer day, she replied, "I suppose. Yes."

"She does. Mary, for the next while of your life, you may very well have no more devoted friend than Fiona. You both need each other. Remember that."

Mary cast her eyes down a moment, then looked up and nodded. "All right. Thank you."

When the whistle blew two shorts, the shiny crows on the depot roof exploded upward with bellicose cries, then flapped toward a grove of nearby cottonwoods.

Ailse winked at Morag. "When the corbies gang thegither, spring's not far."

Morag gave a nod, then turned back to Mary. "I'll be back in May, in plenty of time for you and your babe."

Mary stepped forward and clung to Morag, her fingers sinking into the folds of Morag's tweed coat. Isobel moved silently away and Catriona dropped her gaze. Only Ailse continued to watch as Morag stroked Mary's hair and held her close.

The whistle sounded again. Hugs went round, and with that, Morag boarded the train for Great Falls.

With Fiona dozing in Catriona's pillowed chaise by the fire, Maude was at liberty to talk with Rory about their father's plans. It was a Saturday, and Rory was not expected at the warehouse, but John and Mac were busy, supervising the replacement of one of the lambing sheds.

"When will you go?"

"Dad can hardly stand it. He wants to go as soon as we can. Late next week, maybe."

"I suppose I would do the same thing if I were in your shoes. I mean, let's face it. Paul is a criminal. A fugitive. It's very likely he won't stay in one place very long. Jack says he's in New York State?"

"Yes. Buffalo. He's doing the same kind of work as before. Easements, but this time for the Erie Railroad."

"Father isn't going to try to bust in there and handle this on his own, is he? I mean, you're going to contact the authorities when you get there, right?"

Rory smiled. "I had some work to do with Father John in that regard."

"You're joking. He wanted to ride in there like a vigilante and . . . lynch Paul?"

"Lynching. That brings quite a picture to mind, now doesn't it?" A sardonic smile curved Rory's lips. Suddenly he shoved back his chair and felt the side of the stove. "It's gone out. I thought it was getting cold in here." While he busied himself shoving newspapers and kindling into the firebox, he continued. "I'm not exactly sure what Dad was thinking, but it may have been something just like that. You know, Maude, if it were my daughter who had been used the way Mary has been, I would probably feel the same way. This kind of crime brings out the darkest side of people."

The deep rumbling sound of warm air tunneling up the chimney meant the stove was drawing again. As Rory ministered to the fire and shoved the coffeepot back over the flames, Maude looked past him to the white landscape that lay beyond the window. *The darkest side of people.* Her thoughts went to her father, and to what might happen to him if he killed Paul. He could go to jail. No one would want that. She would stand by Rory in preventing her father from taking such a risk.

But just now, her heart swelled in her chest. *Why, thirteen years ago, couldn't circumstances have been such that some family member might have risen up and brought to justice the man who had ill-used the eldest Graham girl? Why indeed.*

She stared at the contours of the rolling foothills and the fans of ruddy dogwood rising from the streambeds, giving way to the dark rumpling mountains beyond. However much things could have, should have, gone differently for her, danger and pain were behind her at last. McNaughton had been shamed completely out of her life.

While she talked to Rory about managing their father's rage, she had to admit that, with her father scenting Paul's trail more and more strongly now, she often felt a compounding of her own dark injuries, and even took some gruesome pleasure in visions of John horsewhipping Paul within an inch of his life. *Here, in this grievous crime, at least someone would be punished. Someone's sins would be brought publicly to light, and he would be, as were the shamefaced citizens of old, dragged into the town square and shackled into the stocks to feel the humiliating consequences of his own reprehensible acts.*

"Anybody home?" Rory was watching her.

She swung her head back to him. "Yes. Any father would have difficulty behaving rationally. So I repeat, you will be contacting the Buffalo police?"

"I had to compromise a bit with Dad on that one. He insists that we not contact them until we get there. He wants to take Paul by surprise and he's afraid some well-intentioned constable might bungle the plan if informed ahead of time."

Maude nodded. "I don't blame him there, really."

"He has a point, although it leaves us at a disadvantage if Paul does move his lodgings while we are en route. Jack has someone keeping an eye on him, but this fellow isn't on Jack's payroll. He's just a friend, so our information isn't very consistent."

Maude steepled her fingers and tipped her chin onto them.

"There is an element of risk. You don't think he will be dangerous
. . . I mean, armed?"

"No idea, really."

She lifted her brows. "So let's say you snare him and manage to
keep Father from murdering him. What then?"

"Dad's been talking with Ed Brassey. His legal opinion is that
we can seize Paul's assets on a number of fronts. Emotional cruelty,
misrepresentation, abandonment, and so on."

"Provided he has assets. He seems like the squandering type."

"We'll just have to find out. That's why it's important to take him
by surprise. We don't want him to have time to hide his bankbook
or any important papers that might be helpful to Mary."

"Ailse and I will be . . . praying for you."

Rory set his cup down on the stove and drummed his fingers
on the edge of his chair. "You can pray, or you two can brew up a
damn spell if you want."

The flat, wide spot in the river near Dawson's attracted a number of
children from around Judith Basin, but by the time Isobel had her
fill of skating, the only remaining family was waving good-bye from
their spring wagon and rumbling down the road. Ailse had left the
buggy across the footbridge on purpose, wanting to take her time on
the walk back, looking for lichen in the woods near the bridge.

After insisting that Isobel take a different path away from the
skating area than the hazardous one Fiona had chosen, she waited
for her granddaughter to approach, then took her arm. Ailse studied
the ground, using her stick to poke away branches of juniper and
deadfall, looking here and there as they meandered idly toward the
bridge, entirely unaware that the two of them were being watched.

Ailse cut a somber figure in her black worsted, but Isobel, in her
new scarlet coat and polished boots, with her dark curls blowing in
the crisp afternoon air, was striking.

The tall figure astride the black horse, hidden in the ponderosa pines, held a brass telescope to his eye, studying the girl, and felt the turning pages of time. Back they flew, back to an earlier day, when he had young sons, when he himself was far younger and held the course of his life tightly in his grip like the well-crafted stock of a prized weapon. He had been a powerful man. Born to the good life, he was part of Scotland's landed gentry. He had traveled Europe, had hunted with royalty. Now he had created a fine life for himself and his family in the American West. Education, privilege, good company—all these things were his. Unswerving business sense had enriched his position; virility had pounded through him every waking hour, and he had given it free rein whenever he liked, the way a rider lets a fine horse have its head.

Yes, he had had everything he wanted, except one thing. He'd tasted it, once. How sweet that bit of ambrosia had been. The sight of her—the fine waist on her, those trim ankles in the black boots as they strode along the deck, swishing among the chairs and along the ramps. And that glorious mane of silken curls, the color of a blackthorn sapling.

And here, just now, on the arm of a stooped old hag, was the same girl. A vision in scarlet, in high-button boots, with a dark nimbus of curls haloing her head. Through the telescope, even her face was the same.

Ailse's head came up before she heard the horse's hoofbeats. Something was amiss. It came to her just as she and Isobel reached the bridge. Her buggy was in sight, but Ailse knew they would not get there in time. "Isobel," she said, her voice as hard as stone.

Isobel turned and fixed her ice blue eyes on her grandmother. "Something's wrong, isn't it, Gran? I can feel it, here, in my chest."

"Aye, child. I want ye to hold onto me and dinnae let go, nae matter what." Her voice was suddenly hoarse with urging. "Set your skates doon. We'll get them later."

Isobel had barely dropped her skates when the black horse and its rider came thundering from the pines. "Gran, we must try to get to the buggy!" She held fast to Ailse's arm as the two of them began to run across the bridge.

McNaughton's horse shied at the beginning of the bridge planking. They heard him curse. The horse came on, its hooves clomping and ringing on the wood and metal.

Ailse's steps were small and halting. Isobel flung a look back. "His horse hates him," she breathed.

"Ye micht have to let go and run withoot me," Ailse croaked. "Tak' the buggy."

"Never!"

McNaughton was directly behind them. Isobel spun around, still holding Ailse's arm. The railing of the bridge was the only thing that separated them from McNaughton and the icy currents below.

"Lassie!" McNaughton trotted up, calling out to her in a husky voice. "Miss Graham, a word with you."

Staring into the horse's eyes, Isobel focused all her strength on the ill will she sensed between horse and master. McNaughton peered down at her with basilisk eyes. Bending over, he curled his long fingers around her upper arm like a manacle. "Ride with me today, won't you?"

He is so strong! Isobel's heels left the bridge deck. She closed her eyes, returning her thoughts to the wounds she knew the stallion had suffered. Tension snapped and popped like wild threads of lightning in the air all around them. *Now. I must act now.*

In the quiet darkness of her mind, she grabbed Ailse's worn stick and, wielding it like a sword, she held it aloft. She saw herself tear a hole in the pale sky and stir the chalky clouds to silver madness, whipping them into a crackling maelstrom. She summoned things she'd never considered in all her life, sucking down the energy of the stars behind the broad light of the sun, raining shards of it onto the bridge, hailing the white blessings of the universe into the space between herself and the horse.

The black horse reared up and stayed up, pawing the air. McNaughton lost the reins and cursed at his mount, but fell forward instead of back, as Isobel had so dearly hoped. As the stallion bolted away, McNaughton catapulted against her. The railing gave a loud crack, like a rifle shot, and Isobel began shedding her hold on Ailse. Her slender white fingers opened, letting go of the black worsted sleeve and the bony arm inside.

But Ailse had hold of Isobel's arm and would not release her. "Let go, Gran," screamed the girl, her voice muffled against McNaughton's jacket.

Conquest still written on his aging face, he clung to Isobel, holding her body tight, but the railing cracked and splintered. He watched the brilliant blue eyes, only inches from his own, grow wide with terror, and he felt his balance shift.

Gravity had wrested his precious prey from him; he had to save himself. He lifted his hands away and regained his footing, but Isobel was gone, tumbling past the shattered railing, falling straight toward the jade green water and ice below, with Ailse holding fast to her right arm.

Maude clucked softly to Bobcat and watched a red fox pick up speed in the field near the river. Rob was saying something about the tools he wanted to find on her father's workbench once they got to Stony Creek. The tail of the fox, level with the horizon, was also level with the bridge across the creek, some distance away. As the bridge came into focus, Maude's eyes widened and her hand went toward Rob's arm. Then she shot up from her seat and let out a scream. "It's Isobel! She's fallen off the bridge! I know it's her—I can see her red coat!"

Rob stood up, holding on to the frame as the buggy careened along the road. "Someone's gone over with her. Christ, I think it's your grandmother."

"Sweet God in heaven, go!" She flogged the horse . . . once, twice, three times, she lashed Bobcat's flanks.

Rob yanked the whip from her hands, nearly falling out. "Maude! He's going as fast as he can. We're almost there."

"I'm jumping out. Across the field . . . I'll get to the river before the horse . . ." As she uttered the words, Maude flew from the buggy with Ajax at her heels.

Reining in the lathered and quivering horse, Rob jumped down and tore through the field after her, leaping over clumps of sage and dodging patches of snow and rock.

Maude ran through the willow breaks, over uneven hummocks of grass at the high water mark, then skidded down over the pebbly scree until she hit the shoals of ice banked up around the boulders at the edge of the creek. She cursed the recent cold spell, which had left swathes of ice everywhere on the spring-fed river. Ajax danced at the edge, a thin whine coming from his throat.

There, in the middle of the wide, half-frozen creek, she caught a glimpse of red fabric. It nearly surfaced at one point, then skimmed down again beneath a thick plateau of ice. She couldn't be sure . . . had there been another, darker shadow near it?

Calculating how fast the forms were moving, she took several bold steps downstream, into the river's midline. Rob was fifteen yards farther down, moving in tandem with her. They were thinking the same thing. If she couldn't snare the fabric through one of the openings in the ice where she was aiming, then he could do it, God help them both. She moved fast, watching her feet. A hairline crack, like a thread of white silk, shot out from her left foot. She didn't care. She would die saving them.

Nearly at the middle now, she saw the red form coming, a rusty stain in the moss green water coursing beneath the ice. Aiming her hands at an opening dead center in the river, she knelt down and braced her right foot against a boulder.

But it was Ailse's face that bobbed out of the water first, gasping for air. Maude pitched forward and grabbed, hauling as hard as she could: an armpit, an elbow, a waistband. Dragging, heaving, she had Ailse's torso up on the ice when she saw the red coat slithering close. She plunged away from her grandmother, nearly diving into the hole. "Isobel!" She clawed at the coat, but her fingers were so cold they would not bend, let alone form a solid grasp on the red fabric. She stared at her hands, horrified that such numb and useless appendages could belong to her. "Isobel!" She flailed at the water, screaming so hard that blood rose in her throat.

She threw her head back and let out a keening cry as the scarlet fabric trailed under the ice and drifted past the boulder. "Rob, get her! You must!" Sobbing, she sprawled on the ice, her fingers splaying uselessly on the slippery surface. Then, drawing herself to her knees, she turned back to Ailse, forcing her stiff hands and arms to haul the rest of the semiconscious woman out of the water. She kept her eyes on Rob.

"I'll get her." His voice was hard, steady.

Maude shook her head, then flung her face into her hands, unable to bear the consequences of what might happen. She shut her eyes tight, closing out everything except the bitter cold and the horrid sounds around her. Seconds later, hearing Rob's loud grunts and a drenching thud, she opened them to see Isobel's sodden form and bluish white face.

"Ailse is breathing," she called out, struggling to her feet, afraid to ask about Isobel. Half running, half slipping and falling the six yards downstream to where Isobel lay, she slid on her knees to the limp girl. It was as she feared: Isobel's chest was completely still. Maude reached a stiff hand beneath her head and tipped it back.

"Rob, if your fingers work, you've got to pinch her nostrils shut. Don't ask me any questions, damn it, just do as I say."

"They work. Pinch?"

"Take hold of her nose and just hold it shut."

Rob awkwardly reached out and did as he was told, watching in amazement. He'd heard stories about this kind of thing but had never seen it, never believed in it. Maude exhaled into Isobel, then pushed down on her chest slowly and gently, then rolled her onto her side. She then rolled her on her back again, exhaled into her mouth, and repeated the procedure. After she'd been at it for nearly a full minute, Rob thought he saw a trace of color coming back to Isobel's face, but he knew he must be crazy. It couldn't be. Then a miracle happened. Isobel's body erupted in a spasm of choking and coughing, and a gush of water poured from her mouth. Maude rolled her onto her side and pounded on her back.

Maude looked up at him, her eyes brimming with hot tears.

"Get the buggy, please. Neither one of them is out of danger. We could still lose them."

On Big Spring Road, they met Mac, who'd come to search the road and to see how Ailse and Isobel were doing, because the strangest thing happened, he said. Laird McNaughton's black horse had come galloping up Stony Creek Lane, riderless, and had trotted off to stand with the Graham horses as if he'd lost his wits. He reared up and ran if anyone tried to go near him.

Mac wheeled his horse around as soon as he understood, racing back to Stony Creek to get the covered carriage and blankets. When he returned, Isobel and Ailse, shaking violently, were loaded in. Catriona and Maude stripped both of them naked, casting the soggy clothing on the floor, and buttoned them into John's long underwear, following that with woolly cardigans for each.

While Rob followed with Maude's buggy, Maude and Catriona rattled along inside the carriage, rubbing furiously at the wet heads, trying to mop up every trace of moisture. At last they glimpsed the big house and made the sharp turn onto Stony Creek Lane.

"Fiona and Mary are warming the bedroom," said Catriona. "Mac will go after Doc Attix."

Maude nodded, eager for the doctor's help and opinion. She knew that if Ailse's thin frame could not be brought up to proper temperature soon, she would perish before dawn. Isobel stood a better chance because of her youth, but she had taken a lot of water into her lungs. For the present, Maude felt it best to keep silent on the details of Isobel's somewhat miraculous revival.

Catriona peered over at Maude through the dim light of the covered carriage with a dull, questioning look. Maude leaned stiffly into the corner of the carriage, her chin resting on Isobel's head and her arms folded tightly around the shuddering form. She returned her mother's gaze. They both knew McNaughton was behind this. Catriona lowered her lashes and shook her head, tucking the gray blanket around Ailse, who seemed no bigger than a bird in her lap.

Catriona seemed about to say something, but Maude looked away. Her mind had darted elsewhere, someplace distant and dark, where she gathered herself inward and began to whet the blade of revenge.

Chapter Thirty-One

Fiona gave up her bed, moving into Maude's old one, so that Isobel and Ailse could be together in the room normally shared by the two youngest girls. At first, when Catriona began paying great attention to Ailse's and Isobel's ice-cold hands and feet, going back and forth from bed to bed, chafing and rubbing their limbs, Maude's fist went to her mouth.

She reached out, laying her hand firmly on her mother's arm. "We'll get to the hands and the feet, Mother, but it's the vital organs that we must concern ourselves with right now."

Catriona chattered away, her hands moving rhythmically over Ailse's knotted fingers. "So cold! And me with my loom and my weaving. Think of the socks and gloves I could have knitted this last while."

Maude tightened her grip on her mother's arm, digging her fingers in. As Catriona felt the sudden bite, her head snapped up and she dropped Ailse's hand.

"The heart, the blood at the core of the body, Mother. These are the important things when we are faced with preserving life. *Heat*, Mother. We need linens in which to wrap the hot stones."

Catriona nodded and left, returning with a pile of flannel just as Rob entered with a bushel of flat stones from the oven. "There's more where these came from," he said, then helped wrap the stones while Maude and Catriona tucked them close around the shivering bodies. After twenty minutes, Maude noticed that the spasms seemed to have lessened.

Fred Attix arrived, but not until after eight o'clock. "Mrs. Britten's baby came," he said, tossing his hat onto the trunk in the hall. "These things happen. How are they?"

"We think they are out of danger," Maude said. "They've both had ginger tea within the last hour. Their teeth aren't chattering anymore. But so many things can proceed from this kind of exposure. Mother and I are desperate for your opinion."

Maude was also desperate for something else, and that was to find out exactly what had happened on the bridge. Isobel had stammered some odd phrases through clenched, chattering teeth and seizing gulps of air. She said something about trying to help a horse, and about making silver sparks—this made Maude's eyes soften, because she knew intuitively what Isobel meant—then began spattering out how McNaughton had tried to lift her and take her away.

"Then he went the wrong way and f—fell," she coughed out, "I didn't do a very g—good job . . ."

"Hush now," Maude said. "Tomorrow, sweetheart." The full story would come out later, but Maude had heard enough.

She and Rob had taken over the two stuffed chairs at the end of the upstairs hall for the night. Rather than stand over the doctor as he examined the patients, she retired to this alcove and sat down, bone tired. Ajax, who had followed her silently everywhere, sank down at her feet.

The stairs creaked. Weary as she was, Maude came to attention and leaned forward. "Someone's in the house," she whispered. Rob moved silently toward the head of the stairs while she followed.

There, on the landing, was Kibbey, a rumpled handkerchief in one hand and his hat in the other, his shock of fine white hair in disarray. Even from where she stood, Maude could see his gray eyes watering.

"Kibbey," she said. "What is it? Is everything all right with the sheep?"

He frowned at the steps, then looked up. "Isnae the sheep, Miss Maude. I'm worrit aboot the ladies abovestairs."

"Oh, of course." Maude came down to meet him.

"I want them to be weel again. Both of them, mind ye. But I am special worrit—" he stammered and wiped his nose—"aboot Miss Ailse."

Maude's eyes widened. She'd never had any idea. "They are both comfortable, Kib. I'll tell Mary and Mother to let you know how they are coming along." As she placed a hand on his knotty shoulder, he nodded and turned away.

"God be wi' all ye good ladies this night," was all he said as he trudged down the stairs. Maude heard the heavy front door closing behind him. Going back up the steps, she shook her head. Kibbey, fond of Ailse. It wouldn't have shocked her more had she seen Ajax coming up the stairs carrying the tea tray.

She had scarcely sat down when the doctor came out into the hall. "You've done everything right and proper," he pronounced. "Is there someplace we can all visit? I'd like to give you some additional details on the care of the two women over the next several days."

Adjourning to the living room, the group sat in front of the fire. When Rob was conscripted into carrying Fiona up to her temporary lodgings, the girl fell into a paroxysm of blushing and stammering, but at Catriona's stern look, she submitted and was whisked away.

"I think both of them have every chance of a full recovery," the doctor began. "The only thing that gives me cause for concern is the possibility of them having aspirated any volume of water. In any near drowning, this is always an issue. It is complicated in this case by the hypothermic condition of both patients. I do compliment you on how quickly you acted.

"In listening to the respiration of the young lady," he went on, "I do hear some residual water content." He looked around at the assembly. "Who was present at the—accident?"

Maude glanced around the group. "My fiancé and I arrived immediately afterward."

"When you pulled the young woman—"

"Isobel."

"Yes. When you pulled Isobel from the water, was she breathing, or did she begin breathing soon afterward?"

"She . . . was not breathing."

Dr. Attix's brows lifted. "How was she revived?"

Maude made a little clearing sound in her throat. "I take a certain subscription called the *New England Medical Monthly*. In it, I read about a new process that some physicians had previously done mechanically. It used to be called galvanization. It's now administered from one person to another and referred to as resuscitation. I performed this practice on Isobel and it . . . revived her."

"Yes, the literal exchange of breath. Artificial respiration."

Catriona cocked her head and gave Maude an owlish stare.

"You're the first person I've heard of in my practice who has successfully done this," the doctor went on, slapping his knee. "It's not unheard of. A young boy was revived in Helena last summer." He grinned. "And I also take the *New England Medical Monthly*."

He looked Maude up and down, taking the measure of her, but his face quickly grew serious again. "Miss Isobel is young and will probably clear the remaining fluid from her respiratory system, but she may have difficulty. Do keep an eye on her." He wagged a patriarchal finger at Maude.

"What about Ailse? Are her lungs clear?" Maude stared hard.

"Amazingly, she sounds very good. How old is she?"

"Eighty-one," piped Catriona.

"Astounding," said the doctor. "You Grahams are a hardy lot." He pushed himself to his feet. "I've got to be going. It has been an awfully long day." He walked toward the front hall, then stopped and turned back toward the center of the room. "How on earth did they fall off that bridge?"

"We aren't quite sure," Rob put in, "but we're going to find out." He turned to Maude and her mother. "I'm going to saddle one of the horses and get Sheriff Martin. The sooner we report the details of this, the better. By the time I get back with him, your sister or Ailse ought to be recovered enough to give some account of what happened."

Maude nodded, then watched as his broad shoulders disappeared down the stairs.

In the long side shed sloping off the north face of the barn, she found her way through the gloom to the plank shelving where the camping supplies were stored. Dragging out a large canvas bundle, she checked its contents, then heaved it over her shoulder. Grabbing a lantern in her other hand, she retraced her steps to the cavernous center of the barn.

She went about these chores doggedly, with none of her typical contemplative thinking. When she saw her father's work gloves lying atop a sawhorse near the woodpile, she chewed her lip for a moment, thinking, *is it good or bad that Father is gone, looking for that cur Paul Hathaway? He and Rory must be nearly to Buffalo by now. It's good. He has his war and I have mine.*

She heaved the canvas bag into the spring wagon with a grunt, tucking it carefully around the lantern. Numerous forkfuls of hay, a saddle, bridle, and a bulging rucksack went in as well. She'd pondered whether to bring Ajax, but it took only seconds for her to decide this was no mission for a dog. Grabbing her father's gloves, she flung open the door to the herders' tack room and foraged for some warm gear. A pair of lanolin-greased woolen pants, an old Hudson's Bay jacket, and a heavy scarf. There was even a fleece, which she hastily stuffed in next to the mound of hay. In addition to what she'd taken from the house, these things would serve her well.

Her final stop was the gun bench. There were no pistols or rifles kept here; she knew that John kept them locked in the house. But there was ammunition, and that was all she cared about. Her fingers ran nimbly through many years' accumulation of half-used shell and bullet cartons, bottles of oil and bluing, and bits of rag.

As she opened a red and black box of bullets for her Springfield, she ran her fingers over the cold brass cylinders and whispered, "Who's fair game now, Tom McNaughton?"

Climbing aboard, she tapped the sheathed rifle snugly against the toeboard and snapped the reins against Dundee's speckled gray rump. He snorted and sidled roughly against the harness before plunging forward out of the barn. He wasn't accustomed to the wagon—Maude knew that full well—but he was the best horse for what lay ahead. They took the back lane, through dun-colored grass flattened by the January snows. She rode in silence past Ailse's cottage and swallowed hard when she saw a row of ravens squatting like black ducks on the stone wall of the garden. Ailse always said the ancients considered a line of ravens a sign that battle was imminent. The wind gusted from the west, raising their stiff black feathers like plates of armor.

She flung a look over her shoulder. Although the windows of the main house at Stony Creek had begun to glow a warm yellow with the coming night, no one peered out to watch her turn north on Big Spring Road.

Harriet's boy, Strap Wilkins, worked part-time at Wiedeman's. He also had a cart which he hired out for toting any and all items. Whether it be for parcels that needed to go to the depot, groceries for the elderly, or even the occasional youngster needing a piano lesson across town, Strap's cart was available. At times, Strap had been asked by the moonshiners west of town to carry jugs and crates of special products to the Elkhorn Bar and other establishments. Unless one counted the local ragpicker, whose reputation and credibility were both irretrievably tarnished, there was no one more frequently sighted in the niches and crevices of Lewistown, nor more tightly threaded into its commercial fabric.

When Maude arrived in Lewistown, it was late. She had circled into town from the east, in order to avoid Rob and Sheriff Martin, and meant to stay only as long as necessary. The bell tinkled on the door of Mimi's Café as she entered. Her stiff shoulders relaxed when she saw that the place was nearly empty.

"Is that you, Maude Graham?" Mimi LaFontaine lifted her apron up over her head. "What brings you uptown this evening?"

"I'm looking for Strap. Is he still rooming upstairs?"

"Yes. I think I heard him going up a short while ago. I've gotten so I can tell who's who just by the sound of their feet. I can go and fetch him, or you can go up yourself, if you don't mind. I don't think too many tongues will wag if Maude Graham stops by to speak with the likes of Strap." She winked. "Besides, I heard you got engaged. Congratulations. Rob Elliott, isn't it?"

"Yes. Thank you."

"You waited a long time, but you got a good one."

"I think I did, yes." She shifted from one foot to the other. "Well, I'll only be a few moments. I have an errand for him, that's all. If he has time. Thanks."

"There's chicken and dumplings if you decide you're hungry. Strap's room is number three, by the way."

"Thanks, Mimi." Maude pushed through the side door into the narrow hallway and climbed the wooden stairs to the few rooms that Mimi let to boarders. Several minutes later, Maude and Strap left Mimi's and walked through the chill evening air toward the Mint Bar on the corner of Fourth and Main.

Dabbing a kerchief against his long, straight nose, Strap said, "Most of the wolfers have been hanging around either here or at the Silver Dollar, 'bout four doors down. I'll go to both places and see what I can find out."

"That would be grand," said Maude. "I'll be across the street in the lobby of the Griffin. Take your time."

"And it is all in confidence, don't you worry."

Maude smiled and gave him a quick nod, then hurried across the street. The fireplace in the Griffin's lobby was cold and dark. She sat in a leather chair and pored over a tattered magazine, watching the clock. Strap returned, smelling of whiskey, about thirty-five minutes later.

"I had to drink with them. Sorry. I'm sure you can smell it."

"It's all right. Go ahead. What did you learn?"

"McNaughton's headed north, you were right about that. Due north along the Judith River. The Snowy Mountain wolf pack has headed up that way. Some weeks back, folks are thinking. Some hold to the notion they've gone to Coffee Creek, but there's others that think the Adrad's leading them to Dog Cutbank right near the Missouri. At any rate, McNaughton and his oldest boy are tracking him and his pack."

"Did his man Desmarais go with them?"

"Don't sound like it. Someone said Desmarais has the gout . . . went down to Ten Sleep to see his people."

Maude nodded. "Do any of them know how many are left in the Snowy Mountain pack now?" She wasn't sure why she asked, but she knew she'd take the wolves' part in this contest, at least that was clear.

"They say there are a dozen or more. I think his mate—she's the pure black one—had a litter of four or five last spring. Then there's the ones from last year, and a few rogues that have come in with them."

"And what about the Riggs Brothers? I know they want the Adrad desperately. Have they gotten wind of this?"

"Yes. I don't know if McNaughton heard they was getting geared up to go or vicey-versy. But the Riggs boys left first, then McNaughton left tonight. The older fellas in the Silver Dollar was talking about it when I walked in. Someone heard McNaughton say he wouldn't let those 'bottom-feeding cretins' have his wolf. He said it was his destiny to have the Adrad."

Maude swallowed at the word *destiny*.

Strap was saying, "Some of the old fellows in there are done wolfing. They said it's gone sour for them. No purpose to it anymore other than spite, that's what one of them said. Wouldn't want to kill just for that."

Maude had stopped listening. She was thinking about Dundee, who was at Greene's Livery Stable, being watered and fed. They had a long journey ahead of them, and she needed to get moving. Fishing in the pocket of her wool trousers, she dug out three dollars. "Thank you, Strap. You've done well, just like always. Hatty's lucky to have you. I'll see you next time."

When Elijah Greene asked where she was going in the middle of the night, she lied and said she was going east to Ruby Creek to help her fiancé.

Arranging all her goods at the stable, she didn't think about the nature of her errand. With Elijah puttering a few feet away, she kept at her tasks, ramming the rifle sheath into place, adjusting the items on the packsaddle for balance, and tying the half-hitch knots. Then, when it was all done, she mounted up.

Overhead, the light of the half-moon was just enough to help her navigate. She left the spring wagon behind at Greene's and had gotten a half-appaloosa packhorse for her gear. Dundee picked his way briskly through the frozen ruts, uncertain about the new horse but glad to be free of the wagon. As they crossed a small creek, the horses' shoes rang like bells on the river stones and the sharp scent of wood smoke from a nearby cabin cut the air. Maude pressed her knees tight against Dundee's sides, urging him on.

She knew McNaughton and Blair would travel with a retinue of sorts. *Would they pick up some kind of cook along the way, someone to help them with their chuck tent?* The laird was famous for his wall tents, always having one for cooking and dining, the other for sleeping. His normal leisure, however, would be dampened by the looming threat of the Riggs brothers. Something told her he had already managed to absolve himself of any guilt over what happened on the bridge. Her jaw tightened. *No, he won't let the trip be sullied by that little misdemeanor. If anything causes him unrest, it'll be his effort to keep an upper hand over the Riggs brothers.*

When she saw the lights of the tiny settlement of Kendall glowing in the near distance, she knew it had to be close to midnight. It wasn't fair to the animals to push them all night, nor would she aid her own cause by doing so. Turning the horses over to a young man she rousted by means of a bell, she stumbled wearily up the stairs at Borland's Rooming House. As she sank onto a brass bed, her bones settled against the feather tick with a shudder of thanks, but her mind was restive, full of vagrant thoughts about tomorrow.

She propped herself up on an elbow, rallying. *I must use these moments*, she adjured herself, *to repeat the rudiments of my plans: Strive to differentiate between his trail and that of the Riggs pair. Open myself to signs of all kinds. Ask around town in the morning who has come through in the last day or so.* She sank back down, thinking of the wolves. *What will become of them? And when this pack is killed, what will Rob think? He has such a mysterious affinity for them. They are not my affair, yet I feel just as I did last June, when I told Ailse I wished the big gray would never be slain. Alone, strong, isolated—I understand him. He doesn't deserve to die.*

A stiff breeze rattled the windowpane. She turned to look at the moon, knowing that wherever the wolves were, they looked at it too. With that thought, Rob entered her head again. *He wonders where I am, what I'm doing. What madness I'm about. Well, let him. He thinks he has set me free, but he hasn't. I'm not free. Nor is Isobel, nor my family. McNaughton will torment us the rest of our lives, endangering me and my loved ones at every turn. God in heaven, I have won the right to stop him by any means I choose. I confess I hate the man; but this has gone beyond me now. I won't live this way anymore, nor will I let it spread to my family. The accursed taint of him has hovered over me these many years like a miasma, lying in the lowlands along Big Spring Road, clinging like a sickly vapor to every aspect of my life. Within a day or two, it will stop forever.*

She wadded the tick into her hands, whispering to the dark room, "There's only one way to freedom. One way to justice."

Still fully clothed, she drifted. Images came filtering in . . . a massive gray wolf running wild and free, his black companion at his side. Their long, strong legs carried them through the frosted sage, blowing puffs of snow up beneath their feet as they rose along sandstone bluffs to a dawn streaked with purple and gold.

Leal and Adrad rose in the dark. Leal left the four pups curled together in a shallow cave beneath the roots of a ponderosa pine. No longer were they the tiny balls of fur with blunt noses she had watched so vigilantly last spring; no, these were young adults, with intelligent faces and keen eyes. Nearly the same size now as her pups from the year before, they were adept at hunting small prey like sage hens and snowshoe rabbits, although it seemed to her these were now harder to find than ever. The pups would accompany the pack on today's hunt, learning and growing.

She and Adrad had killed a mule deer yesterday and a young elk a few days before, but in recent weeks they had taken two calves from a ranch near Denton. Neither she nor Adrad liked going where people and cattle and sheep lived, but sometimes they had no choice.

Last year, Adrad had shown her a pile of bones that smelled peculiar, not like deer or elk, and certainly not sheep or cow. There was even a scrap of hide and tail partially buried in the prairie shale. As she sniffed these, Adrad communicated to her that once there were thousands of these animals, huge beasts that the wolves fed upon many years ago, but this was before his time. His father had seen them, but only the very last of them. The Indians still had their fur robes, and sometimes at night near the Indian encampments you could smell the hides.

Adrad didn't know how they were all killed. Maybe they were poisoned by the whites, just as the wolves were being poisoned. Curious, Leal ran her nose over the huge skulls and bones, but when she looked up, Adrad was trotting away. She loped off to catch him. He was wise; he could smell poison. Had these big, horned beasts been poisoned? Only something strong and terrible could have killed so many of these kings of the prairie.

She and Adrad tore off some strips of the mule deer, now crisp with frost, and chewed them, then lay down, waiting for the sun.

Leal rose after a while and went off to mark her place. She was surprised when Adrad came after her quickly, marking exactly where she had been. Then she remembered. *It is midwinter, is it not? It is our time.* She swung around, watching him. His amber eyes lingered on her, then he came at her, gently nipping her cheek. She felt the fur on her shoulders rise like feathers, then roll and settle again. She opened her jaws and ran her teeth over his muzzle, leaping against him. The feel of his massive shoulder muscles against her chest sent a surge of something familiar and potent through her belly; it made her feel alive again after the time of darkness and long nights. The song of coming spring rose inside her, strong and triumphant.

They played like this for several minutes, then grew sleepy and curled up next to each other, back to back, in the early slanting rays of the sun. It would be a long day of northward travel, and they needed their rest.

Chapter Thirty-Two

Rob paced the center of the barn as Mac looked on. "I haven't even got a goddam gun," he said, slamming his hand against a post and glaring at Mac. "My pistols are at Kettle Creek and I'm sure as hell not riding all the way over there before I go after her. I suppose no one even knows where your father keeps the keys to that gun cabinet in his den. I've got to have a rifle of some kind."

"I know where the keys are. But we can't very well go in there and start looting the gun cabinet with Sheriff Martin standing there drinking coffee."

Rob ran a hand through his hair. "No. I can't go back in, not like this. Can you—would you—go in and see how things are going?"

"Do you want me to ride with you? I will. I'd like to. Maude . . . Maude's special to me. She and Isobel and I—we're connected somehow."

Rob took a deep, stiff inhale. "I know. There is something about the three of you. But Mac, I think right now it's best to have a man around the house, with both John and Rory gone. Does that make sense to you?"

Mac pinched the bridge of his nose and nodded his head. "Yeah. I'll come back out to the barn in a bit."

Rob had already saddled Glasgow and, at Mac's urging, had fitted one of the secondary horses with a packsaddle and camping gear. When he had returned from Lewistown with Sheriff Martin, it hadn't taken the two of them long to figure out that Maude had embarked on a journey of several days. With McNaughton rubbing his hands in anticipation of a wolf hunt, and now with a reeking scandal coming down on his head, there was no doubt that the man would leave town any moment, if he hadn't already.

It would be easy enough to track him. Today's events also meant it would be easy—at least Rob hoped it would—to track Maude. Her intentions were too dark to contemplate. Although no one who knew her intimately could blame her for wanting revenge, he could not let her throw her life away. To do so would mean giving McNaughton the final victory—and probably losing Maude forever.

He came to the post again and pounded it with his fist, then slung his head around and groaned in anguish. He simply had no time to waste.

Mac ran in, panting. "The Sheriff's leaving. He's going to form a party of riders and start out looking for McNaughton in the morning." He held up his fingers, from which dangled a brass key. "Mother and the girls are all upstairs. I told them you were going to look for Maude. Mother is nearly hysterical. I gave her a drink, but I probably should have laced it with laudanum."

Rob led the horses toward the barn door. "Let's go see what's in that cabinet."

"I know Dad took a couple, but there's quite a few left. You won't have a problem finding something to your liking."

Rob found plenty, including a Colt .45 and a Winchester. Setting out, something told him to head toward Denton and White Cliffs, but he didn't want to rely on his animal senses alone. He went directly to Lewistown and the drinking establishments on Main Street, tossed back a short whiskey, and questioned the local denizens as though he were setting out on a wolfing excursion himself.

Within an hour he was headed north. No one had seen a woman rider, and whenever he asked, people looked askance. He changed his approach and began visiting saloons, listening for word of any passing hunting parties or trappers. In Danvers, a town about halfway to Denton, he got confirmation that the Riggs brothers had come through several days before and that McNaughton had also passed by with two covered spring wagons earlier that day.

That night, he collapsed in a small, unpainted hotel that appeared likely to topple into a creek. In the morning, when he saw the tidy barn across the square where the horses had spent the night, he shook his head, thinking he ought to have crawled into a manger with them.

"Thet wolf pack is around here, no doubt about it," said the stable boy as he handed Glasgow's reins over to Rob. "My uncle's got a place over Denton way and they took two calves right out from under his nose a couple of weeks ago. Someone said they's gone a little farther north since then, but my Uncle Frank ain't resting any easier."

"No. I suppose not." Rob handed the boy a fifty-cent piece. *All right*, he reasoned as he rode along, *I'm on McNaughton's trail, and on the trail of the Adrad and his pack, but where the hell is Maude? She must have gone north through Kendall instead of Danvers. That road joins up with this one a few miles up ahead, and I'm sure she's got at least a five- or ten-mile lead on me. Which means she's probably closing in on McNaughton.*

It wasn't until late that afternoon, well past Denton, that the trail became more distinct. Ranchers and travelers made mention of wolfing parties, and when Rob referred to McNaughton's well-outfitted wagons, eyebrows went up in recognition. One rancher digging postholes along the road reported that McNaughton and his companion had stopped and talked to an old wolfer named Whitman. This Whitman supposedly knew the country "better than the Indians."

Rob dismounted and helped the man chunk a watermelon-sized rock out of a hole. "'Pears you've done a bit of fencing," said the man.

"I know my way around a wire stretcher." Rob flashed a quick smile, then looked up at the sky. "Least you've got good weather. Good for fencing, not so good for us wolf hunters."

"I s'pose."

Rob warmed the clay. "So this Whitman probably has a sense of where the wolves are denning."

"I hear them most nights. They've gotta be up around White Cliffs, making their forays out of there."

"If Whitman knows so much, why didn't they hire him on with them? I hear the McNaughtons are in high feather."

"Whitman's laid up. Horse wreck."

Rob touched the brim of his hat and swung up into the saddle, giving Glasgow a light prod. The road that ran like a ribbon between Wolf Creek and the Judith River was seldom traveled, bending sharply east a mile or so before the confluence of the two. Here they joined to become a tributary of the Missouri, emptying into the great river at the place known as White Cliffs.

He drew the gold pocket watch from his vest. Quarter to six. The skeletal arms of the cottonwoods reached into a sheet-iron sky, and the rugged hills were mottled with dark pines and gray patches of bare aspen. Long slopes of snow-covered prairie, broken by rough buttes and rock outcroppings, dotted the valley. A quarter mile up ahead, he saw a ravine winding its way down an unnamed mountain slope and guessed it might feature a creek, if he was lucky. As good a campsite as any.

Still holding the pocket watch in his hand, he could make out the inscription in the gathering twilight. "O whistle, and I'll come to you." He snapped the lid shut, then let out a soft whistle, like the song of a lark. Borne quickly away, it died on the cold breeze.

He pitched his small tent on a rise near the creek, affording himself a good view of the valley. He chose not to build a fire, wanting instead to watch for other fires in the valley—to see, rather than be seen. Seated near a lightning-blasted cottonwood and chewing on some dried beef, he watched the pale sky deepen to indigo. One by one, stars sparked the cold vault of blue. The taut muscles in his shoulders twitched at every rustle of grass, at any change in the faint plashing of the tiny creek. As the wind died, he heard the cry of a wolf to the north, where he estimated the coulees of White Cliffs to be.

If McNaughton meets his maker, Rob reasoned, *at least he won't kill any wolves. But there could be no blood on Maude's hands. If I have to*, Rob vowed, *I'll do the killing. If there was ever a man who needed to be sent on his way, it's Tom McNaughton.*

Of course, there's jail as an alternative. No question Ed Martin and some of his men must be headed this way by now. McNaughton would be tried and found guilty of something. Attempted kidnapping and rape. But for his other crime, long-buried in the past? What of that? And God only knows what other wickedness he's committed and concealed.

Rob whipped the heavy camp blanket around himself and settled in, propped in relative comfort against his saddle and the tree. By eight o'clock, his vigilance was rewarded. Not one but two fires appeared, separated by a great distance. One was less than a mile from his own campsite, farther south, which surprised him, because it seemed to be back the way he came. The other was to the north, on the opposite side of the valley, also about a mile away. For a moment he wondered if one might be Maude's. A grim smile flickered across his face and disappeared. *As stealthy as I am tonight*, he realized, *she'll be like the very ether, silent as an owl on the air and completely invisible.*

Caching his belongings in a granite crevice and checking the pickets on both horses, he strapped on the Colt and headed off through the buckbrush toward one of the fires.

One of the few things Rattler and Judd Riggs knew how to do in a campsite, Rob concluded from his observation point twenty yards downwind from their campsite, was to keep their foodstuffs tied in a canvas manty and hung in a tree. They also knew how to build a small, hot fire, the way the Indians do. Right now, the fire was untended, and overall, the place looked like a rummage sale.

The once-white canvas wall tent wasn't just dirty, it was dashed everywhere with gray black stains. The flickering light inside revealed strange patterns where rusty chains, wolf traps, and wheel hubs had lain upon its folds. Enamel dishpans and buckets sat here and there around the site, and pieces of long underwear lay spread-eagled on the junipers. One of the sideboards on the wagon had been let down to serve as a kitchen. Rob could see open tin cans and utensils scattered about.

The tent flap opened and both men emerged, each carrying a lantern.

"I ain't setting no meat out in the damn dark. We done that over by Winnifred and you seen what happened there. Like to kilt myself on them rocks."

"It'll be just as dark when we get up to do it. You're so soused you'll probably dump poison in the breakfast beans."

"I don't know why we bother with't anyways. Damn beast. Guns. Mark me, it'll be a gun that gets 'im. I gotta piss."

Rob backed away into the open meadow, having seen all he needed. He knew that these wolfers, and McNaughton as well, would do their serious work just before sunrise, as soon as the hills had the barest shimmer of predawn light. Right now, he had to assure himself of McNaughton's location. He set off across the valley, keeping his gaze fixed on the tiny orange gleam in the distance.

McNaughton's frame of mind was something Rob could only attempt to comprehend. He was certain that the laird had Blair with him. Even so, he had just assaulted two women and was intelligent enough to know that even his good relations with Sheriff Ed Martin wouldn't keep Martin from upholding the law.

A momentary flash of attachment to Thomas McNaughton, mingled with pity, drifted through Rob every now and then. After all, he was Grant's father. But Rob had reached the end of the line with McNaughton and had consigned the man to the fate he had wrought for himself. In a standard criminal case, once the perpetrator's dark deeds lay open for perusal, the courts and the public would take up the questions Rob no longer cared to ask.

But in this case, Rob pondered as he stole silently from one stand of pines to another, McNaughton's account would never be publicly tallied, not without devastating injury to the innocent. *No*, he thought, his jaw clenched tight and his hand hovering close to the butt of his gun, *justice must be meted out differently sometimes. God forgive me, but if necessary, I'm ready to dispense it.*

He slowed as he closed in, taking more care with his footing and listening keenly. As he approached, he realized this camp was closer to the river than he had originally thought. He could tell by the dull rushing sound that the broad, cold Missouri river was only twenty or so yards away from the campsite.

When he made out the silhouette of two covered spring wagons, he knew for certain he'd found McNaughton. Creeping in a wide circle around to the north, he moved close to the river, hoping to discover some trace of Maude. But halfway around, he had to abandon the strategy. A wall of granite rock made further progress impossible, so he doubled back toward the south. En route, he stepped on a brittle twig. The loud snap broke the still night, and voices rose up in alarm.

He ran dead east toward the road, knowing that the two men would not hesitate to come out in the brush looking for a predator. In no time at all, he put a half mile between himself and the camp. Minutes later, he was spreading out his bedroll, banking up a mattress of cottonwood leaves and spruce boughs.

Tossing onto his back, he inhaled deeply, forcing air into his lungs. Then, out of the north, came a long, rolling howl, just like the one he'd heard many months ago on Ruby Creek that had awakened him out of a dead sleep. Another wolf joined in, sending up a low, moaning call to its mate.

He closed his eyes, soaring back to that warm, sleepless night. To the very marrow of his bones, he'd felt as though they were his spiritual kin. That feeling was so strong that he'd gone and found Inii and Medicine Badger to help him learn, at least to begin to comprehend.

Now, with his head resting against the firm roll of blanket, he recalled Medicine Badger's words that strange, crimson night in the forest. "The humans have their nation," he had said. "The owls have their nation, the wolves have theirs. Rob Elliott, you can be Wolf Brother, but you are human nation. Listen to wolf song, and learn what your wolf brothers tell you, but you can never be wolf nation."

The wolf chorus swelled up into the cold blue night, varying in pitch as it bounced off the rugged topography of the Missouri River bluffs. One wolf would carry the message for a few moments, only to be drowned out by a lusty group a short distance away. It was almost as if they knew they could die tomorrow. A dark malaise passed over him, and he knew that when morning came and the first wolf fell, he would feel it. He squeezed his eyes shut.

For now, they are alive. The Adrad and Leal are singing tonight. As he listened, he felt the tension begin to leave him. Fatigue edged in, tugging at him like gravity. Feeling his limbs twitch and relax, he drew the sougain blankets up around his shoulders. As he sank into sleep, he knew that, as the wolves find one another in the wilderness, he would find Maude.

Chapter Thirty-Three

Through drowsy eyes, Leal watched as Adrad's haunches disappeared through the low opening in the rock shelf, out into the crisp morning. Even in the darkness of the cave, her eyes made out the forms of the other wolves and her nose detected their unique scents. They were all present, a mass of folded paws and tucked tails: her four youngest and all five of the full-grown pups. Then there was the big tawny maverick who so desperately wanted to best Adrad, and two more slender latecomers.

She had grown thinner. As she stretched, her belly let out a gurgle that rose in her throat. They hadn't had a kill in two days, and although the bones of a carcass lay on the ground outside the crevice, she was hungrier than ever.

Something was different, and she knew exactly what it was. She and Adrad had been together, and of their union would come another litter in the spring. Blind, stumbling little things they would be, at first interested only in nursing and coddling. But they'd begin tumbling around their grassy world at the age of three weeks or so, when their ears would begin to straighten. She'd have a little of her free time back when the pups began to nip at the jowls of the other adults to stimulate a partial regurgitation of a recent meal. Each wolf sleeping in the rock crevice was raised like this—cared for by its elders—and each instinctively followed these ancient ways.

Rising to her feet, she ducked through the opening and went out into the frosty predawn. The full-grown wolves came next, yawning nervously, then the yearlings. Adrad wasted no time in setting out, moving rapidly down the slope of one of White Cliff's countless rocky bluffs. He didn't need to look back over his thick gray ruff; he knew they would follow.

There was a band of mule deer on the flat, but it was a good three miles away. Both open space and thick stands of timber lay between the pack and its destination. Adrad had crouched on a worn, sage-crusted butte the day before, watching his prey. One of the deer was limping. If chased, it could be taken easily.

Once the bottom of the hill was reached, the pack began to run. Leal saw the first opal tones of dawn tint the eastern horizon. The moon was a pale, dissolving ghost. Eyes forward now, she stretched out her legs and felt the cold, firm earth beneath her. Her pink tongue lapped up the wind and the cold air poured into her dark nostrils, filling her with the new day. Adrad's huge, tufted paws flew across the patches of crusted snow, but she kept pace, running just even with his shoulders.

After a mile and a half, the pack fanned out, picking up the musky scent of the deer herd on the west-borne wind. Leal struck east, circling around a stand of timber, slowing to a steady trot, curving gently toward the center of the wide loop the pack had formed. They would move together, as they had done many times, like a tightening noose.

A whiff of blood, pungent and aromatic, made her skid to a halt, one paw raised. *If there is something to be had here . . . something to be dragged back in addition to the deer . . .* she lifted her head, looking west toward the pack, but she knew whatever she scented was close, so close that she could find it within a few steps. Sinking to a near crouch, she slunk through the low-hanging branches.

There it was—a bloody calf carcass, partially gutted. It looked newborn. Odd that an infant calf would be here. She nosed it, lapping at the frozen blood on the rib cage. It was scarcely enough to feed her, but she smelled the guts through the open rib cage and forced her snout inside, grabbing, yanking. Just a few bites and she would be on her way. As she gulped and turned away, a faint taste passed over the scent glands in her mouth, and she knew.

Her jaws closed and she looked west, feeling a thin film of saliva gather in her jowls. There was Adrad, on a ridge less than a quarter mile away, his massive shoulders hunkered in a crouch. The pack was closing fast on the small band of deer. Her mate needed her; she had to move quickly. Perhaps she had not eaten enough poison to do any harm. Wheeling away from the carcass, she bounded through the trees to the edge of the ridge.

From here, her vantage point offered a perfect view of the broad coulee where the deer grazed. Just as she was about to leap forward from a patch of junipers and begin her descent, there was a slight movement among some rocks on her right. *A man.* In the gray wash of morning light, she saw his coat, his motionless arms outstretched, resting on the rocks. She moved her eyes back across the coulee to Adrad. A deafening crack tore the stillness of the valley. Adrad's massive body flew up in the air and tumbled backward.

Leal bolted straight down the hill, her paws firing out, tearing up the earth between herself and her mate. Her eyes were on the place where he had fallen. Midstride, she catapulted forward with a yelp as her left front foot landed squarely in the center of an iron-jawed trap. Snarling at the fierce metal teeth, she would not be stopped. She dragged the trap with her, only to be snapped like a fish when she reached the length of the anchor chain. She sank onto her right shoulder, writhing in rage and agony, gnawing at the trap.

Something new took hold of her. The poison from the carcass had made its way to her belly. Within minutes, the pain in her paw began to worry her less than the fire that threatened to burn her from the inside out. She nipped at her gut, then licked her bleeding foot, then nipped her scorching gut again. She looked for Adrad, but the horizon swam before her. The sun was up now, slanting across the coulee. It seemed as though summer had come. It was warm, even hot. She felt a thirst unlike any she'd ever known.

Adrad. Adrad.

Tension in her core stacked up against her spine, piling up to her head, making her skull want to split. Her dark body began to shudder, wringing the air from her lungs. She rolled into a ball, whimpering and howling, then convulsed repeatedly, until her eyes lost their focus. Her legs stiffened. Finally, her head lolled back and her eyes found only darkness.

"Leave 'er be. Check the other traps, up on the ridge. We'll circle back and get this one."

"Christ, she's big. That's his mate, I'm sure of it." Rattler rubbed his hands.

Judd Riggs nodded, saying nothing. The big black female had met her match. He took a wad of long cut out of his pocket and stuffed it into his cheek. The sun was high in the sky and they were at their last three traps. It looked like the day would yield them a total of nine pelts. A hundred and thirty-five dollars.

He moved the tobacco around in his mouth and shifted his weight in the saddle. They'd call them the White Cliffs Pack. Ought to be the last pack in central Montana. Might be a few renegades still around, but the days of bringing in four dozen pelts after two weeks' work were over. No more proud displays of shimmering pelts set out like curtains on a long lodgepole in the center of town for the women to stroke and the men to envy.

He let out a sigh and pushed his hat back, mulling over the place they'd come to. Change was working on him; he could feel it. *Might be time to light out. Canada, or California, even. We aren't getting any younger. Montana has come to be a strange place. Take that rich sonovabitch Thomas McNaughton. The Laird, as everyone down in the Judith Basin calls him. Who'd have thought he'd come into our camp yesterday afternoon and hand us two hundred dollars just to lay off the Adrad? Two hundred dollars. And now the grand old creature is most likely dead. It's a sign, that's what it is. The wolves are gone, and it's time for Rattler and me to move on.*

His throat tightened for a moment as he considered the possibility that McNaughton had more than likely killed the Adrad.

What if the great gray wolf, who had been the subject of so many ardent chases, strategies, and campfire councils, was dust? What if that crafty mind, all that efficiency of movement and cleverness, had been erased from the landscape forever? His worthy opponent of many years, eliminated. If that were true, it didn't matter who had taken him; it only mattered that life would be different now, in a way he had never fully anticipated.

As he watched his brother lead the salt-and-pepper packhorse back from the ridge, he could see two dead wolves slung across the packsaddle. Yes, that makes nine. Judd shook his head and shot a stream of rusty juice through puckered lips. Rattler approached, puffing his way up a small incline toward the wagon. Judd's eyes moved quickly over the two new wolves, experiencing some relief as he verified that neither was the Adrad. Both were young and lean, probably about a year old.

"I guess," huffed out Rattler, "that the Adrad avoided poison one more time. That is one smart wolf. Two hunnert dollars notwithstanding, I hope the old bastard got away from Laird High and Mighty." He leaned back on his heels and held onto his lapels, mimicking McNaughton: "It'll gi'me a lifetime of pleasure to have the craiture stuffed and mounted, for my bonny wee huntin' lodge."

"Well, we did hear some shots. He may very well have got the old vagabond."

Rattler chewed the inside of his cheek. "Well, we'll find out if we take him up on his offer to go over there for a skinnin' party."

Judd shrugged. "He'll have some damn fine whiskey and good victuals. We'll bring our fat pile over and slice them from tongue to tail right in front of that pearl-buttoned prig. Whet his appetite."

Rattler grinned and heaved the large black female onto the wagon.

Field glasses against her brow bone, Maude watched from a thick stand of pines as the Riggs brothers' wagon, loaded with slain wolves, lurched down the road. She shook her head and swallowed. They seemed to be headed directly for McNaughton's camp. She'd heard gunshots that morning, just about the time she located the camp. It had been empty, but she recognized the character of his wagons and horses. *Had he killed the Adrad?* She would find out. *And as for the Riggs brothers, well, from the looks of that wagon, they appeared to have gotten the rest of the pack, or most of it.*

Lowering the glasses, she rubbed her eyes. If the Riggs brothers went to the laird's encampment, chances are they'd be there all afternoon. This could be a blessing, though, because it would keep McNaughton just where she wanted him—far away from any well-traveled byway and ill-prepared to strike camp any time soon.

Pulling her hands away from her face, she stared at her dirty palms and fingertips, then thrust them into the pockets of her jacket. She winced and thought of home. Isobel's pale face came to mind, then Ailse's. "I have to remember why I came," she told herself, her voice like flint.

Checking the air again to make sure she was still downwind, she visited the horses, then removed her rifle from the scabbard. With the field glasses around her neck, she ducked into the thick brush and set off for a well-concealed place she had found earlier.

Moving along a wooded bluff, she kept to hard surfaces whenever she could, making no sound as she traveled. Finally, she reached a small cirque, a bowl-like structure of rock with a small gap on one side. Here she could lie on a stretch of dry moss in the sun, unobserved, and watch the proceedings at the McNaughton encampment.

The sun shone down, thawing the mounds of snow among the rocks. At first she lay there winded from her climb, listening only to her breath and the sound of her heaving chest. Then she became aware of the steady dripping of a melting slab of snow as a tiny rivulet made its way along one course of granite to another.

Only the slightest breeze moved the leafless cottonwoods, while the occasional croak of a jay drifted through the jack pines. Her eyes made a quick sweep of the campsite and discovered the great body of the Adrad stretched out on a snowbank. Her heart sank. The very image of wild freedom, lying motionless in someone's camp, appearing to sleep in the presence of man.

What was it about that head that seemed familiar? He had been a loner. Of course he had a family he cared for and protected, but he was a symbol of something that would not last into this new century. He would never fly across the prairie again; the big rib cage would breathe no more; that great shaggy head would never lift to scent the wind. Yes, that head, defended so often by . . . her father. Tears came quick and strong as she realized how much the two of them had in common. Wise fathers both, seasoned by years of hardship, by making a place in a raw and rugged land.

McNaughton stood over him, holding the rifle that had killed him, pointing to a red hole in the skull and another in the neck. Maude's own rifle, warmed by her grip, felt solid and sure in her hands. She could do this thing, yet as she looked at him, she began thinking about the precise action of it. *Just how would it be done, when the moment arrived? Where, exactly, ought she have the bullet enter McNaughton's head?* From her vantage point, she would have her choice. The temple, the forehead, the neck. She would be humane. She'd do as much for a dog, or a horse that was down and suffering. He deserved far less.

What would happen afterward, though? He would topple over, of course. Would he convulse? She might need to make a second shot. She had not thought of that. The angle would be difficult.

She slid the rifle up along her arm, close to her face, getting acquainted with the posture she'd take when the moment of firing came. She drew her elbows beneath her and watched intently as McNaughton gestured, talking to the Riggs brothers and Blair. Blair pulled a measuring tape from his pocket and, with the help of the others, straightened the heavy body and measured it from its nose to the tip of its tail. Even Maude could tell from where she lay that the Adrad was enormous. The head was easily twelve inches across and the overall length must have been well over six feet.

Something familiar surged up in her. Even as she felt it, she shook her head, willing it away. Her hair waved before her eyes as she whispered between clenched teeth, "No! Let nothing come between me and what I must do." But the sensation came on, and she could not stop it. She had to roll onto her back and lay flat and let the air move over her, filling her lungs. She gasped as her breath came strong and ragged, in and out. The hair bristled on her arms and she winced. *What now? What on God's green earth will happen in the next hour, the next several hours? Whatever it is, I won't sit around like a mystic and await further divination. Nothing's going to deter me from this task. Nothing.*

Her chest heaving harder than it had after she'd climbed the hill, she brought her fist to her mouth, fearing they would hear her panting. Resting her teeth against her knuckles, she lay stock-still. After several minutes, she was calm enough to twist around and look. Seeing them busily occupied around the campsite, she relaxed, and her fingers found the rifle once more.

The men had gathered around a wagon sideboard where McNaughton poured a round of whiskey and proclaimed some kind of toast. Blair stepped away toward the shoal of the river and relieved himself, after which the group gathered around the Riggs brothers' wagon and conferred about the skinning to be done.

McNaughton took his glass of whiskey and strode toward the center of the campsite, stripped off his coat, and stretched. It was almost as if he were posing, inviting her to shoot. The air took on a haunted, crackling sizzle. *Now. It's time. This is it.*

She tried to swallow but her throat stuck to itself. Strange thoughts darted through her head. She could almost hear Ailse's voice, whispering in her ear, "Thair's some eldritch things gang on."

He wasn't looking at her, but he was standing right there, perfectly positioned. She slid the rifle up, sighting him in. *I'm ready. I'm going to push everything out of my mind except the memories of the horror.*

I'll use them like a needle, to prick myself with all the hateful things he's done. As she took aim, he reached up and brushed his silver-streaked auburn hair back, exposing his high, regal forehead. There was the fair, faintly freckled skin, with its horizontal creases.

A feeling like nausea struck her in the pit of her stomach. It wasn't the strong dose of special wits she'd just experienced moments ago. No, this was something else. She was in Ailse's garden. It was a scene from long ago. Ailse was chatting away, in her gravelly little voice, about special wits, and Maude was listening half-attentively, but listening well enough, as she always did where Ailse was concerned. The line was well rehearsed, and it went like this: "The thing ye've always got to know, my little Maudie, is that we are sworn to harm nae one."

The wave of nausea rose higher, and Maude blinked. Dizzy, she could not see McNaughton anymore; she only saw and smelled the roses and the lavender in the wild toss of greenery around Ailse's cottage. She felt the worn smoothness of Ailse's hands settle lightly on hers, loosening her trembling fingers. With that cool, easing touch, every bit of intention she had to kill Thomas McNaughton drained out of her whitened fingertips onto the mossy stones. A whimper escaped her. Chilled and exhausted, she fell into a stupor, barely able to watch the scene below.

Her lips moved, like a supplicant chanting, as she whispered to the air. "And so it all goes away, just like that, does it? Ailse, look what you've done. You've unraveled me like an old sock. Should I feel angry at having failed, or relieved for having been saved?" She stared at a patch of deep green moss, thinking of Scotland. *Look where life has brought me. Not just across the wide ocean, but to a lonely place among these rocks to kill a man.* Her fingers left the rifle and touched the velvet softness of the moss. "The forces that created the universe shall deal with McNaughton," she whispered. And it seemed in that moment that a great heaviness left her, the heaviness of many years.

She had cried moments ago when she looked upon the dead wolf, but the tears that came now were like nothing she'd ever felt before. She wept for the child she had once been, the girl who'd been attacked and ruined. Once pure and innocent, she admitted that perhaps she was not so far from that stainless girl as she had grown to believe. She had needed protection when no one was there to provide it. Tears streamed into her hair for all the lost years spent hating herself for not being able to stop McNaughton. She cried for all the baths she took trying to make herself clean again, for all the frozen family silences, and for the desolate conviction that her wholeness would never be restored.

She had never allowed herself to be angry, because anger would mean she had indeed been maimed and that what happened was real and irreversibly poisonous. It would have meant the laird had won, that her shame was real, and that the child inside her still carried his venom in the rosebud place no man should ever touch.

Why had her passionate hatred worked against her, tying her to him, when she wanted to let go? Now it was clear, clear as the droplets of snow-water dangling like gemstones from the twigs. She may have hated McNaughton, but even more, she'd hated herself.

As she lay on her back staring up at the afternoon sky, she slipped into a soft gratitude toward Ailse, who had somehow carried her to this place. She knew that Catriona and Morag had helped, but it was Ailse's unconditional love—and Rob's too—that had saved her from herself.

She shivered. *What will come now*, she wondered, *to fill my life? Now that this nightshade has been purged from me? I am a blank slate, an empty glass.*

There would be a new kind of Maude Graham, she knew that. Little by little, she sank back into the world around her, less aware of her inner world and listening once again to the sounds of the thawing snow and the wind gathering in the trees.

She rolled onto her stomach again and looked down upon the encampment. The men lifted the wolves' legs this way and that, stretching various animals out to full extension. It was clearly time for skinning. Maude had skinned sheep and knew how to get through the grisly business. She'd learned to empty her mind and think with her hands. When it was over, she always went directly to the garden to dig, or to the most basic barnyard chore she could find, in order to connect with the dirt, to discharge any spiritual tension into the forgiving neutrality of the earth.

But as these men began their work, they could stop their knives midstroke to point to the length of a leg or the volume of a tail, even to joke or step away for another drink. McNaughton stood awhile, then walked toward the river, where chunks of ice drifted past on the dark water.

As arrogant as the men were, with all their posturing and bravado, she felt a current of something humming around the campsite, as though something or someone might be holding them accountable for dispensing with the Adrad.

Back again, McNaughton directed Blair to help the Riggs brothers while he watched each man's work to see who handled the knife most deftly. Clearly, she realized, he was choosing who would do the work on the Adrad.

Finally, the large black female was hauled off the wagon. Leal, loyal to the end, Maude thought with a tightness in her chest. With no conscious intention, her heart dragged her thoughts straight to Rob, and tears scalded her sunburned face.

She stared at the wolf as the lush black pelt began rippling away from the bloody carcass. In minutes, it came away free, held high by the hand of Rattler Riggs. He and his brother lifted the she-wolf, now only a blood-streaked mass of muscle and tendon, and slung her across the damp pile of flayed animals beneath a jack pine.

Maude rested her chin on her forearms. *It's not like I didn't know they would come to this end*, she thought, *yet my tears are all the more bitter because they are in vain. I grew up listening to stories of families who'd grown to detest wolves, and by God, many of them had a right to. The Adrad and Leal had forebears who struck hard at sheep and cattle holdings in the Basin for dozens of years. My own neighbors. But to witness this.*

The men hauled the Adrad over to the skinning area, where Rattler dropped to one knee and began his work, drawing his blade carefully around the genitalia. Maude winced and jammed her face back down into her arms. She prayed that there might be yet another gallant wolf left somewhere in the Rockies, leading a small renegade pack, but cut her prayer short when she realized that any alpha male and his family would soon come to a similar end.

The afternoon sun beamed down on her as she cradled her aching head in her arms. Drowsily, she reasoned that the Riggs brothers would leave before long, eager to display their pelts in Lewistown. Her eyes grew heavy, and try as she might to keep them open, her head sank to the ground and her lids closed. Two sleepless days of stalking her prey, combined with the effort of laying down a long-wrought burden, at last overcame her.

Chapter Thirty-Four

It was leather, shoved against her face—someone's glove, tight over her mouth. She cried out, but the sound died against the deerskin. Her useless hands were pinned against her by a muscular arm. Whoever it was, he was so close that she could not focus on his features. *McNaughton . . . or Blair?*

The head dropped down, close to her ear. "It's me, you little fool. Be quiet."

Rob.

He pulled his hand away from her face and drew his head back to look at her, then sank down on one elbow. "I see McNaughton still lives." He nodded toward the campsite.

She rolled into him and flung her arm around his neck. "Oh Rob, I just want to go home. I'm so sorry."

He held her for a moment. "You've come a long way."

She nodded, then stared at him. "You're pale. How are you?"

"I could have found you faster if I hadn't felt so low. Cold sweats. I saw the Riggs brothers on the road. They had to show me the alpha female's pelt. The black one I knew from the forest. Damn if I didn't get weak in the knees." When his eyes met hers, they were bright. "You found yourself one crazy cowboy."

"It's the end of an era. At least you were never placed in a position of having to kill her or one of her kind."

"No. They took care of that."

He looked down through the rocks and the tangle of wild clematis into the camp, where McNaughton had pulled his campstool near the edge of the river for a cigar. Blair appeared to be on the verge of joining him, but instead picked up his rifle and pointed downriver, trudging off across the gravelly shoals.

"Blair must be going after some dinner," Rob said.

Maude leaned forward to look. "Ed Martin will come, won't he?"

"Yes, he'll come. We'll get justice soon enough."

"I'm worried. He and McNaughton are tight as ticks. My father says that McNaughton gives the Sheriff's Fund a thousand dollars every Christmas, and then Ed Martin shows up at the Rocking M Christmas party with a bottle of the laird's favorite scotch."

Rob lifted his shoulder and said, "We have to have faith in Ed. The whole community knows what happened."

As they watched McNaughton sitting alone on his campstool, something stirred on the right-hand edge of the encampment. Some other creature must have come into camp, because the pile of wolf carcasses seemed to quiver. Maude blinked, adjusting her eyes to the late afternoon light. Maybe Blair had come back and was rooting around in the dead pile of meat. Perhaps a varmint of some kind.

But no. Maude watched in disbelief as one of the topmost corpses stirred, wriggled its legs, then lifted its bloody head. "My God," she said.

Rob jerked his head around and looked at her. "What?"

"Look . . . look at the pile of skinned wolves." Her fingers clutched his arm.

They both stared in amazement as a corpse slid down off the pile and fell on its knees, then righted itself, yellow eyes glaring into focus. Rob knew, as did Maude, from the size and proportions of the body, that this had to be the Adrad's mate.

Lifting her head to scent the air, the she-wolf quickly identified the foreign odors of both McNaughton and his cigar. With enough blood still circulating in her veins and just enough feral vitality to move the twenty paces between herself and McNaughton, who sat in his wool shirt on a campstool near the river, she loped straight toward him, limping on her broken right foot, but with the full, single intention of completing a desperate final act.

Leal flew into the air, landing at the back of his neck in a flash of blood and gristle and fangs. From deep inside her came a gurgling snarl, the voice of hell unleashed. McNaughton shrieked and attempted to rise from his seat, but under her weight he could only manage to stagger to the side, one clumsy step after another, over and over as he struggled not to fall.

As the wolf held on, working her jaws farther in, blood spurted forth. Her long incisors had found McNaughton's jugular vein. Bright red stains spread rapidly down his chest and splattered onto the wolf, so different from the rusty, clotted blood of her exposed musculature. McNaughton fell once, then regained his balance, and fell again. He batted and yanked at the wolf, but he could not get a grip on the slick fascia covering her body. He continued scrambling over the gravel, locked in a horrible embrace with the mate of the animal he had so passionately sought to destroy.

As they spun together in a morbid dance of death, it seemed for a moment that McNaughton might break free, but suddenly man and wolf were at the river's edge. Maude watched as McNaughton's boot stopped, poised on the sandy bank, teetering. Then they were gone, in a splash of white droplets that fanned up and fell away.

Maude went from frozen shock and disbelief to a short, keening scream. Arms wrapped around her rib cage, she rocked back and forth, unable to comprehend what she had just seen.

Rob darted around the maze of boulders that formed the cirque, down through a warren of deer and rabbit trails, ducking past willows and buckbrush until he finally blew through the brittle foliage into the meadow. He shouted for Blair, whom he spied a short distance away, standing like a statue with his gun half-aimed, half-sagging. Clearly, Blair had seen everything and had not been able to get a good shot. Both men ran to the river's edge, hoping to catch McNaughton floating by. Rob knew it was unlikely. Mortally wounded, with the wolf in a death grip at his throat, McNaughton would probably never be found.

Rob skidded along the gravelly shore, past the toppled campstool to the sandy bank where they had gone in. Nothing but dark, icy water, churning past in its slow, wintry current, carving its millennial path away from the Continental Divide.

He dashed downstream to meet Blair, who was running up and down the shore staring at the water, seeking any glimmer of human form and shouting, "Father! Father!"

"I can't believe it," Rob said.

Blair ignored him, wheeling away, kicking up a spray of pebbles as he ran farther downstream. His plaintive shouts of "Father! Father!" died on the wind.

Rob winced as he watched, unable to say or do anything. He shook his head. *There's no trace of the man who ruled the Judith Basin for so many years, who ruined lives on whim, and who came damn close to destroying the woman I love.*

Maude had come down from the bluff. She stood calmly in the camp as Rob returned. "My God, Rob. If Blair hadn't seen this, no one would ever have believed our telling of such a tale."

Rob compressed his lips and let out a long, whistling breath.

"Do you think we should . . . go to him?" she asked.

"I don't think so. Not yet."

"I guess not." Maude watched the river, then turned her head slowly to Rob. "I didn't run to this river with the same eagerness I ran when Ailse and Isobel were drowning."

"Maude."

"I wanted him to die. I . . . I think I even had a prescience of this happening, earlier today. I didn't know what it meant."

"You told me you almost never know what that uncanny feeling means, that you only know that something might happen."

She looked back at the river, staring vapidly. It was true. This time she hadn't known anything. When she felt Gran lift her fingers from the gun, she thought that had been it—the decision to harm no one. Wasn't the complete reversal of her mission a powerful

— 358 —

enough message from the air? But that *hadn't* been it. At least not all of it. She hadn't known that Leal was still alive, destined to kill McNaughton.

Rob took her arm. "Maude, you had a chance to kill him and you chose not to. Am I wrong?"

"No."

"Then let that be the end of it."

She shook herself and put both hands in front of her, parting the air. "Let's walk out to the river so we can be there when Blair comes walking back upstream. It's the least we can do."

They walked slowly down the bleached shoal, listening to the low, grinding sound of the Missouri. Glancing at the water, Maude marveled at its force. It was so heavy, so deep; it seemed to be a dark, stationary thing, yet it changed every second—one moment fathomless and black, other times malevolent green. In a few places, ice still covered the river from one side to the other, but in most areas it was choppy with ice melt and swift-moving slush.

Blair emerged from a band of willows, eyes forward. "He's gone. Doubt we'll ever find him. He's just . . . gone."

"We're both terribly sorry," Rob said.

Blair trudged along the cold gravel in silence.

"We'll help load everything up."

"Thanks."

Rob began loading the McNaughtons' goods into the long hunting wagon, moving around the clearing and striking camp with an air of authority. Fire tools, water kettle, kindling hatchet. Handing Maude the canvas rain fly to fold, he advised her in low tones that the sooner they got the wagon onto the public road, the better.

Blair was distracted, incapable of even the simplest task. When he went to pick up the campstool on the pebbly bank, Rob suggested that they might want to leave it be. "If we need to ride back and show Sheriff Martin what happened, the Sheriff will appreciate having the stool left exactly as it is." Rob noticed several sprays of blood on the gravel and a bloody paw print on a rock slab, and made a mental note to mention this to Ed Martin.

Blair lifted his shoulders and went back to the wagon, puttering with his father's personal things.

Three hours later, after they had pulled off the southbound road at dusk and made a campfire, they heard approaching horses. Dundee whinnied, and within minutes, Sheriff Martin arrived with two deputies. After hearing the news that Thomas McNaughton had been killed, Martin instructed his deputies to take Blair McNaughton for a walk, then turned his unremitting gaze on Maude and Rob.

Rob told Martin everything, looking him straight in the eye throughout the grisly tale. "No doubt it's the most bizarre thing you've ever heard, Sheriff Martin, but as God is our witness, it truly happened. Blair was there, too. He was some distance away, but he saw it as well." Rob waited for a reply.

Ed Martin rubbed the back of his neck and raised his eyebrows. He directed his first question at Maude. "You were mighty upset with the laird."

"I was."

"Mad enough to do some damage your own self."

"I seriously contemplated it, after what he did to Gran Ailse and Isobel. I came to my senses when I realized what it would mean to my family and to my future with Mr. Elliott if I threw everything away in an act of revenge. My Gran taught me to harm no one, and that's the creed I will live by as long as I breathe."

Martin let his eyes linger on her a moment, then turned to Rob. "And you, Mr. Elliott, you wouldn't have done some foolish thing out of a misguided sense of chivalry, or some other plumb stupid notion?"

"That, Sheriff, would have been too plumb stupid even for me."

Ed Martin stood up and dusted himself off. "To do this right and proper, I will now go and have a little chat with Blair."

Maude's eyes rested heavily on Rob as the Sheriff walked away. "Blair doesn't like either of us. I shot at him once."

"What?"

"I fired a warning shot at him when he was spying on my sisters. He was on my property."

Rob threw up his hands. "Well, I pinned him in the dirt in Fenton's barnyard and made a public spectacle out of him, so we've done ourselves no favors, I guess. Still, I think there's a shred of decency somewhere in that raw-boned body of his. He seemed to be in a different state of mind when I saw him at Christmas. We can only hope he's not the bad seed his father was."

Maude shook her head and broke a twig between her fingers, then leaned back to look at the stars. "Whatever happens, we just have to tell the truth as we know it, and we've done that."

Within minutes, they heard the crunch of boots on pine needles as Martin approached in the dark. As soon as he entered the campfire's circle of light, Martin announced, "Blair told me the same story that you did. I'll go to the scene in the morning and look it over. It's still damn hard to conceive."

He studied Maude for a moment. "As for you, Miss Graham, you need to get back to your kin. Your grandmother is coming out of her accident all right, but your little sister is faring worse. I think your family could use you right—"

"Isobel?" Maude jumped up and clamped a hand on his arm. "What has happened?"

"Doc Attix said inflammation of the lungs, I think. Fever. When I left town he had just put her in the hospital."

Pneumonia. Maude's heart went into her throat. "Rob, we have to go."

"Not at night, Maude, it isn't safe. We'll go at first light."

"I won't sleep. You know I won't." She paced to the wagon where her rucksack lay.

"You'll have to try. It's a long ride."

Sheriff Martin and his men agreed to visit the fatal campsite in the morning with Blair, then travel together with the wagon back to the Rocking M and deliver the news of McNaughton's death. He dismissed Rob and Maude, telling them to leave as early as they chose.

If anything happens to Isobel! I had begun feeling sorry for Thomas McNaughton, but now, I almost resent the wolf for killing him. He deserved everything he got. Oh, Ailse! Am I really so full of wickedness?

Such were Maude's thoughts as she rode along, with only the clopping of hooves and the creak of saddle leather to break the early morning silence. They passed through Denton at six o'clock, stopping only to water the horses and down a cup of scalding coffee at the tavern. Her hands were doubly cold, both from the morning chill and from worry. She kept them wrapped around the heavy china cup as long as she dared, then she and Rob were off again.

Many hours later, with the sun tinting the western sky a bronze gold, the horses' heads lowered in fatigue, they plodded into Lewistown. Maude nudged Dundee to pick up his pace as they turned onto High Street, where the new hospital loomed like a fortress. She could think of nothing but Isobel.

Dismounting, she waited impatiently while Rob tied the horses, then took his hand and ran up the walk. Inside, it did not take long to locate the area where her mother and Mary sat on an overstuffed bench in the wide hall.

"My God, child! You're back, and safe." Catriona folded Maude in her arms.

Mary gave her a weak smile, using the arm of the bench to help her rise. "Mac is at home with Fiona and Ailse," Mary said. "We've been here all day."

"How . . ." Maude's tongue stuck in her mouth. She kept her hand tight on her mother's. There was something in both Catriona's and Mary's eyes that she didn't like. The puffy redness, the dark pools of the pupils, the lavender shadows above the cheekbones.

"She's going to be all right," Maude asserted stubbornly, not liking what she saw and felt in the cold, quiet hallway.

"Maude." Catriona's voice was calm. "Sit down." She placed

both hands on Maude's forearms and drew her to the bench. Rob took a step back.

Maude went forward and sat, her eyes welded to Catriona's. "It is quite serious," began Catriona. "Isobel's fever has gotten so high that she has lost consciousness. We have done everything we can. We must pray. That is what Mary and I have been doing all day. Father Wakefield was just here and prayed with us."

Maude stared. *Prayer. It has come to this? Prayer and clerics and winding sheets?* She twisted away and stood up. "I want to see her!"

"They won't let us go to her right now," Catriona said beseechingly. "She's in the intensive ward."

Maude smashed her face into her hands. "If I had been here . . ."

"You couldn't have kept this from happening, Maude. It was the water in her lungs. Dr. Attix said you brought her back from death. That in itself was a miracle. He's going to be back in a little while. You can talk to him yourself."

Rob's hand closed over Maude's. "Walk with me." He drew her close to him and marshaled her into step along the tiled floor, down the long hallway toward the window at the far end. They made several circuits, saying nothing.

When she heard the metallic sound of the ward door opening, she turned to see Fred Attix coming down the hall.

"I've just been in to see Isobel again." His familiar, balding head and kindly face were a relief, but he was not saying the things Maude wanted to hear. "There is no change since I was here earlier this afternoon. Her fever has risen very slightly—two-tenths of a degree. They gave her a cool bath at six o'clock and are applying fresh cold cloths to her head continually."

For the first time in her life, Maude wished she were a nurse, working here at St. Joseph's.

Dr. Attix looked at them all and took a deep breath. "It is my opinion that, if she makes it through the next twenty-four hours, she may live. This is a very critical time."

Maude's eyes welled with tears. "Is it true that we cannot—cannot see her at all?"

Dr. Attix tilted his head and gave her a paternal look. "I am afraid that in cases like this, responsible medical advice severely restricts visits to a gravely ill child. I can only permit the child's mother to see her."

Maude's eyes went to Catriona's. Dr. Attix smiled and called out to a nurse who sat at a desk down the hall. "Bring us a gown, will you, Nancy?"

The nurse pulled a folded white gown from a cart and brought it to the doctor, then walked away. Dr. Attix unfolded the gown and held it toward Catriona. In one fluid motion, Maude shed her old hunting coat on the floor and extended a slender arm between Dr. Attix and her mother and took the gown.

For a moment, all Maude could do was to hold the gown against her chest while tears streamed down her face. Her mouth opened, but no words came out. The tears just kept coming. At last, she looked at Dr. Attix and stammered out, "You . . . said the child's mother . . . should be the one."

"I did."

"Then will you . . . please help me on with this?"

Catriona's hand went to her mouth. Mary turned pale and leaned against the wall, slack-jawed. Rob stood tall and silent, a slight furrow on his brow.

"Mother, I brought her into the world," Maude sobbed. "And if this is to be the end of her life, I must be there to help her go."

Catriona nodded dumbly, then cradled her face in her hands and wept.

"Oh, my God." Mary sank onto the bench.

Maude laid her hand on the doctor's arm. "Please take me to my beautiful girl."

Chapter Thirty-Five
MAY 1909

Kibbey sat on the steps of his sheepwagon, coaxing an old melody out of his fiddle on a cool Friday morning. Today wasn't just any Friday. This morning, a fresh coat of green paint was drying on two sheepwagons—his own familiar wagon and a brand new one he and the Stony Creek hands had just finished.

Within a few days, both would follow the Graham packstring up the Two-Track, as John called it, into the Snowy Mountains, bringing two bands of sheep—two thousand in all—to summer pasture. The Two-Track, a barely distinguishable grassy road, consisted of parallel paths worn side by side from years of wagon travel. In May, the road and the flanking meadows were just as green as the braes of old Scotland. Unlike Scotland, though, the countryside would be dusted with pale blue forget-me-nots and the cherry pink flowers the Montanans called shooting stars.

How many years had it been? Fourteen now, he figured, since they had arrived in ninety-five. Of course they didn't go up into the high country that first year, with John going to Wyoming to buy the starter sheep. More than a baker's dozen years gone, anyway.

They'd intended to line out some of the packstring goods today, but everything had come to a halt early that morning when Catriona came fluttering out of the house in her fancy white wrapper, calling for her husband. Kibbey had lightened the pressure on his bowstring at that point, letting the note linger a moment and die on the breeze. Watching Catriona descend the steps off the veranda, he rested the instrument on his knees, figuring that fiddle music might not fit with this particular drama.

"John," she had shrilled out, blurring through the apple orchard, her form hardly distinguishable among branches bursting with pink and white blossoms, "it's Mary's time! You've got to send Mac over to Kettle Creek for Maude."

John turned away from the twitching, stamping horses and mules to look at his wife, then back again, peering over the array of canvas-wrapped bundles and tidy wooden panniers spread around the barnyard. "You've got Morag, Trina."

Catriona's mouth pruned up. "Of course we've got Morag," she fumed. "But Mary wants her sister." She snapped a dishtowel in the air and pulled herself to her full matronly stature. "Birthing, John Graham, is a sacred trust among women."

John shifted his weight and dabbed at his nose. Mac and the other herders straightened up from their work. The mood of the barnyard shifted.

"A baby. Well, yes. We cannae argue with a bairn, can we, Kib?" John turned to Mac and tossed his head toward the road. "Take your pal Dundee."

That morning, Maude had risen early, earlier than Rob. She left him snoring lightly in that position he seemed always to have— left arm extended beneath his head, wavy hair tossed across his perfect muscles, fingers draped over the side of the bed. He'd be up soon enough, and on his way to Stony Creek to help.

Sleep had eluded her; she'd shivered several times in the night. Wondering if it was the window they'd left open, she rose at three o'clock to close it, but still felt a vague chill run over her skin. When her breath quickened at four and Mary's voice came rushing into her mind like wind through a harp, her heart pounded as though she'd run to Big Spring Creek and back.

Today. The baby will come today.

With Rob asleep, she went first to the pasture south of the house to check on the three dozen new lambs. There was Flourface, who had been safely delivered of a dark little lamb last week. The little fellow was butting against his mother's belly, nursing gustily, as Maude slipped out the lane gate and dropped down to the creek where the wild plum trees bloomed.

It was still strange, after four months, to wander about the place with no fear. To think that she had an entire lifetime of this ahead of her was nearly incomprehensible. It was a luxury she couldn't understand, not yet. Any dark shadow on the periphery of her vision, like the tarpaulin that flapped off a wagon in town the other day, made her whirl around. She still kept the rifle in the buggy or in her saddle scabbard. But life was different now, different in a way she could never have imagined.

She wouldn't say anything to Rob about this morning's intuition. She could be wrong. She'd wait for the summons, if one was to come. The last thing she wanted was to ride to Stony Creek and be wrong. Things were far different between her and Mary than they'd ever been, but it was a tentative peace. Probably would be forever.

That night in the hospital, when none of them knew if Isobel would live or die, she hadn't cared—at least at that moment— who knew and who didn't know that Isobel was her own child. The look of benumbed shock on Mary's face hadn't mattered to her; she only wanted to get into the intensive ward and see and touch Isobel. The doctor allowed her to stay only a short time at the bedside, where she summoned every bit of will and spirit she possessed, praying over the hot, pale form beneath the sheets. She conjured Ailse's face, and Morag's, and even the long-dead Gran Callie, rallying them into her prayer circle, commanding them to lend their strength and transcendent wisdom, conferring it into the hands of everyone who would touch Isobel over the next twenty-four hours.

She kissed the flaming cheeks, stained at the center with a red blush, and laid her own cool hand across the purple-hued eyelids, then tore herself away.

"Doctor—" she rested her fingers on his arm before they reentered the hall.

"Yes, Miss Graham?"

"You . . . are now privy to a secret I have carried many years. It may shock you to know that while my mother and grandmother are aware that Isobel is my child, my father and brothers know nothing of it. They were away from our family for quite some time when we first settled in Montana. You see my father often. He believes Isobel to be the child of himself and my mother. To protect our family, and especially to protect Isobel, I want things to continue as they are."

"Miss Graham—Maude—you have no idea how many family confidences I shall take to my grave," said Fred Attix, raising the brows on his high forehead. "This is but another of the many treasures I shall lock in my heart until I breathe my last. You have my word, as a physician and as a man of honor."

Maude's lower lip trembled. "Thank you."

"You must think no more about it. Let us concentrate our thoughts in prayer for Isobel."

In the hall, Maude's eyes flickered over Mary's. Unable to tolerate the inquisitive fervor she saw there, she looked away, but was soon drawn back. She could tell Mary yearned to speak. Taking a breath, she waited for her sister to approach.

"Maude. Mother won't tell me anything. I . . . I guess I don't blame her. She says it is for you to say, if and when you choose." Her desperate eyes searched Maude's face.

"It was a long time ago, Mary. Suffice it to say, I most certainly didn't choose what happened to me." She didn't want to be unkind, but she turned away, wanting to think of Isobel, not of that voyage across the ocean.

Mary covered her face with her hands as her shoulders began to quake. "I have been so unkind to you, Maude."

"Yes, Mary, you have." The words tumbled out. "You've thought that no one but you has ever borne a great difficulty."

"But you never said anything to dissuade me from those beliefs. Oh, Maude!"

"What could I have said to you, Mary?"

"If you had revealed this to me, it would have made such a difference."

Maude sighed and looked at Mary dead-on. "Mary. Think about this. Maybe having this information about me and Isobel would have helped you in some way, but the cost to my daughter would have been far too high. Who would have benefited except you?"

Mary's face tightened as she felt the rebuke, but new tears spilled down her cheeks.

Maude softened. "Mary, I have always loved you, and I always will. If you have any trace of love for me, you will do one thing."

"Of course. Of course I will."

"You will never breathe a word of what has happened here tonight to anyone. Not to a living soul, and especially not to Isobel. Do I have your word, as God is your witness?"

"Why . . . yes. I can give you my word. I mean, I *do* give you my word."

"Now that you've felt your child move inside you, surely you understand something of what it feels like to want to protect that child at any cost. Once it's born, that feeling multiplies a thousand fold. You will—at least I believe you will—be overcome with an instinct that drives you harder than anything you have ever felt in your life." She leveled her eyes straight at Mary's, imbuing her next statement with unmistakable fierceness. "You would do anything, and I mean anything, to prevent any pain or suffering from being inflicted upon your child. Do you understand my meaning?"

Mary drew back, sensing a potent force. "Yes. Maude, I would never do anything to hurt Isobel. I love her. To me, she is a sister. She always will be."

Maude nodded in return, then looked around, as though someone had tapped her on the shoulder. "I suddenly feel that Isobel is going to be all right. I don't know why, but I do."

Catriona and Rob, who had been talking some distance away, came over and proposed that the four of them spend the night in the Bright Hotel.

Maude waved them on. "It makes no difference where I am, I won't sleep. Go ahead and go. I mean it."

"But Maude—" Catriona began a protest, albeit a weak one.

"Go. If I sense a change in her—and you all know I might—I'll just be leaving the hotel in the night and running up here. Leave me be." She sat down on the bench and laced her fingers in her lap.

Mary and Catriona picked up their coats and made their good-byes, but Rob would not go. He brought another bench from a nearby hall and went in search of pillows and blankets.

A nurse came to Maude at four o'clock in the morning to tell her what she already knew: Isobel's fever was down. Maude had spent much of those waiting hours telling the story of the past thirteen years to Rob, explaining that John Graham's time spent buying sheep and investing in land in Wyoming during the fall and winter of 1895 had made it impossible for him to know that Catriona had not borne Isobel.

He had taken the two boys with him. The little girls, Fiona and Mary, were too young to piece together the tumbled events of that winter and to realize that Maude's time in Great Falls with Morag was far more than part-time employment. Isobel had appeared, as babies do, in their mother's arms, and from that moment on, she was their little sister.

"Even when she's older," Maude said, "perhaps about my age, if I choose to tell Isobel that I'm her mother, I won't tell her who her father was. I may tell her it was someone of good breeding back in Moray who took advantage of me." She shook her head, shoving back her curls and blowing out a weary sigh. "I don't know. But I don't want to tell her who it really was."

Rob listened, his hand wrapped around hers. "Whatever you want to do. You've done everything right so far, as far as I'm concerned."

That was her Rob. Given the turmoil, they put off their marriage until Easter, and made their vows on Good Friday, two days before Rory and Antonia's wedding.

Rob had asked Grant to come to their ceremony. Grant had been his closest friend ever since he'd set foot in Judith Basin, but he knew when he issued the invitation that Grant would probably decline. He also knew it wasn't because Grant didn't want to come, or didn't care. Thomas McNaughton's body had never been found, and the raw scrape of grief was still keenly felt at the Rocking M.

So he had asked Roy Akeley, the lanky, unassuming ranch hand from the Ingersoll place up on Ruby Creek. Roy had trouble getting away, because old Per Ingersoll was ill, and the ranch required even more attention than ever. But he came. Rob had warned Maude about Roy's interest in Mary, so they both hid their smiles as Mary's eyes grew round when Roy took his seat behind her in the second pew at the church.

Walking back up the creek path, Maude smiled again at the memory. Roy had seen Mary's pregnancy full well that day, but it hadn't seemed to bother him. He stopped and chatted with her on the church steps after the wedding, then politely took his leave. The pink in Mary's face had faded, but the luminous curve around her lips had stayed.

Maude found Rob in the grassy front yard between the house and the barn, brushing and watering his blue roan. His hair was wet, tightening into crisp, bronze waves in the morning sun.

He looked up and gave her one of his crooked smiles. "Couldn't sleep?"

She shook her head. "I needed to check on the lambs. It looks like the last ewe might drop hers today or tomorrow. That'll be a relief."

"I forgot to tell you that I told Roy I'd go to Ruby Creek this weekend. Per is failing. Can't walk at all. Roy wants me to try to talk Hildy into hiring more help. The Ingersolls have more money in the bank than they let on."

Maude nodded. "Good. They're lucky to have that kid."

"I think they know it." He lifted the saddle off the fence and fitted it onto the horse. "Well, I'm off to see my new partners. Still can't believe I let your dad talk me into the sheep business."

Maude smiled and waved good-bye, wondering for a moment if she might have been wrong about Mary's baby coming today. *Maybe I was just thinking about the white ewe, and it was a lamb's imminent birth I was sensing.* But as Rob rode away, she heard another horse's rhythmic footfalls. Both sounds stopped and she knew the two riders had met in the lane.

Lifting her head to the sun, she smiled at the translucent shimmer of tender new leaves on the tall cottonwoods behind the barn. Better get my bag, she thought, picking up her skirts and heading for the house.

Rob watched Maude enter the big house at Stony Creek with her satchel, then notched his hat back on his head and looked around. The military sense of order in the broad open area among the barns and corral had evaporated. John Graham had abandoned the crew and had gone off for a walk up the creek with the dogs. Click Hawkins was feeding the bum lambs, and Lou Beck was toting a bundle of shingles toward the bunkhouse.

Normally, he had no trouble figuring out what to do or where the daily thrust of work was on this four-thousand-acre operation. He'd adapted to his new role here as son-in-law and partner, well pleased at John Graham's invitation. It wasn't an honorary role, either. John had made a real financial overture, with Rory's and Mac's blessing. Rob was to become a full partner in Stony Creek if he wanted the opportunity.

He'd had to think it over hard. He decided to accept, but to hang onto Ruby Creek too. Roy Akeley was still running things up there for him, even staying at the cabin. Roy came down to Stony Creek every chance he got, ostensibly to talk to Rob, but Roy's eyes searched the main house every chance he got for a glimpse of Mary's coppery hair. When she did appear, her belly as round as a melon, she'd wave and duck back inside again.

Rob surveyed the tidy barnyard. Despite the orderly array of goods, the announcement of the baby's arrival had sent the boss off on private cogitations and had scattered the rest of the crew like loose spokes. Bluebirds swooped and twittered around the barn, some carrying bits of grass in their beaks. *They seem to know their business*, he thought with a grunt.

He spied Rory, as aimless as the rest since Antonia had offered to do the cooking during Mary's lying-in. The two of them went to work on the new sheepwagon, fitting the tongue to the axle. The trip to set up sheep camp in the mountain meadows would come soon enough, and Rob wanted the wagon to be ready.

Rory was in a talkative mood, and since Rob had never heard the details of how it had gone, that business of tracking down Paul Hathaway last January, he was fine with listening.

"Father didn't want to bring the police into it at all," said Rory, tapping on a cotter pin. "He thought they might bungle things. So when we got to Buffalo, we met Jack's friend at the Bigelow Hotel, who showed us the lay of it all. The worst part of it was that Paul was already engaged to another gal." He glanced at Rob. "We'll never tell Mary that, mind you."

Rob shook his head. "No."

"We had to make sure we set up our snare when this other woman wasn't around. Paul's lodgings were three blocks away in another hotel. Nice place. Paul always did put on the dog. We observed him for two days, coming and going, before we contacted the authorities. Father insisted on being present for the confrontation, and I sure as hell wasn't going to sit in the lobby.

"We went to his room and knocked. It was Father and I and the Inspector, whose name was O'Neill. And there was another officer there, in uniform. Paul opened the door and the look on his face was a sight to behold. Wide round eyes, like a 'herring in a net,' Father said later. He invited us in, all graciousness. But his face was red as a lantern."

"You didn't tell him about Mary's—"

"No. He doesn't know about the baby. But wait till you hear what happened next. Father confronted him with the facts, and

I could tell from the way Father's voice was shaking he wanted to pound him right then and there. Paul's face went from red to white. Then Inspector O'Neill says to him, 'Young man, you're under arrest.' Then Paul said, 'I would like to get my coat and hat, from the bedroom.' So he steps into the next room and by the time we knew what had happened, he was out the window and down the fire escape."

Rob whistled. "Damned weasel."

"O'Neill and his officer went out after him, and shouted to us to go down to the front of the building and run him down if we saw him. From there it was a mad chase. We went around the building to the back and saw the policemen chasing Paul through the alleys. We ran for five blocks, then saw Paul duck into a mean-looking private residence. The police were right on his heels, though, and later told us they got him just as he was climbing out the roof scuttle."

"Can his assets be seized?"

"Father wanted to seize more than that, if you take my meaning."

Rob chuckled. "I've no doubt of that."

"Paul has fewer resources than one might think, for all his puffery. But it turns out that, although his parents are deceased, he has an uncle of some means who wants to make good on at least some of this. This uncle has been contacted by Inspector O'Neill and the attorney will be getting ahold of our Ed Brassey right here in Lewistown. Mary's not to know about it."

Rob nodded. "What exactly has she been told? Maude said Mary knew they'd found Paul, and that it was very clear to her he had no intention of ever coming back here."

"That's about it." Rory shook his head. "Mother and Father just want her to know that he has no attachment to her. They think that's best."

"Was the marriage legal?"

"We aren't sure yet. If it was, a divorce or annulment will take place."

Rob nodded and locked the wagon tongue into place.

"We h'ant got a want o' women, that's sairtain," said Ailse, who sat in a rocking chair, surveying the sunny bedroom with Mary at its center, propped by several pillows in a wide white bed. "Has she ta'en her raspberry leaf tea today?"

"I'm sick of that stuff," moaned Mary. "I've drunk enough of it to float a ship."

"Tones the womb, is all. Trina took it reg'lar, with each of ye bairns."

Maude sat on Mary's left, with Morag on the opposite side of the bed. Mary turned her face toward Maude, her eyes glistening. Maude leaned in, her hand on Mary's arm.

"I'm . . . I'm afraid, Maude." Her eyes reflected the sunlight that filled the room and her fingers found Maude's, clutching tight. "I'm afraid because of what I did last fall. What if the baby . . . isn't right?"

"Mary." Maude's voice was firm. "You can't think thoughts like that right now. What's done is done. You need to think about something beautiful and true, something that will carry you through this."

"Is that what you did," she whispered, "when you were with Morag all those years ago? Oh Maude, you were just a girl!"

"Yes, it's exactly what I did." She felt her own eyes dampen. "And I was young, but it's all right now. Very much all right." She smiled at Mary. "Maybe you need to think about that moment when you stood in the snow on Christmas Eve and looked at the Virgin Mary, and felt your baby move inside you."

Mary nodded as tears plummeted from her eyes onto the pillow. "My namesake. It did seem that she was looking at me, with real eyes."

"If it seemed real to you, then it *was* real."

"Oh, here comes another pain." Mary's face screwed into a wince.

Catriona stood at the foot of the bed, holding a watch. "They are much closer now. It won't be long. I've got the water boiling, and we've got plenty of sterile flannel here."

The intervals grew closer for the next hour, with Morag and Maude checking frequently to see if Mary was ready to push. Mary, now irritated and scowling, said, "I think my body has something to say about this pushing business."

"Try not to." Morag was official and kindly at the same time. Maude was glad to have her aunt here, saying the things a sister might not be able to say with authority.

"I can't stop it." Mary's voice sounded like a gurgle and a groan. "It's doing it all by itself."

"Hold back, Mary." Morag leaned in.

But Mary groaned, louder and louder. For a moment, Maude wondered where Isobel and Fiona were. *What if they hear all this? So be it,* she thought with a wild shrug. *This is what happens when women have children.*

She and Morag, with Catriona urging too, succeeded in keeping Mary from pushing for another five minutes, then there was no holding her back. Mary glared at the three of them and growled, "Stop telling me what to do. I've got to push!"

Maude saw the clock when Mary started. It was quarter after one. The pushing went on for over an hour, and Maude grew concerned as she saw Mary's increasing fatigue. For the dozenth time, Morag checked between her legs. This time she popped up and said, "Mary, I can see the head! You've got to give a few more really good tries. I know it will come."

Groaning fiercely, Mary put herself into the next contraction and wailed with effort. Again with the following contraction, and once more, and Maude had the baby's head in her hands. "Mary, the head is out!" She cried. "The worst is over. Another good push and the shoulders will come. You can do it."

The shoulders slithered out, then the entire perfect little body. Catriona carefully lifted the baby while Morag snipped the cord. "You have a beautiful boy," she said.

"John Jamie Graham," breathed Mary, "after my father and my grandfather." Wet with sweat and wearing a little smile of victory, she sank back into the pillows.

Rob and Maude huddled on the steps of the new sheepwagon as evening tinted the sky a faint lavender over a grove of pointed firs. The air was rich with the fresh scent of pine and the tart smoke from their modest campfire, where an old gray kettle sputtered near the glowing coals. The sheep were everywhere, quiet now save for a few bleats as lambs and their mothers reconnected after the long climb up the trail.

"They're calming down," said Rob. "I hope Kib's bunch are doing all right in the lower meadow. He's amazing, isn't he?"

"You know he's fond of Ailse, don't you?"

"Yes, that's been made clear."

"So peaceful here. It's odd to think the wolves are gone," Maude said ruefully. "I know it's good for the sheep and the cattle. And the farm dogs," she added, thinking of Harriet and Sport.

"I know there are still a few packs left around the state, but it won't be long. They'll never survive what's happening throughout the Rockies."

"There are still some wolves in the Canadian wilderness," Maude mused. "They'll be allowed to survive, I think." She felt a quick tremor move through Rob. Drawing her head back, she stared. "What was that?"

"I . . . well, when you said that, I remembered a dream I had, probably a month ago. I'd completely forgotten it until what you just said about wolves in Canada. I dreamed about a young Montana wolf who crossed the Missouri River, running over the ice. I can see it plain as day in my mind. He was tall and gray, with a scar on his left shoulder. He stopped to look up at the sky, then took off like blue blazes for Canada."

Maude puckered her lips wistfully. "I hope that dream comes true."

"So do I."

She let her head fall onto his shoulder. "Rob?"

"Hmm."

"I would never ask you to tell me what happened during that time you . . . spent in the woods. But do you think you found . . . " she stopped, not wanting to tread where she shouldn't.

"Did I find what I was looking for?"

"Yes."

"Well, I learned something. Not sure if it was more about myself or more about the wolves. I got a few things into my head. I really do believe there is more than one culture governing this world of ours. Not really governing . . . that's a poor word." He rubbed his chin, thinking.

"Medicine Badger helped me see things more broadly," he went on. "I mean, I think the wolves have a truth, like humans have a truth. And the wolves have their journey, just as we have ours. Because I have a blood bond with an ancestor who once made a connection with the wolves, I guess something drove me to do the same thing. And I did, for a moment in time. But I discovered that my inability to understand the wolves and my separateness from them is actually the greatest gift of all.

"What's different now is that I *want* the awe I feel for them, the wonder I have for those instincts we'll never fully comprehend, and for the profound secrets they knew before man even scratched a symbol on a stone. If I ever hear the wolf howl again, I will feel nothing but gratitude for the gulf of mystery that separates me from them."

Maude listened, watching Rob's profile against the setting sun. *Who is this man,* she wondered, *who came to me and insisted on staying? This wonderful soul who challenges me and defends me, who shares my bed, who listens to me and loves me?*

Resting her chin on Rob's arm, she saw the skin around his eyes crease into a smile. *What was amusing him?* Then she heard it.

From the valley below them came the lilting strains of a Scottish ballad. Kibbey. The wind shifted, bearing the melody louder and stronger. As she felt her body begin to sway from side to side, she looked down at her boot tops and saw the new petticoat Gran Ailse had given her, trimmed with rows of lace. She wanted to laugh and cry at the same time.

Rob turned to her and lifted her up, swinging her out on the grass and into a waltz, bringing her hips close. Maude gave herself up to the rhythm of the music and the feel of his body next to hers. Clove-scented shooting stars bloomed pink and bright in the meadow, forget-me-nots trailed over the stream, and an eyelash moon winked above.

The End

Acknowledgments

It is my pleasure to thank the people who either contributed directly to this story by supporting my work or who enriched it with their knowledge and wisdom.

First is my husband Douglas Mackay, whose unconditional love is my anchor and touchstone. Many friends have given me insight, among them John Potter, who shared his personal knowledge of American Indian ways and spirituality. Marvin Weatherwax of Blackfeet Community College was indispensable with his knowledge of the Blackfeet language.

In learning the ways of wool growers, I was assisted by Joreen Mills and her father, the handsome Ben Reifer, who is now tucked up with the angels. Also gone to her rest is the flinty but affectionate Kathryn Kern of Absarokee, who taught me about beaver slides. I thank Marilyn Weast as well, for touring me around her sheep operation northwest of Red Lodge on a brisk spring day. John Paugh, former president of the Montana Wool Growers Association, was a superb resource over the telephone.

I deeply appreciate the counsel and technical skill of both Judy Arnstein, my proofreader, and Judy Gilats, my book designer and typographer. Jenny Zimmerman of Creative Designworks provided talented cover design services.

Many writers and authors—and innocent bystanders—inspired me and gave me colorful thoughts and words. The Lewistown Area Chamber of Commerce and the Lewistown Public Library were valuable resources, as was Robert Dissly's book on the history of the area. I give a very special thank-you to verbivore Chrysti Smith and to author Gary Ferguson.

And I thank the land—that wild, living, breathing source that always moves me to write.